A SUDDEN CHANGE OF HEART

Barbara Taylor Bradford was born in Leeds, and was a reporter for the *Yorkshire Evening Post* at sixteen; at eighteen she became women's page editor. By the age of twenty she had graduated to Fleet Street as both editor and columnist. In 1979 she wrote her first novel, *A Woman of Substance*, and that enduring bestseller was followed by fourteen others: *Voice of the Heart, Hold the Dream, Act of Will, To Be the Best, The Women in his Life, Remember, Angel, Everything to Gain, Dangerous to Know, Love in Another Town, Her Own Rules, A Secret Affair, Power of a Woman* and *A Sudden Change of Heart*. Nine have been made into television mini-series and three more are currently in production. Her novels have sold more than 60 million copies worldwide in more than 89 countries and 39 languages. Mrs Bradford lives in New York City with her husband, film producer Robert Bradford. Mrs Bradford received an Honorary Doctorate of Letters from the University of Leeds and an Honorary Doctorate of Letters from the University of Bradford.

BARBARA TAYLOR BRADFORD

A Sudden Change of Heart

HarperCollins*Publishers*

HarperCollins*Publishers*
77–85 Fulham Palace Road,
Hammersmith, London W6 8JB

www.harpercollins.co.uk

This paperback edition 1999
1

First published in Great Britain by
HarperCollins*Publishers* 1998

ISBN 978-0-00-790990-2

Typeset in Minion by
Palimpsest Book Production Limited,
Polmont, Stirlingshire

Printed and bound in Great Britain by
Clays Ltd, St Ives plc

For Bob, with my love

AUTHOR NOTE

Two paintings described in this novel do not exist in real life. *Tahitian Dreams*, by Paul Gauguin, is part of the imaginary collection of Sigmund and Ursula Westheim, fictional characters from my novel *The Women in his Life*, who were victims of the Holocaust in that novel. Sir Maximilian West, their son and heir, and claimant of the invented painting, is another fictional character from the same book. *Moroccan Girl in a Red Caftan Holding A Mandolin*, by Henri Matisse, is part of the imaginary collection of Maurice Duval, a fictional character in this novel. I took literary licence and invented the two paintings for the dramatic purpose of the story, and because I did not want to name real paintings by Gauguin and Matisse. I have no wish to make it appear that actual paintings by Paul Gauguin and Henri Matisse are under any kind of dispute, or in jeopardy.

Barbara Taylor Bradford
New York 1998

CONTENTS

PROLOGUE

Summer

1972

PROLOGUE

The girl was tall for seven, dark haired, with vivid blue eyes in an alert, intelligent face. Thin, almost wiry, there was a tomboy look about her, perhaps because of her slimness, short hair, restless energy and the clothes she wore. They were her favourite pieces of clothing; her uniform, her grandmother said, but she loved her blue jeans, white T shirt and white sneakers. The sneakers and T shirt were her two vanities. They must always be pristine, whiter than white, and so they were constantly in the washing machine or being replaced.

The seven-year-old's name was Laura Valiant, and she was dressed thus this morning as she slipped out of the white clapboard colonial house on the hill, raced across the lawns and down to the river flowing through her grandparents' property. This was a long wide green valley surrounded by soaring hills near Kent, a small rural town in the northwestern corner of Connecticut. Her grandparents had come to America from Wales many years ago, in the 1920s, and after they had bought this wonderful verdant valley they had given it the Welsh name of Rhondda Fach . . . the little Rhondda, it meant.

Once she reached the river Laura slowed her pace as she usually did, meandering along the edge, walking under the branches of the weeping willows that dripped down over the water. She paused for a moment to watch the wildlife here. There were ducks circling around on the surface of the water; it was a whole family, with a mother duck nosing her ducklings along; and there were several Canada geese searching around for food on the edge of the lawn nearby. Laura scanned the river, her hand over her eyes shading the sun, as she sought out the blue heron. It was not here today, but it often came and strutted along the far bank, a proud bird. She couldn't help laughing out loud as she watched the mother duck tending her babies. What a fuss the mother was making.

Moving on, Laura hoisted the string bag slung across her body, and made for the drystone wall and the copse where giant oaks and maples grew in abundance. Years before when *he* was a boy, her father and his siblings had built a tree house in one of the giant oaks. It had remained intact, and it was Laura's favourite spot, just as it had been for other young Valiants before her.

Laura was a strong girl for her age, athletic, agile and full of boundless energy. Within seconds she had scrambled up the rope ladder which dropped down from the fork in the branches where the tree house was built.

Scrambling inside the little house, she made herself comfortable in her leafy lair, sat cross-legged, gazing out at the early morning sky. It was six o'clock on this bright and sunny July day and no one else was up, at least not in the house. Tom, the caretaker who ran the farm, was outside one of the red barns near his cottage cleaning a piece of farm machinery. She had seen him out of the corner of her eye as she had run across the lawns a few minutes earlier.

Laura sniffed. Tom had cut the lawns yesterday, and she loved the smell of the newly-mown grass and of new-mown hay. She loved *everything* about Rhondda Fach, much preferred it to New York, where she lived with her parents and her brother Dylan.

Imperceptibly, Laura's young face changed as she thought of her parents. Richard, her father, was a well-known composer and conductor; he was usually travelling somewhere to conduct a symphony orchestra and her mother invariably went along with him. 'Those two are inseparable,' her grandmother would say, but she said it in such a way it sounded like a criticism; Laura understood that it was. And it was also true that they were hardly ever around. When her mother Maggie wasn't travelling, she was painting her famous flower pictures in her studio on the West Side. 'She gets good money for them,' Grandfather Owen kept saying, making excuses for her mother because he was always kind to everyone.

And so it was that Laura and her brother Dylan, three years younger than she, were frequently left in the care of their grandparents. She loved being with them, they were her favourites, really; she loved her parents, and she was quite close to her father, when he was around to be close to, but most of the time her mother was distant, remote.

Laura thought of the rope ladder which dangled down to the ground, and she moved towards it, intending to pull it up the way her father had shown her, then changed her mind. Nobody was going to invade her private lair. Dylan was too young at four to get much farther than the first few rope rungs, and her friend Claire was afraid to climb up in case she fell. It was true that the ladder was a bit precarious, Laura knew that. She had often offered to help Claire climb up into the tree house, where Claire longed to be, but her friend never had the courage to go beyond the first few steps at the bottom.

Claire was scared of other things even though she was twelve and much more grown up than Laura. She was small, dainty, fragile, and very pretty, with deep green eyes and red hair. 'A Dresden doll,' Grandma Megan called her, and it *was* the most perfect description.

Laura loved Claire. They were the best of best friends even though they were so different. 'Chalk and cheese,' Grandpa Owen said about them; Laura didn't know if she was the chalk or the cheese. Her grandfather encouraged her to be athletic and adventurous; he had taught her to ride a horse, taken her climbing in the hills, given her swimming lessons and instilled in her a confidence in herself. And he had taught her to be unafraid. 'You must always be brave, Laura, strong of heart and courageous, and you must stand tall.'

The problem for Claire was that *she* wasn't at all athletic and she shrank from most physical activity. She couldn't swim and she was unable to ride, being afraid of water, afraid of horses. And yet they were best friends because they shared so many other things, and Claire, despite her physical fragility, had strong mothering instincts. She was warm and loving with Laura and Dylan, and this was especially meaningful to Laura.

Claire was a master storyteller, inventive and imaginative, always weaving yarns, telling them ghost stories and other fantastical tales. They played charades, wrote plays and acted in them, and they shared a love of films and music and clothes. In certain ways, Laura was in awe of Claire. After all, she *was* five years older and knew so much more than they did. Dylan, being only four, didn't know much of anything, and he was very spoilt, in Laura's opinion.

Pulling the strap of the string bag over her head, Laura fished inside for the plastic bottle of orange juice which Fenice, the housekeeper, left for her in the kitchen every morning. After taking a gulp or two, she put the bottle on a small ledge, took her diary from its secret hiding place and began to write her private thoughts, which she did every day.

Soon it began to grow warmer inside the tree house and several times Laura found her eyelids drooping; finally she put down her diary and pen, rested her head against the wall. And although she tried hard to stay awake, she began to doze.

Laura was not sure how long she had been asleep, but quite suddenly she opened her eyes and sat up with a start. Just now she had heard screams coming from somewhere in the distance. Had she been dreaming?

Then she heard it again, a faint scream, and an even fainter voice calling, 'Help! Help!'

It had not been a dream; someone was in trouble. Crawling as fast as she could, Laura backed out of the tree house, bottom first, dangled over the edge until she found her footing on the ladder and climbed down swiftly. She was well practised in this descent and soon reached the ground.

The cries were increasingly fainter, and then they stopped altogether. But Laura knew they had emanated from that part of the river which was wide and deep, beyond the drystone wall, near the meadow where all kinds of wild flowers grew. Sensing it was Claire calling for help, Laura ran at breakneck speed, her long legs flying over the grass. It had to be Claire who was in trouble in the river, Laura was certain. Who else would be in the valley?

Coming to a stop when she saw the flower basket, Laura quickly pulled off her sneakers and jeans, and scrambled down the muddy bank just as Claire's pale face bobbed up above the surface of the water.

'I'm here, Claire!' Laura shouted, dived in and swam towards her friend.

Claire's head went under again, and Laura took several gulps of air and dived once more. At once, she spotted Claire floating underwater.

Swimming to her, Laura grabbed her under the arms and swam them both up to the surface as best she could. She was tall and strong for her age, and she managed somehow. But then when she started swimming them both towards the bank Laura was pulled back along with Claire who was clinging to her.

'It's my foot,' Claire managed to splutter. 'It's caught on something.' Terror etched her stark white face and her eyes were wide with panic.

Laura could only nod. The girl glanced around frantically, wondering what to do. She had to get Claire's foot free from whatever was holding it underwater. Yet she could not let go of Claire, who would sink if she released her. Laura spotted the branch of a tree a short distance away from them. It was a large limb, half on the bank, half in the water, and she was smart enough to know it was probably too heavy for her to lift. But she decided she must attempt to swivel the part which was in the water towards them. If she was successful, Claire could hang onto it, use it as a raft.

Staring at Claire she said, 'I've got to let go of you, Claire, so that –'

'No, no, don't! I'm scared!' Claire gasped.

'I've got to. I'm going to get that branch over there, so that you can hang onto it. Then I'll get your foot loose. When I let go of you, start flapping your arms in the water and keep moving your free leg. You'll stay afloat, you'll be okay.'

Claire was unable to speak. She was terrified.

Laura let go of her, shouted, 'Flap your arms! Move your leg!' Once Claire started to do this, Laura swam upstream in the direction of the branch. It rested on top of the water, and after a bit of tugging and pulling it began to move; unexpectedly, the other end came away from the bank. It flopped into the river with a splash. Grasping the leafy part of the branch, Laura tugged and tugged for a bit longer until it began to float alongside her. Dragging it with her with one hand, she struck out, heading for Claire.

Although she had gone under several times, Claire had kept on moving her arms and leg in the water and had managed to hold her own. As soon as Laura pulled the branch nearer to her, Claire grabbed for it and hung on tightly.

So did Laura, who needed to catch her breath and rest for a few minutes. When she had recouped, she dived underwater, went down to the bottom of the river bed and slowly came up, swam closer to Claire to see what had happened.

Laura was frightened when she saw that Claire's foot was caught in a roll of wire netting, part of which had unravelled. Claire's sneaker was wedged in, entangled with the loose part of the netting. Laura attempted to free her foot, but she could not; nor could she get the sneaker off, try though she did. She floated up to the surface, took several big gulps of air and rested her arms on the branch.

Peering into Claire's worried face, she said, 'I'll have to go and get Tom to help me.'

'Don't leave me,' Claire whispered tremulously, sounding more nervous than ever.

'I have to. Just don't let go of that branch,' Laura instructed and swam across to the river bank.

After hauling herself up out of the water, the girl pulled on her jeans and sneakers, and set off across the meadow. She ran at a good speed, heading for the farm's compound of buildings in search of Tom. When he was nowhere to be found, and knowing there was no time to waste, Laura dashed into his tool shed, found a pair of garden scissors and headed back to the river. After undressing once more, Laura dived into the river, and swam over to Claire who still clung to the tree branch, looking scared.

Showing Claire the garden scissors, Laura explained, 'I can't find Tom. I'm going down, I'm going to cut your sneaker off.'

Claire nodded. She was shaking uncontrollably and goose bumps had sprung up all over her body from being too long in the cold water. Laura dived down into the river, but it was hard for her to reach Claire's foot at first, and she had to try from various angles. Finally, she managed to manoeuvre her right hand and the garden scissors underneath the wire netting. Her first attempt to release the trapped foot was to cut up the front of the laces. She succeeded, but Claire's foot would not come out of the sneaker; after struggling for a few seconds longer Laura had to rise to the surface to breathe in air.

Within minutes she dived down again. This time she cut each side of the sneaker, tugged at Claire's ankle and finally freed her foot. Filled with relief, Laura swam up, flopped against the tree branch, holding onto it and resting, breathing in large gulps of air.

'I'm sorry,' Claire whispered. 'Are you all right, Laura?'

Nodding, Laura continued to rest for a minute or two. Then reaching for Claire, she towed her back to the bank and dragged her up onto the grassy slope.

Both girls were dripping wet and shaking with cold. Although Laura was exhausted, she wasted no time, pulling on her jeans and sneakers swiftly. Supporting each other they made their way back to the house.

Once they reached the back door which led into the kitchen, Laura stopped, and stared at Claire intently. 'Before we go in tell me what happened. How did you get in the river?'

Claire nodded and pushed back her wet hair. Her freckles stood out like dark blotches on her ashen face. 'I was picking wild flowers and got too near the edge of the river, Laura. I suddenly slipped and rolled down the bank into the water. I was scared and I panicked, floundered. I just don't know how I drifted into the middle of the river.'

'Gran says that part of the river is dangerous because there's some sort of current out there. But come on, you're shaking.'

'So are you,' Claire said, her teeth chattering.

Fenice was the first person they saw as they stepped into the big family kitchen.

The housekeeper, tall, red-haired and colourful in her white Austrian blouse and floral dirndl skirt, swung around from the stove as they entered. She gasped out loud at the sight of them.

'Good Lord! What happened to you two?' she cried rushing towards them. 'A couple of drowned rats, that's how you both look!' She saw they were cold and shaking, most especially Claire, and drew her closer to the big kitchen stove where she was cooking breakfast. Glancing at Laura, Fenice added, 'Get some big towels out of the linen press in the back hall, please, Laura. I'm afraid Claire's a bit worse off than you.'

'Yes, I know she is,' Laura said and ran and did as Fenice asked. She returned with an armful of large towels.

'Come on, Claire, wrap yourself in this and let's get you

upstairs. You too, Laura. What you both need is a hot shower immediately.'

'What happened? What's going on?' Megan Valiant asked from the doorway of the dining room which led directly into the kitchen.

'Claire was picking flowers and she fell into the deep part of the river near the meadow,' Laura explained quickly.

'I would have drowned if Laura hadn't fished me out,' Claire interjected. 'I'm sorry, Grandma Megan, for making trouble.'

Megan Morgan Valiant held herself very still, remembering ... remembering another child, her grandson ... Mervyn, who had drowned in the lake in Connecticut. She felt a chill run through her. But at once she pushed aside her memories, and stared at Claire. She was puzzled by the girl's apology and by the way in which she seemed to cower next to Laura, as if seeking protection.

Hurrying across to the two girls huddled together near the big range, Megan looked them over quickly and said in a brisk tone, 'Neither of you seem to be too much the worse for wear, but you'd better go upstairs and have a shower, as Fenice suggested. And Fenice, please put the kettle on, I think the girls need something hot to drink. Grandpa Owen's miner's tea, that'll do the trick.'

'No sooner said than done, Mrs V.' Fenice went to get the kettle, filled it with water at the sink and put it on the stove.

'Come on, Claire,' Laura said, shepherding her friend out of the kitchen.

Megan followed the two young girls, still pondering Claire's demeanour. No wonder she seems frightened, Megan thought, she's had a terrible scare. Falling into the river must have terrified her, since she can't swim. It struck Megan that Claire might well be suffering from shock, and she wondered whether to call the doctor. Perhaps Claire ought to be taken over there to see him. Laura also looked pale, and she was shivering, but otherwise there didn't seem to be too much wrong with her granddaughter.

Climbing the stairs behind them, Megan remarked, 'I see you lost a sneaker, Claire.'

'It's in the river, Gran,' Laura said, glancing over her shoulder.

'I see. Never mind, we'll drive over to Kent later and buy you another pair, Claire.'

'It doesn't matter,' Claire answered rapidly. 'I have my sandals with me.'

'Sneakers are useful in the country, comfortable, and they'll be a gift from me,' Megan told her as they reached the landing at the top of the stairs. 'Now, girls, into the shower both of you.'

Claire hurried off to the blue-and-white bedroom where she always stayed, and Laura went into hers.

Megan followed her granddaughter, and once she had closed the door behind them she said, 'Out of those wet clothes at once and into the shower, Laura. Later you can tell me exactly what happened.'

'But I *have* told you, Gran.'

'Claire could be suffering from shock,' Megan said. 'I think I ought to drive you *both* over to Dr Tomkins.'

'We're both okay, Gran,' Laura protested.

'I'm going to pop along to Claire's room, I want to see how she's feeling.'

'Yes, Gran,' Laura said and went into the bathroom.

Megan knocked on the door of Claire's room and when there was no answer she went in. From the bathroom she could hear the sound of water running in the shower. Turning, she caught sight of herself in the mirror hanging on the wall above the antique French chest.

Pausing for a moment, Megan smoothed her hand over her dark chestnut hair and then straightened the collar of her pale blue shirt. Leaning closer, she stared at herself. How white her face was. But that was no surprise. Claire's misadventure had upset her greatly, even though she had not let the girls see this. Laura had not yet given her the details of the accident, but obviously they had been in a precarious situation. And Laura had put herself at risk because she had run to Claire's rescue.

The wide part of the river was dangerous, and the outcome might have been very different. Megan shivered and goose bumps flew up her arms as she realized how terrible the consequences might have been. Little Mervyn . . . he hadn't been so lucky when he had fallen into the lake . . .

She walked across the floor, stood gazing out of the window for a moment, waiting for Claire to emerge. At sixty-seven, Megan Morgan Valiant was a beautiful woman. Tall and slender, she held herself erect, and in her carriage and deportment she was very much the great Broadway musical star. Although the colour of her rich chestnut hair needed help from her hairdresser these days, it was, nevertheless, thick and luxuriant; her face was relatively free of wrinkles and had remained youthful. Her eyes were her most arresting feature. They were a deep vivid blue, large and set wide apart. Her granddaughter had inherited them, as well as her height and colouring. Lithe and full of energy, Megan was a woman who had remained young in spirit. Her career in the theatre was somewhat curtailed these days, through choice, but her popularity as a star had never waned.

'Oh, it's you, Grandma Megan,' Claire said, sounding surprised as she stepped into the bedroom wrapped in a towel. 'I'm feeling better after my shower. And *warmer.*'

Megan nodded. 'But perhaps we *should* go and see the doctor in Kent –'

'No, no, I don't need a doctor,' Claire interrupted. 'I'm fine, honestly I am.'

'What happened? Why did you venture into the river when you can't swim, Claire dear?'

'I didn't. I fell in. I was picking flowers and slipped. I rolled down the bank. And I somehow got swept into the middle, into the deep part of the river.'

'There's some sort of strange current there,' Megan explained. 'And it *is* very dangerous. We've been aware of it for years. You're very lucky Laura was with you.'

'Oh but she wasn't! I was alone. She must've heard me shouting for help. She dived in, but at first she couldn't get me out of the water. My foot was caught in a roll of wire netting. She had to cut my sneaker off.'

'My God, it's worse than I thought! You were very lucky indeed!'

'Yes, I was. I'd better go and dry my hair.' Swinging around, Claire headed back into the bathroom. As she did the towel slipped down at one side, revealing part of her body.

'Claire, whatever happened to your back?' Megan exclaimed, staring at the yellow bruises under her shoulder blade.

'I must have hurt myself when I fell into the river,' Claire muttered, pulling the towel around herself swiftly.

'Claire, those are old bruises,' Megan answered, her voice gentle but concerned.

'I fell off my bicycle in Central Park,' Claire replied, and disappeared into the bathroom.

A few minutes later Megan found her husband in the dining room, where he was breakfasting on boiled eggs, thin buttered toast and his famous miner's tea, which was very strong and sweet.

'I heard all about it,' Owen said as Megan hurried into the room. 'Fenice told me, and from what she said they're both all right, aren't they, Megan?'

She nodded. 'They are, but it could have been fatal for Claire,' she replied, and then went on to explain what had happened to her.

'Laura's a plucky one, and strong for her age,' Owen exclaimed. 'And thank God she had the presence of mind to jump in and help Claire, rather than running back here for me or Tom. You say Claire's foot got caught in a roll of wire netting. God knows how that came to be in the river. I'll talk to Tom later, and he can lift it out.' Owen gave Megan a pointed look and added, 'But I'm afraid I'm going to insist Claire learns to swim. Laura and I will give her lessons in the swimming pool.'

'That's a good idea . . .' Megan paused, leaned back in her chair and looked off into the distance.

Owen, watching her closely, said slowly, 'I know, I know, my darling, this mishap has brought back bad memories for you . . . you've been thinking of poor little Mervyn.'

'Yes, I have,' Megan answered, her voice as quiet as his. Sitting up straighter, finding a smile, Megan went on, 'I think I'll have a cup of tea. I need it after all this.' As she spoke she reached for the teapot and poured herself a cup.

Owen said, 'I'm glad I helped Laura to become an athlete. It's served her well, and will in the future.'

'Laura's always been brave, Owen, even when she was a small child. And quick thinking, as well.'

'She idolizes Claire,' Owen remarked, thinking out loud. 'She'll always rush to her rescue whatever the circumstances.'

'I know.' Megan sighed and looked across at Owen.

'What is it?' he asked, frowning. 'You look troubled.'

'Claire's back is covered with old bruises.'

'What?' He sounded startled.

'I saw them when she came out of the shower. She said she'd fallen off her bicycle in the park,' Megan explained.

'But you don't believe her?'

'I don't know whether I do or not.'

'I've always thought the Bensons were a bit odd,' Owen said, bringing his hand up to his generous mouth. He rubbed it thoughtfully, his dark eyes narrowing. 'She *could* have fallen, you know.'

'Yes . . .' Megan was silent, but eventually she said, 'I hope you and I live a long time, Owen, so that we can look after Laura and Claire, be there for them.'

Reaching out, he put his hand over hers and smiled at her lovingly. 'So do I. But remember this . . . those two will always be there for each other.'

PART ONE

Winter

1996

1

Whenever she was in Paris on business and had an hour or two to spare, Laura Valiant inevitably headed for the Musée d'Orsay in the seventh arrondissement on the Left Bank.

Today was such a day. The moment her lunch with two prominent art-dealers from the Galerie Theoni was over, she thanked them, promised to be in touch about the Matisse, and said her goodbyes.

Leaving the Relais Plaza, she crossed the lobby of the Plaza Athénée Hotel and stepped out onto the avenue Montaigne.

There were no cabs on the rank in front of the hotel and none in sight, so she decided to walk. It was a cold December day with a hint of rain in the air. She shivered and shrugged further into her black overcoat.

Laura was dressed entirely in black, from the topcoat to her smart woollen suit underneath and soft leather boots that stopped just short of the knee. Her jet-black hair, styled in a short, sleek cut, accentuated both her pale face and her eyes of a blue so brilliant they seemed supernatural. A slender tall young woman, she looked much younger than her thirty-one years.

Laura was a striking figure as she hurried along; many a male head turned. But she did not notice those admiring glances, so intent was she in her purpose.

She lifted her head and looked up at the sky. It was leaden and grey this afternoon; a watery sun was trying to push through the clouds without much success. But the weather was irrelevant here. To Laura, Paris was a city full of nostalgia and memories, memories happy and sad . . . so much had happened to her here.

First love – oh, how she had loved him and willingly lost her virginity at eighteen – and first heartbreak, when he had said it was over and had left her with such sudden abruptness that she had been stunned. And oh, the terrible jealousy when she had gone to see him a few days later and found him in bed with another girl. But there was more self-love than love in jealousy, de la Rochefoucauld had written long ago; she had taken those wise words to heart on that awful day and made them her own personal motto over the years. And she *had* fallen in love again, more than once, even though she had believed she never would. Miraculously, or so it had seemed to her at the time, she had eventually recovered from her broken heart to discover that there were other attractive young men in the world, and many were available.

It was her mother who had first brought her to Paris when she was twelve, and she had been captivated. At the age of eighteen she had returned to study art history and literature at the Sorbonne. In the two years she had lived in Paris as a student she had come to know it as well as she knew New York, where she had been born and raised. Whether shrouded in spring rain, wrapped in the airless heat of summer or coated with winter snow, Paris was the most beautiful of cities.

City of Light, City of Lovers, City of Gaiety, City of Artists . . . it had so many names. But no matter what people chose to call it, Paris was a truly magical place. She had never lost her fascination with it, and whenever she came back she immediately fell under its spell once again.

Mostly, Laura thought of Paris as the City of Artists, for had they not all worked and lived here at one time or another, those great painters of the nineteenth and twentieth centuries? Whatever their origins and from wherever they sprang, they had eventually come here, armed with their palettes and brushes and paints, and their soaring talent. Gauguin, Van Gogh, Renoir, Manet, Monet, Matisse, Cézanne, Vuillard, Degas, Sisley and Seurat. The Impressionist and Post-Impressionist painters she most admired, and in whose work she was an expert, had all converged on Paris to make it their home, if only for a short while.

The world of art was *her* world, and it had been for as long as she could remember. She had inherited her love of art from her mother Maggie Valiant, a well-known American painter who had studied at the Royal College of Art in London and the École des Beaux Arts in Paris.

But Laura was the first to admit she lacked her mother's talent and vision as a painter, and when she was in her early teens painting became an avocation rather than her vocation. Nonetheless, she had decided she wanted to work with art once she had finished her studies, and after her graduation from the Sorbonne she did stints with several galleries in Paris before returning home to the States. Once back in New York, she did gallery work again, and then completed a rewarding four years at the Metropolitan Museum of Art.

One of her superiors at the museum, impressed by her unerring eye, superb taste, and knowledge of art, encouraged her to become an art-adviser. And so three years ago, at the age of twenty-eight, she and Alison Maynard, a colleague at the Metropolitan, had started their own company. The two of them had made a great success of this venture, which they had named Art Acquisitions. She and Alison bought art for a number of wealthy clients, and helped them to create collections of some significance. Laura loved her career; it was the most important thing in her life, except for her husband Doug, and the Valiants.

A few days ago she had flown to Paris from New York, hoping to find paintings for one of their important clients, a Canadian newspaper magnate. Unfortunately, she had not found anything of importance so far, and she and Alison had agreed on the phone that she would stay on a bit longer to continue her search. She had a number of appointments, and she was hopeful she would find something of interest and value in the coming week.

Increasing her pace, Laura soon found herself turning onto the rue de Bellechasse, where the Musée d'Orsay was located not far from the Eiffel Tower and Les Invalides. She had made it from the hotel faster than she had expected, and as she went into the museum she experienced a little spurt of excitement. Inside were some of her favourite works of art.

The museum was deserted and this pleased Laura; she disliked crowds when she was looking at paintings. It was really dead this afternoon, so quiet you could hear a pin drop. The only sound was the click of her heels on the floor; her footsteps echoed loudly as she walked towards the hall where the Renoirs hung.

She stood for a long time in front of *Nude in Sunlight*. Renoir had painted it in 1875, and yet it looked so fresh, as if he had created it only yesterday. How beautiful it was; she never tired of looking at it. The pearly tints and pink-blush tones of the model's skin were incomparable, set off by the pale, faintly blue shadows on her shoulders which seemed to emanate from the foliage surrounding her.

What a master Renoir had been. The painting was suffused with light – shimmering light. But then to her, Renoir's canvases always looked as though his brush had been dipped in sunlight. Lover of life, lover of women, Renoir had been the most sensual of painters, and his paintings reflected this, were full of vivid, pulsating life.

Laura moved on, stopped to gaze at a much larger painting, *Dancing at the Moulin de la Galette*. It represented gaiety and young love, and there was so much to see in it – the faces of the dancers, merry, sparkling with happiness, the handsome young men, their arms encircling the beautiful girls; how perfectly Renoir had captured their *joie de vivre*. His use of colour was superb: the blues and greens in the trees, the blues and creams and pinks in the girls' dresses, the soft, clear yellow of the men's straw boaters, and the . . .

'Hello, Laura.'

Believing herself to be alone with the Renoirs, Laura jumped when she heard her name. Startled, she swung around. Surprise registered on her face, and she froze.

The man who stood a few feet away from her, went on, 'It's Philippe, Laura. Philippe Lavillard.' He smiled, took a step towards her.

Laura recoiled imperceptibly. Dislike and a flick of anger curdled inside her.

The man was thrusting out his hand, still smiling warmly.

Reluctantly, Laura took it, touching her fingers quickly to his and then pulling them away. This man had always spelled disaster and trouble. She could hardly believe he had run into her like this.

'I thought you were in Zaire,' she managed to say at last, wondering how to get rid of him. There was a slight pause before she added, 'Claire told me you were . . . living in Africa.'

'I am. I arrived in Paris a couple of days ago. Actually, I'm en route to the States. I'm going to see the head of the CDC.'

'The CDC?' she repeated, sounding puzzled.

'The Center for Disease Control. In Atlanta. I have some meetings there.'

'Claire mentioned you were working on Ebola in Zaire.'

'And other hot viruses.'

Laura nodded, tried to edge away.

He said, 'Are you staying in Paris long, Laura?'

'No.'

'How's the famous Doug?'

'He's well, thanks.'

'This is one of my favourites,' Philippe Lavillard began, looking intently at *Dancing at the Moulin de la Galette*, then gesturing towards it. 'I think I favour it because it's so positive. There's so much life in it, such happiness, don't you think, such hope and expectation in their faces, and a sort of quiet exuberance, even innocence –' Abruptly he cut himself off, and glanced to his right.

Laura followed his gaze, saw a woman approaching. As she drew closer, Laura realized, with a sudden flash of recognition, that it was Philippe's mother: a dumpy middle-aged woman in a maroon wool dress, with a black coat flung over her shoulders. She was carrying a handbag on one arm and holding a Galeries Lafayette shopping bag in her hand. She moved at a measured pace.

A second later, Rosa Lavillard was standing next to her son, staring at Laura with undisguised curiosity.

Philippe said, 'You remember Laura Valiant, don't you, Mother?'

'Oh yes, of course,' Rosa Lavillard responded in a cool tone. 'Good afternoon.' Rosa's lined face was impassive, impenetrable; her pale eyes were frosty, and there was a degree of hostility in her manner.

'Hello, Mrs Lavillard, it's been a long time,' Laura answered, recalling the last time she had seen her. At the wedding. Trying to be polite, she added, 'I hope you're well.'

'I am, thanks. Are you here on vacation?' Rosa asked.

'No, this is a business trip.'

'Laura's an art-adviser, Mother,' Philippe explained, glancing down at Rosa and then across at Laura. 'She helps people to select and buy paintings.'

'I see. You like Renoir, do you?' Rosa murmured.

'Very much. He's a great favourite, and I try to come here whenever I'm in Paris,' Laura replied.

'Such beauty,' Rosa remarked, looking about her. 'All these Renoirs . . . they nourish the soul, calm the heart. And they are reassuring . . . these paintings tell us there is something else besides ugliness out there. Yes, such beauty . . . it helps to baffle the clamour of cruelty.' She waved a hand in the air almost absently, peered at Laura and asked, 'Do you like Van Gogh?'

'Oh yes, and Degas and Cézanne, and Gauguin, he's another favourite.'

'His primitives are deceptive. They appear simple yet they are not, they are complex. Like people.' Rosa nodded her head. 'It's obvious the Impressionists appeal to you.'

'Yes, that's my area of expertise. The Post Impressionists, as well.'

'I like them myself. If I had a lot of money that's what I would do, how I would spend my life. I would collect paintings from the Impressionist school. But I am just a poor woman, and so I must make do with going to museums.'

'Like most other people, Mother,' Philippe pointed out gently.

'That's true,' Rosa agreed, and turning, she began to walk away, saying over her shoulder, 'Enjoy the Renoirs.'

'I will,' Laura said. 'Goodbye, Mrs Lavillard.'

Rosa made no response.

Philippe inclined his head, gave her a faint half-smile, as if he were embarrassed. 'Nice to see you again, Laura. So long.'

Laura nodded, but said nothing.

He stared at her for a moment, then he swung on his heels and followed his mother out of the hall.

Laura stood watching the Lavillards depart, and finally went back to her contemplation of the Renoirs. But the Lavillards had ruined her mood. Their intrusion on her privacy had brought too many memories rushing back, and most of them bad memories. Suddenly she felt nervous, unsettled, unable to concentrate on the paintings. But she didn't want to leave the museum just yet; she might not have another chance to come back during this trip to Paris.

Glancing around, Laura spotted a small bench placed against the far wall, and she went and sat down, still thinking about the Lavillards. What a strange woman Rosa Lavillard was. She remembered a few things Claire had told her years ago, mainly that Rosa was unpredictable, a sick woman who had been hospitalized for long periods. Hadn't Claire said she had once been in a mental institution?

From what Laura now remembered hearing, Rosa had led a troubled life ... there had been a painful childhood in France, growing up during the war, the loss of her family in the Allied bombing raids, later a volatile marriage to Pierre Lavillard, then emigration to the States in the 1950s, where Philippe was born. Their only child. The doctor. The prize-winning virologist whom the medical world called a genius.

Claire had once said in a moment of anger that Rosa was a crazy woman, and should have been kept in the mental hospital. She had been very vehement about it at the time.

Laura closed her eyes, her thoughts settling on Claire Benson: her best friend and confidante, the elder sister she had never had, her role model. Claire had been living in Paris for a number of years, which was one of the reasons she liked to come here, to spend time with Claire.

Opening her eyes, Laura stood up. She began to stroll down the long gallery, determinedly pushing aside all thoughts of the Lavillards, mother and son. Within seconds she had forgotten them, once more enjoying the Renoirs hanging there. Soon she was lost in the paintings, soothed by their beauty.

And then once again she was no longer alone. Unexpectedly, there was Claire standing by her side, taking hold of her arm.

'What are you doing here?' Laura exclaimed, startled to see her friend, filling with a rush of anxiety. Oh God, had Claire run into the Lavillards? She hoped not; they usually upset her. She searched Claire's face, looking for signs.

Claire explained, 'You told me you were coming to the museum after your lunch, so I thought I'd join you.' She peered at Laura. 'What's wrong? You look odd.'

'Nothing, I'm fine,' Laura answered. 'You took me by surprise, that's all.' She was relieved to see that Claire was calm;

obviously she *had* missed the Lavillards. But probably only by a few moments. Forcing a smile, she went on, 'So, come on then, let's walk around together.'

Claire tucked her arm through Laura's. 'I like seeing paintings through your eyes. Somehow I get much more pleasure from them when I'm with you.'

Laura nodded, and they moved on, gazing at the masterpieces on the walls, not speaking for a short while. At one moment, Laura lingered in front of a painting of a mother and child, frowning slightly.

Claire, always tuned into her best friend, said, 'Why are you looking so puzzled?'

Shaking her head, Laura replied, 'I've often wondered lately if any of these paintings are stolen –'

'Stolen! What do you mean?' Claire asked.

'Thousands and thousands of paintings were stolen by the Nazis during the war, and that art, looted by them, hangs on museum walls all over the world. It's from some of the world's greatest collectors, such as the Rothschilds, the Kanns, and Paul Rosenberg, who once owned one of the most prestigious galleries in Paris, to name only a few.'

'I read something about that recently. I guess it's hard for the heirs of the original owners to get their paintings back if they don't have proof of ownership.'

'That's it exactly. And so many records were lost during the war. Or were purposely destroyed by the Nazis in order to blur provenance.' Laura grimaced, and said, 'A lot of museums are fully aware of the real owners, because many of the paintings are coded on the back of the canvases. It all stinks. It's morally wrong, but try and get a museum to give a painting up, give it back. They just won't . . . At least, most of them won't . . . Some are starting to get nervous, though.'

'Can't any of the original owners sue the museums?' Claire asked.

'I suppose they could,' Laura answered. 'But only if they have proof a painting is theirs. And even then it's dubious that they'd ever get it.'

Claire nodded, 'I remember now, Hercule knows something about this . . . He mentioned it only recently. I believe he has a client who is the heir to art stolen by the Nazis from his family in 1938.'

'Oh, who is it?'

'I don't know . . . He didn't say.'

'A great deal of the looted art is in private hands, and try and get *them* to give it back. They never will, not when they've paid millions for it. There's going to be a lot of trouble in the next few years, now that it's all coming to light. You'll see.'

Claire said, 'You're repeating what Hercule was telling me not long ago. Maybe you should talk to him about it.'

'I'd like that.'

'Maybe we can get together with him this weekend. Anyway, do you represent someone with a claim to stolen art?' Claire asked curiously.

'Not at the moment, but I may well do so in the not too distant future.'

They fell silent as they continued to stroll around the museum, at ease with each other. Laura, forever worried about Claire, stole a quick look at her. In her years of living in Paris Claire had acquired a certain kind of chic that was uniquely French. This afternoon she wore a dark purple wool coat, calf length and tightly belted, over matching pants and a turtleneck sweater. The purple enhanced Claire's large green eyes and auburn halo of curls. Big gold hoop earrings and a dark red shoulder bag were her only accessories, and she looked stylish, well put together. Laura admired Claire's style, which seemed so natural and uncontrived.

Glancing at Laura, Claire came to a halt and said, 'I'm glad you're in Paris for a while, Laura, I miss you.'

'I miss you too,' Laura answered swiftly.

Looking at her watch, Claire went on, 'I think I'd better be getting back to the photographic studio. I'm doing a shoot for the magazine, as you know, and Hercule's coming over later. I need his advice about one of my sets.'

'He's turned out to be a good friend,' Laura said. 'Hasn't he?'

'Yes. But not my *best* friend. That's you, Laura Valiant. Nobody could take your place.'

Laura squeezed Claire's arm. 'Or yours,' she said.

Laura heard the phone ringing above the sound of the water pouring into the bath, and she reached for the receiver on the wall.

'Hello?'

'Hi, sweetie.'

'Doug! Hello, darling.' She sat down on the small bathroom stool near the make-up table, and glanced at her watch. It was six here. Noon in New York.

Her husband said, 'I called you earlier but you weren't there. I'm off to lunch with a client in a few minutes, and I wanted to catch you before you went out again.'

'It's such a clear line, you sound as if you're around the corner!' she exclaimed warmly, happy to hear his voice.

'I wish I were.'

'So do I. Listen, I've got a great idea! Why don't you come in for the weekend? Tomorrow's Friday, couldn't you take it off and fly over? It *would* be lovely, Doug.'

'Wish I could, but I can't,' he answered, his voice changing slightly, growing suddenly brisk, businesslike. 'That's another reason I'm calling you, I have to fly to the coast tomorrow. Meetings with the Aaronson lawyers. The merger's on, after all.'

'*Oh.* It's unexpected, isn't it?'

'Yep, it sure is. But what can I do, I'm needed out there.'

'Never mind. But it would have been nice to have you in Paris if only for a couple of days.'

'Sorry, darling, it can't be helped. When do you think you'll be back?'

'I have appointments set up for the early part of next week, Doug, so I'll probably leave for New York on Thursday or Friday.'

'Great! You'll be here next weekend, and so will I. This is probably going to be a quick trip to LA. In and out.'

'Where are you staying?'

'Er, the Peninsula, in Beverly Hills, as usual.'

'Doug?'

'Yes?'

'I've really missed you this week.'

'I've missed you too, darling. But we'll make up for it, and you know what they say, absence makes the heart grow fonder.'

She laughed. 'I guess it does . . . the way I'm feeling right now, I wish you were here . . .' She laughed again, a light, infectious laugh.

He laughed with her. 'Got to go, sweetie.'

'When are you leaving tomorrow?'

'My flight's at nine in the morning, and I'm going straight into meetings once I've dropped my luggage off. I'll call you.'

''Bye, darling.'

''Bye, Laura. And a big kiss,' he said, before hanging up.

Laura sat soaking in the bath longer than usual. There had been no cabs on the street when she and Claire had left the museum earlier; they had walked all the way back to the hotel where Claire had finally found a cab.

The water was helping Laura to thaw out and to relax, and she luxuriated in the hot bubble bath for a while, thinking of Doug. She had married Douglas Casson when she was twenty-five and he was twenty-seven. They were a perfect fit, compatible, attuned to each other in the best of ways. But lately he worked too hard. She smiled at this thought. Didn't he say the same thing about her?

To his way of thinking, they were both workaholics, and he seemed to relish announcing this. It was true, of course, but she didn't like that particular word. It smacked of obsessiveness, and she was quite sure neither of them was that. Not exactly.

Anyway, Claire had always said that the ability to work hard for long hours was the most important thing of all, and that this was what separated the women from the girls.

But Laura thought that love was important, too. Hadn't Colette, her favourite writer, once written that love and work were the only things of consequence in life. Certainly she believed this to be so. But Claire didn't – at least not the love part, not anymore. Claire had been burnt. 'And they were third-degree burns, at that,' Claire had said. Those burns had taken a long time to heal. 'Now I have built a carapace around me, and I'll never get burnt again. Or hurt in any way. My shell protects me. Nothing, no one, can ever inflict pain on me.'

Laura loved Claire. She also had enormous compassion for her, because of all the bad things that had happened to her. Laura was well aware that Claire was raw inside; still, she couldn't help wishing her friend would open herself up to love again instead of retreating into her shell the way she did. There was something oddly sterile about a woman's life, if she did not have love in it, if she didn't have a man to cherish and to love.

These days, whenever she broached this subject, Claire only laughed hollowly, and responded swiftly, 'I have Natasha, and she's all that matters. She's my life now, I don't need a man around.'

But a fourteen-year-old daughter wasn't enough, was it? Laura wondered. Surely not for a loving, passionate, intelligent woman like Claire.

Claire. The dearest friend she had ever had. And still her *best* friend, the one she loved the most, even though they lived so far away from each other now. Claire and she went back a long way. Almost all of their lives, really.

She had been five years old when Claire and her parents, Jack and Nancy Benson, had come to live in the apartment opposite theirs in the lovely old building on Park Avenue at Eighty-Sixth

Street. She had instantly fallen in love with her in the way a little girl of five falls in love with a very grown-up ten-year-old. She had worshipped Claire from the start, had emulated her. Once their two families had become acquainted, Claire had taken Laura and Dylan under her wing, had been baby-sitter, pal, and confidante.

Cissy, the Valiant nanny, had had her hands full with Dylan, who was then only two and very naughty. So Claire had been a welcome addition to the Valiant household. An only child, Claire had loved being part of this extended family, especially since Laura's grandparents, Owen and Megan Valiant, were very much in evidence. They all helped to make Claire feel like a very special member of their family.

Because Claire attended Miss Hewitt's School, Laura went there as well. And there came a time when the five years difference in their ages suddenly seemed negligible. As teenagers and young women they were as inseparable as they had been as children, bonded together as sisters in soul and spirit, if not blood.

Claire had married young, at twenty-one, and her daughter Natasha had been born a year later. Two years after that she had moved to Paris with her husband and child. But nothing, not distance, husband or child, had ever come between them or changed the nature of their friendship. Very simply, they loved each other, and, as Claire was wont to say, they would always be sisters under the skin, no matter what.

The sad part was that Claire's life had gone horribly wrong seven years ago. Her marriage had foundered and she had divorced; her parents had died within a few weeks of each other, not long after this, and then Natasha had been in a car crash and had suffered serious injuries. But thanks to Claire's nursing, the girl had made an amazing recovery.

Laura roused herself, pushing herself up in the bath. Here she was daydreaming about the past when she should be getting dressed.

No time to dawdle now.

2

'Don't you like the room, Hercule?' Claire Benson asked, pausing near the grouping of Louis XVth chairs, resting a hand on the back of one of them. 'Is it the chairs? Do you think they're inappropriate? Don't they work?' She shot these questions at him as she glanced down at the silver-leafed wood frame under her hand, and then at the silver-grey upholstery. 'Yes, it *is* the chairs, isn't it?' she asserted. 'Maybe they're totally wrong for the setting.' She looked across at him questioningly.

The Frenchman chuckled. 'Ah, Claire, so many questions you fire, rat-a-tat, and you make the jest, *n'est-ce pas?*'

'No, I'm being serious.'

'The room is superb. *Formidable, oui.* You have the wonderful taste. The furniture, the fabrics you have chosen, this Aubusson rug, everything is perfection. But –'

'But what?' she cut in before he could complete his sentence.

'The room is incomplete, my dear. A room is never finished until it has –'

'Art,' she supplied, and then immediately laughed when she saw the amusement in his face, the twinkle in his eye. 'I need paintings on these walls, Hercule, I know *that*. But what kind of paintings? That's one of the reasons I wanted you to see the setting, to help me make some decisions about art. Shall I use a

Picasso? Or a Gauguin? Or go for a modern work, such as Larry Rivers? A Van Gogh? A Renoir, maybe? On the other hand, I could look for something really old, like a pair of Canalettos.'

'A Van Gogh or a Gauguin would give the room strength, but I do not think it is a strength you require here, Claire. And Canalettos would be wrong. A soft painting would be the ideal choice, something in the pastel tones. It would underscore the stillness, the sense of . . . quietude you have created. Also, this space has a light look. Airy. A Renoir, most definitely. *Oui. Parfait.*'

'Perfect, yes, I agree. But where am I going to find one? And who would lend me one for the photography? People don't normally let their Renoirs out of their sight.'

Hercule Junot smiled. 'There is a possibility that I might be able to find one for you. A few months ago, I was shown a Renoir which was for sale –' He paused, shrugged lightly, raised his hands. 'Well, I do not know, *chérie*, perhaps it has been sold.'

'If it hasn't, do you think the owner would agree to lend it to me?' she asked, her face eager.

'*Mais oui.* The owner is a friend, a former client . . . I am happy to speak with her. If she still has it, she will allow me to borrow it. For a few hours. If that is enough time for you, Claire. Because of its great value, she would not want to leave the painting here in the studio overnight.'

'And *I* wouldn't want it to be here overnight! Not unless I slept with it. I wouldn't want the responsibility, although we will insure it, of course, even if it's here for only a few hours. Too risky not to.' Claire stepped out of the set, went to join Hercule Junot, who was standing on the studio floor. 'When can you speak to your friend?'

'I shall be happy to telephone her this evening.'

Claire said, 'My lead time is three to four months, as you know, and I'm shooting this for the March issue. It's going to be the cover shot.'

'If she has not sold it, that might be an inducement for her to lend the Renoir. Having the exposure in the magazine could serve a purpose.'

Claire nodded. 'Good thought. What's the painting like?' She grinned. 'Although who needs to know that, a Renoir's a Renoir.'

Hercule's face had lit up at the thought of the painting, and he beamed at her. 'It is beautiful, *bien sûr*, a semi-nude, a bather sitting on a rock. But this is not a large painting, Claire. It would only be suitable to hang over the fireplace or above the console. You will need a larger one ... for the wall where the sofa is placed.'

'I'm pretty sure I have one already. My assistant found a Seurat at one of the galleries, and they're prepared to lend it to us.'

'That is good. A Seurat will be compatible. It will sit well with the Renoir. I shall telephone you tomorrow, after I've spoken with my friend.' He picked up his dark overcoat, which was thrown over the back of a wooden chair. 'I must return to my *bureau*, Claire. Will you come with me? Can I take you to the magazine? Or are you staying here at the studio?'

'No, I'm not, Hercule. I've finished for today. I'll just have a word with my staff who are still working on another set, and then I'll come with you. I'd love a lift to the Plaza Athénée, if that's not out of your way.'

'*Ce n'est pas un problème*, Claire.'

Claire had known Hercule Junot for twelve years, having met him when she first came to live in Paris as a young bride. They had been seated next to one another at a posh dinner party, and the renowned older man and the unimportant young woman had taken to each other at once. He had found her irreverent, saucy, provocative, and challenging, and her knowledge of art and antiques, coupled with her journalistic flair for telling a good story, had been impressive. She had been the most interesting and entertaining dinner companion he had had in many a year, a sheer delight to be with.

Hercule Junot, who was now seventy-six years old, was one of the most famous interior designers in the world, on a par with his peers Stéphane Boudin, a fellow Parisian, and the Italian, Renzo Mongiardino. Renowned for his elegant and glamorous formal interiors, he had great taste, immense flair, a discerning and critical eye, and was considered to be one of the foremost experts on Fine French Furniture. Another area of his formidable expertise was Impressionism, most especially the paintings of Van Gogh and Gauguin, the latter a great personal favourite.

Rather than lessening as he grew older, his business seemed to be flourishing even more than ever, and he was in constant demand by those who appreciated his extraordinary gift for creating tasteful but eyecatching interiors full of style, wit and comfort; those who had the vast amounts of money required to pay for the antiques and art of the highest pedigree and quality which he favoured in his designs.

Claire had been at a crossroads in her career when they had met. She wanted to continue working as a journalist, but she felt more drawn than ever to the world of visual and decorative arts.

At that first meeting over dinner she had found herself confiding her concerns about her career and the route it should take, and Hercule had made up his mind that he must somehow help her.

The following morning he had talked to a number of influential people, pulled a few strings, and in the process had contrived to get her a job on *Decorative Arts and Design,* a glossy magazine devoted to art, antiques, and interior design which was popular with the French and with the international public. It was owned by a friend of his who had long owed him a favour.

Claire had started out in a most lowly position, that of caption writer, but such was her creative talent and energy that within eight years she had risen to the top of the hierarchy of the magazine.

Four years ago she had been named publisher and editor-in-chief, answerable to no one but the owner. Hercule Junot, not unnaturally, was proud of her success and the name she had made for herself.

In the ensuing years since that first meeting, most propitious for her, these two had remained staunch friends, and Hercule had become her mentor. Claire trusted his judgement about everything in the world of design, and whenever she was doubtful about a project she ran to him for his opinion and advice.

Such had been the case today; a sudden lack of confidence about the set, an unprecedented occurrence for her, had induced her to invite him to the photographic studio to give his opinion.

The set had been painstakingly designed and skilfully installed with the utmost care; nonetheless, she had been unusually critical of her own work when she had seen the finished result. She had also been suddenly hesitant and indecisive about the art she should choose to complete the room.

Hercule had been impressed by the beauty and quality of the formal salon and the splendid choices she had made, and more so than he had actually said. Now he wondered if this had been an error on his part. Perhaps he should have expressed himself more volubly. She was certainly quiet, preoccupied, a silent companion in the Mercedes, and this was most unlike her.

Hercule sighed under his breath, leaned back against the leather upholstery and glanced out of the window. It had snowed earlier, but the light flakes had melted, leaving the dark streets wet and glistening. Under the bright lights of the boulevard du Montparnasse the road looked slick as a mirror, as his chauffeur manoeuvred the car carefully through the busy traffic of the Left Bank.

If he had any regrets about Claire professionally, it was only that he had not brought her to work for him as his assistant all those years ago. She would have been a godsend to him today, the perfect right hand. She had flair and taste, and her skills as a designer were wasted at the magazine; they only came into play when she created a room to shoot for one of the magazine's covers. The rest of the time she was plying her trade as a journalist. *C'est dommage*, he thought. My mistake.

Hercule had one other regret about her, and this was intensely personal. He never ceased to wish he had courted Claire when she and her husband had separated seven years ago. He had wanted to do so, but he had been ... afraid. Yes, afraid of looking foolish ... of being rejected ... of spoiling the friendship. Better to have her in his life as a friend, than not there at all.

There was his age to consider: he was forty years older than Claire. What could she possibly want from him? he had asked himself innumerable times. His late wife Veronica had always said he did not look his age, and he had believed her. He was fit and trim, mercifully not as lined and ancient-looking as some of the men he knew who were his age. Admittedly his hair was white, but it was a full head of hair. And sex was not a problem, not at all.

Initially, he had not pursued Claire or pressed his suit because she had been so distraught at the time of the divorce, a state he had found most odd since she purported to detest her husband. And so time had slipped by, other things had intervened, and the opportunity had been missed. They had fallen into a pattern of loving friendship, and he did not know how to change this without upsetting her unduly.

Veronica had been dead for fifteen years. There was not a day he did not miss his wife; yet he had known, when Claire had separated, that this young American woman could so easily fill the void created by his wife's death. Veronica had been an American too; they had that in common. There any resemblance between them stopped. Veronica had been tall, long-legged, an all-American beauty, blonde, blue-eyed and wafer-thin, one of the great post-war models in Paris, on Christian Dior's runway showing his New Look and on the cover of every fashion magazine in the world. When he had met her it had been love at first sight, a *coup de foudre,* and a most happy union until the day she died.

Hercule stole a look at Claire, surreptitiously, out of the corner of his eye, and for the second time today he thought she did not look well. She had faintly bluish smudges under her eyes, and the short, curly auburn hair, the bright burnished halo he found so attractive, did not have its usual glossy lustre.

What struck him with such force when he had arrived at the studio this afternoon was her weight, or rather loss of it. Always slender, she appeared thinner than ever. *Maigre.* A waif, that was how she appeared to him. An appealing gamin in looks and style, somehow she had become bony. Had she looked like this last week when he had lunched with her at Taillevent? No, she could not have; he would have noticed. He wondered if she were ill? But no, he did not think this was so; she had been full of her usual energy at the studio.

Worries of another nature? Money? If this were the problem then there was no problem. He would readily give her as much as she needed. Instantly, Hercule dismissed the thought that Claire lacked money. The mere idea of it was ludicrous. Her husband provided for Natasha, and she was well paid by the magazine. Could it be that Natasha was causing problems for her? No, no, he did not think this possible either. The girl was unusual, very steady and practical, older than her age in a number of ways. Whenever she had been concerned about her daughter in the past, Claire had discussed it with him and he had given the best advice he could. Since he had never been a father, he felt somewhat inadequate in doing so, and yet how kind she had been, always so appreciative of his interest in Natasha.

He began to formulate an opening sentence in his mind. He wanted to pose certain questions. How he longed to make whatever it was that ailed her go away. He knew he could do that. If she would let him. He loved her. He had loved her for a long time now. He would always love her, and because of this he had the need to ease the burdens of her life, if he could. And if she would permit him to do so. Women, ah, they were so contrary. He was a Frenchman, and he knew about their natures only too well.

Claire had always felt exceptionally comfortable with Hercule Junot, and there was a great sense of ease in their relationship. And so she did not think twice about drifting along with her thoughts, as his car eased its way through the early evening traffic, heading in the direction of the avenue Montaigne.

She considered the older man to be her dearest friend in Paris; and they never stood on ceremony with each other. To Claire, the silence between them was perfectly normal, acceptable; she never felt the need to talk to him, to entertain him. And she knew he felt exactly the same way about her.

She was thinking about Laura; she was looking forward to having dinner with her tonight. Laura was the only family she had, except for Natasha. Her parents were dead; Aunt Fleur was dead; her husband was ostensibly dead since they were long divorced. Momentarily, his face danced before her eyes, but she pushed it away. She did not want to think about him now; it would spoil her evening.

On their walk from the museum she and Laura had planned the weekend. It was going to be fun. Natasha was as excited as she was about Laura's unexpected sojourn in Paris, and without Doug in tow for a change. Not that she minded Doug, he was fine. But having Laura to themselves was a very special bonus.

'Is there something troubling you, Claire?' Hercule asked, cutting into her thoughts.

Turning to look at him, Claire exclaimed, 'No, of course not, Hercule! Why do you think there is?'

'You've been very quiet on our drive across Paris,' he remarked, touching her arm. 'And I have to confess to you, I was most forcibly struck by your appearance this afternoon. You've lost weight, Claire. You're like a . . . a waif.'

'No, wafer-thin!' she shot back, laughing, pleased with her

play on words. 'Remember what the Duchess of Windsor said: "You can never be too rich or too thin."'

'But *you* are *too* thin.'

'I'll confess, Hercule, I've been on a diet. I want to be slender and chic for your New Year's Eve party.'

'You are a lovely young woman; all this dieting is not necessary. Starving, starving, starving, and all for a size four dress. *Mon Dieu*, you could slip through the eye of a needle.'

'It is easier for a camel to go through the eye of a needle than for a rich man to enter into the kingdom of God,' she murmured, smiling at him, grasping one of his hands. 'I first heard those lines from the Bible in that old Tyrone Power movie with Gene Tierney, Anne Baxter and Clifton Webb.'

'*The Razor's Edge*,' he said. 'How could I forget it? Ever. I have seen it a hundred times with you.'

'Not quite a hundred,' she laughed. 'But we're getting there, and I'm fine, Hercule, really I am. Actually, I'm as fit as a fiddle. A bit overworked, that's all. But listen, I want to talk to you about the Renoir. If it's not been sold, Laura might well be interested. For one of her clients. I know she has her heart set on a Matisse and a Bonnard, if she can find them, but why not a Renoir as well? She has several big collectors as clients.'

'I know she does, and that is an excellent idea, Claire. I have a feeling that the painting is still hanging in my friend's house. I am sure she would have told me if she had sold it.' He gave her the benefit of a wide smile, and nodded his head, looking pleased. 'I shall tell the countess there is the possibility of a sale.'

3

'It's going to be like old times this weekend,' Laura said. 'The way it was when I was studying at the Sorbonne, and you'd just arrived here with a husband and a baby. We really had a ball in those days, didn't we?'

Claire laughed. 'Yes, we did. And some baby she is today! Fourteen going on forty, taller than both of us and into make-up, clothes and boys. You'll get a shock when you see her, Laura, she's really sprung up in the last couple of months.'

Laura nodded, settled back against the chair and took a sip of her champagne.

The two women were sitting in Laura's room at the hotel, lingering over their drinks before dinner. In the half hour they had spent greeting each other effusively and discussing the Renoir, the weather had turned nasty. By the time they had been ready to go to Benoît, one of their favourite bistros, it was snowing hard and, according to the doorman, an icy wind had blown up. And so they had agreed it would be much wiser to stay at the hotel and have room service.

'What do you feel like eating?' Laura now asked, picking up the menu on the coffee table. 'I'm going to have *anything* with their *pommes frites*. They make the best, as you well know.' She grinned. 'If I eat too many meals here I'm going to start putting on weight. I just can't resist them.'

'I know what you mean. I'm going to have grilled sole and *pommes frites*, too.'

'That's what I'll have. Want anything first, Claire?'

'Just a green salad. Hercule thinks I look like a waif, far too thin. What do you think? I don't, do I?'

'You're a bit thinner than you usually are, but you look great, Claire, honestly, and very chic. I love you in deep purple. It sets off your red hair.'

'Thanks. I must admit, I have been dieting a bit more strenuously to fit into my dress for Hercule's New Year's Eve party.' She shrugged. 'He gave me a bit of a lecture on the way from the studio. About my weight, I mean.'

'He fusses about you, I know that. But then, he loves you.'

Claire looked at her. 'Like a father, yes, I realize that.'

'Not like a father, *no*. Like a lover, or rather, a potential lover, potential husband.'

'You've got to be kidding!' Claire exclaimed, looking askance. 'Hercule and me. Don't be so silly.'

'I'm not being silly. I've always known he has . . . well . . . a thing about you, Claire. It's written all over his face. Even Doug has mentioned it to me and more than once.'

'So I'm the last to know, huh?' Claire shook her head vehemently. 'I love him, as a person. He's been wonderful to me always, my best friend in Paris . . . but I'm not interested in him . . . *romantically*.'

'Because he's too old, you mean?' Laura probed.

'No, age doesn't matter, and in any case he's much younger than a lot of people I know in their thirties, even though he's seventy-six. I'm just not interested in men anymore. I've told you that for years now. Shall we order dinner?'

'Yes, let's, and I'm going to have another champagne. What about you? Another martini?'

'God, no! I'll be drunk. One's enough for me.'

Laura went to the phone, dialled room service, and gave their order. Then she went on carefully, 'Look, just because you had one bad experience doesn't mean you've got to close up shop, close your heart to another man. Okay, so you're not interested in Hercule, but maybe there's somebody else out there who's just right for you, Claire, if only you'd give yourself half a chance –'

'No!' Claire cried softly but emphatically. 'I'm not interested. Marriage is a battlefield, and I have the scars to prove it. I won the war by leaving the battlefield, and I've no intention of putting myself in the line of fire ever again.' She laughed hollowly. 'Being in harm's way is being no place . . . no place at all.'

'Marriage doesn't have to be a battleground,' Laura argued. 'Mine isn't.'

'You've been luckier than most, Laura. You met Doug and fell in love, and somehow, for you, it all went smoothly. No arguments and fights, no big differences of opinion. The two of you perfectly in sync, leading nice, orderly, happy lives together.'

'You make it sound awfully dull!' Laura exclaimed. 'Doug's not all that easy to live with, you know he isn't. He's pernickety, a perfectionist, and he can be very opinionated. And he's a nag! God, he never stops nagging about my having a baby –' Laura broke off and pursed her lips, shook her head. 'That sounds disloyal,' she finished lamely, looking chagrined. She sat back against the sofa.

'I know he nags you about having a child, but it could be his fault you don't get pregnant. Why does he blame you?'

'I don't know, but he does. At least, that's the way it seems to me. We've both been tested again, and there's nothing wrong with either of us, seemingly. But pregnant I'm not.'

'Do you *want* a baby?' Claire asked, looking at Laura intently.

'Yes, I do, I've always wanted a child. But I'm only thirty-one, so there's time. It's not as if I'm ancient, on my last legs.'

'Perhaps Doug's just too uptight about this, Laura,' Claire suggested quietly, her face reflective. 'That often happens. A couple don't make a baby, and they get overanxious and that works against them.'

'I'm not overanxious.'

'No, but perhaps Doug is, darling.'

'Maybe he is. He's certainly highly strung these days.'

'He's going to have to learn to relax.'

Laura laughed. 'Tell that to the marines. *Relax.* My God, he's a bundle of nerves, and always on the go, rushing hither and yon, as Grandma Megan says. She told me recently that Doug doesn't stay still long enough to make a baby.'

Claire burst out laughing. 'Good old Grandma Megan! I must admit, I do miss her pithiness, and her forthrightness. She comes out with some marvellous lines.'

'She told me the other day that her great age gives her licence to say anything she wants. And to anybody, too.'

'Old people are a bit like that. I guess they get to the stage where they don't care anymore. And their bluntness can be amusing.' She punched Laura's arm lightly. 'Hey, do you remember what we used to say when we were growing up? That when we were old ladies and had finished with men and all that nonsense, we'd live together on the French Riviera and sit on the beach wearing large picture hats and caftans, having our toenails painted purple by beautiful young gigolos.'

Laura nodded, her face lighting up. 'Sure I do. We were a fanciful pair in those days.'

'We might still do it, you know,' Claire said, grinning. 'When we're old enough.' She took a sip of her gin martini and said, 'I can't wait for you to see Natasha. I told you, she's sprouted lately, and since you saw her in the summer her face has changed. She's sleeker looking, has lost some of the puppy fat, and it helps. She's just become very, very pretty.'

'Like mother like daughter.'

Claire merely smiled. 'She's a very special child, Laura, even though she's mine and I shouldn't say it. Nonetheless, she *is* special, sort of . . . well, *magical.*'

'You may have lived on a battlefield, but you got something out of it, after all, didn't you now?'

'Yes, I certainly did. Natasha has made it all worthwhile . . . the spoils of war are veritable spoils indeed. She's a jewel, and I love her dearly.' Claire's voice changed, became extremely tender, as she continued, 'I don't know what it's all about, this world we live in, this life of mine, but whatever it's about, my child has given my life whatever meaning it has. And she's the best part of me. I thank God every day that I had her, and that I have her with me. She's very caring of me, in a funny sort of way. Sometimes she behaves like the mother, treats me as if I'm the child.'

'I've always thought she was an old soul,' Laura murmured, and then ventured softly, 'Does her father ever see her?'

'No.' Claire shook her head and grimaced. 'Well, not very often. She doesn't care anymore. She used to, of course, but she's adjusted now.' A small sigh escaped, and Claire added, 'But I can't fault him on the money. His cheques come every month, and he's never missed a payment.'

'I always thought he loved her,' Laura murmured, and stopped abruptly when she saw Claire's expression.

'Mmmm.' Claire twisted her martini glass by its delicate stem, the reflective look in place in her green eyes again. She gazed into her drink.

Laura decided not to say anything else about Natasha's father and his feelings for their child. It had always been a sore subject with Claire.

A moment later, the room-service waiter materialized at the door. Laura went to let him in, and clearing her throat, remarked, 'Here's our dinner, Claire. Oh, should I order some wine?'

Claire said, 'I'll have a glass of white wine with the fish, that'll be nice, Laura, thanks.'

After ordering the wine, Laura sat down at the table and turned her attention to the salad. The two friends ate in silence for a moment or two, until Laura said, 'Did Hercule give you any idea about the price of his friend's Renoir? Or rather, what she wanted?'

'No, he didn't, and to be truthful I'm not sure that he even knows.'

'It won't be cheap,' Laura muttered, raising her eyes from her plate, staring at Claire. 'A Renoir is a Renoir is a Renoir, to paraphrase Gertrude Stein.'

'Well put. Listen, Hercule could be a good source for you. Many of his clients are art-collectors, and they might well have something they want to sell: that's of interest to you, I mean, such as a Matisse or a Bonnard. You said your client craves these two artists.'

'That's right, and I have another who always says he'd give his right arm for a Gauguin, at least that's the way he put it to me.'

'Well, you know Hercule's the great expert on Gauguin, so if there's anything knocking around, he'd know. We should talk to him about it. Over the weekend. I'll invite him to dinner one night.'

'I like Hercule, and I enjoy talking to him about art. About anything for that matter. He's very interesting.'

'Great, I'll ask him to come to dinner on Saturday.' Claire put her fork down and leaned back. 'I forgot to tell you, I saw Dylan a couple of weeks ago.'

'Oh, and how is my baby brother?' Laura asked, sounding surprised.

'Recalcitrant, as usual, even a bit contentious, to be honest. He took me to dinner at Espadon. He was staying at the Ritz, and he seemed determined to pick a fight with one of the waiters. I felt a bit uncomfortable at first, but then he finally calmed down after I'd kicked him on the shin under the table, *and* punched his arm. I hate it when he picks on people who can't answer back.'

'What a pity he hasn't outgrown that nasty little habit yet. Anyway, how's he doing? *Really?* Mom constantly says he's behaving himself at last, and that things are working out for him, but he's always managed to pull the wool over *her* eyes, as you know.'

'I think he *is* doing well, Laura, as surprising as that might sound to you. In a funny way, living in England has ... what's the phrase I'm looking for? It's settled him down, yes, that's it, and it's sorted him out. I think he's come into his own. He says he loves working on *Time*, and I believe him.'

'That's good to hear. But I bet his personal life's a mess.'

Claire grinned. 'He says it's a full-blown calamity, and I'm using his words. He told me his girlfriend Minerva has split, and he's worried that she might be pregnant and is depriving him of his child. And his former girlfriend Nina is stalking him, he insists. He's just met a new young woman, Inga, a Swede, and he was thinking of having her move in with him. Oh, and he's bought a farm in Wales.'

'Par for the course, all this,' Laura said, and she couldn't help laughing. 'We were right, you and I, when we gave up on Dylan years ago. He's just a bad boy, as Gran's forever announcing. And you *know* the way he feels about *us*. He resents us and our friendship, yours and mine. He's never forgiven us for sending him away when he was a little boy, cutting him out of our fun and games. Don't forget that, and his tantrums. He's all mixed up, that brother of mine.'

'Aren't we all?' Claire eyed Laura carefully.

'I guess so. The Valiants are probably as dysfunctional as any other family.'

'Better not let Grandma Megan hear you say that, or she'll have –'

'My guts for garters, to quote dear old Gran,' Laura said.

'I'm glad you let me be part of it, though.'

Laura gazed at Claire, her eyes quizzical. 'What do you mean?'

'Part of that dysfunctional, crazy, wonderful family of yours. Without the Valiants I might have turned out to be quite different.'

'Sane for one thing.'

'No, ordinary and dull.'

'You ordinary and dull, never! You were born special, Claire, take my word for it. And I'm glad you were part of it, *are* part of it, part of us. You've brought a lot of wonderful stuff to the Valiants. And to me especially.'

Laura awakened with a start.

She was bathed in a cold sweat, and her nightgown was clinging to her body. Struggling up into a sitting position, she threw back the bedclothes and swung her feet to the floor, turning on the bedside lamp as she did.

She could not help wondering, as she made her way to the bathroom, if she were coming down with something. To be perspiring like this was not normal; she hoped she was not in for a bout of the flu, or at the least a bad cold. She couldn't afford to get sick; she had far too much work to do, and Christmas was only a few weeks away.

After taking off her nightgown and drying herself, Laura put on a terrycloth robe and padded back to the bedroom. Wide awake, she punched up the pillows and got onto the bed.

Zapping on the television, she found CNN, and sat drinking the glass of carbonated water which she had put on the bedside table earlier but had not touched until now. Leaning back against the pillows, she stared at the set, grateful for the continuing stream of news out of Atlanta. At least it gave her something decent to watch in the early hours of the morning.

Laura put the glass down with a clatter, and sat up a bit straighter, suddenly remembering her weird dream . . . She had dreamed about Rosa Lavillard. The dream had been frightening, oppressive. She had been with Rosa in a vast building in some unknown city, and they had been lost within its maze-like corridors which seemed to lead nowhere. The corridors were endless, and there were many, many doors. Every time they opened one a startled occupant would look up, stare at them, and tell them, in answer to their question, that the way out was at the far end of the corridor. But it never was. Another door led only to another corridor. Nervous and distraught, she had begun to panic, but Rosa Lavillard had not. The older woman had remained calm.

'There is always a way out,' Rosa kept repeating, and yet they could not find the door that would lead them to the outside . . . and freedom.

It had become hotter and hotter in the windowless corridors, and she had grown overheated, tired. But Rosa was stalwart, stoical, forever promising she would get them out of this maze, no matter what. The final door opened onto a slide; Rosa had pushed her onto it, and she had slid farther and farther down into terrifying blackness. And as she had slipped into this bottomless pit she could hear Rosa singing in French, but she couldn't make out the words exactly . . . Suddenly Rosa herself was on the slide, hurtling down behind her, singing for all she was worth.

And then she had woken up. Bathed in sweat, and with good reason. She had been afraid in the dream.

Laura was baffled by the nightmare. What could it possibly mean? And why had she dreamed about Rosa Lavillard, a woman she hardly knew? The answer to the latter was relatively simple. She had run into the Lavillards earlier in the day, and obviously they had remained in the back of her mind.

When they were having coffee after dinner, Laura had been about to tell Claire she had bumped into them in the museum, and then the moment had been lost. Claire had started to talk about the Renoir, and Hercule, and the weekend plans. But I should have told her, Laura admonished herself, and she felt suddenly guilty that she had not done so. It's lying by omission, she thought.

Her mind lingered on the Lavillards for a second or two, and then it leapt to her brother Dylan.

She knew she should call him in London, just to say hello, but she was afraid to do so and had kept putting it off for the last few days. And for a simple reason. Invariably, they always managed to quarrel. Her brother was contentious by nature, and she wasn't a bit surprised when Claire had told her he had tried to pick a fight with the waiter the night they'd had dinner at Espadon. He loved picking fights with everyone. He was troubled, filled with demons. But weren't they all? Their lovely Welsh grandparents had always claimed, no, boasted, that they were *different* because they were Celts, and Laura had believed this, at least part of her had.

But she was smart enough to know that she and her sibling *were* odd, troubled, dysfunctional to a certain extent, in part because of a fey, neglectful, if loving mother, who was bound up in her husband and her painting at the expense of her children, an overcompensating father who smothered them with love, and a famous actress for a grandmother who surrounded them with her own theatricality and extravagances and mythic tales of ancient Wales.

Laura smiled. Whatever it was they had made her, she was very sure of *who* she was. A Valiant. And proud of it.

4

'I am happy you were available to meet with me, Laura,' Hercule Junot said, bestowing his warm smile on her. 'My friend is leaving tonight for her château in the Loire, and this afternoon at three was the only time she had free to receive us.'

'No problem, Hercule, I'm looking forward to meeting her, and really excited about seeing the Renoir. I'm thrilled she still owns it.'

'It was lucky for you, and for Claire. But come, let us not waste another moment.' Taking hold of her elbow, he ushered her across the lobby of the Plaza Athénée, continuing, 'My car is waiting outside. My friend lives on the Faubourg Saint-Germain in the *Septième*, not too far for us to go.'

'It's one of my favourite areas of Paris,' Laura confided as they went out into the street and made for the car. Once they were comfortably settled on the back seat and driving off, Hercule remarked, 'Yes, I know what you mean about the seventh. I myself have always found it very special, perhaps because of its diversity as well as its beauty ... an enclave for aristocrats in their beautiful houses, and yet an area where students, artists and writers abound.'

'I used to haunt the seventh when I was at the Sorbonne, Hercule,' Laura told him. 'When I wasn't trotting around the

Rodin Museum I was at the Café de Flore or the Deux Magots, or heading in the direction of the Hôtel des Invalides to visit Napoleon's tomb.'

'Ah yes, he is a favourite of yours,' Hercule said. 'Claire has told me how much you admire our famous Emperor.'

Laura smiled. 'Napoleon and Winston Churchill are my two great heroes.'

'Not Lincoln or George Washington?'

'Well yes, but in a different way. Churchill comes first with me, then Napoleon. I was tremendously influenced by my Welsh grandfather, who believed that Churchill saved Western civilization from extinction, quite aside from pulling the whole of Europe through evil times in the Second World War. Until the day he died my grandfather Owen Valiant said that Churchill was the greatest man of the twentieth century. And I believe that, too.'

'And Napoleon, the great dictator, how did you come to him?'

'Is that how you think of him . . . as a dictator?'

'Not I. Neither do most of the French, for that matter. The rest of Europe?' Hercule gave a small shrug and lifted his hands. '*They* think of him as a monster, but I do not believe he was.'

'I agree. And I came to him when I was living here as a student. I'm a Francophile, as you know, and I fell upon a wonderful biography of him, by Vincent Cronin, and I was just captivated. He was a genius, in my opinion.'

Hercule nodded. 'There is no half measure when it comes to Napoleon. He is either loved or loathed. Now, to move on, Laura, I must tell you about my friend, who you will be meeting in a few moments. Her name is Jacqueline de Antoine-St Lucien. I have known her for many years. Her late husband Charles was a dear friend, and he indulged Jacqueline in her grand passion . . . collecting art. She has the great taste . . .' He paused, kissed his fingertips. 'Superb taste . . . *formidable*. Her collection is enthralling. You will be seeing some of the greatest paintings in the world in a few minutes.'

'Why does she want to sell the Renoir?' Laura asked, filled with curiosity.

'She has not really confided the reason to me, but I do know the family château near Loches is expensive to run. Last year she sold a Van Gogh.'

'I wish I'd known about that!'

'And I, too, wish I had known, Laura. Certainly I would have informed you. *Immediately.* From what Jacqueline told me later, she did not even have it on the market. Someone saw the Van Gogh and made an offer, and so it was sold – just like that.' He snapped his thumb and finger together. 'From what I understand she had not thought of selling it, but the offer was so tremendous she found she could not refuse.'

'My favourite of all the Van Gogh paintings is *White Roses.*'

'Ah, *mais oui*, the most beautiful. And now it is hanging in France again, at least for the time being.'

'In France, but in the American Embassy.'

'And therefore on American soil, at least technically speaking,' he answered. 'Actually, it is at the Ambassador's residence.'

'I'd give anything to see it.'

'Perhaps that can be arranged. I know the Ambassador, Pamela Harriman.'

'That'd be wonderful, Hercule. By the way, how much does your friend want for the Renoir? Or don't you know?'

'When I spoke with her last night she mentioned that she was thinking of somewhere in the region of four million, or thereabouts.'

'Dollars?'

'Yes, US dollars. Ah, here we are, Laura. This is the house where Jacqueline lives. It has been in the family for many, many years.'

The private house, known as an *hôtel particulier*, was one of a number of similar residences standing on this famous street, hidden behind high walls built of pale stone. Immense wooden doors, studded with huge nails and painted dark green, were opened by a man in a striped uniform a moment after the chauffeur had rung the bell.

As the Mercedes rolled into the cobbled courtyard Laura saw that there was a concierge's cottage to the right, a fountain in the centre of the yard, and two wonderful old white chestnut trees growing against the ivy-clad walls. The trees had shed many of their leaves and so looked somewhat bereft on this cold December afternoon.

Hercule helped Laura out of the car and together they walked up the wide front steps. These led to double doors made of thick glass encased in wrought iron, which had been worked into a scroll design. Before he had even rung the bell the doors were opened by a manservant dressed in a dark suit and a bow tie.

Nodding, Hercule said, '*Bonjour*, Pierre.'

The butler inclined his head. '*Monsieur, madame. Entrez, s'il vous plaît.*' As he spoke he opened the door wider to give them access to the foyer, which was like a long gallery in its architecture. French windows on the wall facing the front door where they had just entered led outside. Laura glanced through them quickly as they were taken down the gallery by Pierre; she could see gardens, a lawn surrounded by trees, and in the centre a fountain that echoed the one in the front courtyard.

'*Madame la comtesse* attends you in the *salon vert, monsieur*,' the butler murmured.

Laura could not help smiling warmly when she saw Jacqueline, Comtesse de Antoine-St Lucien. She was the daintiest, prettiest little woman Laura had ever set eyes on. She could not have been more than four feet ten or eleven inches, and she was slender, with widely-set, bright green eyes, blonde hair, stylishly cut, and an almost cherubic face, hardly lined at all. There was something very girlish and pretty about her, even though Laura guessed she must be in her early seventies, or thereabouts.

Jacqueline was standing in front of the fire in the *salon vert*, pale green in colour, and she smiled back at Laura and hurried forward.

'Hercule!' she exclaimed. 'So nice of you to come, and to bring your friend.'

Hercule kissed her on both cheeks and said, 'I am so happy to see you, Jacqueline. And may I present Laura Valiant. Laura, this is the *Comtesse* de Antoine-St Lucien.'

'I am delighted to meet you, Mademoiselle,' Jacqueline said, shaking Laura's hand.

'And I you, Countess,' Laura responded, smiling at this perfectly groomed and elegantly-dressed diminutive woman.

'May I offer you something? Coffee, tea, a drink perhaps?'

'No, thank you,' Laura said.

Hercule shook his head. 'Nothing for me either, Jacqueline. But thank you.'

'Then do let us sit down,' the countess replied, smiling graciously and leading them across the room to a grouping of comfortable chairs near the fireplace.

Almost at once, Hercule began speaking to her about the château near Loches in the Loire Valley, where she was having some repair work done to the roof. This gave Laura a chance to look around.

Her eyes scanned the room quickly, took in the eau-de-nil walls, the pale green silk upholstery on the chairs and sofas, and the matching taffeta draperies. The pale green walls made a soft and beguiling backdrop for the paintings in the room, which included a Bonnard, a Degas and a Cézanne. And of course the Renoir, which was hanging above a *bombé*-fronted chest set against a small side wall.

Laura was itching to get up, to go and look at it, but her natural good manners forbade this.

It was Hercule who suddenly rose and said, 'Ah, the Renoir, Jacqueline, I must look at it again, if I may.'

'But of course, Hercule,' she answered. 'Please do, and you also Mademoiselle Valiant. Please, go and see it.'

'Come, Laura,' he said, turning to her. 'I know you are anxious to look at all of the countess's works of art.'

'Yes, I am,' she admitted.

They walked over to the Renoir and stood gazing at it, both of them entranced by its beauty and grace.

Hercule said, 'I have seen this many times over the years, Laura, and I must admit I never tire of it. But then Renoir was the great master, as we both know.'

'And this is just gorgeous,' Laura murmured, sounding slightly awed. Nonetheless, she could not help wondering if her Canadian client would find the painting too small. In her dealings with him in the past, he had usually favoured larger canvases. On the other hand, the painting was a little jewel; the skin tone of the model glowed like luminescent pearl under the picture light, and the woman truly came alive, as did the landscape and the pool near the rock she was seated on. Laura hoped that her client *would* buy it.

After another moment or two lingering in front of the Renoir, Hercule took hold of Laura's arm and drew her across the room, first to look at the Degas, then the Bonnard and finally the Cézanne. All three paintings were, like the Renoir, total perfection, prime examples of the artists' work. Laura couldn't help wondering if any of these were for sale, especially the large Cézanne.

Eventually they went and joined the countess in front of the fire, and Laura turned to her and said, 'The Renoir is exquisite, and so are your other paintings, Countess. It is quite an experience to be in a room which contains four such masterpieces. A room in a private home, I mean.'

'*Merci*, Mademoiselle Valiant. You are very kind, and I must say, they are all paintings which make me feel happy when I look at them. But then I have never liked anything that makes me sad or depressed. I have the need to be uplifted by art.'

'Absolutely!' Hercule exclaimed. 'I agree with you, Jacqueline. Now, I would like to take Laura to the dining room, to show her the Gauguins. He is one of her favourite painters. Is he not, Laura?'

She nodded.

Jacqueline stood up. 'I shall accompany you,' and so saying she glided across the Aubusson rug and led them down the gallery to the dining room at the far end.

Its walls had been sponge-glazed in a cloudy, dusty-pink colour, and this shade also made a wonderfully soft background for the paintings. In this instance they were breathtaking primitives by Paul Gauguin, three altogether, each one hanging alone. There was one on the long central wall, and the others had been placed on two end walls. The fourth wall in the room was intersected by windows which filled it with natural northern light, perfect for these particular works of art.

All three paintings were of dark-skinned Tahitian women, either by the sea or in it, or sitting in the natural exotic landscape of the Polynesian islands. The dark skin tones were highlighted by the vivid *pareos* the women wore around their loins, the colourful vegetation and the unusual pinkish-coral colour Gauguin had so frequently used to depict the earth and the sandy beaches of Tahiti. The dusty-pink walls of the dining room echoed this warm coral, and helped to throw the dark-skinned beauties into relief.

Laura was mesmerized. She had never seen Gauguins like these outside a museum, and they were impressive. All three paintings were large, dominant, just the type of art her other important client Mark Tabbart would give his right arm for, as he so frequently proclaimed to her. 'They are magnificent,' she exclaimed, glancing at the countess, and before she could stop herself, she rushed on, 'I would buy any one of these, or all of them, if you would consider selling.'

'They *are* the most fabulous Gauguins,' Jacqueline murmured. 'Gauguin painted all three in the same year, 1892, and what extraordinary examples of his work they are. I could never sell them, I love them far too much. But even if I had the desire or the need to auction them to the highest bidder, I am afraid, Mademoiselle Valiant, that I could not. The paintings belonged to my husband, and he left them to our son Arnaud and his wife Natalie. I have them to enjoy for my lifetime, but I do not own them.'

'I envy you living with them,' Laura said. 'They are so beautiful they are . . . blinding.'

'Perhaps we should talk about the Renoir,' Hercule interjected. 'As you know, Jacqueline, Laura has a client who may well be interested in it, and, of course, there is Claire Benson, who wishes to photograph it on Monday.'

Jacqueline said, 'Let us go back to the *salon vert*, where we can sit and discuss everything in comfort.'

Later that afternoon when Hercule dropped Laura off at the hotel, she thanked him profusely, then said, 'I will phone my client in Toronto, and hopefully I will be able to give the countess an answer by Monday, perhaps even sooner.'

Hercule nodded. 'That will be perfectly all right, Laura.' After helping her out of the Mercedes and walking her to the door of the hotel, he said, 'I shall come in with you for a moment, if I may. I want to talk to you about two things: about paintings. And about Claire.'

Taken aback, Laura stared at him. 'What about Claire? Is there something wrong? You sound odd.'

'I think perhaps I sound worried, Laura, but let us not stand here. Please, let us have a cup of tea, or something else if you wish.'

'Yes,' she said swiftly, 'yes, of course, Hercule,' and she was unable to keep the sudden concern out of her voice as she spoke. 'I don't think I want tea. I'd prefer a drink. Can we go to the bar, please, Hercule?'

'*Mais oui*, let us do that,' Hercule replied, and they walked on quietly without saying another word, and went downstairs to the bar. It was only when they were finally settled at one of the small tables in the dimly-lit, rather clubby-looking Bar Anglais that Laura spoke.

'Why are you worried about Claire? Please tell me, Hercule.'

'I will, in due course. First, let us order. What would you like?'

'A glass of white wine, please.'

Hercule beckoned to the waiter, ordered for Laura, and asked for a Scotch and soda for himself. Then he sat back in the black leather chair and said, 'I'll get to Claire in a moment. First, I want to talk to you about paintings.' He paused and added, 'Something serious about paintings.'

Looking at him alertly, she nodded. 'Please tell me, Hercule.'

'It is about Gauguin's paintings. It is very important that you let me know whenever one comes onto the market in the States. Providing you know this, of course, and if you are interested in it for a client. I am asking you to do this for your own protection.'

'Of course I'll tell you. What's this all about?'

'There are several Gauguin paintings that are, well . . . *questionable*. I know your great interest in him as an artist, and how much you love his work, and I do not want you to make any mistakes. I do not want you to make a commitment without talking to me.'

'You mean there are some fakes around?'

'I am going to tell you a story about a Gauguin, and you will find it interesting, I believe.' He paused, stared at her intently. 'Laura, this is confidential. What I am about to tell you is for your ears only, it must remain between us. At least for the moment.'

'I would never discuss it with anyone,' she reassured him. Her eyes were eager, the expression on her face expectant.

'Many years ago, there was a collector,' he began. And slowly, carefully, he recounted a story to her.

She was rapt, hung onto his every word.

When he had finished, he said, 'Now to Claire. I don't think that she is well. In fact, I would go so far as to say that she is ill.'

Laura gaped at him, then said, 'She told me you'd given her a lecture about her weight.'

He nodded. 'She has lost much weight. She says she has been on a regime. However, it is not so much the weight loss that troubles me. It is . . . the *look* of her, Laura.'

Frowning, shaking her head, Laura murmured, 'I don't understand what you mean.'

'Yesterday, at the studio, there was a moment when she was talking to me from the set, and she had . . .' He stopped, looked off into space, as if trying to remember something, and then he said, 'She looked very peaked, no, that is not it. What is the word I am looking for . . . she looked pinched . . . drawn . . . as if the skin of her face were stretched very tightly over her bones.' He took a deep breath, and added, very quietly, 'Her face was like a death mask; it frightened me, Laura.'

'Hercule! That's awful! An awful thing to say,' she exclaimed, and shuddered.

The waiter brought their drinks, and they were silent until he disappeared behind the bar again. Then Hercule continued, 'I have the most terrible apprehension for her. I cannot explain it. You see, I love her –' He cut himself off, and stared at Laura, suddenly at a loss.

She said swiftly, 'I know you love her, Hercule, I've known it for a long time. You don't have to be embarrassed or feel shy with me. I do understand. And I'm glad you love her, glad you care so much about Claire.'

Looking relieved, he answered, with a slight nod, 'I am pleased I have told you this, and I thank you, my dear, for your understanding.' He lifted his glass and took a sip of his Scotch.

Laura, also sipping her drink, asked, a moment later, 'What do you mean when you say you feel apprehensive?'

'As I told you, I do not think she is well, but I cannot explain why I feel this, not in a rational way. I thought she looked tired, worn out, yesterday, with the black smudges underneath her eyes, and so very thin. At one moment, when she turned to speak to me, the light fell upon her and she looked . . . like a skeleton, and so *ill*. I was frightened.'

'Perhaps it was just the way the lights on the set hit her face; you know that can happen.'

'Yes, that is true. I tried to tell myself this last night. I reviewed the time I had spent with her at the studio, and certainly she had been energetic, as she always is. But –' He cut himself off again, sat back drinking his Scotch and soda; his eyes were troubled, his shoulders taut with anxiety.

Laura could see how upset he was, and she waited until he had collected himself before she said slowly, 'What do you think is wrong with Claire? You say you think she's ill, but with what?'

He lifted his hands in that typical gesture of his and shook his head. 'Alas, I do not know, Laura.' He sighed and continued, 'I push the worry away, as I did when we were at Jacqueline's earlier. Yet it creeps back into my mind. Has she . . . has she confided anything in you?'

'Nothing, Hercule, and I'm sure she would if she were sick, or worried about herself. She did mention you'd chastised her about the weight loss, and she *is* thinner, I agree with you. But I didn't think she looked ill last night over dinner.'

'The cosmetics, they help,' he said pointedly.

'That's true. She's very . . .' Laura paused and did not continue, changing her mind all of a sudden.

Hercule, looking at her intently, asked, 'She's *what*?'

Laura shook her head and answered softly, 'She's still very angry. About her bad marriage, about men, or perhaps one man. It seems to eat her up at times, consume her. Perhaps it's just that, the anger, the disappointment. Plus working hard, being tired occasionally.' Leaning forward, Laura put one hand on his arm. 'Try not to worry so much. I don't think she's sick, Hercule, I really don't.'

Her words seemed to help him to relax, and the tight lines around his eyes eased slightly. 'I hope you are correct. When you love a woman as I love her, it *is* worrying if she seems . . . well, not herself.'

Taking the plunge, Laura said, 'Why don't you tell her how you feel, Hercule? Tell her you love her?'

'Oh but I could not do that, Laura. Never, never. Claire does not feel the same way about me as I feel about her. *I am afraid.* Yes, I admit that to you, Laura, I am afraid to tell her. I do not want to lose her, you see, and I might, if she . . . knew how I truly felt. Being her friend, and part of her life is so important to me.'

'You ought to tell her. You might be surprised how she reacts.'

'Laura, how can you of all people in the world, say that to me? *Mon Dieu!* You have just told me that she is angry about her failed marriage, about *him*. No, there is no room for me in her life, as much as I want there to be.'

His gently-spoken words seemed to strike at Laura, and she flinched inside. She sat back in her chair, thinking how sad it was that Claire was being so cruel to herself, and was, in a way, punishing herself without reason. *No room for me in her life.* She replayed his words of a moment ago in her mind, and she knew it was true, and that this was indeed a tragedy. Hercule was much older, but he was a good-looking man, well-built, tall, and strong as an ox, and he was a kind and loving human being. He would have looked after Claire, protected her, given her so much.

He said, 'Maybe I worry about nothing. Is that what you are thinking?'

She shook her head. 'No, I was thinking how sad it is that Claire has this attitude about . . . life.'

'You do not think she is ill?'

'No, I do not. In fact, I'm positive she isn't, at least not in the way you mean. Not physically.'

'Mentally?' he asked, his voice growing slightly sharper; he stared at her intently.

'No. I don't mean that either. She's very sane, our Claire. But she is a *tormented* woman, Hercule, and I don't know how to help her. I have tried for years.'

'Do you think . . . she still loves her ex-husband?'

'No. I think she is filled with hatred for him.'

Hercule was silent for a moment, sat nursing his drink. Eventually he lifted his head and looked into Laura's eyes, and his own were moist with tears. 'What a terrible waste. How tragic that is . . . to cut yourself off . . . to deny yourself the possibility of love in that way.'

'Yes,' Laura said, her voice a whisper.

Later that evening, after a light supper in her room, Laura worked on her papers for a while. But for once in her life her concentration was fleeting. Finally, she put down her pen and sat back in her chair.

She was troubled about Claire.

Not in the way that Hercule was, not about her physical health, but about her mental state. Claire had harboured a dislike of Philippe ever since their break-up, perhaps even before that. But now it had turned to hatred and Laura couldn't understand why.

Claire had changed in the last six months. In the summer, when she and Doug had been in Paris, Claire had been much more relaxed, more at ease with herself. Now Laura realized that Claire was taut, full of tension, and at times she could be quite volatile.

Laura could not help asking herself why there had been this change. She's alone and lonely, Laura thought, rising, walking across the room to the window. Parting the curtains, she looked down into the courtyard below. In spring and summer it was a garden restaurant; now it was devoid of flowers and furniture, a simple paved yard flooded with light from the windows of the rooms that looked down onto it. Empty, cold, uninviting. Like Claire's life. If only she could meet someone. A nice man of the right age with whom she could fall in love, perhaps settle down with. But Laura knew instinctively that this would not happen because Claire would not permit it. She's her own worst enemy, Laura muttered under her breath, loving her friend but at the same time feeling suddenly somewhat disturbed and critical about her behaviour. I want to help her and I don't know how to do that, Laura said to herself, remembering how difficult that had always been, even when they were children. Claire had tried to be so independent and brave, but Laura had always sensed, even then, that she was afraid. Claire had been . . . timid. That was a good word to use to describe her. Her grandmother had once said that: 'Claire's a scared little thing, isn't she? So *timid* and reluctant.' She had often wondered what Claire was frightened of when they were little, and once or twice she had asked her, but Claire denied her fear. There was one thing, and it came rushing back to Laura. Her grandmother had never really liked Claire's parents. She had said her mother was ineffectual and her father a womanizer. But those were not reasons for Claire to be *frightened*, were they?

Sighing under her breath, Laura turned away from the window, got undressed and went to bed. Feeling wide awake she zapped on CNN and lay watching it for an hour. She had just turned it and the light off when the phone rang; reaching for it she said, 'Hello?'

'Hi, darling,' Doug answered.

'I wish you were here,' Laura grumbled.

'I can be there if you want.'

'But not fast enough for me.'

'How's three seconds?'

'Three seconds? What are you talking about?'

'I'll be right up,' he replied, and laughed. 'I'm in the lobby.'

5

'What are you doing in Paris?' Laura asked, smiling at Doug as he came through the door. 'You're supposed to be in Los Angeles.'

'I was never going there. I lied. I wanted to surprise you, darling.'

'You succeeded,' she said, and came into his arms.

Pushing the door closed with his foot, Doug held her close to him for a moment then bent down and kissed her on the mouth. Finally pulling away, he said, 'I thought a weekend in Paris would be great for both of us. So here I am.'

'I'm thrilled, it's just wonderful, that's all I have to say.'

He walked across the room, his arm around her shoulders, and said, 'So whatever you have planned I think you should cancel it. I want you all to myself.'

'I'm glad you do, and I feel the same way. There's no problem about cancelling things. All I have are two appointments with galleries, but they don't matter all that much. Oh but Doug, I told Claire I'd have dinner at the apartment tomorrow night. I can't really cancel that.'

'I don't want you to, and you know I love Claire. It'll be good to see her and the Shrimp.'

Laura laughed. 'I'd forgotten that you call Natasha that. She's not much of a shrimp anymore, though. More like a . . . golden salamander.'

'Mmmm. So she's growing up gorgeous, is she?'

'Absolutely.'

'There's the bell. It's my bag,' Doug said and went to open the door. The porter placed his suitcase, briefcase and overcoat in the room, thanked him for the tip, and left.

Laura said: 'Are you hungry? I'm sure the Relais Plaza is still open. I'll get dressed and we can go down for a bite.'

'No, don't bother, darling. I ate dinner on the plane. But I would like a drink. White wine would be great.' Leaning into her he kissed her on the cheek, took off his jacket and tie. 'I'm going to have a shower and then I'll be right with you. Order a bottle of Pouilly Fumé, sweetheart.' He continued to undress and Laura went to call room service.

She was propped up against the pillows on the bed sipping a glass of carbonated water when Doug came out of the bathroom swathed in a bath towel which he had wrapped around him toga style.

'The wine's over there on the chest,' she said. 'I had the waiter open it.'

'Thanks. Do you want a glass with me?'

'But of course.'

Doug poured two glasses and carried them over to the bed. After giving one to Laura, he strolled around to the other side, climbed onto it, sat propped up next to her. Turning to look at her, he lifted his glass and touched it to hers. 'Here's to our weekend together, darling,' he said and smiled.

Laura smiled back at him over the rim of the glass. 'To the weekend. And to you, darling. You're a crazy fool, flying all this way just for two days, but I love it.'

After a few sips of the white wine, Doug placed his glass on the bedside table; drawing closer to Laura, he kissed her cheek, then her neck.

Immediately putting her wine on the nightstand next to her,

Laura shifted her body around to face him, and a moment later he was pulling her into his arms. Doug renewed his kisses, showering them on her neck, her shoulders, her bare arms; reaching inside her nightgown he began to caress one of her breasts sensually, drawing small sighs from her.

Moving closer to him, Laura loosened the towel wrapped around him, let her hand trail down over his flat stomach, making gentle circular movements; her fingers fluttered down, and she began to stroke him.

Doug lay very still, his eyes tightly closed; he luxuriated in her touch, drifted with his sensual thoughts. He felt a slight movement against his legs as Laura slithered down the bed and crouched over his thighs. She was still stroking him and then unexpectedly her moist lips encircled him and he let out a long sigh as she took him fully in her mouth. Suddenly he was aroused. After a second or two, she stopped, lifted her head, kissed his stomach, and then pushing herself up the bed she brought her mouth to his.

Doug's excitement was mounting. He returned her fervent kisses and with suddenness, almost abruptness, he rolled them over so that he was on top of her. Their mouths stayed locked together. Her tongue grazed his and they shared a moment of intense intimacy before Doug pushed his hands under Laura's buttocks, fitted her long, lean body into the curve of his. And at last he was hard enough to slip inside her, easily and expertly, and within moments they had a rhythm, were rising and falling together, their movements swifter, almost frenzied. Her legs went high around his back and he shafted deeper into her, sinking deeply into the warmth.

Soon Doug felt as though he were falling through dark blue water, falling down, falling further and further down into a bottomless dark blue sea. The waves washed over him, beat against him. He squeezed his eyes tighter shut. Images danced behind his lids. Oh yes, he thought, oh yes, and as he began the long slide down into total ecstasy he saw that face, trapped as it was in his mind . . .

'Doug, oh Doug!' Laura cried. 'Now. Please. Oh please don't stop, darling.'

Her voice came to him from far away. And yet it was clear, sharp, the voice he knew so well. And it brought him down. Instantly he lost his erection. His fantasy shattered. Falling against her, Doug lay still, breathing heavily. He was flaccid, drained of energy all of a sudden. And he was mortified.

After a long moment, Laura whispered, 'Why did you stop? What happened?'

'I don't know,' he whispered back. 'I'll be all right in a minute.' But he wasn't, and after a short while he slid off her, and lay on his back, still breathing deeply.

'Are you all right, Doug?' she asked, concern giving her voice an edge.

'I'm fine,' he replied in a low voice. He felt vitiated, sapped of his strength.

Laura's hand reached for him; she began to stroke him, endeavouring to arouse him once more. But a moment later when her lips encircled him, he knew her efforts would be in vain. This happened a lot with her these days, this loss of strength and vitality at the crucial moment. Doug got off the bed, hurried into the bathroom.

Snapping on the light and locking the door, he went and looked at himself in the mirror. What in God's name was wrong with him? Why couldn't he bring the act of love to its true culmination for them both? He had always been proud of his prowess as a lover, his staying power.

It was odd how he fell apart, though, somehow never reached fulfilment these days. Panic struck him. Was it always going to be like this? For the rest of his life? Was he always going to be an ineffectual lover, a man incapable of satisfying a woman, satisfying his wife? Suddenly, Doug was hit by a rush of embarrassment. He had flown all this way to make love to her and he had failed her, failed himself.

And then he thought: It's all in the mind, of course. That's where all this begins. And ends.

6

Laura had always thought of herself as an observer. She would sit back and watch, saying very little but hearing everything. And there had been a great deal to see and hear, whether she was observing her brother Dylan, the rebel, her father, the composer and conductor; or her mother, the artist.

Then there was her grandmother Megan, the once-great musical star, and her grandfather Owen, theatrical manager and professional Welshman. And Claire Benson – her heroine, role model, and best friend.

Each one of them was highly individualistic, a complex personality, and therefore a fascinating study.

The two people she most enjoyed observing were her grandparents, Owen and Megan Valiant. They were the greatest influence in her life, especially her grandmother; and, because she loved them so much, she saw them through eyes that were not in the least critical. So many of her values had come from them, and it was on her grandparents that she had based her own notions of romantic love.

Grandfather Owen would boast, 'Ours is one of the greatest love stories that ever happened. I fell in love with Megan when I first heard her singing in the Chapel at Port Talbot, and I've loved her truly ever since.'

And whenever he said this, which was very frequently, her grandmother would blush prettily and smile at Owen with adoration. 'It's true, Laura. The day I set eyes on your grandfather I was kissed by the angels. It was the luckiest day of my life, meeting him.'

When she was young she was well aware that her parents loved each other, too. But unlike Owen and Megan, who never quarrelled, Richard and Margaret were often engaged in roaring battles.

'It's a feast or a famine with your parents,' her grandmother would say. 'They're either in each other's arms or at each other's throats. Goodness me, I've never before seen such goings on in my life.'

Her parents' way of making up after one of their regular tempestuous falling outs was to go off on a trip for a week or two. 'Another honeymoon,' Claire would say, and she would become a kind of surrogate mother to the two of them, aided and abetted by Mae, the housekeeper, Dylan's nanny, Cissy, and Grandma Megan, who would swoop down in full force to take charge of the household.

Claire had been the other important influence in her life, and she had observed her dearest friend through loving eyes and hardly ever found fault.

'Always the observer, Laura,' her lovely gran had often said in those days, laughing lightly, and then Megan would go on to predict that her favourite grandchild would become a writer. She hadn't, of course; nonetheless, she continued to be the observer, forever watching everyone, and assessing.

She was doing exactly that tonight as she sat on the stool in Claire's kitchen, where Claire and Natasha were preparing dinner. As she looked from mother to daughter she saw the enormous love and friendship flowing between them. It was so potent, such a palpable thing, Laura felt as though she could reach out and touch it. To see them in such harmony made Laura happy. Neither she nor Claire had been close to their own mothers, a situation which had often saddened Laura. But then she'd had Grandma Megan, and so had Claire, for that matter. And they still had her, in fact.

Everything that Claire had said about Natasha earlier in the week was true. Laura had not seen her goddaughter for almost five months, and in that time she had lost her puppy fat and grown even taller. Like her mother she had bright auburn hair, although hers was full and flowing, unlike Claire's which was cut short. Her resplendent locks gave her the look of a girl who had stepped out of a Renaissance painting. Her large eyes were a peculiar golden brown, a sort of amber colour, which Laura had always found unusual, and there was a faint dusting of freckles across the bridge of her slender nose. Otherwise, her creamy skin was without blemish.

Natasha had a short torso and long legs, and, as Claire had pointed out, although she was only fourteen, she dwarfed them both these days. She's growing up to be a real beauty, Laura thought, then turned her attention to Claire.

Contrary to what Hercule believed, Laura was quite convinced there was nothing wrong with her friend. Tonight she was full of her usual bountiful energy; her face was flushed, her eyes shining brightly, and her short auburn curls were like a burnished halo around her pretty face. No, there was nothing wrong with her, Laura decided, filled with a sudden sense of relief. Her dearest friend was the picture of good health.

Claire was wearing a red wool tunic over matching leggings, and she was full of laughter and gaiety as she skilfully prepared Navarin of lamb, her famous lamb stew with vegetables. Simultaneously, she was putting finishing touches to another speciality of hers, Strawberries Romanoff.

Claire had always been a marvellous cook. This was the one thing Laura envied, since she herself had little talent in that direction. Although Claire had been an enormous influence on her in other ways, she had never been able to teach her the simplest rudiments of gourmet cooking.

On the other hand, Claire had shown her such important things as how to put on make-up, pluck her eyebrows and paint her toenails; it was also from Claire that she had learned how to walk properly in high heels when still too young to wear them, and most importantly, how to flirt with boys.

Flirt with boys. Laura smiled, thinking that before long Natasha would be doing that. She almost laughed out loud; in all probability, Natasha was flirting already.

Shifting slightly on the stool, Laura said, 'Please let me do something to help.' As she spoke she glanced across at Claire and Natasha, and added, 'I feel like a spare wheel.'

Claire laughed. 'Everything's under control, I promise you, so just relax and keep us company until Hercule gets here, then you can entertain him while we finish up.'

'All right, that's a deal. But let me know if you need me to peel a potato, chop something, or whatever.'

'I've done all the whatevers for Mom,' Natasha said, laughing as she looked up. Then she returned to the task of dropping dollops of chocolate-chip-cookie mixture on a metal cookie sheet.

'It certainly smells delicious, Claire,' Laura remarked. 'I like your lamb stew better than Dina Zuckerberg's famous specialities.'

Claire burst out laughing on hearing this, and Laura started to laugh with her; their peals of laughter rang out, echoed around the kitchen.

Puzzled by their sudden and unexpected hilarity, not understanding it at all, Natasha asked, 'Who's Zina Duckerberg?'

'It's not Zina Duckerberg, it's Dina Zuckerberg,' Laura corrected. 'She used to live in the same building in New York when we were growing up, and she was always inviting us to dinner when her mother was out or away travelling.'

'And she always "cooked" the same thing, pizza from Ray's Pizza Parlor and Dayvilles vanilla ice cream,' interjected Claire, who began laughing again, as did Laura.

Natasha shook her head wonderingly, smiled indulgently at the two women, whom she thought were suddenly slightly crazy, and immediately changed the subject. 'You could do one thing to help, Laura. Would you go and ask Doug if we need more ice?'

'Good idea,' Laura replied, and slid off the stool. She found Doug on a sofa in front of the fire, nursing a drink.

'Do we need more ice, Doug?'

'No, darling, there's plenty in the bucket.'

Laura glanced around, once more admiring the room. Claire had decorated it with a great deal of style and flair, and a little help from Hercule. It was easy for Laura to spot his touches here and there, such as the bouffant taffeta curtains at the windows. 'Dance dresses,' he called them, because they were narrow at the top and flared out like a skirt before they reached the floor. And the large silk lamp shades, the urns of twigs and leaves were also Hercule's well-known imprints.

The room was old-fashioned, traditional, with spacious, rather grand proportions. A highly-polished wood floor met crisp white walls, with bookshelves soaring up to the ceiling on the long wall facing the fireplace.

On the other walls were hung oversized framed prints, all of them colourful reproductions of Toulouse-Lautrec's Moulin Rouge Can-Can girls. A cream Savonnerie rug, patterned with red, black and green, covered part of the dark floor, and there were two large cream velvet sofas and several chairs arranged in an airy seating arrangement.

Claire had been collecting French country antiques for a number of years and their ripe woods gleamed in the lambent light, adding a touch of elegance and warmth to the room. She had arranged lovely old pieces of porcelain on some of the antique chests and tables, and grouped together a large collection of silver-framed photographs on a Provençal sideboard. Laura gazed back at all of the Valiants, as well as herself. And Natasha, Claire and her parents were also captured in different poses on celluloid.

The air was fragrant with the scent of fresh flowers, bowls of potpourri and Rigaud candles, all of which were trademarks of Claire's. It was a lovely room at any time, but especially so at night, with the candles burning, the silk-shaded lamps glowing and the fire blazing in the hearth. There was a welcoming warmth here, and a great deal of love.

Walking across to one of the tall windows, Laura stood looking down at the place de Fürstemberg, which she considered to be one of the most picturesque little squares in Paris. It was a cold night. The inky sky was clear, without cloud, and the stars were few. But a curving crescent moon was bright as it cast its silvery light across the shadowy square.

Directly below the apartment windows was the solitary, old-fashioned lamppost with its five globes which gave off the only other illumination, except for the light streaming out from the windows of the adjacent apartments. Laura had always thought of the lamppost as a charming little sentinel standing next to the ancient Paulownia trees which were much treasured by every inhabitant of the square.

Laura knew the Sixième, the sixth arrondissement, very well and especially this quaint square with its great charm and old-world atmosphere. It was she who had found the apartment for Claire seven years ago, just after she had separated from her husband. It had belonged to Madame Solange Puy, grandmother of her old friend Marie-Louise Puy, who dated from her Sorbonne student days.

Marie-Louise had inherited the apartment from her grandmother and had just put it up for sale. Fortuitously for Claire, as it turned out, Laura had been in Paris at this particular time, and the moment she heard about the apartment going on the market she had told Marie-Louise that Claire might well be interested in buying it.

The three of them had met at the apartment and Claire had instantly fallen in love with it. Within a couple of months the sale was complete with all the documents signed, and the place finally belonged to Claire. As soon as the deed was in her hands she began to decorate. Hercule, as always, was the chief adviser and initiator of ideas, and together they had created what Claire called, 'My first real home as a grown-up.' And it *was* beautiful, Laura was the first to acknowledge.

It had pleased Laura to see Claire so happy on the day her friend had shown her the finished apartment. Claire's excitement about her new home had wiped the anger and pain off her face, for a little while at least.

'Laura.'

At the sound of Natasha's voice Laura swung around. 'Yes?'

'Your lipstick . . . well, it's not right . . . not the right colour. I've brought you this . . . one of mine. It's much better for you.' Natasha hurried forward and handed the tube of lipstick to Laura.

Laura automatically took it, startled as usual by Natasha's candour. The girl was breathtakingly honest, blunt even, but then weren't most fourteen-year-olds today? 'What's wrong with the colour I'm wearing?' Laura asked, after a moment.

'It's too red for you. Anyway, bright red's *out*. Old-fashioned. Look at the one I've given you. It's sort of brownish with a hint of pink, and it's much more *in*. Just ask Mom. She uses one of my browns now. Red is definitely gross.'

'Thanks for your beauty advice, darling. It used to be your mother passing on tips, now it's you.'

'You're not mad at me, are you, Laura?'

'No, of course not,' she answered with a light laugh, amused by the girl's seriousness and look of concern about the lipstick.

The doorbell rang, and Natasha exclaimed, 'That's Hercule, he's always on time!' She glanced at the clock on the mantelpiece. 'Just two minutes past seven,' she added as she ran across the floor to the entrance hall.

Laura followed at a slower pace.

Doug jumped up and straightened his jacket.

Natasha wrenched open the door and cried, 'Hercule, we

were –' Her sentence was bitten off abruptly. Natasha stood stock still, gaping at Hercule's companion. It was Philippe Lavillard.

Laura stared at Philippe, as speechless as Natasha.

Philippe looked from Natasha to Laura, and then took a step forward, drawing a bit closer to the threshold. It was obvious that he was about to say something; he opened his mouth then immediately closed it. The words remained unsaid.

The kitchen door had flown open with a clatter at this moment and Claire now rushed into the living room; she was laughing. 'There you are, Hercule, as punc –' She, too, instantly cut off her sentence midway, when she saw Philippe Lavillard; she was flabbergasted at the sight of him. 'What the hell are you doing here?' she exclaimed, but the words sounded more like a snarl than anything else.

'We met, he and I, on the doorstep,' Hercule began, already sensing trouble, wishing to keep things at least civilized; he knew they would never be amicable. That was an impossibility between these two antagonists. 'We came up the stairs together,' he finished somewhat lamely, and shrugged.

Claire stared at her old friend without uttering a word, blinking rapidly, as if suddenly afflicted with a nervous tic. Then her eyes swung to Philippe. 'What do *you* want?' she demanded, her voice shrill.

It struck Laura that Claire was spoiling for a fight with Philippe, and she wondered how best to diffuse the situation before it spiralled out of hand, became a full-blown row. She glanced at Doug; he stared at her pointedly.

In answer to Claire, Philippe said quietly, 'You know what I want.'

'What you want and what you'll get are two entirely different things. You can't just come here without warning and make demands on me. And you know that,' she snapped, her eyes icy.

'I'm entitled to see Natasha.'

'Huh! *You*! You don't give a damn about Natasha. If you did you wouldn't bury yourself in darkest Africa, tending to the natives and their Bubonic Plagues and Black Deaths or whatever other horrendous diseases it is they have. You'd be here, living in Paris, and *available* to be with your daughter whenever she needs you. Instead, you're thousands of miles away, half the time incommunicado because of your deadly viruses, and of no use to her or me when we might need you urgently.'

'You know if there were an emergency I'd be here as quickly as possible, if you asked me to come. And I do have a right to see my daughter,' he answered, cool and reasonable in his tone.

'You gave those rights up when you ran off!'

'I didn't run off, as you put it, Claire, and you know it. And don't forget, I do have visitation rights.'

'If *I* say so. And don't *you* forget that I have sole custody, and that I control your visitation rights. They're at my discretion. The judge said so. And you accepted that stipulation without a murmur.'

'I don't wish to fight with you, Claire,' he replied, sighing imperceptibly, holding his temper in check, knowing it was futile to squabble with her. Invariably her rage turned into a terrible verbal violence that frightened him because he never knew where it was going to lead. Again, he said, 'Look, I just want to see Natasha for a while.'

'But she doesn't want to see you, do you, Natasha?' Claire turned to their daughter.

At first Natasha did not answer, then she said softly, 'No, Mom.'

'You see!' Claire cried triumphantly, and threw him a smug smile. 'You've even antagonized your own daughter, not that she really knows you as a father. Basically, she never had a father. You were always away, far too often, ever to be one of any consequence. In fact, you're a stranger to her.'

'That is not true,' Philippe shot back swiftly. He shook his head and shifted slightly on his feet, wanting to be gone from her. 'And let us not dredge up the past,' he went on, his control still tightly held, his voice steady. 'I just thought we could spend a bit of time together, she and I. I'm only here for a few days.'

'*Now*? At this hour? Why *did* you come at this particular time? I'm not going to ask you to stay to dinner, if that was your intention.'

'I don't want to stay to dinner. I want to see my daughter.'

'You can't. Not now. You should have phoned me. That would have been the proper thing to do.'

'I knew you'd say no, or slam the phone down if I called you.'

'I'm slamming the phone down now. You're not welcome here. Please leave.'

'Claire, be reasonable,' he begged, his tone now becoming even more conciliatory. 'Please agree to –'

'No way,' she cut in swiftly. Her hatred for him flooded her eyes, washed over her face. He saw it and flinched.

He said, 'Tomorrow, Claire. For a short while. For lunch?'

'*No.*'

'For coffee, then? In the morning. Here at the apartment. Or at a café. Whatever you say.'

'Please go, I don't want you in my home,' Claire almost shouted and she stamped her foot.

Laura was not only appalled but troubled. She had never seen Claire behave like this before.

Hercule said, 'Perhaps it would be more appropriate to have this discussion inside the apartment, rather than out here in the hallway.' He took a long stride into the foyer, and carefully closed the front door of the apartment behind him. At the same time, he managed to give Philippe a gentle push into the room. Then he struggled out of his overcoat, which he hung in the cloakroom.

Philippe spoke in a coaxing tone, making a last ditch effort as he said, 'Let me spend an hour with Natasha tomorrow. That's all I ask.' Growing bolder suddenly, he took another step towards his former wife.

Claire backed away.

They glared at each other.

There was a rush of immense dislike flowing between them like waves. It filled the room.

Hatred, Laura thought. They have only hatred for each other. How terrible that they should end up like this. Once they so loved each other, shared all their hopes and dreams, planned a future, a whole life together. Now they are embattled.

Natasha also felt the hostility flowing between her parents, and as always it dismayed and troubled her. But she managed to diffuse it to some extent by saying, 'It's okay, Mom. Coffee tomorrow is fine.'

'No!' Claire exclaimed. 'I don't want you to do this, Natasha, just to placate him.'

Natasha went and put her arm around her mother, who was so much smaller than she, and held her close to her, as if somehow protecting her. She couldn't stand her mother's pain. It broke her heart. 'Mom, I don't mind, honestly I don't, and it's better this way.'

Claire did not respond, simply leaned into her daughter, taking sudden comfort from her close proximity, her warmth and the love she exuded.

Looking across at her father, Natasha continued, '*Ten o'clock.* I'll be ready. We can go to the café on the corner.'

Philippe nodded, and an unexpected smile struck his sombre mouth. 'Yes, that's perfect, and thank you, Natasha. Thank you.' He cast a glance at Claire. 'Is that all right with you? You're not going to throw a spanner in the works, are you?'

'Everything will be all right,' Natasha answered swiftly, suddenly in command here, in charge of this volatile situation. 'I promise. No problems.'

Relieved, reassured by the oddly grown-up girl who was his daughter, Philippe relaxed a little. For a moment he gave his attention to Laura. 'Nice seeing you the other day,' he murmured, and then nodded to Hercule: knowing it was wise to disappear before Claire did indeed find a way to object to the date their daughter had made with him, he let himself out without further ado.

The moment he was gone, Claire pulled away from Natasha, and swung her head to look at Laura. She frowned and said in a puzzled tone, 'You *saw* him the other day?'

'I ran into him at the d'Orsay, just before you arrived. He was looking at the Renoirs.'

'And you never told me when *I* got there . . . never told me he was in Paris. Why not?'

'I was going to, Claire darling, but then I decided against it. I realized you didn't know Philippe was here, passing through, as he'd told me, otherwise you would have mentioned it to me. And to be honest, I didn't want to upset you. Mentioning his name is like a red rag to a bull, you know that, and I was just . . . Well, I was waiting for you to tell me you'd had a phone call from him. But when you didn't, I decided not to say anything. Obviously he hadn't been in touch with you. Why open a can of worms?'

'Lying by omission,' Claire pronounced, her mouth drooping. 'I can't believe it,' she added in a low mutter.

'Oh, Claire, come on, don't take exception like this,' Laura exclaimed. 'It wasn't lying by omission.' She cleared her throat. 'Well, not really,' she now thought to say, remembering that she herself had thought the same thing two nights ago, when they were having dinner at the Relais Plaza. 'Surely you understand, Claire?'

But Claire remained silent.

Laura continued, 'Look, I didn't want to bring up Philippe's name, to say I'd run into him accidentally. What good would it have done? You'd only have been as mad as hell that he was in Paris and not calling you, not asking to see Natasha.'

'I'm mad now.'

'Mom, don't take it out on Laura. She hasn't done anything,' Natasha said gently, a worried expression clouding her eyes.

'Never a truer word spoken, my dear,' Hercule agreed. 'I don't know about anyone else, but I'd like a drink.' He moved further into the room, and glanced at Laura. 'Actually, I *need* one, don't *you*?'

'Absolutely, Hercule. Go and sit down, I'll fix them,' Laura answered, walking across to the drinks table. 'Scotch and soda, as usual?'

'*Oui. Merci.*'

'What about you, Claire?' Laura asked, as she dropped ice into two glasses. 'I'm fixing myself a vodka, for a change.'

'I won't have anything thanks,' Claire responded, her voice suddenly back to normal. 'I think I'd better go and look at the dinner.'

'I'll come with you,' Natasha cried, rushing into the kitchen after her mother.

'What about you, Doug? Do you want something?' Laura asked.

'I'll have a glass of white wine, please.'

Laura carried the drinks over to the sofa in front of the fire, handed the Scotch to Hercule, and the wine to Doug, then sat down on a chair opposite them. 'Cheers,' she said, lifting her glass. Doug lifted his, and smiled at her.

'*Santé,*' Hercule replied and took a sip. Leaning back against the cream velvet sofa, he stared at the fire for a brief moment, a look of abstraction on his face.

Laura sat observing him, giving him a few minutes to collect himself, to relax.

Eventually, she said in a low, concerned tone, 'I've never seen Claire act in that way before, not in all the years I've known her.'

'A dreadful scene,' Hercule replied, shaking his great leonine white head. Turning to look at her, he went on, 'I've not witnessed anything like it, either. However, I must tell you, Laura, she now harbours the most terrible hatred for Philippe.'

'I've never been able to get to the bottom of *that*, Hercule. I mean, after all, a lot of marriages fail and people get divorced. But there isn't always this hideous acrimony.'

'That is true, yes. I am rarely if ever with Claire and Philippe when they meet, but Natasha has told me that it is always stormy, and that Claire rages on and on at Philippe.' He shook his head; there was a hint of bafflement on his face. 'It seems to me she has grown to hate him more and more as the years have passed. Extraordinary, I think.'

Laura made no comment; she was at a loss for words. But she knew deep down within herself that Hercule was correct. A sense of dismay suddenly lodged in her stomach, and she said slowly, 'I hope this hasn't ruined the evening. Claire was so lighthearted in the kitchen before Philippe showed up. But then –' She cut herself off, sipped the vodka.

'But then?' Hercule's eyes rested on her quizzically. '*What?*'

'Philippe Lavillard has always spelled trouble. And I've never really liked him.'

'Oh, I don't think he's such a bad fellow, Laura,' Doug interjected.

Hercule smiled at her, and said, 'Perhaps you see him through Claire's eyes, and not your own, my dear.'

'Perhaps,' Laura had the good grace to admit.

Hercule chuckled softly to himself and glanced into the fire, his face grown contemplative again.

'What is it? Why are you chuckling?'

'We can control so much in our own lives . . . except what other people say and do. And their actions and their words affect us tremendously. Therefore we do not have as much control as we think we do, Laura.'

'No, we don't,' Laura agreed.

'You can say that again,' Doug said.

7

Natasha could see her father standing on the far corner of the place de Fürstemberg, and she ran across the square to join him.

'Hello, Natasha,' he said, when she drew to a standstill in front of him, and hugged her to him.

'Hi, Dad,' she responded, hugging him back, and when they drew away, she went on, 'Let's go somewhere else for coffee, not the café on the corner, and then maybe we can go for a walk.'

'But your mother . . .' he began and then stopped, peering at his daughter, his dark eyes suddenly worried. 'Won't she expect you home soon? Within the hour?'

'Oh no, it's okay, Dad, honestly,' Natasha reassured him. 'I told Mom I wanted to have a longer visit with you today, and she said it was all right.'

Philippe Lavillard continued to regard his daughter for a moment, assessing what she had just said. Although he did not know her as well as he wished he did, he was, nevertheless, quite sure she would not say anything to him which was untrue. Claire had brought her up well.

'All right,' he said at last. 'Since you say your mother's agreed, let's walk for a bit and find a place for breakfast. I haven't had any yet, have you, darling?'

Natasha shook her head, smiling up at him. She tucked her arm in his and they set off at a brisk pace. Natasha loved her father, and she did not think he was the ogre her mother constantly made him out to be. And she was baffled by her mother's perpetual anger, who would never discuss her past relationship with Philippe. But then she was often baffled by adults, whom she considered to be very strange at times, to say the least, and most especially when it came to relationships.

'I'm planning to leave Africa,' Philippe announced out of the blue.

Taken by surprise, and startled by this statement, Natasha exclaimed, 'Why Dad? I thought you enjoyed working there.'

'I have enjoyed it and I've done some good work there, but I want to get out now. I'm tired, Nattie. Anyway, I want to be near you, able to see you more frequently. Would you like that?' he asked, and was suddenly trepiditious. He had always believed she felt the same way he did, that she loved him in return, and now he hoped he had been right in this assumption.

When she did not immediately respond, he asked, 'Well, how *would* you feel if I were around more?'

'I'd like it, I really would,' Natasha said, meaning this. 'And I think Mom would let me see you more often, wouldn't she?'

'I'm sure of it, Natasha. Your mother is angry with me, not you and if *you* ask her then I know she'll agree.'

'Why is she angry with you, Dad?' Natasha asked, voicing a question that had nagged at the back of her mind for the last couple of years.

'She thinks I let her down, I suppose that's it.'

'Did you?' the fourteen-year-old asked, gazing at him, her eyes questioning.

Philippe sighed. 'We let each other down in so many ways, and you suffered as a result.' He glanced at her, smiled ruefully. 'It's children who always suffer in a divorce.'

'I guess.' Natasha hesitated, and then blurted out, 'Is it true what she says? About other women?'

'No, of course not. But Claire was always suspicious of me, especially when I went away to do research.'

'But why, Dad? I don't understand why she didn't trust you.'

He shook his head and a sigh escaped again. 'I don't know, Nattie. But she believed it, she truly did, and she wasn't pretending to be angry. It was genuine, is genuine.' They walked on in silence for a few minutes, and then Philippe volunteered, 'I have a feeling . . .' He paused, wondering if he should continue.

'Go on, Dad, what feeling do you have?'

'I have a feeling your mother has an enormous and deep-rooted distrust of men for some reason. It seems to me that it's very well ingrained in her, and I think I fell victim to this in some way. I'm not saying I wasn't also at fault in the disintegration of our marriage, but I was often accused unfairly of things I didn't do.'

Natasha nodded quickly. 'I know you're not the villain Mom makes you out to be. Actually –' She stopped abruptly, looked up at him and suddenly grinned. 'I think Mom's still in love with you, Dad.'

Momentarily Philippe was startled, and he exclaimed, 'I doubt it, Nattie! That's your romantic imagination running away with you.'

'No, it isn't, Dad. I just feel she is.' Natasha shrugged, and made a *moue*. '*You* think it's wishful thinking on my part, but I don't think it is.'

He was silent, and she hurried on, '*That's* why Mom's so angry with you . . . that you're not *here*, living with us. I know she still loves you, Dad.'

'Well, in a way, I still love her.'

'That's already something. Don't you think you should try to get back together?'

Philippe came to a sudden standstill, took hold of his daughter's arm and turned her to face him. Very gently, he said, 'I wish it *were* possible, Nattie, for your sake, but I can't. And in all truthfulness, I don't think your mother wants me back. I said

I still loved her in a certain way, but it isn't the kind of love that would support a marriage. Perhaps I should correct that and say I'm very fond of your mother, because of our early relationship and because of you. There's a big difference.'

'I know.'

They began walking again.

Natasha slipped her arm through his, clinging to him as they fell into step. They were very much alike in looks, and Natasha was almost as tall as he was. And to passers-by there was no doubt that they were father and daughter. Philippe was slim, elegant in appearance, and handsome in a quiet way, his lean face sensitive, his dark brown eyes compassionate and kind. Natasha now realized that her mother and father would never get back together, something she had often dreamed about. But she hoped they would be more amicable with each other in the future. Perhaps if her father did come back to work in Paris her mother would see him in a better light, and relent.

'Would you work at the Pasteur Institute again, Dad?' she now asked.

'I'd like to, yes, Nattie, but I'm not sure that this would be possible. However, they're interested in talking to me. Actually, I'm seeing the director tomorrow.'

'You're such a brilliant virologist, they'll want you, Dad. I just know they will.'

He laughed. 'Thank you for that vote of confidence, Natasha. I'm glad I have you on my side.'

'I *am*, Dad.'

'How about going in here?' he suggested, stopping in front of a café. 'I remember it well. They have wonderful croissants and do the best fried eggs. Come on, let's try it.'

Once they were inside the café, Natasha shrugged out of her green quilted-down coat, and Philippe hung it up for her, along with his brown suede jacket lined with sheepskin. After they had been seated and had ordered, he said, 'I'm going to New York later next week with your grandmother.'

Natasha looked across the table at him alertly. 'How is she?'

'Quite well, thanks, Nattie. Longing to see you again.' He pursed his lips. 'Perhaps you and she can get to know each other one day.'

'It could happen if you were living in Paris,' Natasha said, unable to keep the eagerness out of her voice. 'I mean she could come here to see you. And me. Don't you think?'

Philippe nodded. He was glad he had made the effort and had gone to see Claire and Natasha last night. The outcome had been better than he had expected, despite Claire's outburst. And he knew now that he *did* have his daughter's love, and that perhaps his mother would also have it one day. And that pleased him greatly.

'I'm sorry to intrude, Laura,' Philippe said, speaking to her from a phone in the lobby of the hotel. 'But I had hoped we might get together, if only for a few minutes. I need to speak to you about Natasha. And Claire.'

'Just a moment please, Philippe,' Laura said.

Although she had covered the receiver with her hand, he could vaguely hear her speaking to Doug, and then she came back to him. 'Yes, all right. I'll be down in a few minutes. Why don't you go and wait for me in the long gallery where they serve tea.'

'That's fine. Thanks,' he said, and hung up.

Walking across the lobby, Philippe Lavillard headed into the gallery where tea and drinks were served, and found himself a table. He took off his suede coat, put it on a chair and settled in the other one to wait for Laura Valiant.

He had always liked her, and considered her to be a truly good friend to Claire. Many times he had often wanted to ask her if she knew anything about Claire's past that would shed light on her distrust of men, himself in particular. But he had always lost his nerve at the last moment.

Suddenly Laura was there, standing in front of him, looking elegant in a dark red jacket and black trousers. Beautiful as always, he said to himself as he jumped up and stretched out his hand.

After shaking it, Laura sat down and asked, 'Did you have a nice morning with Natasha?'

'Yes, it's always great to be with her, she's a very special girl, very grown-up for her age. We walked, had breakfast and then took another walk through the Luxembourg Gardens. We enjoyed being together.'

Laura said, 'I'm glad. And you're correct, Philippe, she's a terrific girl. Claire's done a good job.'

'Yes, she has, Laura. I'm the first to say it.'

Laura looked at him and asked politely, 'Would you like a cup of tea? Or a drink? It's about that time.'

He shook his head. 'Thanks but I don't really want anything. Except to talk to you for a few minutes about Claire.'

'What about her?' Laura asked cautiously.

Leaning forward, Philippe said in a quiet, confiding tone, 'Look, Laura, I want to spend more time with Natasha, and she'd like that too. But you know how fierce Claire is, and she's determined to keep us apart.'

A thoughtful look crossed Laura's face and she replied, 'I have a feeling Claire thinks you're the one who has created the situation. I mean because you work in Zaire.'

'I know she does. And I'm planning to leave there. It may take me some time to extricate myself and to find a new job, but I've made up my mind to be in the same city as my daughter. If that's at all possible.'

'I see,' Laura said, and added, 'Last night was really awful. I must admit, I was a bit startled by Claire's anger. I've never seen her like that.'

'Neither have I, to be honest, Laura. She's been furious with me for a long time now. And I admit there's been quite a lot of acrimony between us, but last night she was worse than ever. Claire didn't seem like herself. I even wondered if there was something else upsetting her. Was there? Is there?'

'Not that I know of,' Laura answered, and instantly thought of Hercule's concern that Claire was ill. But she refrained from mentioning it. After all, Claire's life had nothing to do with Philippe anymore.

He said, 'Once I'm back in Paris I'm hoping I can establish a better relationship with Claire. Do you think that's possible?'

For a moment Laura was silent, pondering this, and finally she said, 'Perhaps.'

'Only perhaps? You don't sound very certain.'

'I guess I'm not. On the other hand, her complaint is that you're so far away in Zaire. So, once you're back maybe she'll understand how serious you are about Natasha, serious about helping to bring her up. Because that's what you'd be doing, wouldn't you?'

'Absolutely. And I want her to get to know my mother better. She's hardly seen her grandmother in the last few years, and that's not right, Laura. You more than anyone else should understand that.'

Laura merely nodded, but deep down she agreed with him. And she was coming to understand how sincere he was about changing his life in order to accommodate his daughter in it. How obvious it was he wanted to be with her, share time with her. She loved Claire, but like all people, Claire was not infallible. Last night, Hercule had suggested that she had always seen Philippe through Claire's eyes and not her own. Even Doug had pointed out that he was not such a bad fellow. Perhaps they were right. She suddenly adjusted her thinking about Philippe Lavillard.

Now Laura said, 'Yes, I do think it's important Natasha gets to know her grandmother. After all, we all need family. But I thought your mother lived in New York?'

'She does, but she often comes to Paris. She was born here, you know. Anyway, if I were living here she'd probably come more often.' He paused, and looked at Laura intently. 'I know how close you are to Claire, and I almost hesitate to ask this, but do you think you can put in a good word for me? I'm very serious about getting closer to Natasha, being with her in these important years of her life.'

'I know that. Still, Claire might wonder why I'm suddenly intervening.'

'You could tell her I'd been to see you.'

'I suppose I could.'

'You still sound very hesitant, Laura, and I don't want to put you in an awkward situation with Claire. Look, why don't you think about this ... once I've moved here maybe you could talk to Claire and then get her to come around to my way of thinking.'

'Yes, I could do that, Philippe. I realize how important this is to you, and I think it's important to Natasha, as well. She *should* know her father.' Laura nodded. 'Okay. I'll talk to Claire, but not until you're settled in Paris and ready to participate in Natasha's life.'

He smiled at her and his dark eyes lit up. 'Thank you, Laura. Thank you very much.'

8

It seemed to Laura that the rest of the week in Paris flew by. Suddenly, before she knew it, Friday morning was upon her, and she was scurrying around doing last minute things.

By the time she finally arrived at the Bar des Théâtres across the street from the Plaza Athénée, it was one-fifteen and she was late for her lunch date with Claire.

But Claire merely smiled as she began to apologize, and said mildly, 'It doesn't matter, I know what it's like when you're pushed for time. Come on, Laura darling, take off your coat and sit down.'

Laura did this, agreed to the glass of champagne Claire suggested, and then sat back. After taking a deep breath, she grinned and said, 'Everything just piled in on me, all of a sudden, but it was all good stuff! A lot of things came to fruition, *finally*, this morning.'

'So it's been a successful trip?' Claire asked.

'Very much so. Our Canadian client has committed to the Matisse and the Cézanne, and then this morning a private dealer I know came up with a Bonnard that's simply beautiful. I'm sure the same Canadian client will buy that, too. And I think another client in New York is going to buy the Renoir . . . the countess's Renoir.'

'That's great! Hercule will be pleased, and so will the countess. Apparently she needs the money for repairs to the château in the Loire,' Claire said. 'Although I'm not sure why she feels the need to maintain that place. Hercule says it's enormous. She ought to sell it, in my opinion.'

'Hercule said something to me, too . . . about it being in the family for hundreds of years, and there's the countess's son, who inherited the title and the lands. I'm sure the house is . . . well, part of them. It's their heritage, his heritage, actually.'

'I guess so,' Claire agreed. She chuckled suddenly. 'My mother used to say that a house is a thief. It steals all your money. Don't ever forget that.'

'As if I could! When Grandma Megan gave me her house in Connecticut I was thrilled, until I realized that it's a money pit. And that's with Doug doing a lot of repairs and other things himself. You know how handy he is.'

'Give the famous Doug my love. It was lovely to see him last weekend.'

'I will.' Laura took a sip of the champagne, which had just arrived, saying cheers as she did so. With a frown, she then asked, 'Why does everyone call him *the famous Doug* in that way?'

'I didn't know everyone did; I thought it was only me,' Claire replied, looking at Laura curiously, her head on one side.

'Well, actually Philippe said the same thing the other day –' Laura stopped, wondering if she had made a faux pas by mentioning Philippe's name.

'Philippe said, *give the famous Doug my love,* when you saw him in the museum? Is that what you mean?' Claire murmured, her puzzlement reflected on her face.

'No, not that. He said, "*How's the famous Doug?*" And what *I'm* getting at now is why you and he call Doug *famous?*'

'I think I was the one who started it, because when you first met him you talked about him so much, raved about his looks and his brains and . . . his brawn.' Claire laughed as she finished, 'You were so crazy about him, you made him seem like a movie star, and therefore famous. And he *is* so good looking, the proverbial tall, dark and handsome hero, right?'

Laura laughed with her old friend. She said, 'I guess I was pretty bowled over at the time. He was the most gorgeous thing on two legs that I'd ever seen. Still is, really.'

'So, give him my love.'

'I will. And I know he reciprocates. You've always been his favourite.'

Claire looked pleased on hearing this, but she made no comment. Then she asked, 'What do you want to eat? I think I'll have the omelette *fines herbes*, and a green salad.'

'I'll have the same, Claire, I'm not very hungry.'

Once Claire had ordered lunch for them, she confided, 'It's been wonderful having you here, Laura. I'm going to miss you, and so is Natasha. You're the only person she has in this world, you know. After me, of course.'

'And her –' Laura began to cough, covered her mouth with her hand. Once she calmed herself, she finished. 'She has Hercule,' knowing how stupid it would be to say she has her father, which she had just been about to do.

'You started to say her father, didn't you?' Claire said.

Laura felt herself flushing. After a moment, she nodded.

Claire went on quickly, 'But she doesn't have him, you see. She never had him. He's never been a good father to her. Nor was he a good husband, for that matter. His work and his women invariably came first. He was extremely independent, and did what he wanted. And very selfishly so. He was neglectful of me, and of Natasha.'

Suddenly they were right in the middle of something Laura had not intended, had, in fact, wanted to avoid at all cost. She wondered how to respond, was afraid of upsetting Claire by saying the wrong thing. And so she said nothing at all.

Suddenly, Claire leaned across the table, staring into Laura's troubled face. 'I'm so sorry about last Saturday night. I wish it hadn't happened. It was ugly and unnecessary. But Philippe shouldn't have arrived like that, *unannounced*. He knows it upsets me when he does. Somehow he always manages to create problems.'

'I know how hurt and angry you've been, and still are, Claire,' Laura acknowledged in a sympathetic voice. 'But I do wish you could put all that on one side, turn away from it. Philippe is no longer a part of your life, except for seeing Natasha from time to time. It's so . . . *enervating* to hang on to anger the way you do, darling.'

Claire sighed. 'I wish I *could* turn away, Laura, but I can't forget all the terrible things he did to me. I suppose I'm bitter.'

The waiter arrived with their food, which saved Laura the trouble of replying. She was greatly relieved, since she did not know how to answer Claire. At least, not in a way that would please her friend. Laura was aware that to harbour bitterness was deadly: it only bred more pain and hurt in the long run. However, getting Claire to accept this was another matter altogether. Even to attempt it would be a futile exercise on her part.

Deeming it wiser, Laura still did not respond; she picked up her fork and began eating the salad, then took a forkful of omelette.

They ate in silence for a while. It was Claire who eventually broke it, when she said, 'It's funny, I'm very ambivalent about Philippe in certain ways. I want him to see Natasha, to be a father to her, and yet another part of me wishes he would just stay away from Paris altogether, never attempt to see her. That way we would all know where we stand. Perhaps I should say that to him. What do you think?'

'Is he still here?' Laura asked quietly.

'I don't know. He never reveals much to Natasha when he sees her. What did he say to you, when you ran into him at the museum?'

'Just that he was passing through, en route to Atlanta to see the head of the Center for Disease Control.'

Claire nodded. 'That figures. First and foremost, always the great scientist.'

Laura wanted to remind Claire that Philippe Lavillard had done some remarkable work and made some extraordinary discoveries in his field, but she decided to hold her tongue. Instead she said, 'Listen, Claire, I've been thinking about something for the last few days, and I want to pass it by you now. How about coming to New York for Christmas? Or rather, to Connecticut. You and Natasha, and even Hercule, if he'd enjoy it. We'd have a wonderful time . . .' She paused and laughed, added, 'It would be like old times, you know. Mom's coming up, and she's going to bring Grandma Megan. And Doug's friend Robin Knox is bringing his fiancée, Karen. There'll be a houseful, and it'll be warm and happy and fun. What do you say?'

Claire's face had lit up, and Laura could see that she loved the idea. But then she shook her head. 'I just can't get away right now, and anyway, I promised Hercule I would host his New Year's Eve party with him.'

'But you could go back in time for that. It's only the thirteenth of December today.'

'Friday the thirteenth,' Claire cut in, and grimaced.

'Oh, I know, so what!' Laura exclaimed dismissively, and hurried on, 'If you came next weekend, that's Saturday the twenty-first, or Sunday the twenty-second, you could easily stay for a week, even eight days, and then fly back for Hercule's party on the thirty-first. Oh *do* try, Claire! Just think how much Natasha would love it. And *I* would too. All of us would.'

'I'll think about it,' Claire said, and took a mouthful of salad. 'There is something *I* wanted to ask *you*, Laura.' Claire hesitated before saying, 'Could Natasha and I come and stay in the country with you in the summer? I never really know what to do with her then, they have such long school holidays in France. Hercule usually takes us to Brittany, to stay with him there, but normally we only go for a couple of weeks. What do you think?'

'It's a fabulous idea! And of course you can come. But I don't want you to substitute the summer for Christmas. Promise you'll try your damnedest, and that you'll ask Hercule?'

'All right, I'll see what I can do, and of course I'll extend your invitation to him.' She shook her head. 'It's just that I have so much work,' she finished worriedly.

'I understand, I'm sort of snowed under myself. Even though I'm supposed to go to Palm Beach, to see a client's house, to recommend the kind of art she should use, I don't think I'll make it before Christmas,' Laura explained. 'I'll have to go in January.'

'I suppose Grandma Megan still has that pretty little cottage on Island Drive in Palm Beach?'

Laura nodded. 'Mom likes to spend time there in January and February, she says she paints well at Bedelia Cottage. But Grandma doesn't go there anymore, she hasn't been for years. Don't ask me why. Personally, I think the warm weather would do her good.'

'Yes, it would. But you know what she's like. Nobody can tell Grandma Megan what to do.'

Laura smiled, thinking of her grandmother. 'She's just wonderful, that's all I know.'

They fell into a discussion about Megan Valiant, whom they both loved, and who had been such a force in their lives when they were young. Then they reminisced about their girlhood spent together in New York and at the house in Connecticut, and they remembered those days with love and warmth and a great deal of nostalgia.

They were loath to say goodbye to each other, so closely bonded were they, and so they drank another cup of coffee, wanting to be together for as long as possible. Finally, it was Claire who brought their farewell lunch to an end, pointing out that she must return to her office.

The two women walked across the avenue Montaigne, and stood in front of the hotel for a few more moments, still talking, clinging to each other verbally. And then they were doing that physically, as they hugged and said their goodbyes.

'Please try for Christmas,' Laura said, squeezing Claire's arm.

'I will, Laura, I promise,' Claire answered, and then she smiled a bit wanly and hurried off down the street without looking back.

I really will miss her terribly, Laura thought, staring after Claire's retreating figure. Turning, she went into the hotel, and took the lift up to her room. It was time to pack and conclude the remainder of her business.

9

Douglas Casson was well pleased with his handiwork. He had swept the leaves into the centre of the terrace, and all he had to do now was shovel them into the wheelbarrow. He had just begun to do this when a sudden, gusting wind began to blow. The leaves ended up swirling around his feet. He cursed mildly under his breath, accepting that his sweeping had been in vain. And then he chuckled to himself, threw down the shovel and went and sat on the wall.

Oh what the hell, he muttered, I can't compete with the wind. He would have to deal with the leaves later. And what did they matter anyway? Not at all.

He continued to sit on the low wall that encircled the terrace, for a moment enjoying the winter sunshine and fresh air. It was a cold day, bracing, but the sky was very blue, and although there was no warmth in the sun it enhanced the day.

Douglas didn't sit long on the drystone wall. Very quickly he was beginning to feel the cold through his sheepskin-lined suede jacket, and he stood up, put the shovel in the wheelbarrow and trundled it over to the garden shed.

Within minutes he was back in the house, standing in front of the fire in the great hall, warming himself. The weather was deceptive. From the windows the bright sparkling day beckoned beguilingly, but once outside the raw cold bit into the bones. It was a freezing day, as Laura had warned earlier. Not a day to be outside very long, she had said.

He should have listened to her; she was always right about the weather in Connecticut. After all, she had grown up in this old colonial house in Kent, spending many weekends here with her grandparents, as well as Christmas, Easter, and summer vacations.

Dumped on Megan and Owen, he thought now, while her parents went off, doing their own thing. He had never seen a couple as engrossed with each other as her mother and father had been. It seemed to him that they hardly knew that Laura and Dylan existed, although when he had once said that to Laura she had pooh-poohed this idea. 'Dad was always there for us when we needed him. Admittedly he was more involved with us than Mom, but she loved us as much as he did.'

Douglas had never been really sure about that. He thought that Margaret Valiant was a self-involved and selfish woman, although he had never dared to voice this opinion to Laura. She always defended her mother, whatever he said. But then that was human nature, wasn't it? A child could criticize its parents and family, but God forbid if a stranger did. Holy hell usually broke loose.

But he knew he was correct in his assessment of Laura's mother. Her painting and her husband had been the only things of any real consequence to her. Not that he had been around when Laura was growing up, but Maggie had practically told him that herself once in a moment of weakness, when they were sharing confidences of sorts. He was aware that she regretted it later; he saw the regret reflected in her dark soulful eyes.

He wondered what it was like to love someone in this way? He never had. Of course he loved Laura, but not to the exclusion of all else in his life.

Walking over to a wing chair, he sat down heavily, leaned his head against the dark red velvet and closed his eyes.

His marriage was in trouble.

He knew it and had known it for a long time now. But he wasn't sure if Laura was aware they had problems. He didn't know how to tell her, had not the slightest idea how to even broach the subject.

The problems had nothing to do with their inability to produce a child together. This did not even worry him much anymore. Rather, it had to do with *them*, with their relationship, and their future together. Of late they had spent a lot of time apart, travelling because of their careers. And were they not growing apart? Emotionally and physically. *He* believed they were, but he was quite certain Laura had no conception of this. None at all. Not because she wasn't smart, she was one of the savviest people he knew. But because he was different now; he had changed.

'Doug, can you come and help me?'

Laura's voice echoed down from the staircase at the far end of the great hall, and he snapped open his eyes and instantly jumped up.

'Of course, what do you want me to do?' he asked.

'I need you to get a window blind back into its notches, or whatever they're called. It's slipped out and fallen down.'

'Be right there, sweetie.'

Laura watched him walking towards her, thinking how well he looked this morning, very young in his cream fisherman's knit sweater and dark blue corduroys. The time spent outside had brought a rosiness to his cheeks, which enhanced his boyish good looks. Black hair, green eyes, six-foot-two and all athletic muscle. Tall, dark and handsome, as Claire had said in Paris just over a week ago. There was no doubt about it, Doug was an exceptionally attractive man, and looked much younger than his thirty-three years. More like twenty-five, she decided, as he strode down the hall purposefully.

'Sorry to disturb you when you were relaxing,' she said as he bounded up the stairs two at a time. 'But I must get everything finished before Robin and Karen arrive later this afternoon.'

'No problem, I was only whiling away the time, and getting warm after my abortive efforts with the leaves.' He smiled lopsidedly and explained, 'They're hard to handle when there's a strong wind.' He leaned against the bannister at the top of the stairs.

Laura laughed, her blue eyes crinkling up at the corners. 'The leaves can wait.'

'I know. Anyway, isn't it time I started throwing some lunch together, while you do your bit of last minute decorating for Christmas? Your mother and Grandma Megan will be here tomorrow, and before you know it, you'll have your hands full.'

'I'll be finished today. And don't make anything complicated for lunch, Doug. A sandwich is all I'm interested in.'

'That's good enough for me too, but how about a cup of soup? Chicken noodle from a packet, courtesy of the Knorr kitchen?'

'Sounds delicious,' she said, and hurried down the long corridor to one of the four guest rooms situated at the far end.

'It's at this window,' Laura said, entering the yellow room with its four-poster bed, colourful antique quilt and framed flower-prints hanging on the sunny walls.

It took Doug only a few minutes to roll the blind properly, and then slot it back into the notches on the reveals on either side of the window. 'There you go, all done! Now, what else can I fix for you?'

'Nothing. We're in pretty good shape here. But I would like you to decide which room you want Robin and Karen to stay in.'

'Who's sleeping in here?' he asked, glancing around. He had always liked this particular room because it was so cheerful, full of bright yellows and pinks.

'I'd thought of giving it to Mom, but if you want I can put them in here.'

'No, no, let your mother have it. I suppose you're giving your grandmother her old room, as usual.'

'It's hers for as long as she lives, you know that. Listen, she slept in it for almost sixty years, so I'm sure she'd feel disoriented anywhere else.'

'I agree.'

Laura walked out of the yellow bedroom, and said over her shoulder, 'I had thought of putting Robin and Karen in the blue-and-white room, it's so crisp and fresh. But they could have the little suite upstairs under the eaves. What do you think?'

'The suite upstairs! It's cosy, charming, and Robin's going to love it. It has a French feeling to it, and he likes anything French, he's quite the Francophile. Let's go up and have a look.'

Together they climbed the narrow, twisting staircase that led to the top of the house. Doug wandered through the set of four rooms, which were actually the old attics. There was a bedroom, a tiny sitting room, a small den-dressing room and a bathroom. Laura had decorated the suite in red and white, using a *toile de Jouy* in these colours on the walls throughout, and a matching fabric for the headboard. A red-and-white checked fabric appeared on several armchairs, and there was a big red velvet sofa that matched the bright red carpet.

'Yes, Robin will definitely like this,' Doug said, scanning everything. 'So will Karen,' he thought to add. 'Also, they've got privacy up here.'

'Are they definitely staying through Christmas Day?' Laura asked.

Doug nodded. 'Yes. Robin's taken a few days off from the bank, and Karen's closed the shop until January. It makes a nice break for them both.'

'I'll bring some books up,' Laura said, as they went downstairs. 'And the latest magazines along with a bowl of fruit.'

'Let's do it after lunch,' Doug suggested. 'I'll help you finish up once we've eaten.'

In the end lunch became a long, rather drawn-out affair, since Doug decided to make something more substantial than a packet of soup and canned tuna fish sandwiches. Instead he prepared

Eggs Benedict with toasted muffins and Canadian bacon, followed by one of his specialities, caramelized grapefruit and vanilla ice cream.

'That wasn't too bad, was it?' he asked, at the end of lunch, clinking his glass of white wine to Laura's.

'Hardly, it was delicious. You can cook for me any time,' she said, her eyes dancing as she peered at him over the rim of the glass.

'That's what I've always done, or so it seems to me,' he shot back, laughing with her. It was an old story, a family joke really, the fact that she couldn't cook at all and he loved nothing better than to hover over the stove in the big country kitchen.

'I suppose we ought to go upstairs and put finishing touches to the little suite under the eaves,' Laura murmured, lifting her glass to her mouth again.

'I'll help you, but we might as well finish this wine, there's only a drop left. A shame to waste Pouilly Fumé,' Doug said, topping up both of their glasses. 'That's a dead soldier,' he added as he picked up the empty wine bottle and carried it over to the recycling bin.

Returning to the kitchen table, where they were eating, he went on, 'I guess we're going to be ten for Christmas lunch, after all, Laura. My parents now say they'd like to come, and Malcolm and Gloria Mason finally accepted the invitation. Yesterday. I forgot to tell you.'

'Oh good, it'll be fun, and I know the Masons like Robin and Karen.' Swallowing the last of her wine, Laura now pushed back her chair and stood up. 'I suppose you'll do your fabulous goose with all the trimmings, and I'll help you the best I can. But we'll plan the menu later, shall we?'

'Plenty of time,' he replied. 'We don't have to do the shopping until early next week.'

Laura began taking things out of the cupboard, arranging them on a large wooden tray. After putting glasses, small plates, napkins, dessert knives and forks on it, she reached for pieces of fruit in a big wooden bowl on the table, filled a glass dish with apples, bananas, and grapes. 'This should do it, don't you think?' She eyed Doug, who nodded his agreement.

He said, 'I'll go to my den and get a few magazines, some of the books you picked up last week. Do you want me to carry that tray up for you? Or can you manage?'

'I'm fine, darling.' Laura hoisted the wooden tray as she spoke. 'We can take the bottled water later.'

'I'll be there in a minute,' Doug announced before heading in the direction of his den.

Laura was a little out of breath when she reached the suite under the eaves, and after placing the tray on top of a chest of drawers, she flopped down on the large red sofa, endeavouring to catch her breath.

A moment later Doug came in with his pile of magazines and popular books. He burst out laughing when he saw Laura leaning back against the sofa, her breathing still laboured.

'It was a long climb,' she gasped, by way of explanation. 'Three flights. They winded me a bit.'

He smiled at her, shaking his head. And quite suddenly he was captivated by the way she looked at this moment. The last remnants of the afternoon sun were washing over her high cheekbones and delicately-articulated face; she was bathed in a crystalline light. What a truly beautiful woman she was, his wife. He wanted her; he wanted to make love to her.

Doug dropped the books and magazines onto a nearby chair, and went and sat next to her on the sofa. Putting his arms around her, he pulled her closer to him, brought his lips to hers, kissing her gently at first. And then as she responded, and stroked his face, the kisses became more forceful. They clung to each other, their passion accelerating. Doug now kissed her more fervently than ever, his tongue seeking hers in a moment of profound intimacy. It seemed to them both that they were melting into each other.

Doug went on kissing his wife's face, her eyelids, her brow, her neck; his hands went deftly to her breasts and he delighted that her nipples were erect under her cotton blouse.

Pausing, he whispered against her neck. 'Come on, let's go and find a bed.' Taking hold of both her hands, Doug pulled her to her feet; with their arms wrapped around each other they went into the adjoining bedroom.

Within a few seconds they were both naked, lying on top of the antique quilt. 'You're not cold are you?' he asked softly.

'No. This room's always been warm. Actually, I'm hot,' she whispered.

So am I, he thought, but he said nothing, simply buried his head between her breasts. Throwing one leg over her, he pressed his body alongside hers, slowly caressing her arm, and then her thigh. It was true, she *was* hot; he could feel the heat rising from her body.

Encircling her with his arms, he rolled them over on the bed, so that he was on his back and she lay on top of him. Automatically, she went to kneel in front of him, loving him the way he liked her to do.

But a moment or two later he was pulling her up so that she was on top of him. When he entered her he did so with such suddenness, and so swiftly, she let out a little cry. Then they began to move together in the old familiar rhythm that was theirs.

Both of them were carried along by their mutual passion. Rising upward together, they felt as if they were floating ... higher and higher ... soaring ... soaring ...

Far away, as if from a long distance, Doug heard a faint noise. He snapped his eyes open, stared across at the doorway.

Robin Knox was standing there, watching them, his blue eyes startled, his face pale. And then he was gone. In an instant he had disappeared.

Doug blinked, wondering if he'd imagined Robin's unexpected presence. He knew he had not.

Laura fell against him, asking in an almost inaudible voice, 'Why did you stop? What happened? Is something wrong?'

'Nothing,' he said. 'Nothing.' But there was.

There was a long silence. He cleared his throat. 'I guess the wine at lunch got to me,' he lied, hoping she believed him.

PART TWO

Winter and Spring

1997

10

Laura left her office on Sixty-Eighth Street and hurried down Madison Avenue, walking in the direction of Sixtieth. One of Laura's greatest assets was her power of concentration; yet another her ability to compartmentalize matters in order to deal with the single most important problem of the moment. This ability to truly focus on something to the exclusion of all else – she called it her tunnel vision – was one of her strong suits. As she hurried to her appointment her mind was geared to the difficult situation she was certain she was about to encounter.

Laura was thinking about Mark Tabbart, one of America's cleverest, shrewdest and most successful financiers, one of the new mega-rich buccaneers of big business with a lavish lifestyle, money to burn and a high profile. He had been a client of hers for the past two years, and although he was tough, brash, opinionated and dictatorial they had, until this moment, enjoyed a good relationship based on an easy rapport and mutual respect of each other's abilities. For the most part he took her advice and bowed to her better judgement, but she had an uneasy feeling that this was about to change.

Laura and Alison were considered to be two of the best in the business, self-assured, confident in their knowledge of Impressionist art and the international market. They had helped to build fine collections for high-powered business executives and celebrities with newly-made fortunes who wanted to invest in art. All paid strict attention to what she and Alison said and took their recommendations, relying on their professional judgement, knowledge and experience. Their credentials and reputation were impeccable in the art market of the late 1990s, which was enjoying another high.

When she had first been introduced to Mark Tabbart by one of her other clients, he had asked Laura why anyone would feel the need to use her services, or those of any other expert. 'I've got eyes in my head, I know whether I like a painting or not, and I can read the name of the artist on the canvas. So why do I need an art expert?'

Laura had responded with a question of her own. 'Would you sign a binding legal document involving millions of dollars without first seeking the advice of a lawyer? I very much doubt it.'

'You're right, I wouldn't,' he had answered, and encouraged by his straightforwardness Laura had gone on to pose another question.

'Surely then, you would agree that it's foolish to buy an expensive painting without asking advice from someone with a great deal of knowledge about art and the market.'

'Agreed,' Tabbart had concurred and that same day he had become a client.

In the ensuing two years Laura had helped the entrepreneur build a fine collection. She had acquired for him some of the great French Impressionist and Post-Impressionist paintings, including works by Cézanne and Matisse, and such American painters as John Singer Sargent and Frank Benson; and she had picked up two paintings by Dame Laura Knight, the British Post-Impressionist painter.

But the one thing she had not been able to do thus far was to fulfil his desire to acquire a Gauguin. Suddenly, out of the blue, he had discovered one for himself, one that was actually for sale.

Laura had learned about this development four days ago, when Tabbart had phoned her from Aspen, chortling with glee about his extraordinary luck. They had arranged to meet today and she realized as she turned into the lobby of Tabbart's office building that she might have to do battle with him. Taking a deep breath, Laura braced herself as she entered the lift and rode up to the fortieth floor.

Mark Tabbart had kept her waiting twenty minutes already, but Laura was well aware that this did not signify anything special or untoward. Certainly it had nothing to do with her. He was an exceptionally busy man, with endless demands on his time, and this was not the first occasion she had hung around in the reception area until he had finished whatever bit of business he was transacting.

At the exact moment she pulled out her mobile phone to call Doug at his office, Mark's assistant Alec Fulham suddenly appeared at the private entrance to Mark's inner sanctum. She put the phone back in her handbag and stood up swiftly, realizing she would have to call Doug later.

Alec hurried forward, sounding apologetic as he said, 'Sorry about this. Mark's been on a complicated call. He just finished.'

'No problem,' Laura replied. She followed him along the corridor to Mark's office in silence.

When they entered the room Mark Tabbart was standing looking out of the window. He was short, thin and wiry, a baby-faced, balding man who was not particularly prepossessing physically; but he was brilliant in business and considered by his peers to be a financial genius. He was in his shirt sleeves, as he usually was when he was working at his desk, his dark jacket slung across the back of the chair.

He turned around, moved lithely across the thickly-carpeted floor to greet her effusively. His face instantly changed, became genial, although his warm smile was not reflected in his pale grey eyes which, as always, were cold, appraising.

After kissing her on both cheeks and exchanging a few pleasantries Mark went to his desk, picked up several photographs, and began, 'I want you to see these pictures of –'

'*Tahitian Dreams*,' Laura finished for him, swiftly cutting in, wanting to gain the advantage by proving a point to him. 'Painted by Paul Gauguin in 1896. It's the portrait of a Tahitian woman on a starry night, inky-blue sky, brilliant white stars. The woman is reclining under a tree, there's a bowl of fruit by her side, the faint outline of a horse under a tree, and off to the right a Tahitian man gazing at her. Gauguin's wonderfully vivid colours are much in evidence, a lovely deep red in the fan she's holding, the warm coral he often used for his earth tones, a mingling of dark greens in the trees behind her, with pavonine blues in the sky. The woman's nude, except for a strip of yellow silk thrown across her thighs, and she bears a strong resemblance to the woman in Gauguin's painting called *Vairumati* which is in the Musée d'Orsay in Paris, but the actual setting is similar to the one Gauguin used in his painting called *Te Arii Vahine* which is hanging in the Pushkin Museum in Moscow. And, by the way, Gauguin painted *Tahitian Dreams* on his second trip to Tahiti.'

Mark Tabbart made no response whatsoever. He simply sat staring at her.

Laura returned his hard stare unflinchingly; she knew she had the upper hand because, for the moment, he was impressed by her knowledge. When he chose not to make any comment, Laura asked, 'I have described the painting correctly, haven't I?'

His nod was almost curt. 'It seems that you know this painting intimately,' he finally remarked with acerbity, his pale, pellucid eyes still fixed on her intently.

'Yes, that's true, I do.'

'Therefore you must be acquainted with the owner.'

'I am. Norman Grant owns *Tahitian Dreams*.'

'Norman told me the painting has been on the market for

about three months. Did you know *Tahitian Dreams* was for sale?'

'I did. Many people in the art world knew of its availability, Mark.'

'Then why didn't you tell me about it? Recommend it?' he asked, sounding puzzled.

Laura said, very quietly, 'I thought the painting was not right for you.'

'Why not? You know how much I've wanted a Gauguin, been salivating about owning one for years.'

'This is a problem painting. I wouldn't recommend it to anyone.'

Mark frowned. 'What do you mean by *problem*? It's not a fake, is it?'

'No,' she said quickly, shaking her head. 'I didn't mean to imply anything like that. The painting is one of Gauguin's best, in my opinion, and I'd give anything to be able to recommend it to you. But I can't. Please forget this painting, it's not for you.'

Mark Tabbart's fixed scrutiny of her lasted for the longest moment before he finally lowered his eyes and stared at the photographs he was holding. He disliked being thwarted, and suddenly he exclaimed in a cold voice, 'I want it, Laura! I've every intention of making an offer to Norman Grant.'

'I really don't think you should. Please don't go near that painting, it's only going to create problems for you.'

Mark threw the two photographs on his desk and walked around it, sat down heavily in the chair, glaring at her.

When Laura remained standing in the middle of the room, he motioned to her. 'Sit down, Laura, in the chair opposite me, and let's get to the bottom of this.'

She nodded, did as he said.

'Now, please explain. Tell me why I shouldn't make an offer.' Unexpectedly, a grin surfaced and spread across his face. 'It's not stolen is it?'

Laura hesitated, then answered with firmness, 'Yes, it is.'

The grin slid off his face; he sat up straighter in his chair and leaned forward. 'You can't be serious.'

'I'm afraid I am.'

'But Norman Grant is reputable, a man of some standing. He's not going to offer me a painting which has been stolen, for God's sake.'

'But he just did, Mark. Four days ago, to be exact.'

'This is preposterous, and I –'

Laura interrupted him, said, 'Let me explain, so that you fully understand. May I?'

Mark Tabbart settled back in his chair, but his expression was impatient. 'Please do,' he snapped.

'*Tahitian Dreams* is in jeopardy, and it could very easily become the object of a dispute in the not too distant future, that's why I'm trying to steer you away from it.'

'Who was it stolen from?' Mark demanded. 'And how do you know this?'

'I'm a professional art-adviser, Mark, it's my business to know these things. A great deal of information comes across my desk every day, and from all over the world. Very recently, the painting was brought to my attention. *Tahitian Dreams* has a strange history, and incidentally it has changed hands quite a few times, but without much fanfare.'

'I know that. I have the provenance of the painting from Norman Grant,' he pointed out in an irritable voice.

'I would *expect* you to have it. Norman Grant bought the painting from a woman called Anthea Margolis of Boston, about five years ago. She, in turn, had purchased it fifteen years before that from someone called Joshua Lester of New York, or rather, Mr Lester's widow. The Lesters had owned the painting for about eighteen years before selling it to Mrs Margolis. Mr Lester bought the painting from an Arthur Marriott who lived in London and he had owned it since –'

'1950!' Mark spluttered, annoyed with her. 'Look here, I know all that.' He glanced at the paper he was holding, waved it at her. 'I *have* all the relevant dates here.'

'Then read on, Mark, please, and tell me who Arthur Marriott bought it from in 1950,' Laura responded, shifting slightly in the chair, crossing her long elegant legs, looking at him pointedly.

'It doesn't say, only that he had owned it since that particular year. And why does it matter? It's now January of 1997. Forty-seven years are accounted for. What more do you want?'

'Forty-seven years don't mean very much, you know, when you consider that the painting was executed by Gauguin in 1896. That's one-hundred-and-one years ago. Where do you think it was for fifty-four years before that? Before this gentleman called Arthur Marriott bought it?'

'I've no idea,' Mark replied coldly. 'And do we *care*?'

'*You* ought to care, since you've considered buying it.'

'The provenance Norman Grant has provided is good enough for me,' he shot back, glaring at her once more.

'Let me give you a little more information,' Laura murmured, returning his cold stare steadily. He had not been able to intimidate her yet. 'Arthur Marriott was an art-dealer in London, and he bought the painting from the Herman Seltzer Gallery in Vienna, Austria,' Laura went on, then paused, took a deep breath and plunged in. 'The gallery had acquired it about a year earlier, in 1949, from one Josef Schiller. He had been a general in the SS, a Nazi, one of Hitler's top echelon. The painting was, in fact, confiscated by Schiller's lieutenants from the art collection of Sigmund and Ursula Westheim, a wealthy Jewish banking family in Berlin. The Westheim Bank, a private merchant bank, was famous; so was the Westheim Art Collection, which was started by Sigmund's grandfather, Friedrich, in the late nineteenth century. This was immediately following the historic first Impressionist showing in Paris in 1874. Friedrich Westheim was an avid collector, and over the years he acquired some extraordinary art. He bought the paintings of Renoir, Matisse, Manet, Vuillard, Van Gogh, Sisley, Seurat, Monet and Degas, and sculptures by Degas and Rodin, as well. He was also a big collector of Gauguin's primitives, and it was Friedrich Westheim who purchased *Tahitian Dreams,* just after it was first exhibited in Paris in 1897, or thereabouts. In any case, not very long after Paul Gauguin had shipped it to France from Tahiti, along with other paintings he had recently completed. Friedrich happened to be a close friend of Claude Monet's and used to frequently visit the artist at Giverny, and he acquired some remarkable paintings by him. You may not have heard of it, but in art circles the Westheim Collection is well known. It was the greatest Impressionist and Post-Impressionist collection ever put together, in fact. There's never been one like it since, either in private hands or in a museum. And it disappeared in *its entirety* in 1938–9.'

Laura paused, gave Mark a careful look, and finished, 'It was confiscated by the Nazis. *Confiscated* being another word for *stolen,* of course.'

'I see.' Tabbart nodded his understanding, then added, 'And that is why the Gauguin which Norman Grant owns is in jeopardy.'

'Exactly. I'm not sure whether you are aware of this or not, but the World Jewish Congress's Commission for Art Recovery is hellbent on retrieving art which was stolen by the Nazis from the Jews of Europe . . . whenever it turns up somewhere, whatever the circumstances, and *if* there is a claimant.'

'And there's a claimant for *Tahitian Dreams!*' Mark said. 'Of course! That's it. There's a Westheim heir who can prove that the painting belonged to the Westheim family. I'm right, aren't I?'

'Yes. Some new documentation has come to light that leaves no doubt.'

'And where does this development put Norman Grant?'

'With a problem. He could lose the painting.'

'It seems to me he's an innocent bystander.'

'Perhaps. On the other hand, the painting was stolen, and it therefore belongs to its original owner, the person from whom it was stolen originally.'

'Come on, Laura,' Mark said, his tone irate. 'The painting was apparently lost in 1938–9, and that is some fifty-nine years ago now. *Really!*'

Laura shook her head vehemently. 'It can't be reasoned that way. No, no. Listen to me. If I go into your house and steal something, be it a painting or a small object of some kind, and then I go and sell it to someone else, it's still your property. It's not mine. You haven't sold it. *I* have sold it . . . a *thief* has sold it. Am I correct?'

'Yes. But that doesn't wash, in this instance, does it? There are some extenuating circumstances here, Laura.'

'I don't think there are. That painting was seized illegally by the Nazis, and therefore it rightly belongs to the heir of the Westheim family. As does the rest of the Westheim Art Collection, actually. As I just told you, that vanished without a trace.'

'I don't know . . .' Mark's voice trailed off, and his expression was one of uncertainty all of a sudden. He seemed less sure of himself than he had been a moment ago. 'Half the art world's going to be up in arms about this, if the Westheim heir sues,' he muttered. 'It's opening a can of worms, isn't it?'

'Maybe it is. On the other hand, I truly believe it is wrong to shield the provenance of stolen goods from proper scrutiny, which is what happened all those years ago. This problem goes back to Arthur Marriott, who should have asked for, no *demanded*, the proper provenance when he bought *Tahitian Dreams* from the Herman Seltzer Gallery in 1950.'

'And would the owner of the gallery have given it to him, do you think?' Mark asked, a hint of scepticism in his tone.

'I don't know, although I think General Josef Schiller would have had plenty of phoney documentation to make it appear that he had come by the painting legally. The gallery is probably an innocent party to this also. Well, there's one thing I'm absolutely certain of, and it's this. The heir of Sigmund and Ursula Westheim is the rightful owner of the Gauguin, and it should go back to that family, no matter who possesses the painting at this moment.'

Mark was thoughtful for a split second, rubbing his chin with one hand. Then he glanced across at her, his eyes narrowing as he said, 'I suppose you see a string of lawsuits ahead. You do, don't you?'

'Look, I don't know what's going to happen. The situation could get volatile, yes.'

'I can hazard a guess, make a prediction even,' he volunteered. 'Norman Grant will have to sue the woman he bought it from, and she'll have to do the same thing, and so on and so on, right down the line. I can now understand why you don't want me to go anywhere near the painting.'

'I'm glad you do, Mark.'

'Does Norman Grant know anything about the Westheim heir?'

'I have no idea. But the story has begun to make the rounds – at least, it has in the art world. A few people I know are aware of it. But I don't think any legal steps have been taken yet. By the Westheim heir, I mean. I did hear the heir has been doing a lot of digging, investigating, trying to trace the painting's long journey over the years, and so I'm certain that by now he knows Norman Grant owns it.'

'How come *you* know so much about this situation anyway?'

'I explained before, a great deal of material comes to my office, and it's my business to sift through it all. And then a friend in the art world told me something about it, quite a lot actually, and what a story it was. You see, my friend knew how much I love Gauguin's work. He wanted to alert me.'

'I doubt Norman Grant knows anything. Shouldn't he be told?'

'Not by me. Or you, for that matter. Stay out of it, Mark.'

'You know what, Laura, this is all wrong.' Mark settled back in his chair. 'The painting was lost all those years ago, and the Westheim heir should accept that, not expect to receive reparation or to get the painting back. Not only that, let's not forget that Norman Grant paid good money for it, *in good faith*, and now he could be sued for it, could lose a painting which cost him millions. And he's done nothing wrong.'

'*Tahitian Dreams* was stolen by a Nazi general, a member of the SS. It is morally wrong to say that Grant owns it. What he bought is a stolen painting, and now the rightful owner wants it back.'

'But Grant didn't know – and doesn't know – it was stolen,' Mark protested, his impatience with her flaring again.

'As far as we know he doesn't,' she snapped back acidly.

'I bet Norman won't give it up so easily,' he announced and laughed dryly. 'I don't know him, but he looks like a tough son of a bi – son of a gun, and the heir *will* have to sue if he wants to get his hands on that Gauguin. I sort of sympathize with Norman, I must admit. Nobody wants to be out millions of dollars.'

Laura said slowly, 'A moment ago I thought you saw this my way, but obviously not.' She bent forward, drew closer to him, frowning. 'Don't you think that acquiring art from those condemned to die in the death camps, and not paying them or their families for that art, is an unacceptable way to build an art collection?'

'Put that way, yes, I have to agree with you. But look here, this situation had its genesis in 1950, at that gallery in Vienna. The gallery sold the painting to an innocent person who had no knowledge of the provenance.'

'We don't know that, Mark. In those days, people in the art world knew of the Westheim Collection and what was in it before the war. We're talking about only twelve years here, from 1938 to 1950, and remember, the fellow who bought it from the Seltzer Gallery was an art-dealer.'

'Point well taken, but we're dealing with the present, the here and now. Incidentally, just out of curiosity, who is the Westheim heir?'

'Sir Maximilian West.'

'The British industrialist?'

'Yes.'

'He changed his name,' Mark asserted.

'No, he anglicized it. From what I've heard about him, he went to England as a child, grew up there and became a British citizen after the Second World War.'

'I see.'

They both fell silent for a moment or two, and it was Mark Tabbart who broke it when he asked, 'How come he hasn't done anything about the painting before now?'

'According to my information, he only recently found out who owns *Tahitian Dreams*. Also, he apparently just came across some old documents which absolutely support his claim of ownership.'

'I see.'

Laura said, 'Shall I call Norman Grant and tell him you're going to pass on the Gauguin?'

Mark gave her an odd look out of the corner of his eye, glanced down at the photographs, and answered without looking up, 'No, no, I'll talk to him myself.'

'But I don't mind making that call, as your art-adviser.'

'I said I'd handle it myself,' Tabbart snapped and rose. He looked at his watch pointedly. 'I'm afraid I have another meeting, Laura, if you'll excuse me now.'

11

Laura was angry.

She walked back to her office at a rapid pace, seething inside. There was no question about it, Mark Tabbart had literally pushed her out of his inner sanctum, so unceremoniously that his behaviour had verged on the point of rudeness.

Maybe he did have another appointment; on the other hand, he had never propelled her out into the reception area so quickly and in quite the same way before. All of a sudden he had wanted to get rid of her. In order to make a phone call to Norman Grant? she wondered. Obviously she could not be certain about that, but it was a strong possibility.

It struck her that Mark was not going to take her advice. He was convinced he was infallible. Perhaps he was in business, but not in this particular matter. He knew very little about the art world. What to do? How to get him to see it her way?

Then abruptly she stopped in her tracks, as it suddenly struck her that she must get rid of her anger. And immediately. Being angry with Mark for not heeding her was ridiculous. In the end he would do what he wanted, because that was the nature of the man, and it was his money after all. I must be calm, she reminded herself, continuing up Madison, shivering in the cold evening air. Anger blocks all rational thought, and I must think rationally. Yes, that's what I must do now. And I must try to protect Mark Tabbart from himself. If he'll let me, that is.

As Laura let herself into the office and slammed the front door behind her, Alison Maynard, her partner, came out into the reception area to greet her; Alison's pretty face was full of expectancy, and her eyes were questioning.

Slender and petite, with short blonde hair, Alison Maynard gave the appearance of being delicate, even breakable, but there was nothing fragile about her. She was tough, a woman of some force, with strong opinions, good values and, like Laura, she prided herself on her integrity. Also, she too could strike a hard bargain when necessary, and she knew her own mind, her own strengths and weaknesses. The two women made a good team, balancing each other well.

Alison asked: 'How did it go? Uh, uh, need I ask? I can tell from the expression on your face that Mark was difficult.'

Taking off her coat and hanging it in the closet, Laura answered, 'I don't think difficult is the right word. He was quite adversarial at one point. And he asked a lot of questions . . . in the most challenging way. And, of course, he took the attitude that Norman Grant was an innocent bystander.'

'He *is*, in actuality, Laura,' Alison reminded her.

'I know, *he* didn't steal the painting from the Westheim Collection – a Nazi general did – and I wasn't pointing a finger at Grant. We're trying to *protect* Mark, if he'll allow us to do so.'

'From himself!' Alison exclaimed. 'Look, we both know he's a tyrant, and that he thinks he's the greatest. But surely he understands that if he goes anywhere near that painting he'll find himself entangled in the biggest mess?'

'I made that crystal clear.'

'As his art-advisers, how would we extract him, Laura? If, in fact, that happened?'

Laura shook her head, and followed Alison into the latter's office, her expression thoughtful, worried.

It was a large, square room with two windows overlooking a small garden in the back, and a high, coffered ceiling. The antique furniture was handsome, predominantly mahogany, almost masculine in feeling, and the walls were covered with old art prints from the 1920s and 1930s, beautifully framed.

Alison walked around her antique Georgian partners' desk, and sat down in the wing chair upholstered in old tapestry. She stared across the polished mahogany expanse, waiting.

Laura flopped down in the leather chair placed at the other side of the desk; she leaned forward intently, and explained, 'I had a strong feeling that Mark was going to call Norman Grant the moment I left. He practically *hustled* me out of his office. In fact, he couldn't wait to get rid of me.'

'Do you mean he wanted to call Grant to make an offer for *Tahitian Dreams*? Or to alert him that he was about to become enmeshed in enormous problems?'

'I'm not sure,' Laura admitted honestly, and sat back, biting her lip, pondering for a split second. Then she said swiftly, 'I don't think Mark would be foolish enough to make an offer for the painting now. He's a financial genius, and smart as hell, and as a businessman he has great respect for money. So he's not going to spend it casually. He knows the painting has a bad history. I'm sure he's no longer interested in it. But he might feel obliged to tell Norman Grant what I said, explain about Maximilian West and the provenance of the Gauguin.'

'It's possible. No, *very probable*. But according to Hercule Junot, Sir Maximilian is about to put Norman Grant on notice that as the Westheim heir he is the rightful owner of *Tahitian Dreams*, and that he's seeking its return. Isn't that so, Laura?'

'Any moment. Perhaps it's already happened, for all we know. When I spoke to Hercule in Paris yesterday, he said there was no reason why I couldn't explain the situation to Mark, tell him everything. Otherwise I couldn't have done so, since I'd given my word of confidentiality to Hercule.'

'It's a peculiar situation, when you think about it,' Alison murmured, leaning forward, putting her elbows on the desk, propping her chin in her hands. 'Norman Grant *did* buy the painting in the most legitimate way, and in good faith. Now the poor guy's about to find himself in the middle of a major scandal.'

'I feel a bit sorry for him, but our main concern must be our client,' Laura said.

Alison nodded.

Laura went on, 'Mark won't do anything foolish. Having calmed down, I now realize that. But I was furious when I left his office. He can be so superior, such a know-all.'

'That's Mark's personality.'

Laura laughed. 'But knowing that, understanding his quirks, doesn't make him any easier to bear,' she shot back. 'Still, I'd better keep reminding myself he's an important client . . . I guess I'll just have to bite the bullet where he's concerned, and so will you. Of course, we might get lead poisoning in the process.'

'What we must do is distract him,' Alison announced, smiling beatifically at her partner. 'And I have just the right thing for that.'

'*Oh*. What?'

'A small bronze. A ballet dancer.'

'*Not a Degas?*' Laura said, sounding suddenly awed.

'A Degas, yes indeed.'

'Oh my God! Where is it?' Laura's excitement was evident on her face.

'En route to New York from Beverly Hills, as we speak. It's being shipped to us in care of Hélène Ravenel. She agreed to accept it on our behalf and keep it for us at her gallery.'

'That's fantastic! What a *coup*. And aren't you the secretive one. Why didn't you tell me?'

'First of all, I wanted to be sure we could get it. This particular Degas has changed hands several times in the last few years, and there was a question about whether it would go on sale at all. Then again, I wanted it to be a surprise for you. I thought, when

I first heard about it, that we could offer it to John Wells, Laura, but don't you agree it's the ideal thing to distract Mark?'

'You're absolutely right. What a clever girl you are. Go to the top of the class.'

Alison laughed, and so did Laura.

Laura now said, 'I can just picture Mark salivating over the Degas.'

'Instead of the Gauguin.' Alison pushed her chair back and rose. 'I'm afraid I have to go. I promised to meet my sister at the Carlyle for a drink, and I'm already running late.'

Laura also got up and walked towards the door of Alison's office. 'And I'm going to see my grandmother. I must go over some of the papers on my desk, and then I'll be leaving myself in half an hour. So I'll lock up.' Turning, she blew her partner a kiss. 'See you tomorrow.'

Alison said, 'Give my love to Grandma Megan, and tell her she's a fantastic example for all of us.'

Laura nodded. 'I will indeed. It's the truth.'

Laura smiled to herself as her thoughts stayed with her grandmother. What a remarkable woman she still was, formidable really. She had always been proud to be descended from her.

Megan Morgan. The beautiful, feisty gifted girl from the Rhondda Valley of South Wales, who had come to America in 1922, at the age of eighteen, to marry her childhood sweetheart from Port Talbot, Wales. Owen Tudor Valiant. Named for Owen Tudor, legendary Welshman and progenitor of the three great English Tudor monarchs – Henry VII, Henry VIII and Elizabeth I – because nothing less than an heroic name would do for *him*, his doting parents had announced, for wasn't their son going to be a king amongst men.

From the steel mills of Port Talbot to the steel mills of Pittsburgh Owen Tudor Valiant had gone, seeking his fortune and a better life. But it was in New York that he ultimately found it, where the streets were not paved with gold after all, but with opportunity. Those with guts seized it immediately.

Leaving the steel mills behind forever, Owen had cheerfully, and very optimistically, migrated to Manhattan, filled with belief in himself and his darling wife, the incredible Megan.

Loving music as she did – had she not sung three times a day every Sunday in the chapel in Port Talbot since she was a little girl – and being enterprising by nature, the young Megan had used the world of music to make friends and further their fortunes in Pittsburgh. She had entered local singing competitions, appeared in amateur theatrical productions, given renditions of her favourite songs at recitals, many of them Welsh in origin, and had won superlative reviews for her efforts. Everyone loved Megan, taken by her dark good looks and presence, awed and moved by the purity of her voice.

And so it was that one day in 1923, Owen Valiant, twenty-three years old and full of piss and vinegar, drive and burning ambition, made a momentous decision. It was the third most important and decisive step of his life; the first had been proposing to Megan before he left the Rhondda, the second had been emigrating to America. Now came the third: they would go to New York and take their chance in that gleaming metropolis of skyscrapers and seething humanity, the Great White Way and dreams of glory, the centre of the world, as far as Owen Valiant was concerned.

In his mind Owen had no doubt that they would succeed, that Megan would conquer Broadway, soon have her name glowing in lights on a marquee. As it turned out, his faith in her was more than justified. She made a name for herself after only two years of playing small roles and acting as understudy to various leading ladies. Her great chance, the break of a lifetime, came when she was just twenty-one-years old, in May of 1925. The actress she was understudying at the time fell seriously ill; she stepped into her shoes forthwith and never looked back. Megan Morgan had become a star overnight.

'Because she has a bell in every tooth,' the proud young Owen was wont to pronounce about his wife's thrilling voice, one that excited and captivated all those who heard it.

Musically talented himself, he and Megan had decided that he must become her agent and manager. Together they made a wonderful combination, were a great team; they built a happy and successful life for themselves, and raised four children, each one born in between Megan's long runs in a string of Broadway hits.

One of those four children was Richard, Laura's father, and it was from him, as well as from their grandparents, that Laura and her brother heard so many fascinating stories about the Valiants of Port Talbot and their early years in America. They were also regaled with marvellously entertaining stories about Wales, these tales told with relish, amazing flourishes and a great deal of hyperbole. Always heroic, mythic, these were grand tales that glorified the Welsh above all else. 'Nobody like us,' Owen would boast, meaning not only the Welsh race but the Valiants. And so Laura and Dylan grew up on Welsh legend and myth and were made to feel proud of their Celtic heritage. It was this heritage which made them different, Grandfather Owen was swift to point out; by *different* he meant better, special.

Her father had been a composer and conductor, successful, well-known, well-thought of and sought after, but never as celebrated or as popular as his very famous mother, who was *the* great musical stage star of the 1930s, 1940s, 1950s, and even well into the 1960s. Her popularity with the public never waned; the people loved her, and they had for half a century.

If Owen persisted in boasting about Megan, she played down everything about herself, always saying she was, 'Just a little girl from the Welsh valleys who was lucky to be born with something of a voice.'

Amazingly, their grandmother was still alive, a sprightly ninety-two-year-old, going on ninety-three, remarkably clear-headed and healthy, who still went out and about socially in Manhattan, as well groomed and as chicly dressed as ever. Owen had died in 1989, at the age of eighty-nine, but Megan was still going strong, defying the years, much to the joy of her family.

Their grandparents had been dominant forces in their lives, involved and caring and exercising enormous influence over them. But it was their father who had always been there for them until the day he died in 1994, aged sixty-four. Unexpectedly stricken by a fatal heart attack – and he a man with no previous heart troubles – he had been far too young to die.

12

It was cold outside, a very cold night, and windy, she could tell that from the frost coating the edge of her windows, and the look of the East River – turbulent, choppy with waves. Above the ink-dark river the sky was black, without cloud. Stars shone brightly; there was a full moon. It was one of those sharp, clear winter nights when everything appeared pristine, the kind of January night she had always loved.

Her eyes, once a vivid cornflower blue but faded now to a softer, paler hue, settled on the helicopter zooming closer. It looked like a flying saucer, and it was coming towards her unerringly, as if this old landmark building where she lived was its target.

At the last moment, or so it seemed to her, the helicopter veered away, no doubt heading for the heliport, a few blocks up the river in the East Sixties.

The sky was suddenly empty again except for the cold white stars and the Pepsi-Cola sign rising up like a bright red neon sentinel at the edge of Queens. The sign had been part of her life for so many years, she knew she would miss it if it were suddenly no longer there. My bit of pop art, she called it.

Megan Morgan Valiant turned away from the bay window of her library and walked towards the fireplace at the other end of the room. She was a tall, slender woman, regal in bearing; her dark brown hair, lightly streaked with silver, was fashionably styled, and the great beauty of her youth still lingered in her face.

She could not help thinking how good it was to be alive. So many people she had known were dead now. She was ninety-two and still going strong, defying time and the odds. She was luckier than most and in so many ways: well off enough to live as she'd always lived, to do what she wanted. She was also fortunate in that there was nothing much wrong with her, other than a few aches and pains, a bit of arthritis in her feet and a slight deafness in one ear. Nonetheless, she could still hear very well when she wanted to, even when they whispered.

There was no sign of osteoporosis, the curse of so many older women, no senility, no Alzheimer's. She was lucky indeed.

She had outlived her beloved husband Owen, dead almost eight years, and her two eldest children, her sons Emlyn and Richard. Only her daughters left, Rhianon and Cara, and her grandchildren, the children of Richard and Maggie. *Richard.* Her favourite. You shouldn't have favourites, but you always did. It was human nature to favour one above all the others, but you must never let them know. No reason to hurt any of them. Her special child had been her second son. It was curious, she often thought, that his brother Emlyn and sister Rhianon had never had any children. Cara had had two, Mervyn and Lydia, but Mervyn had died in a drowning accident in the lake in Connecticut, Lake Waramaug it was called, and he only twelve. A tragedy. It had haunted the family for years. The loss of a child was always hard to bear. His sister Lydia had never seemed to recover. She had married young and gone to live in Australia, as if she wanted to put great distance between herself and her family, and the memories.

Megan paused at the console table and its silver-framed photographs of her family. The Valiants ... Owen and her, Rhianon and Cara, Richard and Emlyn, so many pictures taken at different ages . . . their children. The children when they were small, in their teens and grown. Funny, she thought, how you could identify each one from the baby pictures. None of them had changed much. The faces were the same in adulthood.

Reaching for a photograph of herself when she was twenty-one, she studied it carefully for a moment. It had been taken the year she had become a star overnight. And thankfully she still had that same face – underneath the wrinkles. Not *that* many wrinkles, though. She had worn well, even if she said so herself. It was easy to see they were all from the same family. Black hair, blue or green eyes; dark Celtic Welsh, the Valiants, yes, the lot of them.

Fey, mystical, sometimes otherworldly, and touched by the magic, that was what Merlin of Camelot had said about the Welsh, whom others called the lost tribe of Israel. Part of that magic was in the throat, in the tongue, in the love of song, the love of language, both the spoken and the written word. Actors and writers and singers, the Welsh were. Special, Owen had said.

Her voice had been *her* magic, a gift from God, was the way she thought of it. She had always played down her success, but it was her voice which had given them their fortune – and seen to their future. In a sense, every Valiant owed almost everything they had to her gift, and to Owen's brilliance as a manager and to his business acumen. He had spun gold for them.

She missed Owen. She would miss him until the day she shed this mortal coil and went to join him.

But not just yet, she added under her breath. Too much still to do here on earth. She knew he'd understand.

Megan placed the photograph on the console, leaned forward, peered at her grandson Dylan. A little sigh escaped her. Dylan had been spoiled by Richard and Margaret, and by Owen and even by Laura, sometimes. But not by me. I've never spoiled him, and I never will.

Next to Dylan stood the silver-framed picture of Laura, taken when she was just twenty-two. A smile touched Megan's mouth, lit up her eyes, brought a sudden radiance to her face. She's the one, she's the best. Strong, reliable, loyal, and steady as a rock. She's the racehorse with the breeding *and* the stamina. I'll put my money on her any day. Megan drew closer to the picture, loving Laura so much, and then glanced at the one of herself taken in 1925. Spitting image, she murmured: Laura looks just like me when I was that age.

Straightening, Megan moved to the fireplace, warming her hands against the flames. Lily, her housekeeper, had kept the fire going since teatime, knowing how much she liked a fire, especially in winter. It cheered up a room. Sitting down, leaning her head against the blue silk brocade of the chair, her eyes fixed on the painting on the opposite wall.

It was a springtime scene of a New York square, painted by Childe Hassam in 1896, one of her better paintings. I'll give it to Laura for her birthday in May, or perhaps she would prefer to choose one for herself. I'll let her decide. Yes, that's what I'll do. That was the best thing.

Now Megan's eyes shifted to the portrait, hanging above the fireplace . . . she had been thirty-one when it was painted. In her prime. The same age as Laura was now.

Closing her eyes, Megan let herself sink down into herself. Remembering, remembering . . . so much to remember, so many memories. They filled her heart. It was still young. Sometimes she thought she was only eighteen in her heart. It was her mind that was old and wise – full of knowledge, too much knowledge, she often thought, of people and their strange ways, of human nature with all its frailties and weaknesses, as well as its strengths . . . She drifted with her thoughts and her memories . . . and she dozed.

'Hello, Megan,' Laura said, gliding into the library.

Megan sat up with a little start and blinked, then she smiled when she saw her granddaughter.

Vivid eyes, vivid hair, vivid personality. Full of vivid life. Her favourite grandchild. Laura bent over, kissed her on the cheek, squeezed her shoulder. She loved her grandmother very much; after all, they had been extremely close ever since she was a child. She had always felt closer to her grandmother than she had to her mother, or anyone else.

'I can smell the cold on you, Laura,' Megan said. 'I hope you didn't walk here.'

Laura laughed, touching her grandmother's cheek gently with one finger. 'All that way, Gran, from Sixty-Eighth and Madison to Fifty-Second and First, and on an icy night like this. You must be joking. I took a cab.'

'Good. Much warmer. Much safer, too. The sherry decanter's over there, darling, in its usual place. Pour for us and let us get cosy for a while. You know how much I enjoy our chats.'

'Sherry coming up, Gran,' Laura murmured over her shoulder as she walked to the round table standing in a corner of the room.

A moment later she came back, carrying two glasses. After giving one to Megan, she sat down in the chair opposite, reached forward to clink her glass against her grandmother's and said, 'Here's to you, Grandma Megan, and another new year. May there be many more.'

'Well, I hope so, Laura dear, I don't want to leave this earth just yet. I've more damage to do, you know. Much more,' she laughed.

Laura laughed with her.

After taking a sip of sherry, Megan continued, 'Is your mother feeling better? I thought she seemed a bit glum at times over Christmas.'

'Yes, I agree, she *was* in a strange state of mind, but she's all right now. I think she cheered up once she got down to Florida, and she's apparently felt much better, is in good spirits.'

'How is that little cottage of mine?'

'As charming as ever, Gran.'

'Your grandfather and I bought it over thirty-five years ago, before you were born, and it was always a pretty place, my beach cottage where I could potter around and relax, be myself.'

'Why don't you go down there for a week or two, Gran? The weather's warm, much warmer than New York. It would do you good. And Mom would love your company. Please think about going, I'll take you there, if you want.'

'I can take myself, thank you very much, my dear girl! But I don't want to go, I don't want to be there, Laura, not without your grandfather. It was always our place, a very *special* place, and it brings back too many memories, makes me feel sad.'

Laura stared at her in surprise. 'But Grandpa Owen lived here, in this apartment with you as well, and surely –'

'The cottage was our very special place, our holiday home. We loved to escape there, it was always just the two of us . . .' Megan lifted her shoulders in a tiny shrug. 'I don't know how to explain it, darling, but I have no desire to go there anymore. As much as I loved it then, now I don't care about it at all. And it'll be yours one day, yours and your brother's, after I'm gone.'

'I hate it when you talk that way, Gran.'

'I know. But we must face reality. I *will* die.'

'Yes, I know,' Laura mumbled.

Megan glanced into the fire reflectively, and after a moment of silence, she remarked, 'Your father's been dead three years now. Don't you think your mother ought to start a new life? She's only sixty, after all.'

'She's trying hard, Grandma. She's gone out and got herself a lot of work.'

'She ought to go out and find herself a new man.'

'Grandma, you're something else!' Laura exclaimed.

'But it's the truth, and sixty is *young*. It certainly looks awfully good to me, from where I'm sitting, and considering *my* age. Anyway, what about this fellow in the Bahamas? The one whose ceiling she's gone to paint.'

'Forget about him, Gran, he's too old. He's eighty-two.'

'The father is, yes. I mean *Harry* Lightfoot, the son. I've met him, and he's very nice. Your mother could do worse.'

'And how old is he?'

'Oh about fifty-five, fifty-six, something like that. Just right for Margaret.'

'Mom'll say he's too young.'

Megan shook her head, took a swallow of sherry, pondered for a second, then announced, 'A younger man keeps a woman young.'

'Speaking from experience, Grandmother?'

Megan had the good grace to laugh. 'No, but I can imagine. Anyway, I'm quite serious, I think your mother should have another man in her life – boyfriend, husband, it doesn't really matter.' Megan leaned forward slightly, pinning her wise old eyes on Laura. 'Margaret's healthy, vital, full of energy, a good-looking woman. Fun, too. Any man would be lucky to have her on his arm, and in his life.'

'I agree, Gran, but try telling that to Mom.' Laura paused, then nodded her head, said with sudden enthusiasm, 'I'm going to encourage her.'

'Good girl,' Megan said.

Laura nodded, sipped her sherry, said nothing.

After a moment Megan remarked, 'But your mother is not the reason why I asked you to come to see me, darling girl. I want to talk to you again about the art collection, such as it is. I've been wondering if we should put it up for auction.'

Laura frowned and her eyes filled with sudden alarm. 'Do you need money, Grandma? Do you have problems? I thought the trusts Grandpa set up were –'

'No, no, there's not a problem about money!' Megan cried, interrupting her granddaughter. 'I just thought it might be more practical to sell the art now. I've been reading about auctions lately: paintings seem to be fetching good prices. The economy's good. If you think we should do it, why not?'

'I don't want to make a snap decision, Gran, not just like that.

I think I ought to evaluate every painting you have and then talk to Jason. You remember him, he gave us evaluations on the small Cézanne and the Sisley.'

'I do remember him. Very well. He was a nice young man. So, you make the decision, and do what you have to do.'

'All right, I will.'

Megan smiled at her granddaughter, loving her so much, full of pride in her. 'In the meantime, let's have another sherry, darling,' she said.

Laura did as she was asked, went and poured more sherry for them both, and carried the glasses back to the fireside. After handing one to her grandmother, she returned to her seat, and said, 'Claire's very excited about coming to spend August in Connecticut, Gran, and naturally she's thrilled that you've agreed to visit for a few days.'

'It'll be nice to be there with you. And Claire and Natasha. I was so very sorry when they didn't come for Christmas. I'd sort of set my heart on it, and when she cancelled I felt sad, quite sad indeed, Laura. After all, I might not be here next Christmas.'

'Don't say things like that, Gran!'

'But it's true, darling, we must face the inevitable.'

'Dylan didn't come either. He's a stinker at times.'

'Oh pooh. Dylan's just a silly boy. He's never grown up. Your parents' fault, too. They spoiled him, especially your mother. I've said it before, and I'll say it again . . . the breeding's there, but no stamina. No backbone.'

'Perhaps if he got married and settled down, he'd grow up a bit,' Laura muttered, eyeing her grandmother over the rim of her sherry glass. 'What I mean is, I think he needs a bit of responsibility to make him pull his socks up.'

'Bah! Don't be a foolish girl, Laura. Responsibility won't change your brother. He'd probably run away from it the first chance he got. As for getting married, I pity the poor girl who takes such a foolhardy step.'

'You sound cross with him.'

'I am in certain ways. But I still love him. He's one of mine, even though he is very silly at times. I haven't quite recovered from his recent venture into real estate. Fancy buying that farm in Wales.' Megan shook her head and grimaced. 'He needs his brains washing.'

'I know. He should have put the money in the bank, as you said at Christmas. But that's Dylan, going back to his roots he calls it. Mythical Wales and the world of legend, Grandmother. He always talked about having a home in Wales.'

'I know, I know, you blame me for filling his head full of fanciful stories and ideas, and your grandfather did it too . . .' Megan looked into the fire for a moment, then lifted her eyes to Laura's, and added, 'But *you* heard the same stories, and you're as sane and practical as I am. I think it's something to do with character, darling girl. And talking of marriage, I'm surprised Claire is still single after all these years. I suppose she hasn't met anyone?'

'She doesn't give herself a chance,' Laura said, and stopped. She shook her head. 'That sounds a bit mean which is the last thing I'd be about Claire.'

'I know how much you care for her. So she's still bitter is she?'

Laura looked at Megan in surprise. 'How did you know? You haven't seen her for a couple of years.'

'She was bitter then and I merely assumed she still was, if she hasn't given herself a chance, as you put it. What a pity really, such a loving girl at heart. And Philippe and she were so very much in love. I thought it would last forever.'

'Didn't we all.'

'I wonder how his mother Rosa is doing these days?'

'Goodness, Gran, imagine you remembering her name.'

'I've always had a good memory. How do you think I learned all my lines when I was an actress, for heaven's sake, child? And I still have a good memory I want you to know, better than most people half my age. I'm not senile yet, Laura.'

'I know, Gran, I know. Don't get excited.'

'I'm not excited,' Megan said, lowering her voice; she took a sip of sherry and settled back in her chair.

Laura said: 'It's odd you should ask about Rosa Lavillard, because I ran into her when I was in Paris.'

'Oh. Was she visiting Claire?'

Laura shook her head. 'Oh no, that would never happen. Claire doesn't like her much.'

'Why not?

'Claire thinks she's . . .' Laura sought around in her mind for the right word, then said, '*Peculiar*. Yes that's it. Claire thinks Rosa is odd, weird.'

'She'd be weird too if she'd had Rosa Lavillard's life, her childhood. Poor woman. Most people would have been in a mental home if they'd gone through what she did. Rosa's a very brave woman. Courageous.'

Laura stared at her grandmother, and asked, 'How do you know about Rosa Lavillard's childhood?'

'She told me.'

'When?'

'Before Claire and Philippe were married. Don't you remember, I gave a small dinner party for them here. It was after dinner. She and I sat in this very room talking for a long time. The rest of you were in the drawing room having coffee and liqueurs.'

'Yes of course I remember the dinner. What did she tell you, Grandma?'

'About the war years in France, what it was like growing up during the Nazi occupation. I was able to sympathize with her, and I also understood because I'd been over there to entertain the troops. That was in 1944 and 1945. Your grandfather hadn't wanted me to go but I really felt I must do something, anything that might help. Those poor boys were over there fighting and risking their lives for us, fighting for the cause of freedom. And so I went. Your grandfather came too in the end. He wouldn't let me go alone because he was afraid something might happen to me.'

'Yes, you've told me stories about when you went to entertain the troops in the Second World War. It must've been exciting, Gran.'

'In some ways. But also heartbreaking . . . it was so dreadful to see the dead and the dying. But I know we helped those who were wounded. We entertainers did manage to cheer them up, show them that we cared, give them a feeling of home. But they were just boys. Soldiers are always so *young*, it's heartrending.'

'I know. At least, I can imagine. How old were you, Grandma?'

'Still in my prime, still good-looking, still able to kick up my legs and sing my heart out.'

'You haven't changed much,' Laura said, leaning over, squeezing her grandmother's hand. 'And you've always been the best.'

'That's nice, darling, thank you. But getting back to Rosa, she suffered greatly when she was a child. She saw too much brutality and evil. In France in those days it was terrible – no food, constant bombings, the Gestapo around every corner. France was under siege then, and it was especially hard for Rosa.'

'She told you all this that night?'

'Some of it she told me, when it applied to her life. But I know what France was like in those days, darling.'

'Why do you say it was especially hard for Rosa?'

'Because she had lost her parents. She was on her own.'

'How old was she?'

'I'm not exactly sure now. Young, Laura, perhaps nine, but no more than ten or eleven. There was no self-pity in her. She told me in a very matter-of-fact way, and then only because I had asked her about her life. I knew she was French by birth and that she and her husband had emigrated here after the war.'

'I see. How sad.'

Megan gave her granddaughter a hard stare. 'You say that in a strange voice. Almost as if you don't believe Rosa's story. I can assure you it's quite true.'

'I do believe you, Gran. I was just thinking it's a pity Claire doesn't understand about Rosa's childhood. Perhaps if she knew more about it she would be more . . . sympathetic.'

'Surely Philippe must have told Claire about his mother and all that she went through?'

'He did tell her certain things, I know that, because Claire once told me. But somehow I don't think she has the full picture.'

'Perhaps not.' Megan was on the verge of telling Laura the whole story about Rosa Lavillard, and then she changed her mind. It was such a harrowing tale, and she suddenly felt that she didn't have the strength this evening. Instead she said, 'If you see Rosa again give her my very best wishes. I liked her.'

'Yes I will. Claire never got on with Rosa. Do you think that's strange in view of your opinion of Rosa?'

'Show me a woman who genuinely gets on with her mother-in-law, and I'll eat my hat.'

Laura had to laugh at this expression, which sounded so odd coming from her grandmother, and then she remarked, 'My mother gets on with you.'

'I'm the exception to the rule, didn't you know that, darling girl?'

'I suppose I did.'

Megan chuckled. 'I'm teasing you, Laura. It was like this . . . your mother and father were so completely besotted with each other they never noticed anyone else. Not her mother, or me or your grandfather, not even you and Dylan. Not really. And when you don't know someone exists, that person can't very well be an irritant to you, can she? And I knew that if I ever voiced one word of criticism or disapproval of your mother, your father would not have spoken to me ever again. Richard meant the world to me, and I couldn't have borne that. All I wanted was his happiness. And your mother made him happy.'

'I understand.' Laura leaned back against the chair, and stared out of the window, seeing very little except the dark night sky, the dark waters of the East River. She was thinking of Rosa

Lavillard and Philippe, wondering about them. Suddenly surprising herself, she confided: 'Claire harbours a dreadful hatred for Philippe these days, it's quite upsetting to witness. He stopped by unannounced when I was there for dinner and there was a terrible scene.'

'That's such a pity, and particularly distressing for Natasha. But children always suffer in divorce, and of course Claire has always been so extreme as well as independent of nature.'

'*Extreme.* What do you mean?'

'Funny word to use, isn't it? But I suppose I do mean *extreme.* Claire is right or left, never in the middle. With her, things are black or white, never grey. She was like that when she was growing up, and I don't suppose she's changed much.' Megan let out a sigh. 'Claire lacks the ability to compromise. Surely you of all people know that, Laura.'

'I do, but I sort of ignore it. Nobody's perfect, least of all me.'

'Oh I don't know about that,' Megan replied in a teasing voice.

Laura smiled at her grandmother and sipped her sherry.

A silence fell between them for a short while. But it was a companionable silence. Laura and her grandmother had been on the same wavelength since Laura had been a child, and they understood each other very well. Grandfather Owen often said that Laura was more like her grandmother than Megan's own daughters, and this was the truth. The two of them were very similar and in so many ways.

Megan suddenly said, 'Is everything all right between you and Doug?'

Taken by surprise, Laura gaped at her grandmother.

'Is your marriage all right? Or is it in trouble?' Megan asked.

Finding her voice, Laura said, 'I don't know, Gran.' Laura had always told her the truth and she was being scrupulously honest now. 'I think there's something wrong, but I'm not sure what it is. Anyway, it's not *right*. Not anymore.'

'I thought as much.'

'You did?' Laura gave her grandmother a puzzled look. 'Did you notice something over Christmas?'

'Doug was preoccupied, abstracted. To me he seemed faraway a great deal of the time, not *with* us.'

'And yet he was very sweet to me, to you, to my mother.'

'That is absolutely true. But there were moments when he thought he was unobserved that he let his guard down, and he looked quite miserable to me. As if he didn't want to be there at all.'

'Oh Gran . . .'

'You must talk to him, Laura. That's the problem with most people, they never communicate their feelings. And they make silent demands.'

'I'll have to pick the right moment.'

'Certainly you will. But don't leave it too long. Don't let whatever it is that's troubling him fester inside.'

'I won't, Gran, I promise.'

13

Laura said, 'So I didn't misunderstand you.'

Turning to look at Alison, she continued, 'When you said a bronze of a ballet dancer, I immediately thought of *The Little Fourteen-Year-Old Dancer* by Degas and I was right. This is from the unnumbered edition of at least twenty-five examples cast in the 1920s. The Shelburne Museum owned one, and if I remember correctly it was auctioned for just over eleven million by Sotheby's last year.'

'Correct. And who owns it now still remains largely a mystery,' Alison remarked, adding, 'and any serious collector would grab this one, don't you think?' She continued to study the Degas Bronze she'd had shipped in from California; it stood on a plinth in the centre of Hélène Ravenel's Madison Avenue art gallery, highlighted by a ceiling spotlight.

'A posthumous, second-generation cast of the original wax sculpture by Degas, done at the Hébrard foundry by the great caster Albino Palazzolo, supervised by Degas's friend, the sculptor Albert Bartholomé,' Laura said, speaking from memory.

'That's absolutely right. The provenance arrived in this morning's mail and I put it on your desk. You can look at it later. So, what do you think?'

'It's an incredible piece, Alison, perfectly beautiful. God, look how dirty and tattered the net tutu is. Mark will want it, I'm sure of that. And even though we have no real reason to distract him now, I think we must show it to him.'

Alison laughed, her eyes filling with merriment. 'Aren't we a couple of idiots, thinking that he would go after a Gauguin against our wishes, and one that was shrouded in problems. He's much too smart a man for that.'

Laura said, 'It was my fault. I was the one who made the judgement about Mark. Flawed, as it turned out.'

'We know he didn't make an offer for the painting, but do you think he told Norman Grant about Maximilian West?'

'It's more than likely, yes, I'm sure he did. But it's of no consequence, since Sir Maximilian put Norman Grant on notice the day after my meeting with Mark. In other words, it wasn't a secret.'

'What do you think will happen about the Gauguin?'

Laura lifted her shoulders in a small shrug. 'I don't know. It's probably going to be a Mexican stand off, an impasse. Both men claim they own *Tahitian Dreams.*'

'It's a terrible situation, it could drag on for years,' Alison murmured and then focused her attention on the Degas again. 'What about John Wells? Do you think he would like this if Mark doesn't want it?'

'Yes I do. John would jump at it, and don't forget our new client Olivia Gardener in Palm Beach. This piece would be perfect for the entrance foyer of her new house on South Ocean Boulevard. I can just see it on a beautiful antique circular table in the middle of the foyer. In any case, Hélène told me she would be interested in buying this herself if we don't place it with one of our clients.'

'I am certainly interested,' Hélène Ravenel exclaimed, coming to join them. 'Very much so.'

The three women stood talking about the sculpture for a few moments and then Laura looked at her watch and said, 'I'm late for my lunch with Hercule. It's a good thing I'm meeting him at the Carlyle.'

'Give him my best,' Alison said, as Laura hurried through the gallery, heading for the front door.

'I will. See you back at the office, Alison, and thanks Hélène, thanks for everything.'

The Ravenel Gallery was only a couple of blocks away from the Carlyle Hotel and Laura set out at a brisk pace; she was soon turning onto East Seventy-Sixth Street, where the front entrance to the famous hotel was located.

After checking her coat she went into the restaurant, where Didier, the maître d', greeted her pleasantly and led her over to Hercule Junot's table.

Hercule was on his feet in an instant, kissing her on both cheeks, beaming at her, pressing her down onto the banquette next to him.

'I am very happy to see you, Laura,' he said, still smiling, 'and delighted that you were able to have lunch with me today, and such short notice.'

Laura returned his smile. 'So am I. It was a lovely surprise to hear from you yesterday. How long are you staying?'

'For about a week. I came to see one of my clients. She has asked me to redecorate her house in Southampton, and so I am going to drive out there on Saturday. To spend the day reviewing the house. Now, Laura, what would you like? A glass of champagne?'

'No, thanks, Hercule. Normally I'd say yes, but I have a mountain of paperwork on my desk and I have to get through it today. I'll have a grapefruit juice, please.'

After ordering their drinks, he continued, 'My client mentioned that she wishes to buy some new paintings, and that she is looking to hire an art-adviser. I immediately thought of you, Laura.'

'That's nice of you, Hercule. Thank you very much.'

'Whilst I was sitting here waiting for you I had this idea ... that you would drive out to Long Island with me on Saturday morning. We could leave the city early, around eight o'clock, meet Mrs Newsam, my client, and speak with her about her art preferences, and you could do a tour of the house with me as well.'

Laura hesitated.

Hercule immediately noticed and said quickly, 'Is it a problem for you on Saturday, my dear?'

'Not really. It's just that Doug and I only get to see each other at the weekends, we're so busy during the week, and –'

'But that is not a problem,' Hercule cut in. 'He could come along with us. My client's house is situated on the dunes, and Doug could take a walk on the beach if the weather is good, whilst we look over the house and chat with Mrs Newsam. And there is no question about it, I know she would love us all to join her for lunch. No problem, my dear, none at all.'

Laura still hesitated and then finally she nodded, gave Hercule a bright smile. 'I'm sure he'll want to come, and thanks for thinking of me. As you know, I'm always interested in meeting prospective clients.'

'Would Alison like to drive out there with us?'

'No, she wouldn't. I'm *positive* of that. She always spends the weekends with the twins, her two little girls, and she never lets anything interfere with her time with them and her husband Tony.'

'I do understand. Ah, here are the drinks,' he said as the waiter placed the glasses in front of them. Lifting his flute of champagne, he toasted, 'Your health, Laura.'

'And yours, Hercule.'

They talked for a few moments about the Southampton house of the client he had flown to New York to see, and then Hercule suggested they order lunch. 'Since it's a working day for you, Laura, I'm sure you don't wish to linger too long.'

Laura smiled at him, picked up the menu and glanced at it. 'I'd like to have the cold asparagus vinaigrette and then afterward the grilled sole.'

'I will join you in the fish, but I will start with *des huîtres*.

To me there are no better oysters than the ones I have in New York, not even in *la belle France*.'

Much later, when the meal was more or less over, Hercule suddenly said in a low, confiding tone, 'I would like to propose a project which would be very profitable for you, if you were to take it on.'

'You know I'm always interested in doing business, Hercule. What's the project?'

'Sir Maxim West.' Hercule smiled, and lifted his hands in his typical Gallic way. 'What I mean is, I want you to meet him. He will be in New York on Monday, and I wish to take you to see him at his office. He would like to totally revamp his art collection – revamp is the word he uses – Laura, and I think you are the perfect person to help him. I have known him a long time, many years, he is a client of mine, and I understand him. He is very low-key these days and doesn't like fuss. I believe the two of you will be . . . compatible. Very compatible.'

Although somewhat taken by surprise at Hercule's suggestion, Laura was excited and she exclaimed, 'Hercule, I would love to meet him! How wonderful of you to do this. Alison will be thrilled when I tell her that we might be acquiring *two* new clients.'

'I am delighted to be of help to you, my dear, and your expertise can only reflect well on me,' he answered, his eyes twinkling. 'Now that we have settled this, tell me your news, Laura.' He gave her the benefit of a warm, avuncular smile and sat back.

'There's not much to tell,' she replied, taking a last forkful of fish, then placing her fork on the plate, also leaning back against the banquette. 'Business is quite good, as I told you last night on the phone, and I've no other news.'

'As I told you, Sir Maxim has informed Mr Grant about the long history of *Tahitian Dreams*, or rather, I should say his lawyers have done so. And now we can only wait and see what is going to happen. However, in my opinion, such as it is, I do believe this is not going to be easy. I doubt very much that Mr Grant will relinquish the painting, hand it over to Sir Maximilian without a protest. Why should he?'

Laura nodded. 'Morally he should, of course, but I tend to agree with you, it's not going to be quite so simple. I'm totally on the side of the original owner, because the work of art was stolen from him. No matter what anyone says to me, or the arguments they make, I believe it's wrong to shield the provenance of stolen goods from proper scrutiny. And by rights *Tahitian Dreams* should go back to the owner, or, if he's dead, the heirs.' Laura paused, then finished, 'But it's going to be a battle. Still, there's a solution to everything, Hercule, although I can't quite envision a solution to this dilemma. At least not at the moment.'

He gave her a long, thoughtful look. 'If you come up with a solution please let me know immediately, I am certain Sir Maxim would want to hear it.'

'Doug's been calling you,' Alison said, walking out of her office into the reception area of Art Acquisitions as Laura came in. 'He tried reaching you during lunch but your mobile was switched off. He called back here to tell me he's now on his way to Teterboro Airport. He'll phone again from the car.'

'Why is he going out there?' Laura stared at her partner, puzzlement flashing across her face.

'He's being sent to the coast. There's an –'

'Just like that, on a minute's notice,' Laura interrupted, walking into her own office, throwing her coat and handbag on a chair. 'Did he say anything else?' she asked over her shoulder, sounding angry.

'Only that there's been an emergency apparently. He told me he rushed home, put a few things in a bag, and now he's heading out to New Jersey. Aaronson International are flying him to LA on their private jet.'

'I see.' Laura sat down behind her desk and looked across at Alison who was leaning against the door frame. 'Did he say how long he's going for?'

Alison shook her head.

The phone rang at this moment, and Laura pounced on it. 'Art Acquisitions.'

'Hi, Laura, it's me. I've been trying to reach you,' Doug said.

'Alison just told me. Why are they sending you to the coast at a moment's notice, Doug? What's the sudden emergency?'

'Will Laxton was out there dealing with the merger for Aaronson, and he had a heart attack. That's why I'm being sent.'

'Oh God, how awful. Poor Will, he's not . . .' Laura paused, took a deep breath, and before she could continue, Doug supplied the end of her sentence.

'No, he's not dead, thank God. He's in intensive care at the hospital. He'll be okay. Out of action for a while, but they say he'll make a good recovery.'

'I'm glad to hear it. How long will you be gone? Will you be back at the weekend?'

'I doubt it, Laura. Today's Thursday, so I'll only have tomorrow as a working day. I'll have to pick up on Monday and keep going for the rest of next week, I'm sure. There's still rather a lot of legal work to be done.'

'Why did they have to send *you*? Couldn't Peter Pickering have stepped in for Will?'

'Pete's there, sweetie, you know what a big deal this is for the firm. We've got half a dozen lawyers on it already. They need *me* to replace Will, to *lead* the team.'

'I understand, I'm sorry, I don't mean to be difficult. It's just . . .' She let her sentence remain unfinished.

'Just *what*?'

'We don't seem to spend much time together these days, Doug.'

'We're both working hard, that's why. But come on, Laura, be happy for me. It's a big boost for me within the firm to be sent out to the coast on this deal. The Aaronson merger runs into billions of dollars.'

'I am glad for you, Doug,' she responded swiftly, suddenly feeling guilty; she realized she had sounded churlish, perhaps even childish.

'I'll call you tonight. I'll be at the Peninsula, as usual,' he told her in his carefree, breezy voice.

'Fly safely, darling, and do a good job. Show 'em what you're made of, Doug.'

'I will. 'Bye, sweetie,' he answered and hung up before she could say anything else.

Laura stared at the phone, frowning, and then she rose and went to find Alison who had returned to the other office during her conversation with Doug.

From the doorway, she said to her partner, 'I think we might have two new clients. Courtesy of Hercule Junot.'

'Come in, come in, and tell me everything!' Alison exclaimed.

Because there was no urgent reason why she should rush home, Laura worked late. After Alison and the two secretaries, Lynne and Joni, had left for the day, she settled in to tackle the paperwork which had piled up on her desk.

At eight o'clock she finally stopped, put down her pen wearily and sat back in her chair, glancing around the room as she did. Like Alison's office, hers also faced out onto the small back garden, and it was similar in size, with the same dimensions and high-flung, coffered ceiling. Laura too had used English antiques and a collection of old art prints exceptionally well framed. But whereas Alison's walls were white she had had hers painted a lovely primrose yellow, a colour that was sunny and cheerful.

Ever since they had leased the ground floor of the town house on East Sixty-Eighth Street Laura had found her office pleasant to work in, but tonight she discovered she'd suddenly had enough of it. On the other hand, the thought of going home to the empty apartment appalled her; it was too late to make a supper date with a girlfriend or to go over to see her grandmother.

A sandwich and a glass of wine, that's my lot tonight, she muttered to herself as she turned off the lights in her office and went out into the reception to get her coat.

As she was taking it off the hanger Laura was unexpectedly filled with a sense of dismay, and for a split second she did not understand why she was experiencing such feelings.

And then she thought: It's Doug. It's because of Doug. Somehow he's drawing further and further away from me and I don't know the reason why.

14

It was windy, bitterly cold. But there was a bright sun in the flawless sky, and so Laura, tempted by the glittering day, had donned her bright red, quilted-down coat and gone out into the garden.

Now, as she walked along the paved path that led to the stone wall fronting onto the dunes, she noticed how lifeless the garden looked. The trees were leafless, dark, skeletal etchings against the azure sky and the lawn was dun-coloured, patched here and there with old snow that had frozen over. Desolate gardens in winter, wherever they were, depressed her, made her feel ineffably sad, and Mrs Newsam's garden in Southampton, Long Island was no exception.

Increasing her speed, Laura hurried, wanting to leave the forlorn landscape behind, and within seconds she was pushing open the gate in the wall and stepping onto the dunes. Shrugging deeper into her coat, her hands thrust in her pockets, she trudged across the dunes and went down an incline onto the beach near the sea.

Icy though it was on this February morning, Laura enjoyed being by the ocean; she was intoxicated by the tangy smell of salt and seaweed, and the fresh, breezy air was a wonderful tonic after being cooped up in her office all week.

This morning the Atlantic was rough and choppy, topped with whitecaps, but as beautiful to her now as it was in the summer months when it was usually much calmer. Being close to the sea had a calming and restorative effect on her, and within minutes she was beginning to feel more at ease with herself. Some of the tension she had been holding for days began to slip away, much to her profound relief. Sunny by nature, she hated being down in the dumps.

There was no real reason for her to be here in Southampton with Hercule, even though Sandra Newsam had just become a client, after the meeting they'd had here last Saturday. But when Hercule had invited her to come along again, if only for the ride out to the beach, he had said, she had accepted without hesitation. She had nothing better to do, and she did not relish the notion of spending the entire weekend alone. And in any case it gave her a chance to look around Mrs Newsam's lovely old grey-shingled house for a second time.

Sandra Newsam had been impressed with her credentials, and had hired Art Acquisitions to buy art for her, after visiting them at their New York office the previous Wednesday. 'I won't be your biggest client,' she had said to her and Alison. 'I don't have millions in loose change to spend. But I do want to start collecting some really good paintings, and your advice is going to be invaluable to me. Once we've found things for the beach house, I'd like to start looking for art for my New York apartment. The whole idea is exciting to me. We might even discover some great new talent between us.'

She and Alison had liked Sandra Newsam, who, they quickly discovered, was straightforward, down to earth and totally lacking in pretence. 'Thank God she's not like Mrs Joyce,' Alison had said after Sandra Newsam had left the office, referring to a client they had felt compelled to drop because she was the total opposite of Mrs Newsam. Laura had grimaced, remembering the dreaded Mrs Joyce and her pretensions of grandeur, bitchy demeanour and acerbic tongue.

As she walked along the edge of the sea Laura continued to think about her work. She and Alison were doing exceptionally well, better than they had ever expected, and their business was in the black, growing more successful every day. They were both aware they might have to hire another art expert to work with them, if only on a part-time basis. They now had more clients than they had dreamed possible; handling them all effectively, *and* finding the right art, could easily become a problem.

'Let's hold off hiring somebody for a few more months,' Laura had said to Alison last night. 'I can handle the extra workload, so you don't have to worry about staying late or travelling. I'm quite happy to do that.'

Alison had been grateful because she liked to be with the twins as much as possible, especially at weekends. Also, she didn't really want to hop on and off planes anymore, or rush around the world seeing clients and scouting works of art. Tony grumbled so much when she went away, that Alison always travelled with a worried and overburdened mind, which Laura thought could affect their business adversely. To balance the workload, Alison had volunteered to handle all of the basics in the office, and do most of the paperwork, which, as she explained to Laura, she could do at home on the weekends if that was necessary.

Laura wasn't sure what Doug would say when he discovered she had agreed to do all of the travelling for Art Acquisitions. As her thoughts automatically swung to her husband she felt a terrible heaviness descending on her, weighing her down. She tried to shrug it off but to no avail.

He had been in Los Angeles for ten days already, and he would be staying there for another week at least. She felt a sudden rush of depression at the thought of this. A few days ago he had asked her to pack a suitcase with extra clothes for him, since he had taken so little when he had left in January. This she had done, and the suitcase had been picked up from the doorman of their apartment building by a lawyer from his firm; the young man was flying to join the legal team working on the Aaronson merger and had been pressed into service by Doug.

Doug called her every day but he did not have much to say; he was even uncommunicative about his work, which was unusual for him. It seemed to her now that all he ever said was, 'Hi, sweetie! How are you? Got to go. Goodbye.'

It's odd, Laura now thought, but he's changed radically in the last few months. So much so, it's even become noticeable on the phone. He used to have so many amusing little things to tell me, odd titbits to share, confidences to make, and now he offers nothing except banalities. And, of course, he usually gets off the phone as fast as he can.

With a rush of clarity, Laura realized that this was *it* exactly, and it brought her to a standstill momentarily. He was only making the phone calls every day out of a sense of duty, of wanting to keep the peace between them, at least for the time being.

On several occasions since he had been in Los Angeles she had tried to speak to him about their life together, the route it was taking, and their problems. But he had brushed her words to one side, told her there was nothing to discuss, that everything was *fine* between them. And then he would hang up before she could argue with him. But it wasn't *fine*. Even if he didn't know it, she certainly did.

Once he came home she was going to sit him down and make him listen to her, make him reveal his thoughts and his feelings. Perhaps then he would share with her whatever it was that troubled him so much. Whatever it was, it was driving a wedge between them.

Doug *was* troubled. Even her grandmother had spotted it at Christmas, although Laura recognized that it hadn't started in December, but dated back to last year, to sometime in the spring, in fact.

Grandma Megan had noticed it, not only because she was a wise old bird who missed nothing, but also because Doug was normally such an untroubled, carefree person, a man who made light of any burdens he might carry. He simply shrugged them off with a cheery laugh, and got on with his life. 'Got to live life to the fullest, enjoy every moment. Because none of us know how long we're going to grace this world,' he would say, and he repeated the words so often they had become his motto. That was his nature, and he had been like that since the first day they had met.

Laura sighed as she swung around and began to walk back along the beach in the direction of the Newsam house. Even though she didn't want to admit it, Doug had become an enigma to her. Here was a man she had believed she knew inside out, but it wasn't true. She didn't know him at all. But how well do we ever really know another person? she wondered, and acknowledged that one never did. Most people were mysteries to others and frequently to themselves.

When she returned to the house ten minutes later, she found Hercule in the library, talking on the telephone. Wanting to give him privacy she started to leave, but he swiftly motioned to her, indicating he wished her to stay. Laura smiled, nodded, and went and sat down on the large overstuffed sofa in front of the fire. She picked up a magazine and flipped through it absently.

After only a second or two, Hercule hung up and came to join her by the fireside. Lowering himself into a nearby chair, he explained, 'I telephoned the Carlyle for my messages and found one from Sir Maximilian West. I have just spoken to him. He has finally arrived in New York after those unexpected delays. He wishes us to join him for lunch tomorrow. Is that possible, Laura? Or are you busy, my dear?'

'No, I'm not, and as you know I've really been looking forward to meeting him.'

'He's going to telephone me tomorrow morning at nine, and he will do so exactly at that time. He is very precise. Once I have heard from him I will let you know where we are to meet.'

'That's fine, Hercule. You told me you'd known him a long time, but you didn't say how long. Is it many years?'

'Ah yes, it is indeed. I first met Maxim well over thirty years ago. I was introduced to him by a friend and client, Margot Derevenko. Her daughter Anastasia was married to him, although sadly they were later divorced. When they remarried in 1990 we all rejoiced.'

'Everyone loves a happy ending,' Laura murmured and glanced into the fire, a shadow of pain crossing her face as she did so.

Hercule noticed the look of anguish, fleeting though it was, and he wondered about her. He thought Laura had seemed both sad and distracted on the few occasions he had seen her in the past ten days. Because he had had to stay longer than first anticipated, to confer with Sandra Newsam about the various decorating schemes for her house, Laura had taken him under her wing. They had dined with her grandmother, seen a movie together, and lunched several times.

It was impossible not to detect her loneliness due to her husband's delay in Los Angeles. Now he asked himself if it were more than that? Could something else be troubling her? He hoped not. She was such a lovely young woman, so good looking and bright, and extremely clever when it came to business. She was also one of the most knowledgeable art-advisers he had ever met. Although he thought of himself as a connoisseur of Impressionist and Post-Impressionist paintings, he realized that this was a small vanity on his part. Although he outstripped her in his knowledge and understanding of Gauguin's work, she knew much more than he did about many other artists from these periods, and her memory was prodigious. She could reel off facts and figures without hardly giving them a thought, or so it appeared to him. Apart from this, she had an extraordinary eye and fine taste in paintings. Perfect taste.

Hercule knew that Laura and her partner were becoming more and more successful, and therefore were accruing power in the world of art. What was it Claire had said to him recently? Ah yes, she had told him that Laura had 'a lot of clout'. Funny expression, but he rather liked it.

Now, as he sat back in the chair studying her surreptitiously, he sincerely hoped that her marriage was in the same good shape as her business. Sadly, women with successful careers were not always so lucky in their personal lives he had noticed over the years.

Sitting up straighter on the sofa, and turning to face Hercule, Laura immediately saw the look of concern in his eyes. She gave him a dazzling smile. 'I'm looking forward to Claire's visit next month,' she said. 'In fact, I'm trying to talk her into staying for a week, after she finishes her shoot for the magazine.'

'Yes, a vacation *would* be good for her,' Hercule agreed. 'She works very hard and she's so intense about it. But then, that is the way she is made. It is her nature, yes. Whatever Claire is doing she gives it everything she has. Her heart and her soul.'

'She's not changed, Hercule, she was like that when we were girls. Ferociously focused.'

He smiled at her, shook his head, looking unexpectedly amused. 'You both are that, Laura my dear.'

'If you're not focused, you don't get anything done, so *I've* discovered.' Laura stood, glanced around the room. 'By the way, what's happened to Yves?' she asked, referring to Hercule's assistant, who had flown in from Paris to help the designer earlier in the week.

'He's upstairs, measuring the windows, and Sandra has gone out to lunch. And I think that is what we should do, once Yves has completed his task. Are you not hungry, Laura?'

'I am, yes. That walk on the beach has given me an appetite.'

At this moment, Yves Pannone walked into the library carrying a yellow pad attached to a clipboard. He addressed Hercule in his careful English: 'The cook wishes to know if we would like to have the lunch, *Monsieur*.'

'It would be simpler if we went into the town. Come, Yves, put on your coat, and you too, Laura, and let us go at once. I myself am ravenous. I will have a word with the cook on the way out so that she will not be offended.'

15

Hercule had insisted that Maximilian West be his guest for lunch on Sunday, and now Hercule sat with Laura in the dining room of the Carlyle Hotel, waiting for him to arrive.

As they waited Hercule told her a few things about Maxim, wanting her to have an inkling of the kind of man she was about to meet, and for whom she might possibly do some work. 'He was knighted by the Queen a few years ago for his contribution to British industry,' Hercule explained. 'It was well deserved. But he wears this honour lightly, almost casually, and like most other truly great people, he has humility and compassion. And he is also down-to-earth, unpretentious.'

'You told me the other day he had remarried his first wife. He had several others in between, didn't he?' Laura said.

'Several. Camilla Galland, the English actress, who died tragically in an accident. Later Maxim married Adriana Macklin, the well-known American businesswoman, but they were subsequently divorced. I always believed that Anastasia was the love of his life. Everyone was stunned when she left him and he was sick at heart about it, very distressed. None of us understood her behaviour at the time, but then we do not know what goes on between two people in their private lives.' Hercule took a sip of champagne, and continued, 'When Anastasia and Maxim remarried in 1990 we were all relieved, especially their children Alix and Michael. Anyway, my dear, you will find Maxim relaxed, pleasant to be with. He has a knack of putting everyone at their ease, making them feel comfortable. Ah, here he is now.'

As Maximilian West walked towards their table Laura could not help thinking what a handsome and distinguished-looking man he was. She had seen photographs of him in newspapers and magazines, but they hardly did him justice. He was tall, lean, with black hair touched by silver at his temples, and his black eyes were brilliant in his tanned face. He wore an impeccably tailored brown-and-beige houndstooth-check sports jacket, pale blue shirt, darker blue tie and grey slacks. She thought: My God, he's gorgeous, no wonder women fall all over him.

After greetings had been exchanged, introductions made, Maxim turned to Laura and started talking about art, and just as Hercule had predicted, she was instantly comfortable with him. Within minutes she was chatting to him as if he were an old friend. Between the first and second courses they covered quite a lot of ground, mostly talking about his art collection in London.

At one moment, after glancing at the dessert menu and then putting it down, Hercule turned to Maxim and said, 'When you told me you had stumbled on new information regarding the Gauguin, you never explained it further, Maxim. You merely said it was old documentation. I must admit, I am very curious to know more.'

'I'll be happy to tell you about it,' Maxim replied. 'I didn't actually stumble on it myself though, to be honest, Hercule. Rather, Aunt Irina did.'

Maxim paused, glanced at Laura and, as though he felt it was necessary to explain, said, 'She's not really my aunt. Irina and my parents were inseparable for many years, and I've known her since I was a small child. Her name is Princess Irina Troubetzkoy.'

Laura, intrigued by this fascinating man, nodded, but before she could say anything, Hercule exclaimed, 'I have met Irina. A most unusual woman. We became acquainted through the Derevenkos, *naturellement*, years ago. She is well, I hope, in good health?'

'Yes, thank you, she is, Hercule. Still going strong at eighty-five, and quite a wonder. And I remember now, you met her quite a few times if I'm not mistaken.'

'That is correct. But please continue with your story, Maxim. I'm afraid I interrupted you.'

Maxim nodded. 'All right. As you know, Irina lives in Berlin, but several months ago she came to stay with me in Paris for a week. One afternoon, wanting to buy a gift for me, she took herself off to the Left Bank. There are, as you're well aware, Hercule, many wonderful bookshops in that area. She spent most of her time browsing in one of them on the Quai Saint-Michel, mostly because the shop has a rather grand collection of art books, art catalogues, and French classics beautifully bound in leather and hand-tooled in gold. She knows I collect old first editions, other rarities, as well as art books, and it was whilst she was browsing amongst the art books and art catalogues that she noticed the name Westheim on the spine of a particular book. The gold lettering was somewhat worn and she couldn't make out what else it said, but because the name was so meaningful to her she naturally pulled it out. And she was stunned when she saw the cover. Inscribed in gold across the front was the title *The Westheim Collection.* The author was my grandfather Ernst Westheim. When she opened it and turned to the frontispiece, her heart leapt, she told me later. The book had been updated by my father Sigmund, but what really took her breath away was the following page. Written on it was my mother's name Ursula Westheim, and even more remarkably, the signature was in my mother's own handwriting. Irina recognized it immediately although the ink was a little faded. She was thrilled, excited, as you can imagine. She bought the book and returned at once to my apartment – in fact she could hardly wait to give it to me. Aunt Irina was in tears. "Such a treasure, Maxim. Ursula's own book," she said as I leafed through it. "Who would have thought I would come across this in Paris, *her personal* copy of a book about your family's great art collection." I couldn't believe it myself, that it had turned up in Paris in this way.'

'What a marvellous find indeed, and how fortuitous for you,' Hercule exclaimed.

'Wasn't it just,' Maxim responded, his eyes lighting up. 'Extraordinary when you think about it. Anyway, the book had been privately printed and only given to friends, and incidentally the signature *is* my mother's. I've compared it with letters I have from her.'

'And when was it printed?' Hercule asked.

'In the mid 1920s originally, and seemingly my father had it reprinted in 1936, and then there was a new edition in 1938. That is the edition in my possession now.'

Laura was amazed at this story. The chances of finding the book were one in a million. Leaning forward, she asked, 'Did you recognize it, Sir Maxim?'

'No, I didn't,' he answered. 'I'd never seen it before. At least, I don't recall seeing it when I was little. I was only four when my father had the book reprinted. However, Aunt Irina began to recollect a few things later that same evening. Vague memories came back to her . . . mostly about my father working on papers to do with the art collection, in 1935 or thereabouts. It was around this same period of time that he told her he had almost finished writing about the art collection.'

'And that's all she could remember?' Laura asked.

'Unfortunately. Those were very bad times, Laura,' Maxim explained. 'Germany was in the hands of the greatest criminals the world has ever known, and death, upheaval and fear permeated everyone's lives. My father was trying to get us out of Nazi Germany to safety. That was his priority, his main concern in those days, and Irina was helping him with the aid of the

German underground, the Resistance movement, of which she was a member.'

'I understand,' Laura replied. 'It sounds as if your grandfather and father created a *catalogue raisonné* about the collection.'

'They did. But it's also a picture book, in a sense, since it has hundreds of photographs of paintings and sculpture from the collection.'

'And *Tahitian Dreams* by Paul Gauguin is one of those photographs,' Hercule asserted, a pleased smile tugging at the corner of his mouth. 'How wonderful, Maxim.'

'It is, yes. And since that painting and the entire Westheim Collection disappeared not long after the book was reprinted, I think it proves beyond a shadow of a doubt that the Gauguin hadn't been sold, that it was still in the possession of the Westheim family.'

'What a pity the book wasn't discovered before,' Laura murmured. 'But never mind, now you have proof of the provenance of the entire collection, should any of it suddenly turn up on the art market.'

'That's true.' Maxim shook his head. 'It's amazing when you think about it . . . that this book survived. It's probably the only one in existence today. I'm quite sure there were a number of them at my parents' home, but they couldn't have escaped destruction. Our house on the Tiergartenstrasse was heavily bombed. Then when Marshal Zhukov marched into Berlin at the end of the war he turned twenty-two thousand guns on a Berlin already battered by the Allies, reduced what was left standing to rubble and dust. The city was flattened. Nobody's possessions could have withstood that kind of bombardment.'

'I wonder how the book found its way to Paris?' Hercule mused. 'That in itself must be an interesting story.'

'Perhaps your mother gave it to someone as a gift, Sir Maxim,' Laura suggested. 'Do you think that's the answer?'

'It's possible, of course. Personally, I think she took it with her when we went to Paris in 1939.' Maxim paused, his dark eyes suddenly intense and reflective. After a moment, he explained, 'My mother had brought Teddy with us, a family friend who acted as my nanny, and in March of 1939 my mother sent us both to England, to safety. And, most fatefully, she returned to Berlin.'

Laura nodded and glanced across at Hercule.

He signalled her with his eyes to be careful, to be still. Laura understood that this was dangerous emotional ground they were suddenly treading on, and so she did not speak. Maximilian West had sounded extremely tense and he seemed stressed.

Abruptly, he sat back in his chair and looked off into the distance, his jaw clenched. But eventually he continued quietly, 'I have my own theory, and Irina is in agreement with me. I believe my father planned to bring some of our paintings out. *Somehow*. He had remained in Berlin after we left, waiting for visas. He finally received them and was about to leave with my grandmother, aunts and uncle, when my mother went back to help him with my grandmother, who was frail and ailing. But I just can't believe that he wouldn't have tried to smuggle a few of the canvases out. He was apparently very resourceful. Rolled-up canvases are not too difficult to transport and he would have certainly had the assistance of Admiral Canaris. The admiral was head of the Abwehr, German military intelligence, but by birth, upbringing, tradition and conviction he detested Hitler and all that he stood for, as did many of the men under him. Canaris and his men were working against Hitler from within, and one of the things the admiral was doing was helping to save people who were in danger from the Nazis, by getting them out of Germany. He helped Teddy and me escape. Subsequently, he paid with his life for his beliefs. He was hanged at Flossenburg concentration camp in 1945,' Maxim finished and sat back; he fell silent once more.

Laura made no comment and neither did Hercule. Both of them were aware that strong memories were assailing Maximilian West and they wanted to give him a moment to recoup himself.

Then suddenly, in a brisker tone, Maxim resumed: 'I am positive my mother took the book to Paris to show it to art-dealers. What better way to present the Westheim Collection to them, just in case my father managed to bring out a canvas or two. She must have left it with an art gallery.'

'That is a perfectly acceptable theory, Maxim,' Hercule agreed. 'Very viable.'

Maxim nodded, lifted his glass and took a sip of Montrachet. 'It seems to be the most probable explanation of how the book got to Paris, although we'll never really know. And it's perfectly amazing to me that it survived at all. The Nazis were not only looting art owned by Jews in Germany, but in France and other European countries as well. They also stole *catalogues raisonnés*, records, and other forms of documentation. Much of the art and its documentation was shipped to Göring and Hitler in Germany. However, from what I understand, a great deal of the documentation was destroyed by the Nazis on the spot in France, and in Germany in the same way. And so the provenance of much of the art became blurred.'

'How terrible that such an awful thing happened, that so much art has been lost, has disappeared into oblivion as a consequence. And if only *you* knew where your paintings are, whose hands they are in today, you could make moves to get them back, since you now have this book,' Laura said.

'That's true, but I doubt that I'd ever be able to track them all down. That's a mammoth task; I would think virtually impossible. The only reason I found out that Norman Grant owned *Tahitian Dreams* was because he put it up for sale. When it came onto the market my daughter knew at once.'

'Is she an art-dealer?' Laura asked.

Maxim shook his head. 'Not exactly. She's an art and antiques broker working primarily with English and European dealers, and she lives here in New York. So she knows what's going on, in the same way, I'm sure, that you do. Naturally, she was aware that we were the real owners of the Gauguin, that it was once part of the

Westheim Collection, because I had told her about it. And these days we do know quite a lot more about the collection. I myself don't remember anything, I was so young when I left Germany. However, Aunt Irina and Teddy have recalled many things, and they've been making notes for years now. They both knew my parents' houses in Berlin and Wannsee, and my grandmother's house in the Grunewald, and they've helped to spark each other's memory. But obviously there was no way I could claim *Tahitian Dreams*, even though I suddenly knew who had it, because I had no proof that I owned it. At least, not until Irina came upon the book by chance.'

'How did you trace the Gauguin back to General Schiller? Through the Herman Seltzer Gallery in Vienna, I suppose,' Laura said.

'Yes, that's right. Alix went to see the painting, and naturally, as a potential buyer she was shown the provenance. She then telephoned the details to me later, and since I happened to be in Paris I flew to Vienna and paid a visit to the Herman Seltzer Gallery. He is long dead, but his grandson Paul was happy to show me all of the records they had in regard to the Gauguin. He bent over backwards to help me, in fact. The provenance stopped with General Schiller. There was no reference to any previous owner before him. Paul Seltzer told me that art stolen by the Nazis was usually stamped on the back of the canvas with a small Swastika, and next to this was written the first two letters of the surname of the owner, and then there was a number. But not all of the art was stamped in this fashion, most especially paintings looted by individuals for their own purposes, such as Schiller. He obviously hung onto it until the end of the war. He then sold it to the Viennese gallery, apparently not an unusual occurrence. According to Paul Seltzer that was happening a great deal in Paris and Switzerland in those days.'

'Yes, it was very systematic, the looting and selling of art, both in France and Germany,' Hercule interjected. 'And why would it not be? It was big business for the Nazis.'

'Of course it was,' Maxim said, and reached for the menu. 'I think perhaps we should order dessert. We've spent the last half hour talking without giving it a thought. What would you like, Laura?'

'I'm not sure,' she answered, smiling at him. 'Everything sounds fattening.'

'*You* don't have to worry,' Maxim said, returning her smile.

'I think I shall indulge myself for once,' Hercule murmured. 'I will have the chocolate mousse. It is delicious.'

'I'll join you,' Maxim said.

'And I think I'll have the fruit salad, please.' Pushing back her chair, Laura rose. 'If you'll excuse me, I won't be a moment.' She hurried off to the powder room.

Once they were alone, Hercule leaned closer to Maxim and confided, 'Laura has an assured taste in art, which I believe springs from her great knowledge of it. In fact, she has a deeper knowledge than anyone else I know. I find that astonishing since she is so young.'

'How old is she?' Maxim said.

'Thirty-one.'

'Really, she looks much younger. Mind you, she seems very intelligent, and she certainly makes sense about revamping my art collection.' Maxim suddenly chuckled. 'Actually, she didn't appear to be impressed when I told her whose work I owned. I think if I hired her she'd then tell me to sell most of it.'

Hercule also laughed. 'She was outspoken, yes, I must agree.'

'Well, she's correct, Hercule, old chap, I do think I should unload most of it, except for the Laura Knights. I do love those, and incidentally, I think your friend can be of help to me in more ways than one.'

'What do you mean?'

'As you know, I'm about to file suit against Norman Grant for the return of the Gauguin. Before I get into any costly litigation, it has occurred to me that I ought to try a different route.'

'Such as?'

'Laura. Earlier, when we were talking, it struck me that she might be better equipped to negotiate with Grant than my lawyers, less intimidating, don't you think?'

Hercule smiled and gave him a knowing look. 'I have the distinct feeling that Laura could be as intimidating as any tough lawyer.'

Maxim laughed again. 'Perhaps so. It wouldn't surprise me at all. But you know, a woman's always got such an advantage, she can be so much softer than a man, most especially when she turns on the charm.'

'That is true, Maxim.'

'I'm seriously thinking of hiring her to handle the matter of the Gauguin, Hercule, quite aside from revamping my art collection in London. She is a personable young woman, obviously very bright, and from what you tell me her knowledge of art is formidable.'

'That is so, and she is well educated and diplomatic. I cannot recommend her highly enough.'

16

Doug came home from Los Angeles the following weekend, and from the moment he walked into the apartment Laura knew instinctively, deep within herself, that their marriage was over.

He was as affable and as charming as he always was, but part of him was simply not there. He seemed more detached and remote than he had ever been before, and it struck her that his interest obviously lay elsewhere. Not for the first time in the past few months, she wondered yet again if there was another woman in his life. It was a distinct possibility and it would certainly explain the changes which had been wrought in him.

Even though she had contemplated this idea before, the thought of it now nonetheless shook her up; she excused herself and left Doug in their bedroom where he was unpacking. Retreating to the kitchen, she stood leaning against a worktop, looking out of the window at the backyard of the brownstone opposite, waiting for the sick feeling inside to go away.

It was a cold grey Saturday night in late February, and the only reason she could see the garden was because light flooded out from the brownstone's windows, illuminating the bare branches of a tree and the garden wall. The scene was bereft, isolated, lonely, and it echoed the way she felt. She shivered slightly, and then an immense feeling of sadness enveloped her like a shroud, and she felt her throat tightening. For a moment she struggled with her emotions and squeezed her eyes tightly shut, pushing back the incipient tears. I won't cry, I just won't, she told herself. I'm going to be mature about this.

For the entire month Doug had been in Los Angeles she had been mindful of his vagueness on the phone, his lack of interest in her and what she was doing, and his ill-concealed impatience, his need to say goodbye and hang up. She was far too smart not to suspect that he might well be having an affair. She wondered whether to come right out and ask him, but instantly changed her mind. Eventually he would open up to her, she felt sure of that, and for the moment she wanted to give him a bit of space.

Opening the refrigerator door, she took out a bottle of carbonated water and drank a glass of it, before returning to the bedroom. Sitting down on a chair, she made idle conversation with Doug as he finished unpacking.

Once he had put his suitcase away, he told her he had a few urgent business calls to make. Excusing himself with a faint smile, he went into his small study at the back of the apartment.

After an hour on and off the phone he finally left the study and found her in the living room where she was working at her desk. She glanced up as he appeared in the doorway and stood leaning against the door frame, looking carefree and nonchalant, as if he didn't have a worry in the world.

'I've booked a table at Le Refuge,' he said, giving her his lopsided smile. 'For nine o'clock. I'm going to shower and put on some fresh clothes. Okay, sweetie?'

She smiled back and nodded. 'I'm surprised you got a table, especially on a Saturday night,' she replied. 'But that's great. And I'm more or less ready. I just have to put on some lipstick and brush my hair.'

'You look great, Laura,' he said, swung around and walked down the hall.

Laura watched him go, thinking how great *he* looked. He was trim and fit, and his face was tanned, as if he had been out in the sun a lot. Well, he had been in sunny California, hadn't he? And apparently not always anchored to his desk, as he had frequently implied. Tall, dark and handsome . . . that was the way Claire had described him in Paris in December, and he was . . . this was the very phrase which had popped into her mind the first time she had met him.

They walked to the restaurant. It was on East Eighty-Second Street, just off Lexington Avenue, not far from their apartment on Eightieth Street and Park Avenue. The evening was pleasant, not too cold, with a bright silver orb of a moon riding high in the black sky.

'Just look at that moon, Laura,' Doug said, glancing up. 'It's a truly *full* moon, perfect! Well, all the loonies will be out tonight, you can bet on that.'

Laura did not respond. Instead, she tucked her arm through his, trying to stay in step with him; he always took such long strides. She was about to tell him she was glad he was home, but instantly she choked back the words. It was too late. In the way that a woman senses these things, she felt she had lost Doug, at least a large part of him. He had started to change last spring, almost a year ago now; and he was a much different man from the one she had married six years ago. This year would be their seventh anniversary, but somehow she didn't think they would be celebrating it. One thing she was certain of, though. Whatever happened between them from this day on, they would always be good friends, and she would always love Doug.

Le Refuge was a charming little French bistro, a favourite of theirs; Laura was pleased Doug had chosen it. As he pushed open the door and escorted her inside, they were greeted by a rush of warm air and the fragrant smells of delicious food cooking, the low-key chatter of the other diners, the bustle of the busy waiters as they hurried about.

After they had shed their overcoats and been shown to a cosy corner table, Doug sat back in his chair and looked at her. 'Champagne? Kir Royale? White wine? What would you like?'

'I think a glass of white wine, please, Doug,' Laura answered, glancing around the restaurant before settling into the chair.

'I'll have the same, I guess,' he murmured and motioned to the waiter. Once he had ordered, Doug went on, 'So tell me more about your new clients. You're getting to be a regular tycoon in the art world, or so it seems to me.'

'You know all about Olivia Gardener in Palm Beach, since we signed her in November, but now we also have this lovely woman, Sandra Newsam. Hercule's doing her house in Southampton. She's recently widowed, and although she won't be spending millions on art, she's going to be a good, steady client; worthwhile, I can tell that. And certainly she'll be nice to work with. But the plum of course is Sir Maximilian West.'

Doug nodded. 'I know. I was impressed when you told me he was considering you. So he took you on, did he?'

'We signed the contract yesterday,' Laura answered, realizing he'd paid far more attention to her on the phone than she'd thought. 'I'm going to reorganize his art collection in London. I'll be weeding out a lot of paintings, getting rid of some, buying new ones. It'll be exciting.'

'It sounds like it. Alison must be really thrilled.'

'She is, and we've agreed that she'll run the office and do most of the paperwork with Joni and Lynne. I'll be on the outside more, seeing clients, tracking down appropriate art, and travelling whenever it's necessary.'

'That'll please Tony. He never did want her to move around much. He likes her joined to his hip.'

'That's true. But it suits *me* this way, Doug. I much prefer to deal directly with the clients, as you well know. The main thing is, Alison's happy with the way we've worked it out and so am I.'

'I understand. And Hercule's turned out to be a really wonderful business contact for you, hasn't he? Quite aside from being a good friend.'

'Very much so, and he's such a lovely person, thoughtful and caring.'

The waiter placed their drinks before them; after clinking glasses they both took a sip and Laura continued, 'I was bowled over when Hercule told me he'd recommended me to Sir Maxim. Having him as a client is a real feather in my cap, and it's good for Art Acquisitions.'

'I should say.' Doug glanced at her quickly and remarked, 'His fame precedes him. What's he like? Really like, I mean?'

'Down-to-earth, pleasant, practical. But charismatic, a genuine presence. And he's suave, charming, extremely good looking. Tall, dark and handsome too, just like you, although he's much older, somewhere in his early sixties, I would think. And he happens to be the best-dressed man I've ever met. *Impeccable.*'

'That's quite a profile you've given him,' Doug said and laughed. 'He's got a helluva reputation as a businessman ... tough negotiator, inspired deal maker, and all that. He used to be a fierce corporate raider in the seventies and eighties, and a very successful one. But I think his son is running the company these days, isn't he?'

'Not exactly. Hercule told me Michael does have a great deal of power, but Sir Maxim hasn't retired yet. They're running the business empire together, I believe.'

'Some team that is,' Doug murmured, and took a swallow of wine. They both accepted menus from the waiter, and Doug asked, 'Do you know what you want?'

Laura shrugged and studied the menu carefully.

Doug studied her, an amused expression suddenly lighting up his green eyes. 'I bet I can guess. You're going to order country pâté with cornichons, lots of extra ones on the side, and then grilled sole to be followed by crème caramel. Your usual.'

'That's right,' she replied, and grinned at his expression. 'I guess I'm very predictable.'

'When it comes to the restaurants you know well.' Stifling his laughter, Doug motioned to the waiter and ordered their food, then asked for a wine list. Once he had perused this for a moment or two, he summoned the waiter, told him which wine he preferred, then turned to Laura once again. 'Robin and Karen have broken up, broken off their engagement,' he said.

Laura was startled, and she sat up straighter in the chair, staring at him. Her surprise showed on her face as she exclaimed, 'My God! When did that happen?'

'About a week ago, but I was so harassed with the Aaronson merger I forgot to tell you. It had slipped my mind.'

'What happened, Doug? I thought they were very much in love, and happy together. Certainly they were well suited. Or so it seemed to me.'

'What happened?' Doug shrugged, shook his head. 'I don't exactly know, Laura. Robin called me in Los Angeles and told me it was off, that Karen had ditched him. She apparently announced it was finished one night over dinner, and the next day she sent the engagement ring back, by bonded messenger. Can you believe it, she didn't even give it to him personally.'

Laura was still somewhat flabbergasted at his announcement of the break-up, and she took a few moments to absorb his words. At last she remarked, 'I suppose she didn't want to face Robin a second time. At least she *did* return the ring, which is more than some women would have done.'

'That's true,' he responded, and shook his head. 'I have to admit, Laura, I was as taken aback as you're looking right now.'

Laura was silent for a moment or two, her expression thoughtful. Then she said slowly, 'If Karen thinks it's not right, then it's better they break it off now. At least this way they won't have to go through a divorce later.'

Doug gave her an odd look, opened his mouth to say something. But at this precise moment the waiter arrived with their first course. He let the moment pass.

Back at the apartment several hours later, Doug went into the living room, poured two brandies and held one of the crystal balloons out to Laura. 'Come on, let's have a nightcap.'

Although Laura was not a big drinker, she did not even hesitate as she might have in the past. 'All right,' she said, walking into the room, taking the glass of cognac from him. 'Why not? We haven't seen each other for a month, we've a lot to catch up on.'

'Mmmm,' was his only comment before he let his eyes wander around their living room. 'You know, you really did a wonderful job with this room, Laura. It still looks great. I'm impressed all over again when I come back after being away.'

Laura followed his gaze, her own eyes scanning everything more objectively than usual. They took in the pale cream walls and cream silk draperies, the matching cream sofas and chairs, the Art Deco wood pieces with their touches of black, the old Aubusson rug on the floor. It was a restful ambience, and her only regret was that their art was not better. The paintings were good, and she liked them, but they were not her favourite French Impressionists; only her clients could afford *those*, which ran into the millions.

Finally Laura said, 'Yes, the room did hold up well, Doug. The scheme is so classic I guess it'll never date.' She lowered herself onto the cream sofa and placed her glass on the Art Deco coffee table, being careful to place it on top of a book and not on the wood.

Leaning back into the cushions, she thought: This is as good a time as any to talk to him. She felt very determined to bring their problems out into the open. Very simply, she knew she had to clear the air; she must know where she stood with him. She couldn't go on any longer in this way. It was far too nerve-wracking, upsetting.

Doug took the chair near the fireplace, and almost as if he had read her mind he said carefully, 'There're a few things I'd like to talk to you about, Laura. I should have mentioned them before, but it's always difficult on the phone, and anyway I *have* been so pushed with work.'

'I know. And we should talk, Doug. I feel you've been very distant, and certainly not too forthcoming.' She shook her head, and made a *moue* with her mouth, finishing, 'I had the feeling you were only calling me out of a sense of duty.'

'Oh come on, Laura, you know better than that!'

'I'm not stupid, Doug. Whenever you've phoned in the last few weeks, you couldn't wait to say goodbye and get off.'

'Mostly because of pressure. The Aaronson merger has been, and still is, very complicated. And it's still not finished.'

'So you've got to go back to LA? Is that what you're telling me?'

'Yes, I do have to go back. To finish the merger.' Lifting his brandy balloon, he sniffed the Courvoisier, took a small swallow, then sat nursing the glass between both hands, staring down into the amber liquid. When he lifted his head, he focused his eyes on her, and said, 'I've had an offer, a very big offer. To go to another law firm.'

Although Laura was surprised, she smiled and exclaimed, 'But that's wonderful, Doug! I'm so pleased for you. Which law firm?'

He hesitated fractionally before saying, 'It's a Los Angeles firm, Laura.'

'*Oh.*' She sat back, staring at him. So it's not an affair after all, she thought. It's business that's been preoccupying him. Frowning, she asked swiftly, 'Does that mean you have to move to Los Angeles? Or would you be at their New York office? If they have one, that is.'

'They do have one, yes, but they want me in Los Angeles.'

'I see. Which law firm is it?'

'Arnold, Matthews and McCall: they're very prestigious. And they've offered me a partnership. It's really a big deal, big for me, I mean.'

She was silent for several seconds, her eyes on him, and then she said, 'You've accepted it, haven't you?'

Doug did not at first answer. He returned her penetrating stare and cleared his throat several times. At last he murmured, 'Not exactly. I've indicated I want to take it, but I haven't actually accepted it. Not formally.'

'Oh Doug . . .' Laura began and then let her voice trail off. She took a sip of the cognac and stared at a painting on the far wall. Finally, with a heavy sigh, she went on, 'You're splitting hairs. You know you want the job and that you're going to take it. Come on, it's me you're talking to.'

Doug bit his lip, looking slightly shame-faced, and then he leaned closer to her, reached out, took hold of her hand. 'I guess you do know me better than anyone, Laura.'

She nodded. '*I* think so. Well, as much as we can ever know another person.' There was a slight hesitation on her part, and then she said softly, 'But I haven't known you at all lately, Doug. You're almost like a stranger to me, in some ways.'

He nodded. 'I haven't known myself at times, Laura, I must admit. I think I've changed a great deal in the last few months.'

'The past year,' she corrected. 'It all started last spring.'

Letting go of her hand, he sat back in the chair, then leaned forward jerkily and picked up the glass of brandy. After a deep swallow, that made him cough for a moment, he said, 'Did it really start then? The change in me, I mean?'

'I believe so, Doug. Look, I've given a great deal of thought to it whilst you've been in Los Angeles, and it *was* then. It became more pronounced around Christmas, even Grandma Megan noticed and mentioned it to me.'

'She did?' He sounded startled; concern flooded his face.

'Oh yes, she doesn't miss a trick, you should know that by now. Anyway, she said you didn't seem to be there, that you were distracted; she even said she thought you wished you were somewhere else.' Laura leaned closer and stared into her husband's face. Very pointedly, she added, 'Did you wish you were in another place? With another person perhaps? With another woman?'

He shook his head vehemently. 'No, I certainly didn't want

to be anywhere else. Or with anyone else. But I wasn't the same anymore. I felt . . . ill at ease with myself over Christmas. And I have ever since. The feeling doesn't go away. Except that I've been too busy working to dwell on it much.'

'I knew it,' she said quietly. 'I just knew you were . . . *different* . . . another person, not *you.*'

Laura flopped back against the cushions and closed her eyes. When she opened them a split-second later she said, 'The marriage isn't right these days, is it, Doug?'

Staring at her, staring into those vivid blue eyes, so blue they were almost blinding, Doug felt himself choking up. His throat tightened to such an extent he couldn't, for a moment, speak at all. He loved her, he would miss her, but it had to be, this end to their marriage.

He got up and went to sit on the sofa, reached for her blindly, tears dimming his vision. Clinging onto her tightly, he tried to regain his composure. He was shaken, much more than he had expected to be. Doug had accepted days ago that this kind of discussion would take place with Laura once he was home, and he hadn't relished it. But he had not realized how upset he would be.

Eventually, when he had full control, Doug pulled away from her slightly, and looked deeply into her eyes once more. 'I love you, but it doesn't work anymore, our marriage.'

'I know. I think I've known that since Christmas,' Laura answered. 'I just haven't really wanted to admit it, I suppose.'

Doug pulled her into his arms again and she clung to him. Against his cheek she said softly, 'You can be honest with me, Doug. Are you having an affair? Is there another woman?'

'No, there isn't, absolutely *not*. I'm telling you the truth. There is no other woman in my life.'

'Then what happened to us, to our marriage?'

'I'm not sure.'

'Is it because . . . we haven't had children?'

'Good God, no! Of course not.'

'Then why?'

'I just don't know. I love you, Laura, I really do, but something's gone.'

'The spark's not there,' she whispered, suddenly understanding, and she sighed. 'You love me, but you're not *in love* with me, that's it, isn't it?'

'I don't know.'

'But I do. Admit it, I won't be angry, Doug, these things happen. You've changed, that's all, and people do change, I realize that.'

'Perhaps you're right,' he finally agreed. 'Maybe the spark *isn't* there any longer.'

Laura made no response. The old familiar heaviness descended on her; it was like a dead weight on her shoulders. And inside she felt cold and empty. Bereft; she thought, I've been bereft for a long time. Like a widow, I've been grieving for him because I've known for months he was gone from me forever.

Doug sighed, aware of her pain. He did not know how to comfort her, there was no way really. And so he did not speak.

Now a long silence fell between them. Neither of them dared say another word, for fear of hurting the other too deeply.

But at last Laura found the strength to mouth the words that had rolled around in her head for weeks. 'I think we should get a divorce, Doug.' There, the dreaded words were out at last. They seemed to hang in the air between them.

After a moment of utter stillness, he answered in a quiet voice, 'No, a trial separation.'

'That's only putting off the inevitable. Look, maybe I've changed too.'

'I don't think you have. Not you. Not Laura, ever true blue.' He drew away, looking at her closely. His heart ached; he was full of regrets, but he could not alter things, not now. It was too late. The die was cast. In a sense it had been cast long ago. He touched her face gently with one finger, running it down her cheek, as he had done so frequently in the past, and then attempted to smile at her, but the smile faltered.

This old familiar gesture undid her. She stared at him and gasped, and fell against him.

As he held her in the circle of his arms she began to cry inconsolably, as though her heart were breaking; and, in a way, it was. She wept for the end of their marriage, for the children they had wanted and would never have, for the future together now lost to them. Suddenly overcome, Laura pushed herself away from Doug and rushed out of the room, her eyes streaming. Running into their bedroom, she closed the door and leaned against it, pressing her hands against her eyes, wanting to stem her tears. She found a box of tissues by the side of the bed, took one and blew her nose. And once she felt in control of herself again, she returned to the living room.

As she walked in she passed the skirted table in the corner, and she paused, glanced at the many photographs of family and friends arranged on it. Prominent amongst them was a picture of Doug, herself, Karen and Robin which had been taken the previous summer in Martha's Vineyard, when the four of them had been on vacation together.

Laura had always thought that Robin and Karen were ideally suited, two intellectuals at heart, sharing a love of the theatre, music and art. In her mind they had always been The Beautiful Couple in capital letters, both blond, blue-eyed and good-looking. Karen, so slender and willowy, stylish and chic, dress designer *par excellence* with her own boutique in Soho. Robin, lean and handsome and somewhat dapper, well-groomed to the point of old-fashioned perfection. He was the cool, precise banker by day, a man who rarely cracked a smile; at night he became the laughing, fun-loving bohemian.

Well, they hadn't been the perfect couple after all, since the engagement was now off. When Doug had told her earlier she had been momentarily taken aback; but she wasn't so surprised after all, now that she thought about it carefully. The pieces had all fallen into place. Suddenly she understood what all of this was about, understood who it was that had come between them.

Doug was sitting on the sofa, his elbows on his knees, his head in his hands. 'Are you all right, Laura?' he asked as she moved into the room, but he did not look up at her.

Ignoring the question, she said, 'It's Robin, isn't it? That's what all this is about. It's Robin who's come between us. You're leaving me for him.'

Doug was silent.

Laura went and stood in front of him, her back to the fireplace. When he did not respond, she exclaimed, 'We've been married almost seven years, and I think you should tell me the truth. You owe me that, at least.'

He still did not respond and his silence infuriated her. She cried, 'I know things have been strained between us; I know we've drifted apart, but at the root of it stands Robin. Don't pretend otherwise, Doug.'

'I wasn't going to pretend otherwise,' Doug said, lifting his head at last. 'I *was* going to tell you,' he went on, and then faltered.

'Tell me *when* exactly,' she demanded. 'Next month, next year?'

'No, of course not, don't be silly. I was going to tell you . . .' He shook his head, his expression chagrined. 'Okay, I lost my nerve a short while ago. But I would have told you before I went back to LA.'

'Would you?' she asked quietly, sounding sceptical.

'Laura, I still love you, and I respect you, and I was going to explain.'

'Then why don't you tell me now?'

He nodded. 'I've always known . . . known I was . . . bisexual. There was another man once, when I was in college, as well as various girlfriends. I wanted very badly to get married and have children; but I never met a woman I wanted to marry. Until I met you. I was totally bowled over by you, and when I fell in love with you I thought everything was going to work out. It seemed to be the perfect marriage. And then I met Robin when I went to that retreat two years ago. I discovered I was very . . . stirred by him, touched by him emotionally and physically. But nothing happened. I thought at the time it was something inside me and only in me. He and I became good friends, and *we* made a great foursome, and that was that. I tried to block out my feelings, Laura, I really did. I tried to concentrate on you, on us, on our marriage; but other things were going on inside me. My attraction for Robin was growing steadily. It simply wouldn't go away. And then last summer, when we were in Martha's Vineyard, Robin and I were alone on the boat one day, and everything exploded around us. It just happened . . . we were together.'

'I see.' Laura sat down on the nearest chair, stunned by what he had told her, and then she asked quickly, 'Were there any other infidelities during our marriage?'

'Absolutely not!' Doug exclaimed, staring at her. 'And that's the truth.'

She nodded. 'Robin's also moving to Los Angeles, isn't he?'

It was Doug's turn to nod.

Laura said, 'What would have happened if we'd had a child? Children? Would you have stayed in the marriage?'

Taken aback by this question, Doug sat back on the sofa and wondered how to answer it. What would he have done? Would he have left a wife and children for his lover? Other men had. But he wasn't sure, and he said quickly, 'I don't know, Laura, honestly I don't.'

'Thinking about it, our marriage was very passionate in the beginning, but the passion . . . sort of dwindled, didn't it, Doug?'

'Yes.'

She was silent, looked off into space. She felt, suddenly, a terrible sense of defeat. Her marriage had started off so well and then it had gone awry, and he had fallen in love with someone else. Man or woman, it really didn't matter because the outcome was the same. He had chosen someone else over her. Sadness trickled through her, and she discovered she had nothing else to say.

Doug said, 'I'm sorry, Laura.'

She looked at him helplessly. She was wordless.

'I didn't mean it to happen, but it did. I can't help it, Laura . . . it's just . . . the way it is.'

17

'It was all handled nicely, Gran,' Laura said, looking across at Megan, then she laughed somewhat hollowly, and added, 'If you can use that word when talking about a divorce. What I meant is we were civilized, grown-up about it, and Doug was thoughtful, very nice really.'

'Doug's always been a nice young man, and in my experience a leopard doesn't change its spots, even when there's a divorce in the offing,' Megan responded. 'So he's gone back to Los Angeles has he?'

'Yes. To finish the Aaronson merger. He's told them at Cohen, Travis and Norris that he's leaving the law firm once the deal has been completed, or rather this particular stage of it. He said he's going to start looking for an apartment, but for the moment he'll be at the Peninsula.'

Laura rose and walked across the solarium, her high heels resounding loudly on the terracotta tile floor. Leaning against the French windows, she gazed out across the lawns; these sloped down to a band of willow trees that dipped their flowing branches into a slow-moving stream which sliced through the property in Kent, Connecticut. In the fading, misty light of the afternoon the grey-green landscape looked ethereal, a Turner painting.

After a moment, almost to herself, she muttered, 'And he's taken all of his clothes with him.'

Megan heard this, and she said quietly, 'Then there's no question about it, Laura, he's gone for good. Is that what you're saying, my darling?'

Laura swung around to face her grandmother; her expression was woebegone. 'Yes. And I feel as isolated and alone as if I'd been abandoned on the Patagonian Ice Cap and left to fend for myself.'

Megan couldn't resist laughing despite the moroseness echoing in Laura's voice. 'You do have such colourful phrases at times. I always did tell you to become a writer. So he's gone, and you're sad, and sorrowing, but that's only natural. Doug has been there by your side, and there *for* you, for almost seven years. You're bound to feel the wrench, especially since I'm quite aware you still love him.'

'I do, Grandma, and I always will. But I've realized for a while now that I've changed in certain ways myself. He's not *in love* with me anymore, and neither am I with him.' At least I don't think I am, she said to herself, as she came back and sat down next to Megan. Staring at her grandmother intently, she continued, 'In the same way that we fell in love, we've . . . grown out of it. And as strange as this might sound to you, Gran, I honestly think we might have killed it off ourselves, working so hard trying to have a baby.'

Megan nodded. 'I can well imagine. Sex became too clinical, too mechanical perhaps, it wasn't romantic sex anymore, is that what you're trying to say?'

'More or less. Anyway, we're friends, and we'll stay friends for the rest of our lives, I feel sure of that. We were both in tears when he went back to Los Angeles last week. All that luggage he took made it seem so . . . *final.* Suddenly Doug didn't want to go. We just clung to each other for ages, until the doorman buzzed again to say that the driver was worried Doug would miss the plane. In the end I had to virtually push him out of the apartment.'

'It must have been difficult for you both. On the other hand, Doug hasn't dropped off the edge of the world. He's only gone to Los Angeles.'

'I know. But there's something quite awful about the end of a marriage, or any relationship for that matter.'

'Oh yes, I know that only too well. However, it's not as if he died. And Doug will always be *there* for you, should you ever need him. I feel that in my bones. That's the kind of man he is.'

'Yes, that's what *he* said, that if I ever needed him I only had to call. He offered to give me alimony, but I turned it down. Why should I do that to him, hamstring him in that way, when I earn a decent living myself?'

'Some women wouldn't be quite so selfless,' Megan responded with her usual pithiness.

'But I'm not some women. I'm *me*.'

'Thank God for that, and I wasn't being critical, I was merely commenting.'

'Yes, Gran. Doug says he wants me to have the apartment. As you know, we bought it together, but he told me he doesn't need his share of the money back. All he wants are his books, the paintings he bought, and his grandfather's Georgian desk and chair.'

'It sounds to me as if the two of you don't have any problems with each other when it comes to the financial side of your marriage, and that is truly quite remarkable.'

'He's bending over backwards to be decent, and so am I.'

'You're a good girl, and I'm proud of the way you're handling this situation.' Megan paused, shifted slightly in her chair, and gave Laura a penetrating glance. 'Forgive me, but I feel I must ask you this. Do you think there's another woman in his life? Has he fallen in love with someone else? Is that what this is all about?'

'Doug denies it. I asked him, Gran. He says there isn't another woman, and I believe him.'

'I trust your judgement. However, he's being so obliging it made me wonder, that's all. Anyway, because your marriage has seemingly gone awry I think it's a good thing you're getting divorced immediately, rather than clinging to it. You're still young enough to start all over again, and the same applies to Doug.'

'I know, but it's a bit hard at times,' Laura whispered, and pushed down the tears which had sprung into her throat. Much to her mortification, her eyes were unexpectedly moist; she brushed her hand across them and blinked rapidly, then cleared her throat.

Megan, ever eagle-eyed, noticed this rush of sudden emotion, but observing how well her granddaughter was handling herself she decided to ignore it. Instead she said, '*Of course* it's hard, but then life *is* hard, and it always has been. And don't let anyone tell you otherwise. It's never been easy, not for anyone. The important thing is how you handle life and all of its hardships and pain. I've always believed you've got to deal with life's troubles standing up, fists raised, fighting hard. It's vital to battle through and come out triumphant. You're a winner, darling, of that I'm absolutely sure.' Megan nodded and her wise old eyes were gentle, full of love, as she finished, 'I have no fears about you, Laura. You'll do fine.'

'Oh Gran, I hope so.'

'You will, because you're a true Valiant. That's the way I brought you up. As your grandfather would have said, a chip off the old block.'

Laura smiled, filled with love for this wonderful old woman who had given her so much love and understanding every day of her life. Whatever would I have done without her, she suddenly wondered; my mother was never around.

Megan said, 'Don't let things drift, start the divorce proceedings as soon as you can. It's better to make a swift, clean cut. Prolonging things gets messy. Anyway, you seem to have worked everything out with Doug in the most amicable way, in a mature manner, and that augurs well for you.'

'We've tried to make it easy on each other, and Doug says he'll recommend a divorce lawyer. He's going to call me regarding one sometime next week.'

Megan nodded and pushed herself up out of her chair. 'I think I'll go and have a rest now, Laura dear. And by the way, lunch was delicious, thank you for making it.'

Laughing, Laura exclaimed, 'You know very well all I did was unpack it and unwrap it. But the smoked salmon *was* lovely, wasn't it?'

Megan nodded. 'Petrossian, I've no doubt. That's another trait you inherited from me. *Extravagance.*' Winking at her granddaughter, she murmured, 'And now I'm going up to my room to daydream about the past. That's what old women do, you know. Live their lives all over again . . . in their dreams. It's a beautiful way to spend an afternoon when you've nothing better to do.'

Laura put her arms around her grandmother and held her close for a moment or two. Then she said, 'Do you want me to help you upstairs, Gran?'

'Get along with you, you silly girl!' Megan exclaimed, sounding irritated as she moved away from Laura. 'I'm not decrepit yet, as I keep telling you. I can manage very well on my own, ninety-two or not. I'm very sprightly, I'll have you know.'

Laura smiled lovingly. 'I've got to come upstairs anyway, to check Claire's room. I know Fenice came in to do a thorough clean during the week, but I want to make sure Claire has everything she might need for the weekend.'

'I'm glad she's coming to stay for a few days, and don't forget to put flowers in her room. Now, come along, Laura, don't dawdle, let's go upstairs.'

A little later Laura put on her Barbour and green Wellington boots, and walked down towards the river. The sky had changed; it was a strange mottled green along the rim, and it looked cold and remote. The dimming light, combined with the mist rising from the river, gave the garden a strange mysterious feeling.

Only a short while ago it had seemed ethereal as she had viewed it through the French windows of the solarium. Now, suddenly, it was distinctly eerie.

Although it was not cold, Laura shivered. Goose bumps speckled the back of her neck. Somebody walked over my grave, she thought, remembering a saying of Megan's, and she shivered again, pushed that dolorous thought out of her head.

Moving away from the river's bank and the dripping willows, she headed towards a small copse where mostly maples and oaks grew, and she caught her breath in surprise and pleasure as she moved forward into the bosky glade. The hundreds of daffodils, which her grandmother had planted over the years, were already shooting up near an old drystone wall that bordered this end of their land. They were early this year, the tender green shoots pushing up out of the rich dark earth. Their yellow bonnets had not yet opened, but she felt sure they would burst into bloom next week, if the weather remained mild.

Years ago her grandfather had placed a green-painted wooden Adirondack bench at the edge of the glade, near the stone wall, and Laura sat down on it, brought her feet to the seat and hunched in a corner, her arms wrapped around her knees. Her thoughts turned to Doug and the end of their marriage, and she sighed to herself.

She had given her grandmother a carefully edited version of everything that had happened. She had not wanted to rehash their parting, or relive it, and so she had shortened the story and smoothed it out and made it sound amicable. Not that it had been a rancorous parting.

Doug had stayed in New York for ten days, working things out with his law firm, and packing; in the evenings there had been any number of discussions, soul searching and endless tears. But finally they had both agreed that everything was truly over between them. There was no way to salvage their marriage; deep within herself Laura knew she didn't even want to try. Perhaps their relationship would work for a while, but Doug would pull away again. Eventually. He would always pull away because he had no wish to be married. Not to anyone. She closed her eyes for a brief moment. She knew he wanted to be with Robin.

She was glad now he was gone: having him around her had been extremely painful; she had felt as if she were living on an emotional rollercoaster whilst he was still ensconced in the apartment. It had exhausted her.

Tears came into her eyes and for a moment she wondered if it was her fault. Had she failed him? She shrugged off this idea. Of course it wasn't her fault. She wished Doug well. She hoped he would be happy. Everybody deserved to be happy. But so few people were.

Groping around in her jacket pocket she found a tissue, wiped her eyes, and then she stood up and walked slowly back to the old white clapboard house on the hill. Claire was coming tomorrow, to stay for a long weekend, and there was so much to do before her arrival.

18

What a blessed relief it is to be here, Claire thought, glancing around the bedroom again, just as she had earlier in the day. She had always loved this room, for as long as she could remember.

When she had first arrived at Rhondda Fach just before lunch she had felt debilitated, terribly worn down after finishing the major photographic shoot in New York for her magazine. It had been a tough assignment, and everything that could go wrong had, but somehow she had managed to pull them all through it, and get the two apartments on film. She was certain they would make good spreads for the magazine. But at what cost, she asked herself, as she wrapped her cashmere cardigan more tightly around her body and went to stand near the fire.

Still, after spending several hours here with Megan and Laura, whom she loved, in this house which she loved, she had begun to feel so much better. Just being in this marvellous old house was such a powerful restorative. She had been coming here to stay since she was ten years old, and this bedroom was known as 'Claire's room'. She did consider it to be hers; she had been its main occupant for all those years, even if other people did stay in it from time to time.

Throwing off her shoes, Claire walked over to the four-poster bed hung with blue-and-white striped cotton, and got onto it, slipping her legs underneath the soft down duvet. Settling back against the mound of pillows in their snow white antique pillowcases, she let her eyes roam around the room, taking pleasure from everything in it.

There was nothing new in her room; each item was familiar and well-loved, and it was just like coming home. Her eyes rested briefly on the lovely old cherrywood armoire, the pretty carved chest from France where Fenice had put her sweaters and underwear earlier, just as she had been doing for twenty-six years. Then her gaze moved on to the collection of paintings on glass. All of them were Chinese scenes; they were very old, Grandma Megan had told her once, painted by Russians, and bought in Shepherd's Market in London's Mayfair over forty years ago by Grandpa Owen.

Her own contribution to the room had been the blue-and-white wallpaper, which Megan had allowed her to choose when she had been redecorating some of the bedrooms at least twenty years ago now. It was an eyecatching pattern composed of Chinese ginger jars, sprays of orange blossoms, men pulling rickshaws and Chinese ladies dressed in cheongsams and holding lutes. All of these images were coloured bright blue on a pristine white background.

When she had first seen the sample, Grandma Megan had said it looked far too busy, and had ordered the rolls reluctantly; once it was up on the walls she had agreed it was as enchanting and as effective as Claire had said it would be. And she had thanked her for choosing it, told her she had a good eye.

Despite the coolness of the blue-and-white colour combination there was a cosiness to the room; earlier, Fenice had switched on the white-silk-shaded blue porcelain lamps and lit the logs and paper in the fireplace. The fire was still burning brightly in the hearth and it brought a golden glow to the room.

Just looking at the logs hissing and spurting and flaring in the grate made her feel drowsy, and Claire closed her eyes, relaxing her tired limbs, drawing comfort from the warmth in these very dear and well-loved surroundings.

As she drifted, her thoughts turned to Doug. Laura had told her only moments after her arrival about their break-up. On first hearing this Claire had been startled, and had found it not only distressing but very puzzling. Now she wondered why she had ever considered it to be puzzling. Nothing that happened between a man and a woman should surprise her, of all people. A small sigh escaped. If men were stupid then women were surely fools. So how could they possibly get anything right?

Nonetheless, Claire couldn't help feeling somewhat saddened because theirs was a marriage she had believed would work. Laura had said she had no explanation for its collapse; did Doug perhaps? Doug would be the loser in the long run, of this Claire was convinced. Laura was such a winner, such a positive and optimistic person she was always going to come out on top. In her opinion, Laura had a much better chance at finding happiness with someone else than Doug did, although she wasn't exactly sure why she felt this. She just did. Doug was far too . . . pernickety. Yes, that was the word that truly applied to him.

Shifting under the duvet, Claire tried to find a little ease. Her bones ached today; she felt as though she were coming down with the flu, but she knew she wasn't. Being on her feet for days on end without a break had been a punishing ordeal, and she was glad there were no more photographic shoots like this in the offing. At least shoots which she had to direct. The next two would be overseen by Giselle Cravenne, she would see to that.

For the next five days she would be here at Rhondda Fach; she knew she would have a wonderful rest . . . doing nothing except reading, listening to music, and basking in the warmth and love of Laura's company, and Grandma Megan's, too. This little vacation was going to be much more than a treat; it would be a great luxury for her.

She wondered when to give Laura her news. Should she tell her later this afternoon, when they had tea, which was something of a ritual with Grandma Megan? Or should she wait until later? After a moment's consideration Claire thought: I'll play it by ear, that's the best way.

Claire couldn't help thinking about the next few weeks ahead of her, all that she had to do, and she began to make lists in her head. It was an old, compulsive habit of hers, especially when she was overburdened, which she was at this moment. She had so much to do before the summer. She wasn't sure how she was going to accomplish it all. But she would. She had to. She had no choice.

Sliding further down under the duvet, Claire turned on her side and stopped fighting the feeling of drowsiness which had slowly crept over her. Within minutes she had fallen off. She slept a dreamless sleep.

The long green valley was surrounded by verdant hills that swept up towards the sky, half of them layered with Scottish pines, oaks and ash. The entire valley and its rolling hills covered over five hundred acres which Owen Valiant had bought some sixty years before, in the middle of the 1930s.

He and Megan had fallen in love with this beautiful fertile valley in Kent, at the heart of the northwestern highlands of Connecticut. They had called it Rhondda Fach, which in Welsh meant the little Rhondda, and it was named for the Rhondda Valley, that most beautiful and famous of all the Welsh valleys from which they came.

The house itself was named Rhondda Fach Farm, although few people ever called it a farm. And it had not been a proper working farm since the day Grandpa Owen had bought it. He had usually referred to himself as a gentleman farmer, and he did so smiling proudly.

Gentleman farmer, though, he had been; he had cultivated apple and pear orchards, herb gardens, and vegetable plots where everything from marrows to potatoes, parsnips and carrots grew; he had also developed fields of corn, and there were large cutting gardens for fresh flowers in the spring and summer. All still flourished, gave bountiful harvests of vegetables and fruit and fragrant blooms. The caretaker Tom Flynn kept chickens for them, and tended to Grandma Megan's greenhouses, where she grew tomatoes, and, most successfully, orchids of all kinds. 'Tom's good with the chickens; we certainly get a lot of eggs,' Grandma Megan would say, adding swiftly, 'but he's a genius when it comes to my orchids. He's got a green thumb. Or perhaps I should say green fingers.'

The old clapboard house, painted white with black shutters and a black roof, had been a small structure when it was first built in 1790; over the many decades it had acquired numerous wings and additions, and these sprawled out at each end. But the house had a lovely symmetry to it and a certain gracefulness which added to its charm.

It stood nestled against the green foothills which rose up behind it in a great swathe like a giant-sized Elizabethan ruff, and it was backed by a copse of dark green firs that threw it into bold relief.

In front of the back terrace, smooth, manicured lawns sloped away to the gardens and a stream which meandered through the property. Beyond were rolling meadows filled with wild flowers in summer, and further beyond there were woods where bluebells, primroses and daisies grew alongside mushrooms under moss-covered trees.

Standing together to the right of the house was a small compound of buildings, including Tom's cottage, the stables and several barns. Nearby was a large pond, which Grandpa Owen had built when he had purchased the valley so long ago, and for years it had been home to all manner of wildlife. To it came Canada geese, ducks and other fowl, and occasionally a blue heron sauntered along its banks. A family of owls nested in a stand of trees not far from the pond, which in summer was filled with pale pink water lilies floating on its surface.

To Claire the valley was a haven of tranquillity and beauty, wide open land with wide open skies and nothing in sight. Lonely perhaps to some, but to her it was a refuge.

As a child she had fallen in love with it, and that love had never wavered. Now, as she walked down towards the river and the weeping willow trees, she hoped that when they came to stay in August Natasha would fall under its spell as she herself had done so long ago. This was such a special place; for her it was also full of memories . . . memories of her childhood and youth, her difficult teen years, of Laura and Megan, and the family who had given her so much love. They had miraculously made her part of them, made her feel so special, so wanted, and a Valiant herself, in a sense. She wanted this for her Natasha . . . a family of Valiants for her daughter.

Claire glanced up at the afternoon sky. It was a clear, bright blue, filled with soft white clouds and the sun was still shining brilliantly. What a glorious March day it had been, more like May, unusually warm for this time of year, a soft day. But Laura had told her over lunch that the weather was going to change radically tomorrow. 'It'll be cold,' she had warned. 'There'll be a frost. Tom's already mentioned that he's worried about the daffodils and the other early bloomers.' Laura, like Tom, was something of a weathervane.

Circling the lawn, Claire began to walk towards the house, but stopped when she came to the group of trees at the edge of the glade where the old drystone wall ran down towards the river, where she had once almost drowned.

Spotting Owen's old Adirondack bench, she went over to it, sat down and found herself watching a squirrel racing up a tree. It disappeared instantly into the upper branches; she smiled to herself, thinking of the chipmunks that used to play around the back porch years ago. They had always sped away under the foundations at the sight of a human being. Now there was one that was fearless, and it came out and waited for nuts and other titbits – so Megan had told her over lunch.

After a moment or two Claire rose and walked to the drystone wall, where she stood looking downstream, her busy mind soothed at last, at least for a few moments anyway.

'Coo-ee! Coo-ee!'

Smiling, knowing it was Laura, Claire swung around and waved to her, and then she sat down on the wall, waiting for her dearest friend.

A second or two later Laura came bounding up, flushed and out of breath. 'I've been looking all over for you, Clarabelle,' she exclaimed, using a cherished childhood name. 'You've been the elusive one. Fenice told me she saw you set off towards the barns, and then Megan told me you were heading towards the hills. And now I find you in our favourite glade.' She shook her head, still laughing.

'I started out that way, heading for the pond actually. But in the end I decided to linger here for a while. I find it so peaceful, and calming.' She paused, shook her head, and there was a hint of a smile on her face as she went on, 'Old habits die hard. Don't you remember, we always came here to think when we were younger; it was a place to struggle through our problems.'

'How could I forget? You've found me here weeping many a time in the past.'

'And so have you, found me I mean. The last time you were so comforting, a rock, Laura. You gave me such a lot of strength.'

'It was when you'd come back from Paris, just after you'd separated from Philippe.' Laura sat down on the wall next to Claire. 'You were distraught.'

'I know. Aren't women foolish?'

'Sometimes.' Laura looked deeply into Claire's face and added, 'We haven't been so lucky, you and I, have we? I mean with men. We've both failed at marriage, but at least you've got Natasha to show for it.'

'Yes.' Claire returned Laura's long stare, and touched her arm.

'You've been such a wonderful friend to me all these years. I don't know what I would have done without you, or how to thank you.'

'Thanks aren't necessary, Claire.' Laura smiled at her lovingly, then glancing up at the sky, she added, 'I'm so glad you came out to Kent today, instead of waiting until tomorrow. It's such a gorgeous afternoon.'

'A beautiful day,' Claire agreed, looking up at the sky herself, her eyes misted. It took her a moment to regain her composure, and she was thankful Laura hadn't seemed to notice. Bringing her gaze back to Laura's, she stared into those startlingly blue eyes, and said in a low but even tone, 'There's something I have to tell you.'

Laura frowned, gazed at Claire more intently. Her expression was quizzical as she asked, 'What is it? You sound funny, *odd.*'

'The other day you complained you hadn't seen me since I'd been in New York, that I'd been far too busy with the photo shoot, and that I should have been able to find time for a cup of coffee with you, at least. You remember saying that, don't you?'

Laura nodded.

'If only you'd told me about Doug on the phone, I would have somehow found a moment to run over, to be with you, Laura. But you didn't, and I was caught up with something vitally important to me. Other than the shoot, I mean.'

'What were you caught up with?' Laura asked, still frowning, looking even more perplexed.

'I was having tests.'

'What's wrong with you?' Laura demanded, her eyes opening wider. 'You're not ill, are you, Claire?'

'I'm afraid so.' There was a momentary pause before Claire said quietly, 'I'm dying.'

Laura recoiled slightly and sat up straighter, blinking. Shock assaulted her and she felt a terrible icy-cold feeling creeping over her body. The sun was still shining and the sky was that marvellous clear blue, but the brightness of the day had dimmed.

Laura leaned closer to Claire and took hold of her hand. 'I don't understand . . . How can you be dying? What's wrong with you?' she asked, her voice breaking.

'I have breast cancer.' Claire answered as softly and as evenly as she possibly could. She was trying not to become hysterical, as she had been several times in the privacy of her hotel room in the last couple of days.

Laura gaped at her. She was disbelieving, unable to properly absorb Claire's frightening words. She exclaimed, 'Oh God, Claire, not you! Not you, darling . . .' Laura stopped mid-sentence, choked-up and unable to continue. Her face had turned ashen and her blue eyes were filling with fear.

Claire nodded. 'But it's true. I've spent the last few days having tests at Memorial Sloan-Kettering Cancer Center.'

'And they told you that you were dying?' Laura whispered, trying hard not to cry, hanging onto her control as best she could. She was shaking inside.

'Not in so many words, no,' Claire answered. 'They never do of course. Doctors don't want to diminish the hope a patient might have, or take hope away. But I know I won't make it beyond this summer. Certainly I won't be alive when . . .' She looked around her, and finished in a voice that had begun to falter, 'When the leaves start changing here.'

'Oh Claire.' Laura shook her head. Her eyes filled with tears. 'I can't believe this is happening.'

'You must. I'm going to need you to be strong, Laura. For all of us.'

'I will be, you can count on me,' Laura replied, the tears trickling down her cheeks. Drawing closer to Claire, she put her arms around her friend and held her close.

Finally, despair got the better of Claire and her control slipped. She began to weep, clinging to Laura, needing her love and friendship more than she ever had in all the years they had known each other.

19

'When did you find out you were ill?' Laura asked, her voice low, echoing with concern. 'Was it in December when I was in Paris? You know Hercule thought you didn't look well, and he was worried about you.'

'It wasn't then, I was fine then. I didn't feel sick at all . . . but obviously I was,' Claire responded, and leaned back in the chair. She closed her eyes for a brief moment, wishing the pain in her back and hips would go away; it had nagged at her constantly for the last hour or two. Making a supreme effort, she sat up, leaned forward and reached for the mug of tea Laura had just brought her, sipped it gratefully. The tea was scalding hot, strong and sweet, and it reminded her of her childhood days spent here. Grandpa Owen had always made tea like this. 'Coalminer's tea', he had called it, and it was addictive.

The two women had not remained in the garden for very long, once Claire had broken her distressing news to Laura. After wiping each other's tears and calming each other as best they could, they had made their way back to the house, had settled themselves in the solarium. The moment Claire had complained of feeling ill, of the general achiness in her bones, Laura had immediately hurried off to the kitchen; a short while later she had returned with Tylenol and the mugs of tea.

Now Laura asked somewhat tentatively, 'Do you feel like talking yet?'

'Yes, it's fine now, Laura, ask me anything you want.'

'I was wondering how you discovered it? Did you find a lump in your breast?'

Claire shook her head. 'No. It was under my arm, and I only found it last week.' Claire grimaced. 'The strange thing is, I had a very small lump under the same arm last month, but it went away. I thought it was caused by clogged pores, you know, from using the wrong anti-perspirant. I didn't give it a second thought, especially since it disappeared almost overnight.'

'And when it came back a few weeks later, you immediately went to Memorial Sloan-Kettering,' Laura stated.

'No, I didn't, I first called my friend Nancy Brinker. You remember her, don't you, Laura? That lovely Texan you met with me in Paris a couple of years ago.'

Laura nodded. 'Of course I remember Nancy. We had lunch at the Ritz Hotel together. Her sister died of breast cancer, and she started a foundation to help fight the disease.'

'That's right, the Susan G Komen Breast Cancer Foundation. Nancy invented Race for the Cure, and she's raised millions and millions. Anyway, since she is the one person I know who has a mountain of knowledge in her head and at her fingertips, I phoned her in Dallas within minutes of finding the lump under my arm again. It was Nancy who made arrangements for me to go to Memorial Sloan-Kettering.'

'And they did tests immediately?'

'Oh yes, a lot of them. The doctor was very thorough. When he discovered the lump was hard and did not move, he tried to put a needle into it, to aspirate it. You see, he thought it might be a cyst. When that didn't work, he sent me for a whole series of other tests.' Suddenly, abruptly, Claire stopped; she shook her head. 'You don't need to hear all this, it's very depressing.'

'I do, Claire! I want to know everything. That way I will

understand, and I will be able to help you, help you to get through this.'

Claire took a deep breath and plunged on: 'When he couldn't aspirate the lump, the doctor sent me for a high-definition mammogram and a sonogram. These were followed by a needle biopsy, bone scans, blood tests and liver scans. The day after these tests had been completed I was diagnosed . . .' Claire came to a halt, before finishing, 'I was diagnosed as having highly aggressive metastic breast cancer. I'm what they call a Stage 4 patient.'

'What does that mean?'

'That I have a very small chance of surviving. A five percent chance, actually.'

'*Claire* . . .' Laura was stunned, and she found it impossible to say another word. Her throat tightened, and she could feel the tears gathering behind her eyes. But in the face of Claire's enormous courage, she took steely control of herself. She said quickly, 'But many women do *survive* breast cancer.'

'That's true, yes, and I'm going to be having very aggressive treatment, but there's no guarantee it will work. The outcome may not be good.'

'Does the doctor want you to have a mastectomy?'

'No. Chemotherapy. The doctors at Sloan-Kettering wanted me to stay in New York, to have several courses of high-dose chemo, but I'm going back to Paris next week, as planned. I can have the same treatments at the American Hospital there. And look, I can't stay here, Laura, I have to get back to Paris because of Natasha, and anyway, there's my job at the magazine.'

'But perhaps it would be better if you stayed in New York, had your treatment at Sloan-Kettering. There's plenty of room at my apartment, and anyway, there's this house. You could stay here if you want, it's only a couple of hours to New York. We could send for Natasha. She could go to school in Manhattan and come here at weekends. Or she could go to school up here.'

Claire shook her head. 'I have to go back, but thank you, Laura, thank you for being so supportive.'

'Please think about it, though. About coming back to New York. *Permanently.*'

'I will, I promise.'

'Do you . . . have any other pain, Claire?'

'No, just the general achiness I've told you about, like you feel when you have flu. My bones ache.'

'Didn't they give you anything for that?'

'Only Tylenol.'

Both women now fell silent, absorbed in their own thoughts.

Claire wondered whether or not to continue, to tell Laura how very bad her condition really was, much worse than she had indicated so far. And then she decided against it. She had said enough for the moment. She did not want to burden Laura any further. Later, before she returned to France, she would confide the rest of it.

For her part, Laura's thoughts were on the future. Her main priority was how to help Claire get through this. She stubbornly clung to the hope that chemotherapy would arrest the cancer. Alison's older sister Diane had battled it through and won; *her* cancer had been chemically destroyed and she was living proof that it worked, wasn't she? Laura shivered, despite the warmth in the solarium. Only now was the shock beginning to recede and even so only very slightly; the surprise, the unexpectedness of Claire's news, and the enormity of it had stunned her, left her feeling helpless and undone. But she knew she must be strong and brave if she were to be of help.

Finally Claire broke the silence when she murmured, 'Obviously, I haven't said anything to Natasha yet, not over the phone. I need to be there with her when I tell her, so that I can reassure her, give her comfort.'

'Yes, that's best,' Laura replied, thinking how devastating this was going to be for Natasha. Then before she could stop herself, she asked, 'What about Philippe? When are you going to tell him that you're sick?'

'I'm not. At least, not for the moment.'

Laura simply nodded, although she wondered about Claire's answer. After a moment's thought, she asked quietly, 'May I tell Grandma Megan? I think she ought to know.'

Hesitating, looking uncertain, Claire bit her lip, shook her head. 'It might be too much of a shock to her, too upsetting, don't you think?'

'She's pretty tough, you know that. And she's bound to guess something's wrong, just from the expression on my face. Concern and worry are difficult to hide, Claire.'

'Then you should tell her. Yes, I agree that it's better that she knows.'

Later, when she was back in her own room, Laura gave vent to her feelings. She sat down on the sofa near the window and wept inconsolably for Claire. Her own shock and heartache were enormous, so she could hazard a guess how Claire must be feeling. She also knew how much suffering her friend was facing, so much so that she found it unbearable to contemplate. Her heart squeezed and squeezed at the thought of it. But, on the other hand, she knew she would have to come to grips with her own emotions in order to help Claire. Already Laura was experiencing a terrible sense of loss; deep within herself she realized that Claire might not win this battle. As she had said herself, there were no guarantees the treatment would work.

Her thoughts swung to Hercule. How right he had been in December. He had noticed something wrong in Claire she had not seen; and neither had Claire, for that matter. He had told Laura that, when he had looked at Claire in the photographic studio at one moment, her face had been like a death mask. At the time she had shuddered. Now she wished she had hauled Claire off to a doctor. Laura sighed and wiped her eyes, and took herself firmly in hand. Weeping wasn't going to get her anywhere, or Claire either. She must be a rock, full of strength, as Claire needed her to be.

My best friend, my dearest friend, Laura thought, and I'm

going to lose her. It didn't seem possible that one day she would not be here, that they would not live out their lives together, grow old together, as they had always said they would. Although they lived in different countries they had remained as close as they were when they were girls, sisters under the skin.

Taking a few deep breaths, Laura rose and went into the bathroom. She splashed cold water on her tear-stained face, brushed her hair, put on a touch of lipstick, then sprayed herself with scent.

A few minutes later she made her way down the corridor, heading in the direction of Grandma Megan's room.

Laura paused when she came to the end of the corridor and stood looking out of the huge Palladian window, her eyes trained towards the distant hills. They rose up in a magnificent sweep to touch the sky, its colour fading now in the late afternoon light, a crystalline light that seemed to emanate from behind the hills, rimming them with silver. Such beauty in this world, she thought. And such pain and heartbreak. Laura felt that icy chill settle over her again and involuntarily she shivered.

Turning, she tapped on her grandmother's door, and then put her ear against it, listening. She was about to tap again, when Megan called, 'Come in, Fenice.'

'It's me, Gran,' Laura said as she opened the door and walked inside. 'Do you need Fenice for something?'

'No, darling girl, I don't. But she said she'd bring me up the *New York Times*. I never finished reading it this morning,' Megan answered and leaned back on the pillows.

'I'll go and get it for you in a moment. Fenice has probably forgotten, or she may be preparing afternoon tea. You know what a production she makes of it when you're here.'

'That's true.' Megan peered at Laura and then patted the edge of the bed. 'You look as if you've come to tell me something serious, Laura, or something important.'

'How do you know that, Grandma?'

'I can tell. That expression. You look as if you've lost a pound and found a sixpence. You're troubled, Laura. Come along, tell me. It can't be all that bad.'

'I'm afraid it is,' Laura said, sitting down on the bed, taking hold of Megan's wrinkled old hand mottled with liver spots.

Her grandmother stared at her, her eyes narrowing. 'Give it to me straight. That's the only way to break bad news.'

'It's going to be a shock. I want you to be prepared.'

'I'm used to shocks, Laura, I've had them all of my life, and somehow I've managed to survive. Come along, get it out.'

'It's Claire, Grandma Megan. She's very ill, she has breast cancer. She doesn't think she'll make it through the autumn.'

Megan gasped, her face draining, and then she fell back against the pillows and snapped her eyes shut, almost convulsively. When she opened them a moment later they were pooled with tears. 'Oh my God, that poor child! And she's so young, only thirty-six.'

Laura nodded. 'It's heartbreaking, Gran.'

'Tell me everything,' Megan instructed tensely, fixing her eyes on Laura.

Once she had finished giving her grandmother all of the pertinent details of Claire's illness, Laura said, 'I tried to get her to move back to New York, but she won't. Apparently she can have the chemotherapy treatment in Paris. At the American Hospital there.'

'I've heard it's a good hospital,' Megan murmured, and frowned. 'But I agree with you, I think it would be far better if she came home. She doesn't really have anyone in Paris, does she?'

'There's Hercule.'

'Oh yes, of course. Such a lovely man, and I'm sure he'll try to help her the best way he can, but she has *us* here. After all, we're the only family Claire's really ever had.'

'I'll try to persuade her, Gran.'

'Yes, do that, darling. I suppose she's going to tell Philippe Lavillard. And Rosa.'

'I don't think so. At least, she said she can't, *not yet.*'

'But she must tell them!' Megan exclaimed. 'They have to know because of Natasha. Perhaps you should tell them.'

'Gran! Don't be silly. I can't do that, go against Claire's wishes. Anyway, it's like playing God with someone else's life. She has to tell Philippe herself.'

'Yes, you're right.' Pushing herself up, making motions to get out of bed, Megan went on, 'Is Claire going to come down to tea?'

'I think so. We agreed I should tell you about her illness first. Do you want me to help you out of bed, Grandma?'

'Yes, for once I do need your help, child.'

'How did she take it?' Claire asked, staring across the room at Laura. She, too, was in bed, or rather lying on top of it under the duvet.

'With her usual stoicism,' Laura answered, and smiled faintly. 'Gran's like an old battleship, I suppose. She's used to knocks and shocks and traumatic bumps, but she manages to stay on a relatively even keel. Naturally, she was upset, and she's very, very concerned about you, Claire. And for you. She agrees with me . . . she thinks you ought to come home. To be with your family, that's the way she put it.'

Claire was touched, and her eyes filled with tears. She passed her hand over them, blinked several times, and said, 'Oh Laura, it's such a blessing having you and Grandma Megan. So comforting, reassuring. But for the moment I think I'll go back and see how it goes in Paris.'

'Okay, but don't forget, you promised to think about moving back home. Listen, Gran wanted to know about Philippe, I mean when you'll be telling him about your illness.'

'I don't know . . . I told you that.' Claire threw off the duvet and got out of bed; she went and sat in front of the fire, staring into the flames. After a moment, she looked up and said, 'Come and sit with me for a minute. I want to talk to you about something else.'

Laura did as Claire requested; she took the other chair near the fire and asked, 'What is it? You sound more anxious than ever, Claire.'

'It's true, I am very anxious, Laura. About Natasha. About her future. She'll be fifteen in the summer, that's so young, even though she is grown-up in such a lot of ways.' Claire brought her gaze to Laura's, and asked, 'When I die will you take Natasha for me? Will you look after my daughter for me? Until she's a bit older.'

Laura was momentarily startled, and she stared back at Claire, and exclaimed, 'Of course I will. You know I love Natasha.'

'She's a good girl, Laura, she won't be any trouble to you, I promise . . .' Claire was unable to say another word. She blinked a bit and cleared her throat and looked away for a moment or two.

Laura, who was also moved, swallowed hard, took hold of Claire's hand and squeezed it. Then she went and knelt in front of Claire, gently turned her face so that they were looking at each other. 'Did you think I would refuse?'

'No, not you, my true blue Laura.' Claire let out a small sigh. 'It's hard . . . knowing I'm not going to be around for her . . . I won't see her growing up, graduating, getting married . . . I'll never see my grandchildren . . .' Her voice broke.

'Oh, Claire darling, please don't give in. We must fight this. I told you, so many women do make it through cancer.'

'I won't.' Claire's voice quavered and once again she had to pause, trying to steady herself. After a moment's respite, and a few deep breaths, she was able to say, 'The cancer has metastasized through the lymph nodes under my arm. I've got twenty-three positive lymph nodes. It's metastasized to my bones, gone through my skeletal structure. It'll spread to my liver soon . . . I told you, Laura, I won't live to see the leaves turn here at the farm . . .' Now facing the reality of her illness, the tears spilled unchecked from Claire's eyes, slid down her cheeks.

Shocked and despairing, and frightened for her dearest friend, Laura also began to weep.

Claire reached out her arms to Laura, and, just as they had in the garden, they clung to each other, trying to give comfort, the one to the other. They stayed like this for a long time, weeping quietly, and it was then that Laura accepted finally that Claire was doomed.

Eventually she went and found a box of tissues in the bathroom; she dried her eyes and her face, and took the box out to Claire, who had remained seated by the fire.

After a while, Claire managed to regain her composure, and she said, 'Sit with me again for a second, Laura, won't you, please?'

Laura nodded and dropped into the chair. 'Now tell me what else is on your mind, darling.'

'Next week, when we get back to New York, can we go and see your lawyer, or a lawyer, and draw up the papers that will make you Natasha's legal guardian?'

'If that's what you want, yes, of course.'

'I do want it.'

'But what about her father?'

'He's never been a father to her, and he won't want her. Trust me on that.'

'But wouldn't you need his permission to make me her legal guardian?'

'No. I have sole custody of Natasha, and his visits are at my discretion. In any case, he wouldn't put up a fight. That's not his way. And how could he manage to look after a daughter in Zaire, when he's in quarantine part of the time? And then there are his women. Natasha would cramp his style.'

Laura was silent.

Claire went on, 'You will take care of her for me, won't you, Laura? It will be an uneasy grave I lie in if you don't.'

'Claire, please don't talk like that. You know there's no question about it. I promise you I will look after Natasha as long as she needs me – all of her life, in fact. She'll be like my own child.'

'It's settled then?' Claire pinned her green eyes on her friend.

'It's settled,' Laura answered, her voice strong.

Claire smiled for the first time in days.

PART THREE

Summer

1997

20

Work, which had always been a pleasure for Laura, now became her salvation. It helped her to keep worry and concern for Claire at bay. And she was so busy and on the move she did not have a single moment to dwell on problems she knew she could not solve. And that was the way she wanted it.

'I've just got to keep going, I can't stop,' she kept telling Alison, who was constantly advising her to slow down. 'This is my way of dealing with Claire's cancer and my divorce from Doug. If I stop for breath I'll become hysterical, and I'll fall apart,' she explained.

Wisely, her partner left her alone after this last conversation; Alison managed to refrain from making any further comments, even when Laura appeared to be overly stressed and worn out.

During the months of April and May, Laura made four trips to London to see Maximilian West, whose art collection she was editing, refining and organizing. Each time she returned to New York she flew back via Paris, so that she could stop off for a day or two to be with Claire and Natasha.

Claire was in the middle of high-dose chemotherapy treatments and trying to keep up a brave front; Laura never stopped praying that the treatments would work and that the cancer would go into remission.

The sojourns in Paris, short as they were, enabled Laura to spend cherished time with Claire and with Natasha as well. Every visit filled Laura with amazement, and her admiration of the fourteen-year-old girl grew. Natasha was handling the heartbreaking situation of her mother's deadly illness in the most extraordinary way; she had become a tower of strength for Claire, a loving and caring companion, always there for her night and day. But the thing which startled Laura the most was Natasha's practicality. She had developed a very down-to-earth way of taking charge and dealing with matters.

'In fact, I'd even go so far as to say she is extremely business-like,' Laura said to Doug one evening in early June. He had come to New York on business, had phoned her at her office and asked her to have dinner with him before he left for Los Angeles. They made their date for his last night in New York.

Now, as they had supper at Felida, their favourite Italian restaurant, Laura was telling him about Natasha and singing her praises.

'*Businesslike* is a curious word to use,' Doug remarked, peering at Laura across the table. 'I'm not sure I know exactly what you mean, especially when you're applying it to a teenager.'

'She's got her feet on the ground, Doug, she's very practical. Efficient. I find it quite remarkable. She takes care of everything, the bills, Claire's banking, all of her mother's paperwork, and she pays the housekeeper, gives her instructions.' Laura smiled. 'She's like a little mother, organizing their lives. Mind you, she's always been mature, as you know, much older than her years. I guess that comes from being with adults a lot of the time, and being an only child. Claire brought her up to be self-sufficient and independent, of course, and it shows.'

'What's Claire . . .' Doug broke off abruptly, looked carefully at Laura, and when he went on, his voice was warm and loving, 'What are Claire's chances of getting better, Laura?'

'Not good, I'm afraid,' Laura responded, her expression suddenly turning sad. There was the faintest hint of resignation in her voice as she added, 'I pray she'll go into remission, but we just don't know yet.'

Doug could not fail to miss her tone and he put his hand on top of Laura's, wanting to comfort her, as he said, 'I'm sorry, so sorry she's ill like this. You two have always been so close. I know how worried you are.'

'Yes, I am, but I'm also very proud of Claire, Doug. You would be, too, if you could see her. She's the bravest person I've ever known, and she's just remarkable the way she's handling the treatments. They're very harsh, extremely strong, and there are so many unpleasant side effects.'

'They're horrendous, from what I've heard.'

'Claire has suffered a lot with nausea and vomiting, and she's lost all of her hair.'

'Oh no, not her beautiful red hair! It was her pride and joy. She always loved it when I called her Red.'

'I know she did. But Natasha and Hercule went out and bought her a wig, a fabulous auburn wig. It's short and curly, made of real hair. It suits her, too. In fact, it's hard to tell it's a wig. They got it at the best place in Paris, a theatrical hair company which actresses use. Claire makes such a big effort. She's trying to lead as normal a life as she can.'

'She's not working at the magazine is she?' Doug asked.

'Sort of. The owner has given her leave of absence, but she does go in when she feels she can make it through the day, or even half a day. She gives instructions and directions from home, and she edits at home. And the staff come for meetings at the apartment. The owner wants her back full time, as soon as she's feeling better, but in the meantime he's being very understanding. And he's still paying her salary, thank God.'

'How's Hercule bearing up?' Doug eyed her over the glass of red wine he was holding.

'Oh God, Doug, don't ask. He was devastated at first. He loves her, as you know. Then again, his wife Veronica died of cancer. Lymphoma, I believe. He was truly wiped out when Claire told him. And then he got angry with himself. He'd spotted something odd about Claire in December, and, as I told you at the time, he suspected she was ill. How right he was. Hercule was so mad at himself for not doing something, pushing her to see a doctor in December, and I know how he feels. I was angry that I hadn't done that either. Got her to a doctor, I mean, since he'd confided his worries in me. He's being the most wonderful friend to Claire. Caring, loving and generous. He can't do enough for her. It's been a comfort to me knowing he's around.'

'He's a good person. A good guy. And what about Philippe? Has she told him how ill she is yet?'

'Yes, she has. I talked Claire into it, with Natasha's help. He has a right to know, and we persuaded her to call him in Atlanta. It was last month actually. In May. I was staying in Paris with them for a long weekend.'

'What was Philippe doing in Atlanta? Visiting the Center for Disease Control again?' Doug's expression was quizzical.

'No, he's actually working there now. Since the end of April. The reason he flew over to see the head of the Center last December was apparently for an interview. He's now got a very big position with the Center.'

'That's a far cry from being a virologist in Zaire,' Doug remarked.

'It is, yes. But being in Atlanta is a relief to him, I think. That's what he conveyed to me over the phone, anyway. He'd apparently grown very weary, he said he was burnt out.'

'I can understand that. But what about the guardianship? Does he know you've become Natasha's legal guardian, Laura?'

'Oh yes. Again, I insisted that Claire tell him. It's only right that he knows, and Grandma Megan was on our backs about it anyway. After all, he is Natasha's father.'

'How did he take it?' Doug probed.

'Very well really. Look, I wasn't face to face with him . . . he was on the phone. But he sounded all right. He seemed understanding. He said a girl of Natasha's age needs a woman around. And naturally Claire told him he could see Natasha whenever he wants.'

'I'm glad she did that . . .' Doug took another sip of the wine, then put the glass down and leaned over the table. 'Listen to me, Laura, this is one hell of a responsibility you've taken on. If Claire . . . if Claire doesn't make it through this, then you're going to be bringing up a teenager. Not the easiest task in the world, especially in this day and age.'

'I know. But I can do it. I just know I can, Doug. And she's a good girl.'

'If it happens, it'll change your life.'

'A lot of things change lives, Doug darling. That's the way life is.' Laura gave him a pointed look. 'Like divorce. That changes lives. It's certainly changed mine.'

He took her hand in his. 'I'm sorry, Laura, so sorry we didn't make it.'

'I know you are. So am I.'

'I worry about you and about this situation, should it develop.'

'Don't, Doug. I'll be okay, really I will. Even if I have to bring up Natasha, I'll be okay. I'll make it, Doug.'

'Yes, you will.' He gave her an appraising look, and continued, 'You're strong and courageous. I've always admired your strength. There aren't many like you, you know.'

She smiled at him. 'Thanks, but I think there are a lot of strong women in this world, women who are brave and dependable, loyal and indomitable. Take Grandma Megan, she's indomitable.'

'That she is. But you're still an original. I spotted that about you right away. In the very beginning.'

'I know. You told me that. Anyway, Claire wants Natasha to be part of a family – well, part of the Valiant family.'

Doug stared at her and a look of disbelief crossed his face. 'But there's only you, Laura.'

She stared back at him without responding, lifted her coffee cup and took a long swallow. Then she sat back in the chair; her gaze was unwavering. 'No, there's my mother and Grandma Megan and Dylan. Not to mention my two aunts Rhianon and Cara.'

Doug shook his head in wonderment. 'Dylan's in London working for *Time Magazine* and wrestling with all of his women. And responsibility is hardly his strong suit. Your mother, never a very reliable family member, is off painting murals in exotic places. Your two aunts you never see, since they're both decrepit and reclusive. And your grandmother's about to be ninety-three. There *is* only you, Laura.'

'But I don't feel that way, I don't feel alone. I just don't, Doug.'

Doug shook his head, sighed. 'Listen, I love you and I'm there for always, if you need me. But let's not forget I'm now living in Los Angeles. It's not as if I'll be around much to help you bring up Natasha.'

'But perhaps *I* won't have to do that either. I'm hoping I won't. I'm rooting for Claire . . . rooting for her to beat this.'

It was two weeks later that Laura found herself having a very similar conversation with Philippe Lavillard. Since she thought nothing of working at weekends, she had gone to the office on a Saturday afternoon to sift through the European art catalogues stacked on her desk.

She was halfway through the pile when the shrilling of the phone startled her. Reaching for it, she said, 'Art Acquisitions.'

'That is you, isn't it, Laura? It's Philippe Lavillard here.'

'Oh hello,' she exclaimed, surprised, for a moment, to hear his voice.

'I'm in New York,' he explained, and as usual got straight to the point. 'I wondered if you could spare me a few minutes to see me? I realize you must be working, so I hope I'm not an intrusion.'

There was no hesitation in her voice as she said, 'No, no, it's okay. Come on over to the office.' After giving him the address, she hung up, went on reading one of the art catalogues.

Ten minutes later she was opening the door to Philippe. 'Hello,' she said, and stepped to one side to let him enter the small reception area.

'Hello, Laura,' he answered, following her through into her office. 'Thanks for seeing me at such short notice.'

She nodded, indicated a chair. 'Please sit down.' Walking around the desk she lowered herself into her chair, asked, 'Are you in New York for the weekend?'

'Just today. Well, actually I'll be here this evening, I'm going back to Atlanta tomorrow. I had a business lunch today with a colleague. I wasn't sure how long it would take, that's why I didn't call you before now.'

'That's all right,' she said. 'I guess you want to talk to me about Claire and Natasha.'

He nodded. 'Mostly Natasha.'

Laura stiffened, staring at him. 'What about her?'

'I think certain things need to be said.' Leaning back in the chair, he crossed his long legs, looking thoughtful.

Regarding him carefully, wondering what he had on his mind, Laura couldn't help thinking that he seemed comfortable, at ease with himself, and with her. She relaxed a little, and sat back herself, waiting for him to continue.

'You and I have only spoken on the phone since . . . Claire . . . became ill, and I wanted to make a few things clear. Face to face, Laura.'

'What things?' she asked, wary again, her eyes narrowing slightly.

'I want you to know that I won't give you any trouble about the guardianship, if Claire doesn't make it, that is.'

'I'm praying she goes into remission.'

'So am I. But she *is* a Stage 4 patient, and that doesn't bode well for her. As a doctor I have to face reality, Laura. Anyway, to continue, Natasha is at that age when she needs a woman in her life. I know you love her, and that you will do the right thing by her. I trust you, Laura, but I felt I had to say that to you. Also, my life is at sixes and sevens at the moment. I'm not really settled in Atlanta, and I don't know where my work is going to take me in the future.'

'I never thought you would create problems,' Laura responded, leaning forward slightly. 'I realize how much you care about Natasha, how much you love her, and I would like to reassure *you* that you will always have as much access to her as you want. After all you are her father, and she loves you. She's made that very clear to me.'

'Thanks for saying that, Laura,' he said, smiling faintly. 'I like the idea of Nattie being in New York, of continuing her education here. After all, she is an American.'

'Yes,' Laura replied, thinking that he made it all sound like a foregone conclusion. But then, as he had just said, he was a doctor and he was not blinded by hope; he looked at the facts and made a judgement. Clearing her throat, Laura continued, 'If I end up taking care of Natasha, I'd like you to be involved in every part of her life, and especially her education.'

'I would be, and that brings me to another point. *Money.* I would take care of her financially, I wouldn't want her upbringing to be a burden to you. And I'll take care of the cost of her education as well. I hope all that goes without saying.'

'Yes, anyway, you more or less indicated that when we spoke on the phone.'

'I also want you to feel you can phone me whenever you need to, Laura, if there's anything to discuss about Natasha and her wellbeing.'

She nodded. 'I think we understand each other, Philippe. But I'm glad we've had a chance to talk face to face, as you said. How's your mother? I suppose you're staying with her?'

'She's good, and yes, I am at her apartment. How's Doug?'

Laura stared at him, wondering how to answer this question. She suddenly felt awkward, and she wasn't sure why. She said,

'He and I, well, actually, we've separated, Philippe. We're getting a divorce.'

'Oh, I'm sorry,' was all he could think of to say, taken by surprise as he was. What a fool Doug Casson must be, to let a fabulous woman like Laura Valiant go. He had always thought her to be exceptional, so intelligent yet a compassionate woman with an understanding heart. Deep down it had always troubled him that she appeared to dislike him, when he had felt just the opposite. But then he knew she had been influenced by Claire's turbulent emotional view of him.

As he continued to regard Laura steadily across her desk, Philippe was struck again by the vividness of her eyes. She was a beautiful woman.

Before he could stop himself, he said, 'Are you going to be working here much longer, Laura?' He glanced at his watch. 'It's almost four o'clock. Do you feel like having a cup of tea?'

For a split second Laura hesitated, and then she said, 'All right, why not? I'd like that, Philippe.' I might as well be cordial with him, she thought as she stood up. After all, Natasha is going to be a common bond between us.

21

Laura was used to being kept waiting by tycoons and Norman Grant was no exception to this rule.

She sat in the grandiose, cold-looking reception area of his humongous offices on Fifth Avenue wondering why he had allowed the architect to use so much white marble. It was the most unflattering material, unless it was gracing a villa in a hot climate, and it made the reception area look like a mausoleum. Or a giant-sized toilet, perhaps.

As she idly flicked through a beauty magazine, she wondered how long she would have to wait this time. On the last occasion she had been here it had taken Grant almost half an hour to admit her into his presence.

Glancing away from the blonde receptionist, who sat at a glass-and-steel desk facing her, Laura smiled to herself. The only one who never kept her waiting for longer than a few minutes was Maximilian West. But then he was quite different from all of the other businessmen she dealt with. He was unique, and a gentleman.

Glancing at her watch, Laura saw that she had been sitting on this sofa for half an hour. Under different circumstances she would now have risen and departed without wasting another moment of her valuable time. But she could not do that today.

Keep your cool, she told herself. You've got to win this. And today's your last chance to pull it off, to succeed.

As she placed the magazine on the coffee table in front of her, Norman Grant's secretary finally came to fetch her. There was no apology, greeting or smile of recognition, and she had been here before. The grim-faced woman simply said, 'He'll see you now,' and led the way down the corridor to his suite of private offices situated at the end.

Norman Grant, sixtyish, silver-haired, red-faced and portly in his dark blue suit, rose from behind his huge modern desk as she entered.

He nodded to her as she was ushered in, and indicated the chair facing his desk. 'Good morning, Miss Valiant. Please sit down.'

'Good morning, Mr Grant, and thank you,' she replied politely, then lowered herself into the chair.

'I don't know why I've agreed to see you a second time, since I've said everything I have to say about *Tahitian Dreams*,' he announced, getting straight to the point at once, without preamble.

'I think I can answer that for you, Mr Grant. You agreed to meet with me today because you want to avoid a lawsuit at all cost.'

Norman Grant glared at her. 'I bought the Gauguin in the most legitimate way. There won't be a lawsuit,' he said.

'Oh but there will be, Mr Grant. Sir Maximilian West plans to file suit at the end of this week. His lawyers are poised to do so, and they have been for months.'

'The case will be thrown out of court because it's not a legitimate case,' Norman Grant shot back.

'Yes, it is. Similar situations regarding Nazi-looted art are coming to light, and a number of cases have already been filed. Not only in Europe but in the United States. Also, an American museum which is in possession of a painting, a Matisse, looted by the Nazis from a Jewish family in France, is prepared to give it back to the family it was stolen from. If the family's ownership of it can be proven. As I told you when I came to see you a few weeks ago, Sir Maximilian West can prove that the Westheim family owned the Gauguin. He can prove provenance because he has the *catalogue raisonné*, which you have been shown.'

'I'm not a museum. Furthermore, I'm not going to *give* him the painting. I bought and paid for it. It belongs to me, Miss Valiant. Any reasonable person would agree with that.'

'Would you really want to embark on a long and tedious litigation? You're a businessman, Mr Grant, these things can become very costly. And time-consuming.'

'I know. But as I just said, the case will be thrown out of court. Because it's not a legitimate case.'

'I think it is, and so do Sir Maxim's lawyers, not to mention a number of museum curators and art experts.' Laura leaned back in the chair and crossed her long legs, outstaring Norman Grant.

He blinked finally, and wondered how to get rid of this unusually beautiful woman in her severe black suit who made him so uncomfortable. He felt uneasy in her presence, and yes, he had to admit it, inferior. 'We're just wasting each other's time,' he snapped. 'I made a mistake agreeing to see you again. I've nothing further to say. I won't change my mind. So don't threaten me.'

'Sir Maximilian and I have discussed this matter at great length and he's given me the authority to deal on his behalf. I'm prepared to make you an offer. And I'm not threatening you, by the way. I was merely pointing out that he will start litigation if we, that is you and I, do not resolve the problem today.'

'What's the offer?'

'We will pay you what you paid when you bought the painting from Anthea Margolis five years ago. We'll pay you the six-point-four-million dollars.'

'I paid more than that!'

'Not according to Mrs Margolis. I went to see her in Boston, and she showed me all the relevant documentation.'

Caught out in a foolish lie, Norman Grant flushed. 'I won't take six-point-four,' he said, and leaned back in his swivel chair, his face set.

'I know you want to triple what you paid, that you want to get nineteen or twenty million dollars. Mark Tabbart told me. But we're not going to pay that.' Laura gave him a long, hard stare and finished, 'And you won't get it anywhere else. I don't think there's a market for this painting anymore. It's tainted.'

Ignoring her last point, he said confidently, 'Sure there's a market.'

'If there is, which I doubt, it will rapidly diminish. The painting will lose its value after my press conference next week.'

'Press conference? What press conference?'

'I am going to hold one next week, on behalf of Sir Maximilian West,' Laura explained softly. 'As his art-adviser, I am going to tell the world about the Westheim Collection, how it was started, how it was illegally confiscated, stolen by the Nazis in 1939. I'm going to tell them all about *Tahitian Dreams*, show them the sequence of ownership, take the press on the journey of the Gauguin, from Friedrich Westheim's purchase of it in 1897, to its looting and illegal sale by General Josef Schiller of the SS to the Herman Seltzer Gallery in Vienna.' She smiled. 'It will make fascinating reading. I am also going to show them the *catalogue raisonné*, tell them the story of how Princess Irina Troubetzkoy found it only very recently in a bookshop in Paris. It's all wonderful stuff, the press will love it.'

'For what reason would you have a press conference? It sounds ridiculous to me,' Norman Grant muttered, giving her a baleful look.

'I don't agree. The story will get the public interested, and certainly there's going to be a lot of sympathy for Sir Maxim, not to mention all kinds of opinions. The Gauguin will become famous. But nobody will buy it.'

'Who cares about the Gauguin except us and other collectors?' He laughed at her. 'The general public don't care about art.'

'Oh really. Is that why museums are filled? Lack of interest on the public's part?' Laura moved slightly, leaned forward and continued, 'From a moral point of view, the painting does not belong to you, Mr Grant. And so this must be a moral decision on your part, not a legal or financial one. I did point out to Sir Maxim that you, too, are a victim in a way, and that is why he is willing to pay for the painting. But you cannot in good conscience make a profit on this art stolen from his parents. Both of them were Holocaust victims who perished because they were Jews. His mother was tortured and beaten to death in Ravensbruck, and his father was shot in cold blood in Auschwitz.' Laura paused, and finished, 'No, no, no, you're not going to make a profit on the dead, Mr Grant.'

'No deal,' he said coldly.

'You're being very unwise. The press will have a field day, especially when they know you're Jewish.'

Grant turned bright red. 'What are you saying?' he spluttered.

'That you're Jewish, Mr Grant. You may go to the Unitarian Church on Lexington Avenue and you may have changed your name . . . and why not? There's no reason why you shouldn't do either. But you *were* born Norman Gratowski and you grew up on the Lower East Side, a nice Jewish boy, of Jewish parents who luckily escaped the Warsaw Ghetto before it was too late.'

Laura gave him a pointed look and sat back.

Grant was silent. He appeared to be floored.

'How will it look to the world if you, a Jew, tries to make a profit on art stolen by the Nazis from a couple who lost their lives in the death camps of the Holocaust? I don't know if it would affect your business, probably not.' She shrugged lightly. 'But you never know.'

Norman Grant said nothing. He sat there in his black leather swivel chair looking sick.

Laura stood up. 'You bought a stolen painting. The rightful

owner wants it back. He's prepared to pay you what you paid . . . isn't that eminently fair?'

'No deal,' Norman Grant said again.

The moment Alison heard the front door slam, she shot out of her office and dashed to the reception area.

'What happened? Did it work?' she cried, her eyes on Laura.

Laura shook her head. 'Not yet.'

'Damn,' Alison said, and motioned for Laura to follow her into her office. Once they were both seated, Alison continued, 'I thought your strategy was brilliant; I was positive it would do the trick. So was Sir Maxim. All that hard work you did investigating Norman Grant's background . . . down the drain.'

'I wouldn't say that,' Laura murmured, shifting in the chair. 'I think we're going to win this. Let's give it time to sink in. Norman Grant's going to wrestle with it for a while, but I have a feeling he's going to come around in the end.'

'I'm not so sure about that. He's a tough guy, and he's not about to budge, in my opinion. He wants a lot of money for the Gauguin. He's going to sit it out,' Alison muttered, her expression suddenly dour.

'No, he won't,' Laura answered swiftly. 'Trust me on this, Alison. First of all, he knows the painting's tainted already. If he didn't before he does now, because I made that clear. Mark Tabbart turned it down because he didn't want problems, and Grant understands that. Nobody's going to buy *Tahitian Dreams* for twenty million dollars or indeed for six-point-four million, not after my press conference next week. It's a painting that's about to be jeopardized. Then again, Norman Grant doesn't want to be embarrassed, he doesn't want the world to think he's a Jew who's insensitive . . . to the Holocaust victims whose art was stolen by the Nazis.'

Alison shook her head. 'I don't agree with you, Laura. He's one tough son of a gun, and I don't believe he gives a hoot in hell what people think of him.'

'Let's see what happens, Alison, let's stay cool and wait.'
'Aren't you going to call Sir Maxim?'
'Yes I will. In a minute. From my own office.'

22

It was Megan who opened the front door of her apartment to admit Laura, who stared at her in surprise and asked, 'Where's Lily?' as she walked into the foyer and hugged her grandmother.

'It's her day off,' Megan replied and then with a sweet smile she added, 'that's why I'm going to take you out to dinner.'

'Oh,' Laura said, sounding surprised, eyeing her grandmother curiously. 'But you told me Lily was making my favourite dinner.'

'That's true, I did, but no fish cakes and parsley sauce tonight for you, darling girl.' Giving Laura the benefit of another sweet smile, Megan walked slowly into the sitting room, remarking, 'Now, let's have a sherry before we go. It's a bit early to leave.'

'All right,' Laura answered, followed her through the sitting room and into the adjoining library, asking herself why she was feeling suddenly suspicious of Megan. Her grandmother was really dressed up tonight, wearing a black silk-shantung dress and jacket, a three-strand pearl necklace and pearl earrings. But this did not really signify anything special; Megan Morgan Valiant was always beautifully turned out whenever she sallied forth to fulfil her social obligations. Like that other nonagenarian Brooke Astor, she was well known in New York for her style and chic.

After filling two glasses with dry sherry, Laura carried them over to her grandmother, handed her one, and sat down on the sofa next to her. 'Cheers, Gran,' Laura murmured, touching her crystal glass to Megan's.

'Cheers, darling girl.' Megan glanced at Laura as she spoke, and then followed her granddaughter's gaze, which was resting on a painting, 'Ah, yes, the Childe Hassam. I gave it to you for your birthday, but you never took it. Do you want it?'

'Oh, yes, I do, Gran, and thank you again, it was so generous of you to give it to me. It's a lovely gift, but I can't take it down until I find something for you to hang in its place. You can't have a blank spot on the wall, over the other sofa.'

'Oh, don't worry your head about it, anything will do, a print of some kind.'

'I'll find a beautiful lithograph for you, Gran. I know the kind of thing you like. By the way, I should have the appraisal for you next week. Jason's put a specific figure on each individual painting, so you can sell one, or all of them, whichever you prefer. Or you don't have to sell any at all. It's up to you.'

'I'll think about it, and thank you for getting him to come over. Such a nice young man.' She peered at Laura. 'Is he married?'

'No, he's not, Grandma Megan, and don't try to be a match-maker. I'm not interested in him.'

'More's the pity,' Megan said, and went on, 'by the by, what's happened to your mother? You haven't mentioned her in ages.'

'Oh, she's still in the islands. Painting away.'

'*Murals*, I've no doubt. Maggie's such a fine artist, she should be painting pictures not walls.'

'She needs the money, Grandma.'

'I know. Your father didn't leave her a great deal. Talking of leaving things . . . do you want that portrait of me over the mantelpiece? I have left it to you in my will, you know.'

'I'd love it, Grandma, thank you. But for the time being I'd like to hang on to the living thing, the flesh-and-blood you.'

'Oh, I'm not planning to go yet, child. But later, when I'm

dead, if you don't want the painting you can always give it to the charity shop.'

'Megan Valiant, I'd never do anything so awful!'

Megan smiled, and muttered, 'I don't know anybody else who'd want it but you.' Then she asked, 'How's Doug? What's happening with the divorce? You haven't said anything about him or it lately.'

'Doug's fine, I spoke to him yesterday. The divorce will be through any time. And as far as his work's concerned, he's doing well at the law firm in LA. He's found an apartment he likes in Century City and he's thinking of buying it. I guess he's enjoying his new life.'

'Well, I certainly hope so, considering that he divorced you to get it!'

'It wasn't quite like that, Gran.'

Ignoring Laura's comment, Megan announced, 'I think we'd better be going to dinner. I don't want to be late.'

'Shall I phone for a taxi?'

'No, I ordered a car for the evening. From the limousine service.'

'Oh.' Laura frowned. 'Where is it that we're going, Gran? What restaurant?'

'It's a surprise.' Putting the empty sherry glass down on the antique side-table, Megan stood up. 'I'll just get my handbag, and then we can leave.'

Laura nodded, watched her grandmother walk out of the library, so erect, so elegant, a miracle of a woman, really. And she couldn't help wondering what she had up her sleeve. Something was afoot, Laura was quite certain of that.

Rising herself, she walked over to the bay window and stood looking out at the view of the East River. It was a beautiful evening in the middle of June; there were several boats on the river, sailing down towards the end of Manhattan Island. What a pretty sight they were, a hint of the summer months ahead.

'I'm ready, Laura,' Megan called from the foyer, and Laura swung around and hurried through the sitting room.

As they went down in the lift, Laura looked at Megan and said, 'Come on, Gran, out with it. Where are we going?'

'I told you before, it's a surprise.'

Laura sighed. 'All right, it's a surprise, but I'm not sure I trust you. There's a certain look about you tonight, one I can't quite fathom. It's a look that tells me you know something I don't.'

'Good Lord, my girl, I certainly hope I *do* know more than you. I'm three times your age, and I've been around the block a few times more than you have.'

Laura laughed, and held her elbow as they went through the hallway to the car waiting outside. Laura had never seen the driver before, but her grandmother seemed to know him.

'Good evening, Peter,' Megan said, adding, 'this is my granddaughter, Miss Laura Valiant.'

'Evening, ma'am,' the driver said, inclining his head politely; he helped her grandmother into the limo solicitously.

Laura decided not to ask any more questions; she sat back against the car seat, glancing out of the window, only half listening to her grandmother who was talking to Peter about his family, asking how they were. But she did notice they were heading uptown on First Avenue, and was somewhat surprised when the driver turned down East Fifty-Seventh Street and then continued up York Avenue. She couldn't imagine where they were heading. As they drove on towards the East Eighties and East End Avenue Laura began to suspect they were going to someone's apartment.

Laura's heart sank as a sudden thought struck her. She hoped her grandmother wasn't trying to be a matchmaker again, as she had several weeks ago. God forbid, Laura thought.

The limo finally came to a standstill in front of one of the grand old pre-war buildings on East End Avenue near East Eighty-Sixth Street. Peter, the driver, parked; helped Megan out of the car and then Laura took hold of her arm and escorted her into the building.

As they entered the hallway, Laura asked curiously, 'So, who are we going to have dinner with, Grandma?'

'Rosa Lavillard.'

For a moment Laura was speechless, then she exclaimed, 'Why have you done this, Gran? I can't have dinner with her.'

'Why not?'

'Claire wouldn't like it, and you know I can't upset her right now. She's fighting for her life.'

Megan nodded, her face grave. 'I realize that, and she's very courageous. But how is she going to know you've had dinner here unless you tell her?'

'*I'll* know, and it'll make me feel I'm being disloyal.'

'I know all about your integrity, Laura dear, but this *is* just a dinner, you know. Now don't let us stand here in the lobby making a spectacle of ourselves.'

'Gran, I really don't –'

'Laura,' Megan interrupted in a stern voice, 'please be sensible, and just listen to me for a moment. You may well be bringing up Natasha and very soon. Actually, I'd say it's more than likely, and you're going to need help, whatever you might think. Rosa's help, and yes, perhaps even Philippe's. After all, I won't be much use to you, even if I'm still around. You're a divorced woman on your own, and you're going to need a support system.'

'But Rosa Lavillard . . . Oh Gran, I don't know . . .'

'I do. She's a very decent woman, kind, warm-hearted, and her great wish is to get to know her granddaughter. You adore Claire, and so do I, but I'm afraid Claire has given you the wrong impression of Rosa. She's not the enemy, you know. Come along, we're late.' So saying, Megan walked on towards the lift, her head held high, her step firm.

Laura had no alternative but to follow her grandmother. They rode up in silence to the sixth floor, and a few seconds later they were standing outside Rosa's apartment. It was she who opened the door to them.

'Good evening, Megan . . . Miss Valiant,' Rosa said, and opening the door wider, she added, 'please come in.'

'I'm sorry we're a little late. My fault,' Megan murmured, walking into the hallway and offering her hand to Rosa.

'Good evening, Mrs Lavillard,' Laura said, also shaking the woman's hand.

'Please call me Rosa. I prefer it.'

'And I prefer to be called Laura.'

Rosa led them into a spacious living room overlooking East End Avenue and the East River. Its high-flung ceiling, many windows and a fireplace gave the room a traditional feeling as did all of the furnishings. Laura, glancing around quickly as she followed Rosa and her grandmother, noticed that the antiques were mostly French. It was a really lovely room, decorated primarily in white and light pastel colours. Handsome porcelain lamps with white silk shades, a glass-fronted china cabinet filled with antique porcelain and two French gilt mirrors denoted fine taste. The overall look, she decided, was definitely old Europe. There were some interesting lithographs on the walls, as well as several good paintings.

'What would you like?' Rosa asked, glancing at them and then at the tray of drinks on a dark mahogany chest.

'Sherry please, Rosa,' Megan said.

'The same, thank you.' Laura went and sat down in a chair next to the large cream sofa on which her grandmother was now seated comfortably, relaxing against a pile of needlepoint cushions.

Rosa gave them each a dry sherry and joined Megan on the sofa. After murmuring a toast, Megan started to recommend a play she had just seen, and it soon became apparent to Laura that the two women had been seeing each other recently, and perhaps even frequently. There was a familiarity between them, a certain ease, the kind of rapport that springs up between women who like each other and have become friends.

When there was a lapse in their conversation, Laura jumped in, saying, 'Have you been seeing a lot of each other lately?' She directed her question at Rosa.

'A little. Megan and I have certain things in common, especially the theatre.' Rosa pushed herself up off the sofa. 'Excuse me a moment. . .' She hurried off in the direction of the kitchen, saying over her shoulder, 'I must check on something in the oven.'

'Keeping secrets from me, eh, Gran?' Laura whispered, leaning closer to Megan when they were alone.

Megan gave her granddaughter a long look through her perceptive, faded blue eyes and merely smiled.

Laura knew better than to press Megan or say anything else, but she realized that the two women were fond of each other. And she was quite certain that it was her grandmother who had made the first move, who had contacted Rosa after all these years. It was just the sort of thing Megan would do.

Laura got up and walked across the room, stood looking at an oil painting which hung on a wall between two windows. 'What a charming Marie Laurencin,' she said to Megan.

'Yes, it is,' Rosa answered as she walked back into the living room. 'I bought it many, many years ago in Paris, and I've always loved it.'

Turning around, Laura looked at her and said, 'You prefer Renoir, though.'

'Ah yes, but Renoir I cannot afford. Only the prints of his work. Now, if you will come to the dining room, dinner is ready.'

The dining room had been decorated in different shades of blue, running from the pale blue of a summer sky to the aquamarine and turquoise of a tropical sea. Laura felt as though she were surrounded by the waters of a Caribbean island, submerged in seawater so clear you could see below the surface of the waves.

The effect was magical, and after Rosa had hurried away

to bring the first course, Laura mentioned it to her grand-mother.

Megan nodded in agreement. 'Yes, I know what you mean. It *is* like being in the sea. Perhaps that's because the ceiling is mirrored and the colours on the walls flow up into it, then flow down. They reflect in the glass top of the table.'

Laura had been looking at the Renoir prints gracing the far wall, and she had not noticed the mirror work in the room. She glanced up at the ceiling and nodded. 'The mirror is reflecting all the different blues . . . what a clever device it is, Gran.'

'She's a clever woman, self-supporting and self-sufficient. She runs the antique porcelain shop, you know. I like Rosa. Actually, I admire her.'

'Self-sufficient?' Laura repeated questioningly.

'Yes, yes. Rosa appears to be perfectly happy being alone. She doesn't seem to need anyone.'

'Not even her son?' Laura asked now, sounding puzzled. 'I thought she was rather possessive of him.'

'I don't think so,' Megan replied, giving Laura a strange look. 'Whatever gave you that idea? Oh, I know. I should have said *who*. It was Claire, wasn't it?'

'Well, yes, but she didn't actually use the word possessive, she just implied it.'

Megan nodded, shifted slightly in her seat, and was about to respond when the door was pushed open and Rosa came in from the kitchen.

'Rosa, the soup smells delicious!' Megan exclaimed, looking up at her hostess and smiling as the steaming bowl of fragrant liquid was placed in front of her. 'Thank you.'

Laura could tell that Rosa was flattered to receive her grand-mother's compliment. Although she didn't reply or smile, or make any kind of acknowledgement, her eyes seemed to brighten as she inclined her head, and then she quickly disappeared again.

'I've had this soup before,' Megan said to Laura. 'It's crystal clear, and delicious. You're going to love it.'

A moment later Rosa was back once more, putting a bowl of the chicken soup on the table for Laura. 'Thank you,' Laura murmured.

'I'll be right back,' Rosa said. 'Please . . . start.'

Laura stared into the soup. It *was* very clear, but a pure golden colour with a few slices of carrot floating in it along with a small matzo ball. Her grandmother was right, it did smell delicious and Laura found her mouth watering.

'Please, let us eat, Megan . . . Laura,' Rosa cried as she finally sat down at the table. '*Bon appetit*,' she added, picked up her spoon and dipped it into her bowl.

Out of the blue, Megan announced, 'It takes twelve chickens to make a soup like this,' and then she looked at Rosa and asked, 'am I not right, Rosa?'

'You are, Megan.'

'How did you know that, Grandma?'

'Oh, I know a lot of things you don't know I know,' Megan answered somewhat enigmatically, and then observing the bafflement on Laura's face, she explained, 'your grandfather and I had a wonderful partner at one point in our theatrical careers. He co-produced a lot of my musicals with your grandfather. His name was Herbert Lipson – Herb we called him – and his mother made the best chicken soup in the whole world. She used to call it Jewish penicillin, and whenever we were in Philadelphia she invited us to dinner and she always served us her soup.'

'Yes, that's what it is, Laura, Jewish penicillin because it does seem to cure everything,' Rosa explained.

The two older women immediately embarked on a discussion about the healing properties of ethnic foods, and Laura spooned up the soup and listened, lifting her head from time to time to scrutinize Rosa.

Laura had been very much aware of Rosa's pleasant and welcoming demeanour from the moment they had walked into the apartment. The last time she had seen her had been at the museum in Paris looking at Renoirs, and Rosa had appeared cold, hostile, wary, and slightly odd. Tonight she was a different person entirely. It was true she had a curious reserve about her, but Laura now decided this must just be her natural manner, perhaps a reflection of her personality. On the other hand, when she had hovered over Megan earlier a lovely warmth had emanated from Rosa, and Laura found this touching; it pleased her that Rosa apparently cared about her grandmother.

Rosa even *looked* different, better, not as old as she had appeared in the d'Orsay, and much less dumpy. Perhaps this was because she was wearing a well-cut, tailored suit of deep purple silk, gold earrings and a matching gold pin. This evening Rosa's dark hair was stylishly coiffed, and the grey streaks she had noticed in Paris were no longer there. They had been carefully tinted out.

Studying her surreptitiously for a moment, Laura decided that Rosa's face was much more attractive than she'd realized; but what she needed was a bit of make-up to define her good bone structure, bring out the luminosity of her large, pellucid grey eyes, the richness of her thick chestnut hair. But perhaps she can't be bothered or doesn't care, Laura thought. Some women didn't, they were content to be as they were, without artifice.

Two things about Rosa were most distinctive, and Laura had noticed them particularly tonight: her beautiful, shapely legs and her voice. The latter was husky, even sexy, and her French accent added a special flavour.

Suddenly she wished she knew a little more about Rosa Lavillard than she did. Unexpectedly, Laura was riddled with curiosity about her. What she did know was that she was Jewish, French born, and had grown up in France during the war. After marrying she had come to America, where her son Philippe had been born. And she had lived here ever since. Laura remembered that Philippe was about forty-one or two, and so Rosa was probably in her mid sixties, even late sixties, perhaps.

Her husband Pierre Lavillard had died some years ago; Laura with her prodigious memory, had an instant recollection of him

She had met him at Claire's wedding, and in her mind's eye she saw a tall, distinguished man with a great deal of Continental charm. His expertise was in French antiques and porcelain from all over the world, she remembered. He dealt in the great marks such as Meissen, Dresden, Herend, Limoges, and the important porcelains of England from Royal Worcester to Royal Crown Derby. He had owned a shop on Lexington Avenue when Claire and Philippe had married, and it was there that he had sold French antiques and antique porcelains.

Laura was roused from her reverie with a small start when Rosa announced, 'I will bring the next course.' As she spoke Rosa pushed back her chair and stood, picked up Megan's plate and her own.

Laura attempted to rise. 'Let me help you,' she said, getting to her feet.

'No, no, I can manage. It is better I do this alone, I am well organized,' Rosa insisted, and was gone before Laura could protest further.

The next course was steamed carp served with home-made horseradish sauce and freshly-baked challah, followed by a chicken which came out of the oven a crisp golden brown and was succulent and moist inside as Rosa carved it at the table. This was served with mashed potatoes, gravy, and peas and carrots.

Finally, Rosa brought in the dessert. It was the most extraordinary apple strudel Laura had ever tasted, topped with whipped cream and cherry sauce. Always a picky eater, Laura realized at the end of the meal that she had demolished everything, and with relish.

Essentially, it had been a simple dinner, but every dish had been meticulously prepared and beautifully cooked, and that was the secret of its perfection. Laura said this to Rosa, adding, 'It's the best dinner I've had in a very long time. Thank you. I really enjoyed it.'

'Yes, it was superb,' Megan murmured, and added her own thanks.

Rosa looked gratified. 'Thank you,' she said. 'I enjoy cooking. And now I shall serve coffee.'

At one moment, over coffee in the living room, Rosa said, 'Congratulations, Laura.'

Laura glanced at her quickly. 'Thank you. I assume you're referring to the return of the Gauguin painting to Sir Maximilian West?'

'Exactly. I read about your press conference in the *New York Times*, and I thought it was wonderful you had negotiated a deal with Mr Grant.'

Rosa Lavillard smiled for the first time that evening, and went on, 'It was a triumph for you, and it gave me great hope that other people will do the decent thing . . . if they *know* they possess art looted by the Nazis. That they will return it to the heirs of those poor souls from whom it was stolen during the war.'

'Some people will. Others won't,' Laura replied. 'I truly believe it's a moral question. Naturally there are those who disagree and think of it in financial terms. They won't want to give up paintings they have paid good money for. That was Norman Grant's attitude at first. He wanted to triple his investment in *Tahitian Dreams*, make a lot of money out of the painting. But I finally convinced him, managed to induce him to accept Sir Maxim's offer of six-point-four million dollars. If you remember the details in the story in the paper, that was exactly what Mr Grant paid for it five years ago.'

Megan volunteered, between sips of her coffee, 'He would not have accepted the money if he'd been really smart. Instead he would have given the painting to Maximilian West. And if he had been wise enough to do that he would have come out a hero. As it is, he looks like a greedy little man.'

'Sir Maximilian must be thrilled to have the painting back after all these years,' Rosa murmured.

'He was,' Laura told her, suddenly smiling. 'And so was I, on his behalf. Actually, looking back, I think I accomplished a miracle

And you, Rosa, I can see that you love art.' Laura glanced around. 'You love beauty in all its forms – that's apparent from all the lovely things you have gathered here.'

'Yes, beauty is essential to me. There is far too much ugliness and suffering in this world. Such immense cruelty. Beauty does soothe the soul . . .'

Laura did not say anything. She had caught the faint echo of words Rosa had uttered in the d'Orsay on that cold December day last year, and there was such great sorrow in the woman's voice it pierced Laura's heart.

Megan said slowly, 'Rosa's father was a well-known art-dealer in Paris, Laura. She inherited his love of paintings, especially the great Impressionists. You and she have the same taste.'

'A gallery in Paris?' Laura began. 'What was its name? Where was it?'

'It was called *Duval et Fils*. My father was the *fils*, the son. But then my grandfather was also the *fils*, the son. For three generations we were art-dealers. The gallery was on the rue La Boétie in the eighth arrondissement, which was sometimes called the French Florence.'

'I know all about the rue La Boétie from my studies at the Sorbonne. It was very famous because every major dealer had a gallery there,' Laura exclaimed.

'That is true. There were the Bernheim-Jeune brothers, who represented your favourite and mine, Renoir. And also the great Paul Rosenberg. Wildenstein, Cailleux, and Josef Hessel all had galleries on the rue La Boétie as well. It was the centre of art through the 1920s into the 1930s, and of course it became the focal point of Hitler's greed for art during the Occupation.'

Laura nodded. 'Yes, I know that altogether the Nazis looted some twenty thousand paintings, drawings and sculpture from France, and that they were all shipped to Germany during the war.'

'Stamped property of the Third Reich,' Rosa muttered grimly.

'Do you feel like telling Laura something about your life, Rosa?' Megan asked in a low voice. 'Or would it be too exhausting for you? Too draining?'

Rosa shook her head. 'No, Megan, it would not. I will recount a little of my life to Laura ... I think that perhaps, under the circumstances, she should know something about the Rosa Duval I once was.' Rosa looked across at Laura, her eyes on her, and finished, 'If you want to hear about that part of my life?'

'Yes, I would like to,' Laura answered. 'But as my grandmother just said, I wouldn't want you to tire yourself out.'

'Oh no, that is all right, I will be fine. But I think I would like to get myself a glass of water first. Would you like one, Laura? And what about you, Megan?'

'Iced water would be lovely,' Megan said. 'And perhaps a little more of the coffee. Thank you, Rosa dear.'

'I'd like a glass of water too, please,' Laura said. 'But let me come and help you.'

Rosa shook her head. 'I can manage perfectly well. I will only be a moment.'

23

'Now I shall tell you about my life when I was a little girl in France,' Rosa said, her attention on Laura. Leaning back in the comfortable armchair, she took a sip of water and then began:

'I spent my early years growing up in the art gallery on the rue La Boétie. *Duval et Fils* was our home, as well as my father's place of business. My father Maurice Duval had inherited the gallery, which was an entire building, from my grandfather who had died in 1934. On the first and second floors my father showed Impressionist and Post-Impressionist paintings, some modern art, and sculpture. My grandmother Henrietta, my father's mother, lived on the third floor with her daughter, Aunt Sylvie. We were on the fourth and fifth floors, and the domestic help was on the sixth. It was a wonderful arrangement, in the time-honoured tradition of old Europe when the family lived above the store, so to speak.

'Grandmother spent a lot of time with us, and so did Aunt Sylvie, who wasn't married. We were six in our little family. Mama, Papa, my brothers Michel and Jean-Marc, and my sister Marguerite. I was the youngest and the favoured child in a sense, everyone's pet.'

Rosa looked off into the distance, as if seeing something very special in her mind's eye, and a faint smile touched her mouth.

'My father called me *mon petit choux à la crème,* his little cabbage with cream, and he adored me. I was the spoiled girl, I suppose, but I was a good girl. Those years were wonderful. My father was a most gregarious man, outgoing, charming, hospitable and very giving of himself. He entertained both clients and artists at the gallery, gave splendid evenings. Picasso was a favourite visitor, and sometimes Matisse came with his model Lydia Delectorskaïa. They all made a big fuss of me, and I have never forgotten them.

'My father's gallery was considered one of the most elegant in that very elegant neighbourhood; it stood at the corner, near avenue Matignon. It had beautiful exposition rooms filled with extraordinary light from the windows, and a glass ceiling in one of the rooms. It was soft filtered light which was perfect for the paintings. My father believed in providing rich back-drops for art and he had walls covered in red silk-brocade and blue damask. The exposition rooms were like a museum, and clients came just to sit there and admire the art ... at different times my father represented Cézanne, Renoir, Degas, Marie Laurencin, and, of course, Picasso and Matisse, to name only a few.

'When France and Britain declared war on Germany on September 3rd, 1939, I was nine years old. My father was worried because we were Jewish, but he did not want to flee the country at first. He was a clever man and he believed in studying situations, appraising everything, and he wanted to see what would happen. And so he continued to study and evaluate the situation before making any rash moves. However, because he was afraid Paris might be bombed by the Germans, fearful that the gallery could be damaged if such an event occurred, he decided it would be wiser to move some of the paintings from the gallery. He began to systematically send them down to the Gironde, to a château in the countryside just outside Bordeaux, which belonged to an old friend of his. He had thought of storing the paintings in the cellars of the château.

and his friend agreed that this was a prudent move. And so arrangements were made.

'Jacques Pointine was my father's right-hand man, and it was Jacques who transported the paintings down to the château. Pointine was married to an Englishwoman, Phyllis Dixon, who also worked for my father as a personal assistant handling many of his art deals. She was very knowledgeable and intensely loyal. A little later Phyllis and Jacques took another collection of canvases to Bordeaux, where they were stored in a bank vault my father had rented. He was sure the paintings would be safe there, and he suggested to several artists that they take the same precautions with their work.

'My father had all of the paintings registered under the name of Jacques Pointine's married sister, Yvette Citrone, again as a precaution. Then he shipped one-hundred-and-twenty more to a warehouse in Grenoble, this time in Phyllis's name. Altogether he managed to move over five hundred paintings out of Paris, some of them from his own personal collection, the rest part of the gallery's considerable inventory. Other dealers were taking similar steps, especially the Jewish dealers and gallery owners, and a number of painters were doing the same thing . . . Picasso, Braque and Matisse included.

'In November of 1939 my father decided we could no longer stay in Paris and so he took the whole family to Bordeaux, which he knew was safe, and where he rented a large family apartment. He insisted that Phyllis and Jacques come with us, and Papa left the gallery under the management of Alain Brescon, who had worked for him for years and was as loyal and devoted as Phyllis and Jacques.

'Our life in Bordeaux settled into a relatively normal routine, and anyway it was the period known as the phoney war when nothing much was happening. Every day I went to school with my brothers and sister; my mother and grandmother supervised our household; Papa worked with Phyllis and Jacques on the inventories of the art, and stayed in daily contact with the Paris gallery. He also talked with many of the other dealers and artists he was close to and cared about. But in a sense, I suppose, we were all holding our breath.

'But by June of 1940 that phoney war had become a real war. The news was suddenly alarming. On June 3rd Paris was hit by 1,100 bombs from 200 Third Reich planes. The Wehrmacht was on its steady, and relentless, march across France. Its destination: Paris. The French Army was almost at the end of its strength and resolve, and the roads were overrun with hundreds and hundreds of refugees fleeing south. The Germans entered Paris on 14 June and France fell. The French Government in Exile in Bordeaux surrendered, and was replaced by the right-wing Vichy Government, under the leadership of Maréchal Pétain. Almost immediately, Vichy passed anti-Jewish laws, long before the Nazis had demanded that any measures be taken against Jews.

'My father had gone down with bronchitis that same June and it turned into pneumonia, as often happens with this kind of illness when it strikes in summer, it took him a long time to get well. Even then he was left debilitated and listless. Certainly he was not in a frame of mind to move out of Bordeaux. In any case we were in the southwest, which was Unoccupied France, and my parents believed us to be safe.

'It was not until July of 1942 that disaster and tragedy struck my family. I have often wondered if we stayed too long, have asked myself what *I* would have done in the same circumstances. But I have no real answers. The times were difficult, the situations hard to gauge accurately, and in any case we were not being bothered.

'I will never forget the date. It was July 16 and I was almost twelve. My mother had asked Phyllis Dixon to take me to the doctor that afternoon, because I had been complaining of my tonsils. We were walking down the street towards our apartment when she suddenly grabbed hold of me and dragged me into the doorway of a building. 'It's the police,' she whispered. 'There is a French Police truck outside the door of your building, Rosa.

I cannot take you home.' I remember that I started to cry and frantically tried to pull away from her, to escape her clutches. But she was too strong for me. She held onto me tightly and wouldn't let go of me. She kept peering out, and it was when I heard her choke on the words, 'Oh my God,' that I knew the police had come for *my* parents. Finally we heard the truck driving off. I wanted to race home to make sure my parents were safe. I kept telling myself that I had been *wrong*, that they had *not* been arrested. But Phyllis wouldn't let me leave the doorway for a very long time.

'When we did eventually return to my family's apartment there was no one there. Not Papa, or Mama, or Grandmama. Aunt Sylvie was gone, as well. And so were my brothers and sister. They had taken them all . . . even the children. Phyllis and I were in a terrible state of shock. Jacques was in Grenoble, checking on the paintings in the warehouse, and we didn't know what to do, since he wasn't coming back until late that night. Phyllis was afraid to leave me alone; anyway, she didn't know who to go and see to find out what had happened. In the end, she grabbed a few of my things, threw them in a suitcase and took me home to their apartment. It was not far away and it was there that we waited for Jacques.

'When he returned home at about nine o'clock in the evening he was as shocked as we had been, and as frightened for my family as we were. He had always been very close to my father. Jacques immediately went to the authorities in Bordeaux. Eventually he discovered that my parents were being held in the prison there, along with other Jews . . . men, women and children. It seemed there was nothing he could do.

'I never saw my parents again. Nor the rest of my family. The next day they were shipped to a French concentration camp in Drancy, just north of Paris. It was the first stop on their fearsome journey . . . to Auschwitz.'

Rosa stopped, her voice suddenly trembling, and then after a moment she continued more steadily. 'They all perished there . . .

Papa, Mama, Grandmama and Aunt Sylvie ... my brothers Michel and Jean-Marc, and Marguerite. Just like that, in the blink of an eye, everyone I loved was gone, ripped away from me forever. I couldn't believe it, I had seen them only a few hours ago, and been with them. Suddenly I was alone, except for Phyllis and Jacques. I will never forget how stunned and terrified I was. And Phyllis and Jacques were terrified *for* me. They feared the police might come back to get me. Later that night, Jacques sent me with Phyllis to his sister's house at the other side of Bordeaux, until he could work out a plan for me, for all of us. The Pointines were not Jewish and Jacques hoped I would be safe with his sister. For a while.

'Jacques Pointine was sharp, clever. I suppose he was the kind of man we would call streetwise today, and he was beginning to worry about the art. But even so he did not fully grasp exactly what was going on, or the extent of it. But then very few people did. It was only later that information about the massive looting of artworks came out.

'Jacques also worried that he and Phyllis could be in danger, because of their association with my father, and he determined that we should all disappear.'

Rosa paused in her sorrowful tale and drank some water before continuing.

Neither Megan nor Laura spoke.

Megan leaned back against the needlepoint cushions and sighed, looking around this gracious room, her mind awash with thoughts of evil and man's baseness and cruelty and inhumanity. Once again her heart went out to Rosa Lavillard, as it had when she had first heard her story so long ago.

Laura wanted to say something to Rosa, but she did not have the right words. There *were* no right words. Words were meaningless. Anything she could say would sound trite, even ridiculous, in view of the enormity of what had happened to Rosa all those years ago. It was beyond human comprehension. Glancing at her grandmother, she tried to imagine what it would be like to have *her* family taken away and murdered in cold blood in a death camp. She *couldn't* envision it; the mere idea overwhelmed her.

In a low, subdued voice, Laura finally said, 'How . . . how did you manage to go on, Rosa? The horror of it . . .' Laura was unable to finish her sentence and she felt sudden tears pricking behind her eyes.

Rosa said, 'I don't know, I have often asked myself that. And there were times when I wished I had been at home, that I had been with my parents, my family, so that I could have shared their fate, been taken with them to Auschwitz. At least we would have all been together. But I wasn't, I was saved by chance, by luck, and by Phyllis Dixon. There were times afterwards, when I was growing up, that I thought I might have been saved because I had a special purpose in life. But I don't know. It's as I just said, fate played a hand, along with Phyllis.' Rosa looked at Laura. 'You asked how I managed to go on . . . I suppose because I was a child. Children are resilient. I wept a lot, I worried about my family, and sometimes I was almost paralysed by fear for them, but we were on the run, moving around a lot, and Phyllis kept telling me I had to keep my wits about me, in order to survive.

'It was soon very apparent that the Vichy Government was deporting Jews to Germany on a large scale. Jacques and Phyllis found it incomprehensible that the French state was so casually delivering *children* to their murderers. There was complicity everywhere. Perhaps you do not know this, but the French Jews were the most assimilated of any other Jews in Europe, they had become, over the centuries, part of the fabric of French life. It was obvious that ordinary French people were turning Jews in . . . without those dossiers at the prefecture, Jews would not have been found. They could not have been deported. Or killed.

'Jacques was conscious of this, and he became convinced that my father and the family had been turned in by a collaborator, which is why he feared for *my* safety. You see, I was not only another Jew to be exterminated, but I was also the heir to

Maurice Duval's immense and valuable art collection. And so we moved around a lot. We went to stay with relatives of Jacques in Mérignac, then we moved on and stayed in Grenoble for a short while, before going to friends of Phyllis who lived near La Martellière. It was there that we moved into a small house. It was on the outskirts of La Martellière, and belonged to the sister of Phyllis' friends. At first Jacques was relieved that we had a respite, could stay put for a while, that we did not have to move around so much. But then it became a nightmare. Suddenly, Jacques was convinced the police were watching the house, and just when he had finished making arrangements for us to leave, Phyllis broke her shoulder and leg when she fell down a flight of steps leading into the cellar. She was incapacitated, and so Jacques had to cancel our plans to go to Bellegarde, near the Swiss border. He thought it was too long a trip for Phyllis.

'One day, about a week later, Jacques was told by a member of the French Resistance to hide me, that the French police were looking for me, that they were convinced I was being sheltered by Phyllis and Jacques. The information had come out of the Bordeaux prefecture . . . the woman from the Resistance told Jacques that they were looking for the Duval girl to deport.

'It wasn't safe to send me to any of their friends, and so Jacques hid me. In a hole in the ground –'

'Oh my God, no!' Laura exclaimed, her voice rising. She stared at Rosa aghast.

Rosa nodded. 'It was the only thing he could do. There was no other place. The hole was actually a small cave in the side of a hillock, at the end of a field. The field abutted the garden of the house, so Jacques felt secure about putting me in the cave. It was dry, and air came in from somewhere higher up, above a ledge in the cave, and so I knew I would not suffocate. But I was always worried something would happen to Jacques and that I would be stuck in the cave forever. You see, in order to properly hide me securely, he had to roll a large stone in front of the opening. I wasn't strong enough to move it myself. Often I panicked, and

I hated being in that dark hole. Jacques would only let me burn candles in the daylight when it didn't matter, because the candle flame couldn't be seen. I wasn't allowed to light them at night. But he always brought me out at night, surreptitiously, cautiously. I was able to go to the house nearby, have a bath, eat, see Phyllis and be comforted by her. But it was an horrendous experience. I've hated dark places ever since.' Again Rosa stopped talking, sipped her glass of water, trying to relax.

'How long were you in the hole?' Laura ventured, her voice strained.

'For a year. Phyllis could not travel, she was ill a long time. Finally we were able to leave the area. Jacques thought we were too close to Mérignac and Dax, where many Jews were still being arrested and deported to Germany. He wanted to get closer to Switzerland, hoping one day to cross the border. But we never did. Anyway, we kept on moving around a lot, until we finally settled in the countryside between Lyons and Bellegarde. Life was hard, we were always afraid of being caught by the police, and food was scarce. And I saw so much killing and ugliness . . . However, I *was* out of the cave, I was no longer living like the troglodytes of Tunisia. But that year was the worst in my life.'

Glancing around the spacious living room awash in pale colours, Rosa added quietly, 'I've surrounded myself with airiness, lightness ever since. Anything dark is forbidding. It reminds me of that hole.'

24

Megan leaned forward and said, 'Are you tired, Rosa? Oh, how silly of me to even ask that! Of course you must be exhausted, telling this story again, reliving your early life. It must be harrowing for you. Perhaps I shouldn't have asked you to do so.'

'No, I'm all right, I'm not tired, Megan.' Rosa glanced at Laura. 'I've tried hard to get past the Holocaust, but it's always there, hidden deep in my heart, because it involves my family, whom I loved, and I can never forget *them*.'

'I understand,' Laura said. 'It must be almost impossible . . . to *ever* forget.'

'Eventually you do bury most of it deep, that's only natural. No one could live with that kind of mental anguish on a daily basis. And once it *is* truly buried it becomes very hard to dredge up. Far too painful. But their memory lives on in my heart . . .' She sighed and shook her head as she continued, 'Anyway, I have never wanted to force all the details of what happened to me on anyone. I've tried not to be bitter, to move forwards always, to look to the future in a positive way. I was spared. I was given a life to live, and I've tried to live it . . . as my parents would have wanted me to, as best I could. The Germans murdered my whole family. But there is no reason why I should allow them to ruin the rest of my life. If I did, then I would be letting them triumph over me.'

'Your spirit is indomitable, Rosa,' Megan murmured. 'I've always admired the way you've managed to cope so well.'

'I've done my best to be . . . *happy*, as I just said. After all, I'm living proof that Hitler didn't succeed, didn't win his genocidal war against the Jews. He lost it, just as he lost the war against the Allies.'

'You've been through so much, Rosa. I don't know what to say to you, how to express my feelings. There are no words to tell you how your story has affected me,' Laura began and hesitated. 'To offer you sympathy, to say I'm sorry, would be . . . banal, in view of the enormity of what you experienced. Your suffering would be diminished, somehow. Well, that's what I think.'

Rosa simply nodded.

Laura hesitated once more, and then she said slowly, in the gentlest of voices, 'You have a brave heart, Rosa, a very brave heart.'

For a few seconds Rosa was silent, her face very still, expressionless; then she reached out, touched Laura's arm. 'That you understand it at all . . . that is enough.' Pushing herself to her feet, Rosa asked, 'Shall I make some fresh coffee? I know I would like some.'

'That'd be great, Rosa,' Laura answered, and this time she did not offer to help, since she knew her offer would be refused.

When they were alone, Laura said, 'It *is* a remarkable story, Grandma Megan, isn't it?'

Megan nodded. 'Yes. But she's left a lot out tonight . . . Perhaps she wasn't up to telling it, or maybe she thought you'd find it too upsetting.'

'Why? What do you mean?'

'Goodness gracious, I can't go into it now, child!'

'I understand. Anyway, what I find strange is that Claire –'

'Not now, Laura dear,' Megan cut in quickly. 'We'll discuss everything when you take me home.'

'Yes, of course.' Laura glanced at her watch. 'You know, it's turned *eleven*, Gran! Perhaps I shouldn't have agreed to have a cup of coffee. Isn't it past your bedtime?'

'No, it's not,' Megan said, sitting up straighter, giving Laura a sharp look. 'And it's not necessary for you to fuss over me, as if I'm an old lady.' Megan laughed. 'Well, I know I am one, but I don't feel old. And in any case, bed is overrated. Furthermore, you die in bed, so I'm quite happy to stay up late. And most nights I do.'

'All right, all right,' Laura said, shaking her head. 'There's no one like you, Grandma.'

'I should hope not,' Megan shot back.

Within a few minutes Rosa returned with a pot of fresh coffee and a selection of biscuits, and as she poured the coffee into the clean cups, Laura said, 'There is something I would like to ask you, Rosa.'

Rosa lifted her head and looked over at Laura. 'Please, you can ask me anything. I will answer if I can.'

'I was just wondering . . . was your family arrested and murdered because they were Jews or were they murdered for the art?'

Rosa did not reply. She passed the cups of coffee to Megan and Laura, and then sat down in the chair again. 'It was for both reasons. That is what I believe,' she said finally.

'What happened to all the paintings your father had shipped out of Paris?' Laura continued.

'They disappeared. When we tried to find them at the end of the war they had vanished into thin air. Stolen, of course, by the Nazis. Jacques and Phyllis were frantic, trying to find out what had transpired, but naturally they met a wall of silence. They did manage to get some information from my father's friend who lived at the Château Le Beauve. Gerard de Castellaine owned the château and he was an old, old friend of my father's. It was he who had stored some of the paintings in his cellars. According to Gerard, one day a truckload of German soldiers came and took the paintings away at gunpoint. That was in the winter of 1942. They had papers which described all of the paintings he was storing, and they knew where to look.'

'But how could that be?'

'We all believed that one of the employees at my father's gallery in Paris had alerted the Nazis about the whereabouts of the paintings which my father had removed. Not everyone was as loyal as Jacques and Phyllis, and Alain Brescon.'

'So it was an act of plunder by the Nazis,' Laura stated.

'It was. Just as they confiscated the Westheim Collection, so they looted the art of Maurice Duval.'

'You read about the Westheim Collection in the *New York Times* when I had the press conference,' Laura remarked.

Rosa inclined her head. 'I did, and I found it fascinating. But at least Sir Maxim has a *catalogue raisonné*. I don't have anything quite so comprehensive, just one record book and a couple of inventories, which Jacques managed to retrieve from my parents' apartment in Bordeaux before we started to move around.'

'And not everything was listed?'

'No. Only about thirty paintings. Jacques couldn't find the other record books and additional inventories,' Rosa explained. 'Maybe my father had hidden them somewhere in the apartment for safety, or maybe they were taken when my family was arrested. It is hard to know exactly what happened to them.'

'But at least you have the details of about thirty paintings. Are they good paintings?'

'A Van Gogh, several Cézannes. Two wonderful canvases by Matisse, and a number of paintings by Picasso, Braque and Marie Laurencin.'

'Oh my God, they're worth a fortune!' Laura exclaimed.

'I am sure of that. But their whereabouts are unknown. I believe they are lost forever, as are all the others. I am certain they were sent to Germany during the war. As you know very well, Göring was looting art for himself and for Hitler. Many private collections similar to the Westheim Collection were taken in Germany, France and other countries. The private collections of the Rothschilds, Paul Rosenberg, the Bernheim-Jeunes and the David-Weills were confiscated in France, as well as the collection of Maurice Duval.'

A small silence descended on the room.

Rosa sat back and looked off into the distance; a sorrowful expression settled on her face. 'My father's great collection is lost to us. I shall never see those paintings again. Who knows on whose walls they are hanging.' There was a small pause, before Rosa ended quietly, 'It would please me to get just one back. It would be like retrieving part of my father, a piece of his soul. And a piece of my family's soul.'

'Are you still annoyed with me?' Megan asked as Laura followed her down the corridor to her bedroom.

'What do you mean, Gran?'

'When we arrived at Rosa's you were put out with me. I don't think you liked my surprise. In fact, I thought you were annoyed.'

'I was startled more than anything else,' Laura replied.

Megan made no comment until they had entered her bedroom, and then she murmured, 'I thought you felt you shouldn't be at Rosa's because of Claire.'

'I guess so, Gran, but I'm glad you arranged the dinner after all. Meeting her was a revelation.'

'I thought it would be.'

'I fully expected her to say something about Claire though.'

'I think she's afraid to, Laura dear. She knows how close you two are, and I believe she was being careful. She didn't want to offend you in any way.'

'I see. But she didn't mention Natasha either,' Laura said.

'For the same reason. She very badly wants to see Natasha, to get to know her better, eventually. And from what she's told me, she wants to see Claire too. But, I happen to know that Rosa is afraid of being rejected,' Megan finished.

Laura was silent as she helped her grandmother to get undressed. It was not until Megan was settled in bed that Laura said, 'There's something I don't understand, Gran.'

'What's that, child?'

'Claire's attitude towards Rosa. In the past I mean. How could anyone feel ill will towards Rosa Lavillard in view of what she's been through?'

Megan shook her head but said nothing.

'Surely Claire must know Rosa's story . . . Philippe would have told her, even if Rosa didn't reveal it herself. Oh, I've just remembered something. Years ago, Claire told me that Rosa had grown up alone in France, that her parents had been killed in the bombings, which I now know is wrong. So perhaps she didn't know the truth.'

'I think she did, Laura,' Megan responded. 'But she probably didn't want to discuss it with anyone. I can't imagine why, but there it is.'

'She told me Rosa was crazy, and that she'd been hospitalized.' Laura frowned. 'Do you know if that's true, Gran? The hospital part?'

Megan said: 'It's true, Rosa was in hospital several times. She was treated for depression. But that's understandable, wouldn't you say, in view of her past? Who wouldn't be depressed, knowing your entire family had perished in Auschwitz? But crazy, no, no.' Megan shook her head vehemently. 'Perhaps Claire misunderstood something Philippe confided. Or Pierre. Rosa and Pierre had a good marriage, but volatile at times, and Claire might have misunderstood him, misunderstood a comment Pierre made. In any case, Laura, Rosa wants to see Claire when she comes here later this month.'

'I hope Claire will see her.' Laura frowned, shook her head. 'I don't know . . .'

'You must arrange it, darling. It's important to Rosa, and it will be important to Claire. You see, Rosa wants to apologize.'

Laura stared at Megan, looking surprised. 'Apologize for what?'

'For always being cold to her, in the beginning, when Philippe and Claire first met. And then later, after they were married. Rosa confided recently that she never liked Claire, that she thought she was totally wrong for Philippe.'

'I told you she was possessive of him,' Laura interjected.

'Protective is a better word,' Megan answered. 'Rosa knew that Claire would not be able to handle Philippe, because he was the child of a Holocaust survivor. That he had his own problems to contend with because of Rosa's history, and Claire would never understand him. But now she feels she should have been warmer, should have tried to like her, even though she knew the marriage was doomed.'

'How could she know that?'

Megan shrugged. 'She says she did. It would be helpful if you could get Claire to see Rosa. I should tell you that she's devastated Claire is so desperately ill.'

When Laura was silent, Megan pressed, 'Promise me you'll try it, darling. It's important for the future, for Natasha's future. She ought to know her grandmother . . . Rosa's the only grandmother she's got.'

Laura went and sat on the edge of the bed. Leaning forward, she kissed Megan on the cheek and said, 'I promise, Gran. I think you're right, Natasha needs a grandmother just as Rosa needs a granddaughter. And Rosa and Claire should make their peace.'

25

Laura worked quietly at her desk in the solarium at Rhondda Fach. She was perusing letters and catalogues about art for sale in England and Europe, as well as in the United States, and making copious notes on a yellow pad.

From time to time she glanced up and looked across at Claire, who was resting on the big overstuffed sofa and had fallen asleep. Laura stood up and walked across the room, wanting to check on Claire but moving softly so as not to awaken her.

It was a hot morning in the middle of July and brilliant sunlight streaked through the many windows. It highlighted Claire's auburn wig, turning it into a fiery halo of curls around her narrow face. Her cheeks were slightly flushed, and in repose she looked better than she had in days. Underneath that wig there was a stubble of hair growing, spiky and still thin, but new hair nonetheless, and it was her natural red. Another good sign, at least according to Claire.

Being here at the farm had worked wonders for her; she had seemed to acquire more energy, both mentally and physically, and Laura was suddenly hopeful once again. Perhaps her dearest friend would make it after all. Maybe she would be one of the lucky ones, like Alison's sister Diane.

Claire and Natasha had arrived three weeks ago, in plenty of time for the Fourth of July picnic which Megan had traditionally given for years; and how they had enjoyed it.

Megan had wanted Rosa Lavillard to come for the picnic and to spend the weekend at Rhondda Fach. Laura had balked at this suggestion, explaining to her grandmother that it was too soon.

Laura knew that Claire wasn't up to it yet, even though she had been settled in at the farm for over a week. 'Not yet, Gran, let's give her a chance to get on her feet, to acclimatize herself.' Megan had immediately agreed that Laura was right; and so she had come up to Connecticut alone.

Laura was relieved that Claire had finally made the decision to come back to New York to live. She had resigned from her job at the magazine in Paris and put her apartment on the market. Hercule was supervising the crating and shipping of her furniture and all of her other possessions. He was constantly in New York because of his decorating and design assignments, and he had accepted Laura's invitation to come and stay at the farm whenever he wished. 'I can't wait to be with you all, with my darling Claire,' he had said to Laura only the other day, and she was now expecting him this coming weekend. Just like Laura, Hercule was trying to be optimistic about Claire's eventual recovery, and he was encouraged by Laura's reports of the improvement in her.

Laura had told Claire she should have the furniture shipped to the farm where it could be stored in one of the outbuildings; she had also offered her an old barn as a weekend home. 'Convert it into a studio for Natasha and yourself,' Laura had said. Claire had leapt at the idea, and in the moments when she had the strength she was creating designs. 'It'll be a place of your own in the place you've always loved the best,' Laura had said encouragingly, praying that the highly aggressive chemotherapy was working. Claire had been thrilled at the idea of remodelling one of the red barns. She saw it as a project for the future.

Natasha had settled in comfortably and quickly, much to

Laura's relief, and Claire's as well. She would be fifteen in a few weeks. Thankfully, she loved the farm and had adapted with ease to the country environment. Next week she would take the entrance exam for the Chapin School on East End Avenue. Laura was confident she would pass and be accepted at the private high school, considered to be one of the best in Manhattan.

Of course Laura knew deep inside that Claire's health was precarious, and that she might not go into remission, that she could die. But there was the slim chance that the heavy doses of chemo were working. She clung to this hope; they all did.

Unexpectedly Claire opened her eyes and stared at Laura. 'I knew you were standing there looking down at me.'

'Liar!' Laura exclaimed, laughing. 'You didn't know I was here. Not at all.'

'Oh yes I did, I can sniff your presence out even when I'm sleeping.'

Laura smiled and sat down on the low-slung Voltaire chair next to the sofa, pleased that Claire was revitalized after her nap and obviously in a bantering mood. 'Men came and went in our lives, but we were always there for each other,' she said.

Claire grinned. 'Bet your ass we were. We were steadfast when it came to each other . . . I'll always be there for you, Laura.'

'As I will for you, darling.'

'You've already proven that. And I know I couldn't have lived through the last few months without you. You've been my rock, my strength, Laura. You and Natasha. She's been so supportive, such a source of help and comfort to me.'

'She's been incredible. Now, what would you like to have for lunch?'

'I'm not really hungry,' Claire murmured, pushed herself up to a sitting position on the sofa and settled against the many cushions.

'There must be something you fancy?'

'Strawberries and cream! I'd love that. And maybe a piece of watermelon for dessert.'

Laura smiled, shook her dark head and sighed. 'My darling Claire, you're not going to build yourself up on a bit of fruit. But all right, it's a deal, providing you'll try and eat a little scrambled egg first.'

Claire nodded. 'Yes, I will, I'd like a taste of scrambled eggs with a slice of bread and butter.'

'That's the spirit. I'll have to go to Balsamos for the fruit. Do you mind if I leave you alone for a while?'

'No, I don't. Anyway, Natasha's somewhere around, isn't she?'

'She's gone riding with Tom's son. Lee has taken her up on the trails through the hills where we used to ride.'

Claire smiled. 'Those trails are so beautiful. Anyway, I'm enjoying resting here, relaxing. Could you lower some of the shades and turn the air conditioning up a bit, please, Laura? The sun's making it very warm in here.'

'Of course,' Laura said, and then bending over Claire she kissed her cheek and hurried out of the solarium, glancing at her watch as she did. It would take her a good half hour, maybe a bit longer, to drive to Balsamos, but the trip was worth it. They had the best produce in the area.

Claire drifted, half dozing, and slowly she tumbled down into herself. Thoughts of the past intruded, memories flooded her mind. Mostly they were happy memories of her younger days, spent here with Laura and the Valiants. At one moment bad memories began to insinuate themselves, but she pushed them away. She wanted to recall only the good times. They filled her with joy . . . remembrances of her childhood and those growing up years . . . spent here at Rhondda Fach . . . All the seasons of the year . . . She had loved them all . . .

Winter days of icy skies and crystal light. Snowflakes blowing in the wind. Icicles dripping from the trees. Cool sunlight on snowdrifts taller than a man. Stalwart horses carrying them up through the trails. Up into the hills high above the valley. The green swathe of spring and summer gone. The splashy red-gold of autumn obliterated. A great spread of white and crystal far below. Stillness. A silent landscape.

The crunch of hooves on powdered snow. The bray of horses. Laura's laughter tinkling in the air. Her own voice echoing back to her. Cooee! Cooee! Calling to the Harrison boys waiting at the top. Geoffrey. Hal. Tall in the saddle astride stallions gleaming dark in the sun. Boyish laughter. Fumbled hugs under the trees. Tender kisses. Shy looks and pounding hearts. Young love blooming under icy skies.

Sultry summer nights. Diamond stars. A sheltering sky like black velvet. Hal's mouth on hers. His gentle hands touching, stroking, learning her. Hands insistent, greedy. Hot breath against her cheek. Strangled cries lodged in her throat . . .

'Mom, Mom, are you all right?' Natasha asked, her voice tight with concern as she peered at Claire on the sofa.

Slowly Claire's eyes opened, focused on her daughter, and on her worried expression. 'I must have dozed off. I was dreaming. Or remembering. Or both.'

'You cried out,' Natasha explained. 'I was studying over there at the desk. Are you sure you don't need anything?'

'I'm fine.' Claire smiled at her daughter. 'I was back here when I was young, when I was your age, darling. Remembering things.'

'What things?' Natasha asked, sitting down in the chair, taking hold of her mother's hand, stroking it.

'I guess I was remembering my first boyfriend, my first love.' Claire shook her head and smiled again. 'So long ago.'

'What was his name?'

'Hal. Harold Harrison. He and his brother Geoffrey lived on the other side of the hills above the valley. They used to ride up to meet us at the top, in the woods up there. His brother Geoffrey was Laura's boyfriend. We often rode up the trails where you've been this morning with Lee.'

'It's so beautiful up there, Mom. *Awesome.* I know why you've always loved Rhondda Fach. I didn't before . . . I guess I was too young to appreciate it, to understand. Now I love it too.'

'I'm glad you do, darling. It's a special place. How's your studying coming along? For the exam?'

'Okay. Laura's been helping me. Do you want me to get you some apple juice?'

Claire shook her head. 'I'll wait until lunch.'

'Mom?'

'Yes, Natasha?'

'I want to ask you something . . . about Dad.'

'What about him?'

'He wants to come and see you, Mom.'

Claire frowned. Her eyes narrowed slightly. 'How do you know that? Stupid question. I guess he's spoken to you on the phone.'

Natasha nodded. 'He's worried about you, Mom. Very concerned. He asked me to call him back at the Center in Atlanta. To tell him if you agree, and let him know when he can come.'

Claire was silent. 'I have to think about it.'

'But he *can* visit us, can't he, Mom?' Natasha asked, biting her lip. 'He wants to so badly.' When Claire was silent, Natasha said, 'And I want him to come, Mom. It's important to me, too.'

'Why?'

'Because I'd like it . . . I'd like you to be friends. You and Dad. You will let him come, won't you?'

'I suppose so, since you seem to wish it so badly. Let me work out a date with Laura. Maybe after your exam next week? How does that sound?'

'It's good, Mom.' Natasha's young face brightened. She would call her father later to tell him her mother had agreed he could visit, but they had yet to settle on a date. She knew he would be pleased. He was extremely troubled about her mother's illness.

Claire said, 'Laura's gone to Balsamos.'

'I know. She left me a note. And then I ran into Fenice in the kitchen. She said I'd have to cook lunch, because Laura can't even boil an egg properly. As if I didn't know.'

Laughing, Claire said, 'Poor Laura, she does get teased about her lack of culinary skills. But why can't Fenice prepare the scrambled eggs?'

'She says she has to go shopping, but actually she did say later that she'd make the eggs if I want.'

'It's up to you, Nattie.'

'Oh, I can do it, Mom, there's nothing much to making a bunch of eggs in a pan.' There was a small silence before Natasha said in a low, tentative voice, 'Do you think the chemotherapy has worked, Mom?'

'I do, my angel. I'm convinced of it; I'm feeling so much better. I want to go into New York next week, to do some shopping. I hanker after Bergdorf Goodman's, it was always my favourite store when I lived here. And I'd like to go to Serendipity too, for a hamburger with French fries, and a banana split. With you and Laura. Grandma Megan says she wants to come too.'

Natasha smiled at her mother. 'I love Grandma Megan. She's . . . *awesome*, Mom.'

'She surely is, darling, and she always was. Later, I'm going to ask Laura to get out Megan's photograph albums and clippings books. From the time Megan was a Broadway star. She was so famous, and totally gorgeous, Nattie. We'll play some of her old records, too. You'll get a kick out of them. Grandpa Owen used to say she had a bell in every tooth.'

Natasha grinned. 'What a funny expression.'

'It's very Welsh. And she did have the most sensational voice.'

'When I start going to school in New York in the autumn, will you be living in the city with Laura as well?' Natasha now asked, her eyes on her mother. 'I want you to be there with us, Momma.'

'I will be, part of the time. I'll be having chemo at Sloan-Kettering. But it's very comfortable for me out here, and Laura thought I might prefer to spend as much time as possible at Rhondda Fach. You'd both come at weekends, to be with me. And Megan would come too.'

'But who'd look after you, Mom?'

'Fenice. She's happy to live here full time, as she used to when Megan came up all year round. In any case, her cottage is only on the other side of the meadow. Fenice'll look after me very well.'

'I certainly will,' Fenice said, gliding into the solarium carrying a large tray. She was a tall, well-built woman, with salt-and-pepper, faded red hair and angular features. Now in her early fifties, Fenice Walton had worked at Rhondda Fach since she was sixteen. She had always idolized Megan, and she loved Laura and Claire like a surrogate mother, had bossed them around for years. Prone to bohemian clothes that often resembled theatrical costumes, Fenice was wearing a colourful cotton skirt that fell almost to her ankles, a fancy white blouse with big puffy sleeves and a huge starched white apron that was obviously Victorian. White ankle socks and red sneakers completed the outfit.

'I've brought iced tea for you, Claire. I know you love it. I found your favourite yesterday at the market. *Honey peach.* And for you, Natasha, I've squeezed fresh grapefruit.' As she spoke, Fenice placed the laden tray on the coffee table in front of the sofa. 'There's some chocolate chip cookies, too. Just out of the oven. And as soon as Laura gets back I'll be fixin' the eggs and the bread. Can't have you starvin', now can we?'

'Oh don't worry, Fenice, you're too busy to do the eggs. I can manage!' Natasha exclaimed. 'I'm a good cook.'

'Get on with you, it's no trouble for me. Stay with your Momma, keep her company.'

'Thank you, Fenice,' Claire said.

Fenice beamed at them both, swung around on her heels and went marching out, looking very much like a woman totally in command of her domain.

Watching her go, Natasha asked, 'Has Fenice ever been married?'

'Oh, no, she's married to Rhondda Fach,' Claire explained. 'At least, that's what Laura and I think. She never got too involved with a man, because she didn't want to leave the valley and this house.'

'And those who live in it, I guess,' Natasha added, sounding much wiser than her years.

Laura was pleased.

She sat opposite Claire in the small dining room watching her eat a plate of scrambled eggs along with a slice of Fenice's freshly-baked bread spread with butter.

'The strawberries look delicious,' Laura volunteered. 'Big and luscious, Claire, and Fenice has whipped up some cream. It's a real treat.'

'I can't wait,' Natasha said, then turning to Laura, she confided, 'Mom says Dad can come and see her. He wants to very much. It's just a question of the right date. Mom said perhaps he could visit after my entrance exam for Chapin. What do you think, Laura?'

'It would be fine,' Laura murmured, and glanced at Claire quizzically. She was suddenly curious about this new development.

'I agreed, Laura.' Claire then explained, 'Natasha told me her father's upset about my illness. And *she* wants him to visit me here as much as *he* wants to come. Whenever you say, Laura. It's your call.'

'Hercule will be here this coming weekend. He could come then.'

'Or during the week,' Claire suggested. 'I don't think Philippe would expect to stay overnight.'

'But maybe –' Natasha began, and stopped when she saw the startled look on her mother's face.

Changing the subject, Claire now said, 'I dozed off when you were out buying the strawberries, Laura. So many memories came rushing back. Do you remember when we painted Dylan gold?'

'Oh my God! How could I ever forget!' Laura cried, shaking her head and laughing. 'Did we get it from Grandma Megan!' Sobering, she added, 'But seriously, we really could have hurt him, you know. I tremble whenever I think about it now.'

'You didn't really paint him gold, did you?' Natasha asked, putting her fork down, looking first at Laura and then at her mother in amazement. 'It's very dangerous. The pores can't breathe through paint, you know.'

'Exactly.' Laura grimaced. 'We were well and truly punished.'

'But why did you paint him gold?' Natasha pressed.

'We were doing a little play, for Grandpa Owen and Grandma Megan. Very short, only two scenes, about Antony and Cleopatra. Dylan was the most beautiful little boy and we decided to make him into a golden idol,' Laura explained. 'And your mother knew enough, even if I didn't, not to paint every part of him. So we fashioned a mask for his face out of cardboard painted gold, and we made him a pair of tiny briefs from a piece of gold lamé Fenice found in the ragbag here at the farm.'

Natasha began to laugh. 'I would have loved to have seen your tiny golden idol. I suppose he was adorable.'

'But sticky. The paint didn't dry very well,' Claire remarked, and then looking across at Laura, she added, 'and it was all your idea.'

'You always blamed me for everything,' Laura complained, grinning at her.

'Only when I thought I could get away with it,' Claire retorted, and began to chuckle.

26

'This is an extraordinary story, Laura,' Hercule Junot said, steepling his fingers, looking at her over the top of them. 'Rosa Lavillard is in the same position as Maxim . . . she's the heir to a great art collection she can't find.'

'*Exactly*. But I might find it for her,' Laura answered. 'Or rather, I might come across a painting or two in the course of my work. After all, an enormous amount of material comes across my desk, as you know, every day of the week. All I need is the right information from Rosa, so I know what to keep my eyes open for . . . names of artists . . . names of paintings.'

'I am quite certain she will be only too happy to give the information to you.'

'She is. She's had the record book and inventories copied, and I'm hoping she's going to give everything to me tomorrow, or on Sunday. You see, Grandma Megan wants her to come up for lunch on one of those days this weekend. And I –'

'But what about Claire, my dear? Won't she object?' he ventured, cutting in. 'You know that Rosa Lavillard is not a favourite of hers.'

'I do. But I'm planning on chatting to Claire about Rosa later today, if she's not too tired.'

'That would be good. Certainly it would be a relief if they

could be on cordial terms. I do loathe dissension of that kind. *Mon Dieu*, Laura! Would it not be wonderful if Natasha got to know her grandmother?'

'Yes, it would. Especially under the circumstances.'

Hercule gave her a worried look and asked swiftly, 'What *are* those circumstances? Please tell me the truth.'

'I would never lie to you, Hercule, surely you know that by now. Claire's about the same. No real improvement, but at least she's not worse. She's finished the course of chemotherapy treatments, and she doesn't have to go back to Memorial Sloan-Kettering Cancer Center for a few months, in the autumn, actually. But what pleases me is that she's been so much better since she's been here at Rhondda Fach.'

'That is good to know, yes,' Hercule murmured.

'I'm praying she's going to beat it, Hercule.'

'So am I.' He sighed and looked away, shading his eyes from the sun with his hand. After a moment, he brought his gaze back to Laura, and went on quietly, 'If I have any regret in my life, it is that I never told Claire how I felt about her, that I didn't ask her to marry me. What a fool I've been. And it has been such a waste of years. Years when I might have been able to make her happy. Perhaps I could have helped her to allay her pain, helped her rid herself of that terrible bitterness. Just to make her mental anguish disappear would have been rewarding.'

'Tell her now,' Laura said, leaning closer to him under the sun umbrella. She touched his arm affectionately, and smiled up into his face. 'Tell her how you've always loved her. You don't have to actually propose, but you could make her understand how much you care. I think it could only be a plus for her. And it may very well make *you* feel better, Hercule. I can guarantee this . . . she won't be angry. Claire's changed. Well, a little bit. Some of her fierce anger has evaporated, at least. *Tell her.*'

'Do you think I really should, Laura?' Hercule exclaimed, his eyes lighting up. 'I will do it, but only if you are certain I will not upset her.'

'Of course you won't. Any woman would be flattered to hear a declaration of love from a man like you, and it's something for her to look forward to . . . getting better, spending time with you.'

'Do you think she would want to do that?'

'It's possible, yes. I do know she cares a lot about you. She's told me so.'

He smiled broadly. 'I could give her a life of ease. We could travel, do anything she wants. I wouldn't expect her to marry me . . . as long as we are together, that is all that matters.'

'Then tell her that.'

Hercule nodded but made no further comment. He sat staring into the distance, his eyes fixed on the willows at the edge of the stream at the bottom of the garden.

He and Laura were sitting on the terrace having an aperitif before lunch on Friday. He had arrived at Rhondda Fach the night before and had been pleased to see Claire looking relaxed, so much more vital and energetic than he had expected.

He thought for a moment or two about Laura's advice, and then putting the matter of Claire to one side, he said: 'It will be a challenge for you . . . seeking Rosa's paintings.'

'Obviously I can't actually go out and look for them, because, like Sir Maxim, I wouldn't know where to even start looking. But if one of them should come onto the market, I'll be poised and at the ready . . . I can go after it.'

Hercule nodded.

Laura said: 'I want to do it for Rosa, but it's for Natasha as well. The art collection is her inheritance.'

'Lunch looks splendid, Fenice,' Megan remarked as she eyed the buffet which had been set up at one end of the dining room. 'You've outdone yourself today.'

'Thanks, Mrs V. But all I did was bake the rolls. Natasha made everything by herself. The salade niçoise, the quiche Lorraine and the caramel custard and raspberries for dessert. The girl's a wonder in the kitchen, a good little chef. My hat's off to her.'

'Thank you, Fenice,' Natasha said as she came into the dining room carrying a bottle of rosé. After putting it in the bucket of ice, she turned to Megan and said, 'Can I sit next to you, Grandma Megan?'

'Well of course you can, Natasha dear,' Megan replied, smiling at her. 'And my congratulations on this wonderful lunch.'

'Mom taught me everything about cooking. She's a much better chef than I am. But I'm striving to reach her level.'

'You will, if you're not there already, and I have a feeling you might be. Where is your mother, Natasha?'

'Hercule's bringing her in from the garden; she sat out there for a while. And Laura went upstairs to change her clothes. Oh, here they are now. At least, here's my mother with Hercule.'

Hercule and Claire came into the dining room together; Claire was well-groomed and looked pretty in a caftan made of amber-and-red printed cotton.

Megan said, 'Where do you wish to sit, dear?'

'Over there, with my back to the window, so the sun's not in my eyes,' Claire answered, and allowed Hercule to shepherd her to a chair solicitously.

Laura finally arrived dressed in a loose, white cotton tunic over narrow black pants and sporting black-rimmed sun glasses. 'It was blistering in the garden, Gran, I'm glad you stayed indoors.'

'Yes, she's right, it was far too hot for me,' Claire interjected.

'You'll soon cool off, Claire,' Megan assured her, and went on, 'you've made a fine little chef out of Natasha. This splendid lunch is all her creation.'

'Not the rolls,' Natasha was quick to point out. 'Fenice made the rolls.'

Everyone laughed at this comment, and then they served themselves the summer fare, except for Claire whose plate was prepared by Natasha. Hercule went around the table pouring the rosé and Laura filled their glasses with iced water.

It was halfway through the lunch that Claire said, 'I'm so happy we're all here together today. The people I love the most in the whole world are with me . . .' She paused, smiled at them.

'We all love *you*, Claire,' Megan said, and reached out and touched her hand affectionately.

'I want to thank you . . . all of you . . . for giving me such support, for helping me to cope with my cancer. For giving me the courage to keep fighting.'

Later that afternoon Claire walked slowly down the corridor to Laura's room, tapped on the door and went inside. 'You said you were going to work, I hope I'm not disturbing you,' Claire said, leaning against the door frame.

'Not at all, I was just looking through some of the art catalogues that came to the office this week. I'm not doing anything very pressing.'

'It's good of you to spend so much time out here with me, Laura. I worry that you're neglecting your work.'

'You know better than that, and in any case July and August are pretty slow months usually. Everyone's on holiday. Don't worry, Alison won't hesitate to give a yell if I'm needed at the office.'

Closing the door, Claire wandered into the room, sat down on the sofa facing Laura, who was perched on a chair behind her big French provincial desk.

Lifting her feet up onto the sofa, Claire gave Laura a penetrating look, and said, 'You advised Hercule to come right out and tell me that he loved me.'

'Yes, I did. Because it was nagging at him, and it has been since last December, probably even before that. I thought it would make him feel better, and you too, Claire. It's nice to know a truly wonderful man cares, isn't it?'

'It is. But there's no future for us.'

'Is that what you told him?'

'No, not in so many words. I sort of fudged it. I didn't want him to become upset.'

'What do you mean?'

'Laura, there is no future for me. So how can there be a future for me with Hercule?'

'But you're so much better!' Laura cried. 'Aren't you? Or are you acting?'

'No, I'm not acting. I do feel stronger than I have for ages, and I don't have much pain. But my days are numbered, whether it's weeks or months or even a year, and therefore I can't offer a man a life with me. *I don't have one to offer.*'

'Doug once said to me that we are all dying, that we die a little bit every day.'

'You're splitting hairs, Laura, and you know it.'

Ignoring this remark, Laura asked, 'Do you love him?'

'Yes, you know very well I do ... as a friend. He's always been perfectly wonderful to me, but I'm not in love with him, not as he is with me. Still, if I weren't so ill I'd probably give it a shot ... I mean I'd live with him, see how it worked out ...'

'Did you tell him this?' Laura asked.

'I told him I loved him, but perhaps in a different way than he loved me. And I said if I were in better health I would be honoured and flattered to be his permanent companion.'

Laura didn't say anything. She sat back in the chair and let her eyes wander around her bedroom. Its pale apple-green walls were gentle, a cool backdrop for the heavy white cotton draperies patterned with red roses, the antique French country furniture, the big bed dressed entirely in white, and the dark green carpet.

'It *is* a charming room,' Claire murmured, following her friend's gaze. 'I've always liked it and for as long as I can remember.'

'Most of your life and mine,' Laura whispered, and pushed down the sudden, incipient tears that threatened to spill.

'Laura?'

'Yes, Claire?'

'There's something ... something I've never told you,' Claire began and then suddenly stopped. She sat staring at Laura, the dearest person in the world to her except for her daughter, and wondered how to go on.

'What is that?'

'I should have told you long ago. Perhaps my life would have been different if I had.'

'You sound very serious,' Laura remarked, returning Claire's intense gaze. 'And what do you mean when you say your life might have been different?'

'Maybe it wouldn't have been so screwed up, and maybe I wouldn't have been so screwed up either, so angry, so bitter and resentful . . .'

Laura seemed baffled. Slowly she said, 'I'm not following you.'

'Do you remember how you sometimes found me here in your room, crying my heart out on that very bed, hugging a pillow?'

Laura nodded. 'You never would tell me what was wrong.'

'I was crying because I was sick at heart. And I was clinging to the pillow as if I were holding onto you. My Laura. You were the only thing I had in my life that was good and decent.'

'Tell me what happened to you, Claire. Tell me what this is all about.'

'It was my father . . .' Claire came to a halt. She stared at Laura. Her face had turned chalk white, and she was unable to continue.

Laura rose from behind the desk and went and sat with Claire on the sofa. Taking hold of her hand, she held it tightly in hers. 'Your father hurt you. Is that what you're trying to tell me?'

Claire could only nod.

'Oh darling, why ever didn't you say anything then? I could have helped you!' Laura exclaimed.

Shaking her head, Claire answered in a whisper, 'How could you have helped me? You were only a little girl, younger than I. My own mother couldn't help me.'

'Did she know?' Laura asked in a horrified voice.

'She tried to stop him!' Claire cried, anger surging through her. She tried to clamp down on it and continued in a calmer tone, 'My mother tried to protect me, to stop him. But he would beat her until she couldn't stand, and then he would turn back to me. He started when I was seven, hitting me, as well as touching me, kissing me. I resisted him as long as I could . . . but he became more and more insistent . . . finally I gave in to him. I had to. It was the only way to stop him from beating my mother. It was easier just to lie there and be silent than to get her involved and see her so badly hurt. Occasionally, I would fight him off. He really had it in for me after that. He would beat me until I couldn't move.'

'Oh God, how terrifying for you! You must have been frightened to death most of the time.'

'I was.

'He was foul, awful. I hated him.' Claire began to weep. Tears trickled down her face as she continued, 'But at least, once I gave in to him, he stopped hurting my mother.'

Laura put her arm around Claire and drew her closer, in an effort to soothe her. 'If only you'd confided in me and Grandma. We could have done something, I know we could.'

'I was afraid to tell you,' Claire gasped between her tears. 'I was embarrassed. Ashamed. It was so sordid. Sometimes I thought it must be my fault. I was torn up. I didn't know what to do. So I just concealed it, pushed it down inside, pretended it had never happened.' Claire began to sob uncontrollably, her body shaking as the dam of suppressed emotion finally burst inside her.

Laura held her closer, stroking her shoulders, saying gentle words of sympathy, giving Claire her love and compassion. Eventually, Claire managed to calm herself; gradually the tears ceased. She sat up, groped for a tissue in the pocket of her caftan, and wiped her eyes, striving for control.

Laura said: 'Your father . . . Well, Grandma Megan once insinuated that your father was a womanizer, and that this was the reason why your mother drank. But she was wrong, wasn't she? He was an abuser.'

'He was both, Laura. Please believe me, he was chasing after women all the time. It broke their marriage. And my mother's heart, I'll admit that. She found escape and solace in the bottle.'

'I'm so sorry,' Laura whispered. 'I'm so terribly sorry you had to go through that alone, Claire, when you were so young. It breaks my heart to think about it.'

'I wasn't alone, in a sense. Because I had you and Grandma Megan. And Grandpa Owen. You were my refuge. Just as this place was. Rhondda Fach was always my safe haven. I always felt secure, safe and loved when I was here with all of you.'

'When did . . . when did he stop?'

'When I was fifteen I told him I was going to tell your grandfather, and ask Grandma Megan to take me to a doctor for an examination. So that she'd know I was speaking the truth. I finally realized I needed words – not fists to stand up to him. He was scared of being exposed to the Valiants. It's a pity I hadn't understood that years ago, because it would have been a weapon I could have used.'

'I think so, and I wish it had been different for you. I can't believe I didn't detect something was truly wrong. I know you cried a great deal, but I thought you were unhappy and worried because your mother drank such a lot of vodka.'

'I was a good little actress, wasn't I?'

'That you were.'

'My father made me hate men, distrust them. He scarred me, and he ruined my life. I know I would have been a very different person if he hadn't abused me. Laura, I was only *seven* when he started . . .' Claire's voice broke, and she had to wait a moment or two before continuing: 'I am sure I would have trusted Philippe, been a better wife, if not for my father's abuse.'

Laura nodded. 'I agree with you.'

Claire now explained, 'Whenever Philippe had to go away

on a trip, to do research, or be in quarantine for his work, I always believed he was really with another woman. Like my father had been. My father was a *genuine* womanizer. Anyway, I was constantly suspicious of Philippe. I was resentful and bitter as well, and I made a lot of mistakes with my husband.' Claire let out a heavy sigh and shook her head sadly. 'I think that in many ways I treated Philippe unfairly. He's not a bad man.'

'Is that why you've agreed to let him come and see you on Sunday? Because you know that you were also at fault in the marriage, and that he never was entirely to blame.'

'Partially. But also because Natasha is so anxious for him to visit me. She longs for us to be friends. Lately I've come to understand that she loves her father.'

'Yes, I know that, Claire. She's conveyed the same to me.' Laura cleared her throat and gave Claire a long careful look. 'Do you still believe Philippe had a lot of women when he was married to you?'

Claire bit her lip, appeared chagrined all of a sudden. 'Perhaps not. I've examined my life a lot in the last couple of weeks, and I realize how very damaged I was as a person. How could I possibly think straight with my history?'

'Your father's behaviour was monstrous! He's responsible for all of the mental anguish you've had to contend with since you were a child.' Laura was angry.

'That's true. And he's responsible for my cancer.' Claire sat up straighter and looked directly into Laura's eyes. 'I mean that.'

'I know you do, and I tend to agree. You believe that your repression of all of this for so many years left you vulnerable to cancer.'

'His acts were reprehensible. The only way I could go on living was to bury them deep inside myself. But nevertheless they still gnawed at me, destroyed me, turned me into an angry, distrustful woman. I was ravaged by a bitterness I couldn't rid myself of. At one point I was really consumed by the memories, but I managed to keep going, somehow. I thought when he died

I'd feel differently, feel better, but I didn't. And the memories just ate at my innards . . . like a cancer.'

'It has been medically proven that mental and emotional stress, plus repression of strong emotional pain can cause all types of illnesses in people. So I'm with you on that, Claire.'

'I feel a sense of relief at last, now that I've confided these things. Perhaps I might start healing . . . and in many ways.'

'I hope so. Didn't you ever tell *anyone* about your father? Not even Philippe?'

Claire shuddered. 'Oh God, no. How could I have told anyone else except you? You're the closest person to me, and look how long it's taken me to speak about it to you.'

'If only you'd unburdened yourself sooner.'

'I should have.'

Laura said, 'You look drained. Would you like a cup of tea?'

'Thanks, that'd be nice,' Claire replied, and forced a smile.

It was true, she did feel very tired, sapped of all energy. And so Claire went and lay down on Laura's bed, nestling herself in amongst the mounds of white pillows. How often she had done this as a child. Waiting for Laura, as she waited for her now, breathing in the smell of her shampoo, the scent of her perfume. Ma Griffe. Laura had worn it for years; a fresh, green smell, that was the way Claire thought of it.

She had always longed to be part of the Valiants, for as long as she could remember, part of that wonderful family and all the love that spilled out of them. Thankfully, they had taken her in, transformed her into one of theirs, and miraculously they had made her forget her father and what he did to her when she was at home. For a short while, when she was with them, she was a different person. And it was Laura who made her feel clean again, just like Laura was herself. Pure. Innocent. Untouched. A good girl.

Claire curled up in a ball in the middle of the bed and closed her eyes for a moment or two. Her thoughts ran amok; but she managed to rein them in, take control of them again. She could not dwell on the past. She had to think of the present and the future. She knew she did not have much longer to live. She was dying.

She kept up the façade, going along with Laura and everyone else, agreeing that she had improved in health. It was true that she had been revitalized here at Rhondda Fach, that she had more energy all of a sudden. But she wasn't getting better. The chemotherapy hadn't worked. The doctors had told her that, confirmed what she already knew herself.

All of the things she had to do had been done. The only outstanding matter was the sale of the apartment in Paris. But Hercule would take care of that and transfer the money to Laura who would put it in the trust account they had opened for Natasha. Her thoughts turned to her daughter. The miracle of her life. Her joy. Claire smiled, feeling warm inside thinking of Natasha. She had gone out for a drive with Megan and Fenice. Actually, they had gone shopping; Natasha was planning a special dinner for tonight.

Claire took a deep breath, feeling unexpectedly dizzy. She closed her eyes once again. After a few minutes she saw her daughter's face in her mind's eye, so fresh, so young, a beautiful girl with her whole future ahead of her. Claire was thankful Natasha had Laura to guide her, to look after her in the years ahead. I can die in peace because of my true blue Laura.

Natasha had been very brave and courageous so far. When Claire had told her that she had made Laura her legal guardian there had been no problem. Natasha had said she understood. But later, from the things she had said, Claire realized there was a good rapport between the girl and her father. And so she had finally given in and said Philippe could visit. He was coming to see them the day after tomorrow. Somehow, she would get through it.

Hercule had told her that Rosa Lavillard had asked to see her. To apologize, that was the way he had put it.

Hercule believed it was important for Natasha to get to know her grandmother, and Claire wondered if he was right about that. In the end it would be up to Laura's discretion, though. After all, she was going to be in control. Just the way I wanted it, Claire thought to herself, and she pushed herself up on the bed as Laura came bustling in with the tea tray.

'Two mugs of Grandpa Owen's famous miner's tea!' she cried. 'Hot and strong and sweet. And slices of chocolate cake, courtesy of Natasha. She made it this morning for you.'

'It's my favourite,' Claire said, smiling. 'And so is this tea.' As she spoke she made an effort to get off the bed.

'Stay there, Claire,' Laura instructed and hurried across the floor. She placed the mug of tea on the bedside table, along with a plate of cake, and then arranged the many pillows behind Claire. 'There, that's much more comfortable, isn't it?'

'Yes, thanks, darling.' Claire took a sip of the tea, and continued, 'Hercule told me about Rosa's request. Why does she want to see me?'

'She's devastated about your illness, and she wants to come here and tell you how sorry she is that she wasn't a good mother-in-law to you.'

'So Hercule was right. I tended not to believe him, Laura. So, she's coming to apologize. Is that it?'

'Yes. Hercule was just repeating what I'd told him.'

'Could she come with Philippe this Sunday? I think I'd like to get them out of the way at the same time, if you know what I mean.'

'I do. And all right, I'll arrange it, if you're up to it on Sunday.'

'I am.'

'Then I'll have Grandma Megan phone her later.'

'They should drive up together,' Claire murmured, 'that would be best.'

Laura stared at her. 'You've certainly agreed very readily.'

Claire nodded. 'I've had a sudden change of heart.' She smiled faintly. 'I'm doing it for Natasha. That's what this is all about really. And also for you, Laura. If I don't get through this bout with cancer, you'll appreciate having them around. And so will Natasha, of course. They'll be supportive.'

'That's exactly what Grandma Megan said to me.'

'She's a wise woman, and she knows the way of the world. She's certainly got everybody's number . . . that's why I believe her theory about Doug.'

'I didn't know she had a theory,' Laura exclaimed, looking startled.

'She says she told you.'

'She never did. When did she do *that*? Did she say?'

'Yes, she told me she mentioned it to you when you first broke up. She said she suggested to you that there must be someone else, another woman, and that was the reason he was being so obliging about the apartment, and the other financial matters.'

'It's true, she did say that,' Laura muttered, remembering, and went and sat on the edge of the bed. 'Doug does have someone else, Claire.'

'Did he tell you finally?'

'I'm afraid so.'

'Who is she?'

'Actually, it's Robin Knox.'

Claire was silent for a moment, a thoughtful expression crossing her face, and then she asked, 'Are you sure?'

'I'm positive. And Robin's fiancée broke off her engagement to him . . .' Laura's voice trailed off. 'Doug is Doug, and a law unto himself. In any case, we're not married any longer, so what he does is his business. I gave him my blessing when we split up, and he knows I'm always there for him if he needs me. Just as he's there for me. That's the way we feel about each other, Claire. We're good friends.'

'I know you are,' Claire said. 'And it's better it happened now, that you ended your marriage when you did. You're still young enough to start a new life with another man.'

'I don't know about that,' Laura said softly.

'You will, Laura, trust me, and in the not too distant future.'

Laura threw her an odd look but refrained from answering.

27

Rosa Lavillard sat very still in the chair near the bed, looking at Claire, wishing she were not so ill, wishing *she* could do something about making her feel better. But she knew she couldn't; neither could Philippe, even though he was a brilliant doctor. Such a pity, Rosa thought. So young. *She's so young.* Her heart filled with compassion, and it took all of her self-control not to start weeping for Claire.

Suddenly Claire opened her eyes, and smiled faintly at Rosa. 'I'm sorry, I didn't mean to fade on you a moment ago.'

'Can I get you anything?' Rosa asked in a worried tone.

'No, thanks,' Claire murmured.

Taking a deep breath, Rosa said, 'I was wrong, Claire, all those years ago. Very wrong to behave the way I did towards you. I should have tried to understand you, tried to get to know you better, before I made any judgements about you.'

Claire blinked and shook her head. 'Whatever your judgement was, it was more than likely correct. I was a very troubled young woman in those days.'

'I didn't give you a chance, and that was unfair. I was being protective of Philippe. You see, I thought you wouldn't understand the complexity of his nature, wouldn't understand his background as the child of a Holocaust survivor.'

'I did love him a lot.'

'As he loved you, Claire. However, you were both volatile, just as Pierre and I were, and volatile marriages don't augur well for the future. Not usually. Somehow mine lasted. But your stormy relationship was something else which troubled me. Going back to the beginning of your courtship, I realize that I wasn't nice to you, merely civil and nothing more. I should have known better, as a mature woman. I should have given you the benefit of the doubt.'

'I guess my marriage to Philippe wasn't meant to be. But at least the most glorious child came out of our union. A truly wondrous gift she's been, my darling Natasha.' Claire's green eyes shone brightly.

'From what everyone tells me she's very special, unique,' Rosa murmured. 'And she's a beautiful young woman. She looks older than her age in some ways.'

'They all do these days. You haven't seen much of her, or spent much time with her, but that's partly because you live in New York, Rosa, and she's lived in Paris most of her life. I'm . . . I'm so sorry you don't properly know your only grandchild.'

Rosa inclined her head, but she didn't respond, simply leaned back in the chair and tried to relax a little. She had wanted this meeting, but she had also been apprehensive about it.

'Natasha's going to be living with Laura in the city, going to the Chapin School,' Claire volunteered.

'That's near me!' Rosa exclaimed, unable to conceal her sudden excitement.

'I know. What I was going to say is that I want the two of you to get to know each other. It's about time, too. I've told Laura she must arrange it in the autumn.'

'I would love to spend time with her, Claire, and with you too. I want to repair the damage. Do you think there's a chance we can be friends?'

When Claire didn't reply, Rosa continued, 'I apologize to you, Claire, with all my heart. I did a terrible thing all those years ago, and I've regretted it for the longest time. Can you see it in your heart to forgive me?'

'There's nothing to forgive. We were all wrong in our different ways.' Claire closed her eyes for a moment, settled against the pillows. A second or two later she opened them and looked at Rosa intently. She said, 'What did you mean when you said you thought I wouldn't understand Philippe's problems?'

'He is the child of a Holocaust survivor, as you know, Claire.' Rosa paused, shook her head as if reproving herself, and went on, 'That was another stupid thing on my part, I should have told you about my life during the war. Since you didn't know much, it was virtually impossible for you to understand anything about me. Anyway, Philippe, like many similar children, has had a hard time coming to grips with what happened to me and to my family when I was a child. He thought he was somehow an insignificant part of my life, nothing of any great consequence in view of the *enormity* of the Holocaust. That horrendous catastrophe somehow manages to overshadow and overwhelm our children. Some children of survivors are even oddly jealous of their parents because they know they will never experience anything so immense as the Holocaust.'

Claire was frowning when she said, 'I don't think Philippe is the kind of man to feel that.'

Rosa nodded in agreement. 'He didn't, and doesn't. What was problematical was the absence of a family, of a family past, and of a family history and inheritance. I know he definitely had feelings about all that. You see, the common element that binds together all of the children of survivors is this unnatural disruption of family history . . . because of that catastrophic occurrence which wiped out so many people.'

'I can understand that, and Philippe *was* odd in certain ways, I agree. He was an angry young man in those days.'

'That is the truth, Claire.'

'He did feel he must do something worthwhile, something for humanity like saving lives.'

'That was always the driving force in his life.'

'Is he still troubled, Rosa?'

'I think perhaps he always will be, but he's learned to live with my past as well as his own life. Just as Pierre did. He and his family were in Switzerland when war broke out in France, and they remained there for the duration. So thank God my husband didn't personally suffer, although his family did. They, too, had many losses. Philippe has learned to control the anger and the despair. He's a good man, a worthwhile man, and I think he is at peace with himself.'

'I hope so,' Claire whispered.

'Are you all right?' Rosa asked, leaning forward, a concerned expression ringing her mouth.

'Yes, I'm all right. Just catching my breath.'

They sat in silence for a while, and when Claire finally opened her eyes again and looked at Rosa, the older woman said, 'Claire, please forgive me, won't you?'

'I forgive you, Rosa. I know you want to hear that, but truly, there's nothing to forgive.'

'Oh, but there is,' Rosa insisted.

Claire reached out, groped for Rosa's hand. 'Grandma Megan told me your story recently, she told me about the hole . . . where they hid you . . . she told me about the things that happened to you. However did you survive?'

'I'm not sure. I often ask myself that. Willpower, determination, the desire to conquer, not to be beaten by the Nazis. Just wanting to live, I suppose.'

'Why didn't you tell me years ago? Why didn't Philippe tell me?'

'I don't know . . . except that once a woman I met said she was sick of the professional Jews who were always showing their numbers . . . the numbers tattooed on their arms when they were in the death camps. Her words stunned me, and I never ever spoke of my past to anyone again. Not that I'd discussed it much at all, but that woman had diminished in the most dreadful and derisive way the suffering of so many . . . millions.'

'I understand,' Claire said, shifting her position in the bed and leaning on her side. 'Rosa?'

'Yes, Claire?'

'Will *you* forgive *me* . . . for keeping your granddaughter away from you?'

'Of course, of course,' Rosa said swiftly, and added, 'but as *you* just said, there's nothing to forgive.'

Claire beckoned with one finger for Rosa to come closer. 'Come and sit on the edge of the bed,' she murmured softly.

Rosa did so; her eyes did not leave Claire's face.

Claire whispered, 'I'm not going to make it,' and took hold of Rosa's arm. 'I'm dying.'

'No, don't say that, Claire!' Tears filled Rosa's eyes; she blinked them away. 'I know you're very sick, but Laura said you'd *improved.*'

'Yes, I did for a while, here at Rhondda Fach. But I can't last much longer, I can't fight any more, Rosa, I'm tired.'

'Oh my poor Claire,' Rosa said and the tears fell from her eyes and splashed down onto her hands holding Claire's.

'Don't cry,' Claire murmured. 'I'll be all right where I'm going . . . it's just that I'll miss Natasha and Grandma Megan and my darling Laura.'

Rosa was unable to speak. She sat on the edge of the bed, holding Claire's hand for the longest time. Finally she bent forward, put her arms around Claire and held her close, just as she had held her son when he was a small boy. And they stayed like that for a long time.

Eventually the two women drew apart and Claire said, 'Don't say anything to the others, will you?'

'No, I won't,' Rosa said and thought: Laura knows, even if everyone else is deluded. She knows but she's keeping up a front for Natasha.

Rosa shifted slightly on the bed and started to get up, when

Claire opened her eyes. 'Don't go, please. Stay for a few minutes longer. I need to gather my strength before I see Philippe.'

Rosa nodded. 'All right. Do you want me to get anything for you, Claire? A glass of juice perhaps?'

'No, thanks. I just need you to stay with me, Rosa.'

Philippe Lavillard sat with Laura in the solarium, drinking a tomato juice and chatting to her. They were alone. He and his mother had arrived at Rhondda Fach an hour ago only to find that Natasha was out with Fenice and Hercule Junot.

Now he said to Laura, with a faint smile, 'They must be buying an awful lot of groceries, it's taking them so long.'

Laura explained, 'It's about half an hour to Balsamos, the best produce stand in the area, and half an hour back, and they did have to go into Kent to pick up other stuff. But they'll be here soon. Don't worry.'

Philippe nodded. 'It's just that I'm anxious to see Natasha . . .' He looked at Laura more intently, and said in a warm voice, 'I haven't thanked you, Laura, for all that you've done for Natasha, and *will* be doing. I'm very grateful.'

'She's a wonderful girl. Certainly she makes it easy for us all to love her. She adores Grandma Megan, they've got quite a little thing going between them. Anyway, we're just happy to have her around. Natasha's got such spirit and warmth, a *joie de vivre* that's infectious. She's always willing to pitch in and help, and she has a great sense of responsibility; she's actually very grown up for her age.'

'Yes, she is, but then I think a lot of European children are. They just seem to mature at an early age. Natasha's been brought up in a single-parent family environment, and that's more than likely made her independent and capable. Anyway, you know what Claire's like . . . she's always treated Natasha as an adult, and expected her to behave like one.'

'I know,' Laura said, and laughed. 'Natasha's always had to stand up and be counted on. By the way, I'm glad you agree with us about sending her to Chapin. Claire selected the school, and I just hope Natasha gets in.'

'I'm fairly certain she will,' Philippe answered. 'Natasha likes school, and that makes her a good student. She seems to be diligent and hard-working.'

'She is.' Laura sipped her apple juice, and then went on, 'Do you like living in Atlanta?'

'Yes, I do, although if I had the choice I'd be in New York. There's no place like one's hometown. But aside from that, New York's such a great city, I get a hell of a kick out of it.'

'I guess you don't miss Africa,' Laura remarked looking at him questioningly.

'Not at all.' He grimaced. 'If I lived to be a hundred I won't miss the sickness and disease, the grinding poverty, the cruelty of the politicians, the barbarity of the soldiers. Nor will I miss the droughts, the famine, the violent wars, the wholesale death and destruction on an unimaginable level.'

'I asked a stupid question,' Laura muttered, looking embarrassed. Suddenly, she felt a bit foolish.

'No, you didn't,' Philippe was quick to assure her, smiling warmly. 'Of course, Africa is beautiful, and the game parks are extraordinary, out of this world. In fact, there's something about being out there in the bush that simply takes my breath away. But I've had my fill of Africa . . . I just became burnt out, Laura. Utterly exhausted. I wasn't functioning properly anymore, and as I said to Francine, I'd better get out before I get sloppy and manage to infect myself with some deadly virus like Ebola or Marburg.'

'Who's Francine?' Laura asked, looking at him alertly.

'Francine Gillaume is a French socialite with a conscience. She's given a lot of money to some of my research programmes over the years. Almost all the time I worked under the auspices of the Pasteur Institute. And naturally she agreed with me, even though it meant I was off one of her pet projects.'

'Being a virologist is pretty dangerous. Hazardous work, isn't it?'

Philippe grinned at her. 'Only if you're sloppy, as I just mentioned. Getting burnt out, becoming over-exhausted, can easily be a death warrant.'

'Claire looks quite good. But she isn't, not really,' Laura said, suddenly changing the subject. 'I know she gave you permission to talk to her doctor at Sloan-Kettering. Did you?'

'Yes, I did. He says she's a real fighter, a tough one, and that she –' Philippe stopped as Natasha came rushing into the solarium, her face wreathed in smiles as she flew across the room to greet him.

Jumping up, Philippe met her halfway, enveloping her in his arms, hugging his daughter to him. Natasha clung to her father, her face buried in his shoulder.

He loves her very much, Laura thought. And what's more, she loves him. Laura suddenly asked herself why she had ever thought otherwise, and she had the answer to that immediately. How alike these two were in appearance. There was no doubt at all whose daughter she was. They were both tall, lean, athletic looking; Natasha had long legs like Philippe. And the shape of their faces was the same, as was the slant of their eyes. Natasha's were golden-amber; Philippe's were dark and full of compassion in his angular face.

Laura was seeing him differently. I'm seeing him as he really is today, she thought, not the way he was when he was young and tempestuous. But we were all different then. I've changed. Claire's changed. And so has Doug. People grow and evolve, and if they're lucky they acquire positive, worthwhile characteristics. I hope I have. I know Philippe has, I can tell. He's become a whole person and his own man. And Natasha knows him, and knows him well.

As father and daughter drew apart, Natasha exclaimed, 'We went to the fishman's stand, and he had fresh lobster. So it's lobster salad for lunch. Mom loves lobster!'

'Yes, she does, and I'm glad you've found something to tempt her.' Glancing at Philippe, Laura went on, 'Perhaps we ought to go upstairs, so you can spend a little time with Claire.'

'I'd like that,' Philippe replied.

Philippe sat holding Claire's hand, his heart aching for her. He knew how much she was suffering, the kind of pain she was in, and there was nothing he could do for her. Except assuage her worry about their daughter. He must reassure her that he would not interfere with the arrangement she had made with Laura, and that he would be there to give his support. As would his mother.

Philippe Lavillard had realized when he walked into Claire's bedroom that Claire and his mother had made their peace. Why does understanding always come too late? he wondered to himself. Why does it always have to be a catastrophic event that brings people together? If there had been this healing long ago, his child's life would have been very different; all of their lives would have been better.

Claire lay against the pillows, staring at him. He was still the best-looking man she had ever met, the famous Doug included. Lean, tough, with a body as hard as a rock, that was Philippe Lavillard. Eighteen years ago she had fallen madly in love with him; it had been a *coup de foudre*, and deep down inside she had never stopped loving him. Very simply, they had been unable to live together . . . because of her terrible secret, her history of abuse, and because of his own troubled background as the only child of a Holocaust survivor. The dice were loaded against us right from the start, she thought. We didn't have a chance.

Tough, determined and ambitious, that was the essential man her ex-husband was, but he was also warm, loving, tender – a man of immense compassion. She understood that now. *Too late. Too late for me now*, she thought, but not for someone else. He's ready finally for someone else, for another wife. All these years he's waited . . . yes, perhaps now it's time for him.

Claire said, 'I'm sorry it didn't work for us, Philippe. I'm sorry I caused you such pain . . .' She broke off; her eyes filled with tears.

'Hush, Claire,' he said very gently. 'It was nobody's fault, not yours, not mine, it was . . . circumstances. And we were too young.' He smiled at her. 'We'd be better off if we met today.'

She nodded. 'Except that I'm of no use to you anymore.'

'Hush,' he whispered, lifted her hand to his mouth. He kissed it, and continued, 'You've done a remarkable job with Natasha. She's a great kid, Claire. I love her, she's my only child, and I've always loved her. You thought I didn't care, but I did.'

'I know. And I was wrong to keep you and her apart. I'm sorry for that, Philippe.'

'No recriminations, Claire. We were both at fault in our different ways.'

'You'll keep an eye on Laura for me, won't you? Be there for her if she needs support? She's strong and resourceful, but even so . . .'

'You don't have to worry about Natasha and Laura. I'll be there for them, I promise you, Claire.'

'Rosa and I . . . we've made our peace.'

'I could tell. I saw it written all over her face only a moment or two ago.'

'Can I ask you something?'

'Go ahead.'

'Why did you never get married again?'

'I never found anybody I loved enough to marry.'

'Oh.' Claire sighed. There was a moment or two of silence before Claire said, 'It's funny, but everything is so clear to me now that I'm dying. What a ridiculous time to find the answers I've been seeking all my life. When they're of no use to me.'

Philippe, listening to her attentively and watching her closely, realized that she was growing tired; there was a strained look on her face, a sudden weariness about her. 'Are you in a lot of pain, Claire?'

'No. Well, a little, but the medication helps a bit. I think I'd like to rest for a while.'

Philippe rose, bent over her and kissed her forehead. 'I'll see you later.'

'Philippe?'

'Yes?'

'Why did you want to see me today?'

'I wanted to reassure you, to tell you you don't have to worry about Natasha. Not in any way.'

She smiled at him and closed her eyes.

Philippe moved a strand of hair away from her face and quietly left the room. He ran downstairs in search of Laura.

Laura was waiting for Philippe in the solarium. The moment he strode into the room she knew before he said anything that Claire was waning. She could read it on his face.

'She's not good, is she?'

Philippe shook his head. 'I'm afraid not. I think she's very weak, exhausted. Although she's trying to keep up a front for everyone. And she certainly can't get up for lunch, I wouldn't really like her to do that. I doubt that she wants anything to eat. I know Natasha's making her lobster salad, but –' He cut himself off sharply, and walked over to the window, stood gazing out at the summer garden for a moment or two. Finally, he turned around, and looked directly at Laura. He said gently, 'Perhaps it's best if you both go up and see her, sit with her.'

Laura nodded. Her throat was tight and she found it hard to speak for a moment. Gripping the chair-back, she steadied herself, and stared at Philippe, still unable to say a word.

Philippe said again, 'Go upstairs, Laura. I'll send Natasha to you.'

Laura did as he said, hurrying up the stairs, pushing down the feeling of panic that was rising inside. Her heart felt tight in her chest, almost constricted. She went into the blue-and-white bedroom, quietly closing the door behind her. Gliding over to the bed, she sat down in the chair next to it.

Her eyes rested on Claire, her dearest friend, her sister under the skin. Laura knew it was over. Claire had put up a courageous fight but the intense battle was finally drawing to its close. Soon she would be at peace.

There was a slight noise and Laura glanced over her shoulder, saw Natasha coming into the room. The girl's face was as white as bleached bone, stark against her red hair, and her freckles stood out like dark blotches. She crept up to Laura's chair, knelt down next to her.

'Mom's dying,' she whispered, looking up at Laura, the tears spilling from her eyes. 'Dad didn't say that, but I could tell from his face.'

Laura nodded, put her arms around Natasha, drew her closer to her knee. 'Yes, she is,' she whispered. 'And it's so hard for us to bear. But her pain's been excruciating lately. Soon ... soon she'll have relief.'

'I know,' Natasha whispered back, and wiped her fingertips across her streaming eyes.

Claire moved slightly and said, 'Are you there ... Laura? Nattie?' She tried to reach for them but her hand fell away, fell against the duvet.

Laura took hold of it, clasped it, and slipped down onto the floor, knelt by the side of the bed next to Natasha.

'Mom,' Natasha said, stifling a sob. 'We're here, Mom.'

'I'm glad I came back to Rhondda Fach, Laura. It's the only place I've been happy,' Claire murmured and opened her eyes.

'I know that, Claire, and *I'm* glad you came back too,' Laura answered softly.

'What would my life have been like without *you*, Laura?' Claire sighed, looked at her very intently, and then at Natasha. Her eyes were suddenly very green, greener than they'd ever been. Claire smiled at them both ... it was a valedictory smile, full of radiance. 'Take care of each other,' she said. 'For me.'

'Always, darling, always,' Laura answered, tears streaming down her face.

Natasha clambered onto the bed and put her arms around her mother.

Claire lifted her face to her daughter, and smiled that radiant smile once again. 'You're the best part of me, the very best part,' she said.

'Mom, I love you,' Natasha cried, her tears falling onto Claire's face.

There was no response.

Natasha cradled her mother in her arms, and Laura knelt by the side of the bed clinging to Claire's hand. Neither of them could bear to leave her, and they sat with her for a long time.

It was Laura who finally released her grip on Claire's fingers. Letting go of her hand, she stood up and bent over her, kissed her cheek.

And then she let herself out of the room and went downstairs to tell the others that Claire was free at last.

PART FOUR

Spring

1998

28

Megan sat studying Natasha, thinking how lovely she looked tonight, rather grown-up in the hand-embroidered burgundy silk dress Laura had just bought for her in London. Her flowing auburn hair cascaded around her face, accentuated its delicacy, and her large golden-amber eyes seemed more soulful than ever. She'll be sixteen this year, Megan thought, yet she seems much older in so many ways. But perhaps that's not a bad thing.

'You're staring at me, Grandma Megan. Don't you like this dress after all?' Natasha asked.

'I do indeed, and the only reason I was staring is because you look very fetching tonight, really lovely, darling girl.'

Natasha beamed at her. 'Thank you. I love my dress, it's cool, sort of medieval.'

Rosa came bustling in from the kitchen at this moment, carrying a large platter, exclaiming, 'I hope it's all right, I hope I didn't overcook this,' and set the platter down on the sideboard. Picking up a spoon and fork she began to put pieces of meat and vegetables on a plate and then took it to Megan.

'Thank you,' Megan said, went on, 'I don't think you can overcook pot roast, can you, Rosa? Anyway, you're such a good cook nothing ever spoils in your hands.'

Rosa laughed. 'We can all have a bad day in the kitchen.'

'I agree with Grandma Megan,' Natasha said, glancing up at Rosa as she came to the table with her plate. 'Thanks, Gran Rosa. And you're the best cook in the world except for Mom. She was the greatest.'

'Start eating, Nattie, before it gets cold,' Rosa said, and went to serve herself.

It was the first day of May, and Megan and Natasha were having their usual Friday dinner at Rosa Lavillard's apartment on East End Avenue.

Whenever she could, Laura joined them, but tonight she had gone to an art exhibition at Hélène Ravenel's gallery on Madison Avenue. And she was dining with Hélène after the show. 'I'll come and pick you up at Gran Rosa's, so wait for me there,' Laura had told Natasha that morning, as the girl had been leaving for school. She had added, 'And you can wear your new dress if you want.' Natasha had hugged her, said, 'Have a wonderful day,' before hurrying out of the front door.

Claire had been dead for almost a year now. Everyone had made a tremendous effort to help Natasha through this difficult period of grief and mourning. And because of the sympathy, understanding and love she had received from Laura, Megan and Rosa, Natasha had managed to cope better than she had expected. She missed her mother and she thought of her every day, but she was mature enough to understand that she had to get on with her own life without dwelling too much on the past.

It was Laura she turned to mostly when she had a problem, and her father whether he was in New York or Atlanta. Philippe came to visit her frequently, staying with Rosa at her apartment, and they had had some wonderful weekends together. Sometimes they were alone, but often Laura was with them, and they always managed to have a lot of fun when they were all there.

Natasha thought of this now, thought of Laura and her father and their growing friendship, and before she could stop herself, she blurted out, 'My father's stupid, and so is Laura.'

Megan was so startled she put down her knife and fork, and looked across at Natasha, frowning. 'Is that what they're teaching you at Chapin? To be disrespectful? And about your father, no less, who bends over backwards to please you. And Laura, who devotes all her free time to you?'

'Megan's right,' Rosa clucked, shaking her head, her expression reproving. 'Why do you speak like this?'

'I wasn't being disrespectful, Grandmas,' Natasha said, looking from Rosa to Megan. 'I was only trying to say what I think, which is what Laura's always telling me to do.'

'So, tell us why they're stupid,' Rosa said. 'Don't keep us in the dark.'

'Perhaps stupid is the wrong word to use. They're being silly . . .' She let her sentence fade away, wondering if she should continue.

Megan's eyes rested thoughtfully on Natasha, and then she glanced quickly at Rosa. The two older women exchanged knowing looks, and Megan said, 'Come along, out with it, child. What is this all about? What are you getting at?'

'Well, they're in love with each other. I know they are,' Natasha confided, her tone suddenly conspiratorial.

'That's wonderful!' Rosa exclaimed, beaming.

'I'm inclined to agree,' Megan said with a huge smile.

'It *would* be wonderful if they told each other,' Natasha exclaimed. 'But they don't. They just go bumbling along, bumbling around each other, looking sort of . . . glazed when we're all together. Dazed, is a better word. Don't you see, my father's being –' Natasha shook her head impatiently. 'There's only one word for it, Grandmas. He's being *stupid*. So is Laura. She should tell him how she feels. After all, a woman can do that today, you know.'

Rosa bit back a smile, and said, 'Perhaps it's not quite the way you think, Nattie. Are you sure they're in love?'

'I'm positive and so is my friend Katie. We *know*.'

'I'm sure you do, in view of your vast experience in these matters of the heart,' Megan said pithily.

Natasha giggled.

'I think I would have noticed something,' Rosa said, looking suddenly thoughtful. 'But I haven't, I really haven't.'

'Neither have I,' Megan said.

'Perhaps the situation will clarify itself, once Philippe is living in New York,' Rosa murmured, thinking out loud. 'I'm so glad he's accepted the Research Fellowship at Columbia University. That's going to be good for him, and for you, Natasha, having your father in New York at last.'

'And it'll be good for Laura,' Natasha said, and began to giggle again.

'You say you know they're in love, but *how* do you know? I mean, what have they actually done to make you believe this, Natasha?' Megan pressed.

'I've seen the looks my father gives Laura, when she doesn't know he's looking at her. And the way she gazes at him when he's off doing something – like helping me in the kitchen at Rhondda Fach. And they're always laughing at the same things, and if he pays her a compliment she goes all red and looks confused.' Again Natasha glanced from Megan to Rosa, and said firmly, 'Grandmas, you've just got to believe me, my father is in love with Laura, and she's in love with him.'

The two women exchanged pointed looks again, and it was Rosa who said, 'You want this to happen don't you, Natasha?'

The girl nodded, smiling, and her eyes gleamed with happiness. 'Yes, I do, I do. I want them to get married and the three of us can live together.'

Rosa said: 'But maybe you're imagining it, Nattie, because you want it to happen so badly.'

'No, no, Gran Rosa, honestly I'm not imagining anything. My friend Katie's seen it too. I just wish he'd kiss her. I've thought he was going to do it when we were in the country. But he didn't. I think Laura thought he might, too, because she looked disappointed.'

'And when was this?' Megan asked. 'I've been at Rhondda Fach every time you've been up there.'

'Yes, but it was when we were outside down by the river,' Natasha explained. 'They were walking ahead, and Katie and I were trailing behind. And they stood looking out across the river, and then they turned to each other, and they were staring. And Katie grabbed my arm, and she said he's going to do it, but he didn't.'

Megan glanced away, hiding a smile. She finally looked directly at Natasha and asked, 'What are we going to do about this? Do you have any ideas?'

'No.' Natasha shook her head. 'Don't you, Grandma Megan?'

'Not exactly,' Megan answered.

'What about you, Gran Rosa?'

Rosa pursed her lips. 'I can't think of anything, not offhand. I mean what can *we* do . . . we can't very well interfere, they're both adults.'

Suddenly, Natasha exclaimed, 'We've got to put them in the right situation together! That's it. And I think I've got it . . . the perfect situation.'

'And what is that?' Rosa asked.

'It's Laura's birthday later this month. We can have a little dinner for her and invite Dad, and somehow it's going to happen, I just know it is.'

Megan nodded. 'Giving a birthday dinner for Laura is quite a good idea, Natasha, I wish I'd thought of it myself. So, let's start making plans.'

29

Rosa Lavillard started to prepare the afternoon tea early. Far too early, she knew that, but she was anxious and excited, and so she couldn't help herself.

After plugging in the electric kettle, she took the damp cloth off the metal tray of honey cakes and glanced down at them. They looked tempting; she knew Laura would enjoy them. Laura also liked macaroons, and there was a plate of these as well, freshly baked that morning.

Laura had telephoned yesterday and had invited herself to tea today, explaining that she had some exciting news for Rosa, news she preferred to impart in person. Rosa had no idea what it could be . . . news of her and Philippe? Was Natasha right about them? *Perhaps.*

Rosa sighed and began to take the best china out of the kitchen cupboard. Philippe and Laura had been thrown together a lot over the past ten months, ever since Claire's tragic death. Their common bond had been, and was, Natasha. She herself had observed them together, and like Natasha she had noticed them circling each other. In fact, she had often wondered if her son would make some move towards Laura. But it seemed to her that he never had. At least, that was her impression of late. And Natasha had confirmed this only the other evening.

Humming under her breath, Rosa put two rose-patterned cups and saucers and two small plates on her best silver tray. She told herself there was no use speculating. In a short while she would know why Laura had asked to see her.

When the intercom rang a few seconds later and Laura was announced from the lobby, Rosa sallied forth, a broad welcoming smile affixed to her face as she headed for the front door. She opened it just as Laura stepped out of the lift, raised her hand in greeting and came down the hallway.

'Hello, Laura, hello!' Rosa exclaimed, taking her hand, embracing her warmly. 'Come in, come in.'

'Hello, Rosa,' Laura answered, hugging the older woman, then closing the door behind her.

'It's such a treat to see you,' Rosa went on, and standing away she gave Laura an appraising glance, taking in the smart navy suit and accessories. 'And you look lovely, very lovely indeed.'

'Thank you, Rosa. You're looking well yourself.'

Rosa smiled and murmured her thanks, and the two women went into the living room. 'Sit down, do, Laura,' Rosa said. 'The tea is ready. I'll go and get it, I won't be a moment.'

Laura glanced around and sat down on one of the comfortable chairs. She smiled to herself, wondering how Rosa was going to react when she heard her news. She'll be surprised but deliriously happy, Laura decided and sat back, the small smile continuing to play around her mouth. She herself was pleased about the turn of events, and could hardly contain herself, so anxious was she to confide in Rosa.

Hurrying back into the room with the tea tray, Rosa put it down on the coffee table, and took a seat opposite Laura. 'I know you like it with lemon, don't you?'

'Yes please, and a sweetener.'

Rosa nodded as she dropped in a slice of lemon. 'I made honey cakes and macaroons,' she told her. 'Your favourites.'

'You're so nice to me,' Laura said with a light laugh. 'Always spoiling me, Rosa.'

Rosa said nothing, merely smiled at Laura as she handed her the cup of tea.

'Thanks,' Laura murmured and took a macaroon, bit into it. 'Delicious. I love coconut. You'll have to teach Natasha to make these.'

'I certainly will, and she's a good little cook, she'll have no problem with the recipe.' Rosa took a sip of tea, put the cup down and sat back in the chair. Looking intently at Laura, she said, 'Yesterday you told me you had some exciting news for me. I can hardly wait to hear it.'

Placing her own cup on the table, Laura said, 'It's wonderful news. *Thrilling.*'

Rosa leaned forward expectantly, her face beaming. '*Tell me.*'

'I've found one of your paintings.'

'Oh.' Rosa pulled back slightly, gaping at Laura. 'You've found a painting,' she repeated.

Laura, returning Rosa's startled gaze, said swiftly, 'You understand, don't you? Understand that I've managed to trace a painting which belonged to your father? A painting which was looted by the Nazis. It's a Matisse, Rosa. Imagine, a *Matisse.*'

Rosa cried, 'Oh my God, one of Papa's paintings! I can't believe it. How did you find it, Laura? What happened?'

'About five months ago, when I was in London working on Sir Maximilian West's art collection, I came across a catalogue from a small museum in Vienna. As you well know, art seized by the Nazis hangs in museums all over the world. Anyway, in the catalogue there was a photograph of a Matisse. It caught my immediate attention because it bore the same name as one of the paintings in the record book of your father's which you lent me some time ago. I'm sure you'll recognize the name too . . . *Moroccan Girl In A Red Caftan Holding A Mandolin.*'

'Oh yes, Laura, yes!' Rosa cried, her hands flying to her mouth. Sudden emotion and memories of long ago brought a rush of tears to her eyes. Blinking them back, she said, 'I remember the name very well. And the painting. It's fabulous, extremely colourful, with a lot of red and violet, deep blue, and a brilliant yellow. A typical Matisse.'

'That's correct. Once I had seen the photograph in the catalogue, I flew to Vienna from London. I went to the museum to view the painting and talk to the curator. I tried to convince him it was your painting. Obviously I had to present clear title to him, the provenance. And so once I got back to New York I sent him a copy of the page in the record book, which listed the Matisse and all details about it. A week later he telephoned me and said he needed more proof. Naturally I was stumped.'

Rosa nodded. 'There is no other proof, not anymore. So what did you do?'

'As I said, I was at a loss, and then an amazing coincidence occurred. I mentioned my experience in Vienna to a client of mine, Sandra Newsam. She instantly recognized the name of the Matisse and said she had recently seen a photograph of it in an old art catalogue. She became very excited when she realized she had come across this at the home of a friend in Switzerland. She phoned her friend, a Mrs Gilda Sacher, and discovered that she had seen the photograph, not in a catalogue, but in an art magazine which had run a story about the Sacher Collection. The Matisse had once been part of that collection.' Laura sat back, pausing for a moment.

Rosa said: 'Oh, don't stop, please, this is so exciting.'

'Obviously I went to Switzerland. To Montreaux, actually, where Mrs Sacher lives. She's a woman in her late sixties, English by birth, and she inherited the Sacher Collection from her late husband, Leon Sacher, a Swiss businessman. During his lifetime Leon Sacher had amassed an amazing collection of art. Naturally, every painting in the collection had its provenance, and listed on the one for the Matisse was the name M Duval, Paris, France.'

'Oh my God! I can't believe it!' Rosa's eyes had widened and she could hardly sit still. 'And so you were able to convince the curator in Vienna finally?' she asked.

'Not exactly. There was a bit more to it than that,' Laura

responded. 'Let me tell you the rest of the story. I asked Mrs Sacher how the Matisse had come to be in the museum, and she told me she had sold it along with a couple of other paintings, to a dealer in Geneva, who in turn had sold it to a client in Vienna. Later it was sold to the museum. She gave me all of the names, just in case I needed them. I asked her if there were any markings on the back of the canvas, and she said there were the letters DU, then a slash and the number 3958. I explained to Mrs Sacher that this was the way the Nazis had catalogued the paintings they had stolen. They used the first two letters of the owner's surname and added a number. She hadn't known this. In any case, she then produced a copy of the provenance. It proved to be quite a remarkable document. According to the provenance, before Mr Sacher bought it, the Matisse had passed from M Duval of Paris to a Madame Wacker-Bondy of Paris, and from her to an H Wendland. Now those two names jumped out at me, meant a lot to *me*, although not to Mrs Sacher.'

'What did they mean to you, Laura?' Rosa asked.

'I will tell you. As I am now very familiar with the fate of Jewish-owned art stolen during the Second World War, those names rang bells immediately. Hans Wendland was notorious. He worked for the Nazis, and he spent most of the war years in Switzerland, where he helped Göring and Hitler exchange "degenerate" art, such as the Impressionists and Post-Impressionists, for the rather pallid old masters the two Nazi leaders preferred. Now it just so happened that almost immediately after my meeting with Mrs Sacher, yet another document came into my hands, almost by chance. It was a British Ministry of Economic Warfare paper, which I got via Sir Maximilian West, and it said that in 1942 one Hans Wendland, working for the Nazis, took delivery in Switzerland of a railway van of art from Paris. And this came from the transport firm of Wacker-Bondy.' Laura stopped and stared hard at Rosa. 'You do see the connection?'

'Yes, I do.'

'What is even more extraordinary, around this time, when I was doing research on your Matisse, Sir Maximilian was given a copy of a memo which had been written in June of 1966, by a woman called Marguerite Gressy, who had been a wartime Resistance heroine in France. She was a curator and she had somehow managed to keep track of many of the paintings which were looted in Paris by the Nazis. Her memo confirms that a painting by Henri Matisse entitled *Moroccan Girl In A Red Caftan Holding A Mandolin* was stored by Maurice Duval of Duval et Fils "chez Madame Wacker-Bondy". Meaning stored in the warehouse belonging to their company.'

Rosa sat looking at Laura speechlessly, trying to absorb everything.

'Mademoiselle Gressy's memo had been sent to Sir Maxim by an old friend in the French art world, a noted dealer, because several Renoirs were listed. However, they were not from the Westheim Collection, as it turned out. But Sir Maxim, very much aware that I was looking for information about the Matisse, passed it on to me.'

'Surely you didn't need more than this?'

'Not really. At least, that's what *I* thought. Armed with a copy of the provenance in Mrs Sacher's possession, a copy of the British Government paper and a copy of the Gressy memo, I returned to the museum in Vienna, and met once again with the curator. This time he was a little less contentious, especially when I showed him the documentation. In fact, I gave him his own set of copies. I also informed him that I would soon start litigation against the museum for the return of the Matisse to you if we couldn't come to an agreement. I also mentioned that I was planning a press conference to announce my findings and my plans on your behalf to the media. He seemed to be quite obdurate, said nothing had changed, and so I left. But I must have scared him because he telephoned me at the hotel that evening. He asked me not to do anything until he had spoken to the board of the museum. After a couple of days, when I didn't get a positive reaction from him or the museum, I left. I flew back to London, then on to New York. Once I was home I started to prepare all of the documentation I knew I would need, and then suddenly three days ago I received a call from the curator. The museum is going to recognize your claim, Rosa. Although they say they bought the painting in good faith, knowing none of its history, they are going to give the painting to you.'

Rosa shook her head. 'Since they bought it legally, why are they giving it to me? Just like that? I don't understand.'

'They're frightened, Rosa. They don't want bad publicity, the kind that Switzerland's had about dormant bank accounts and stolen Jewish gold, and cheating Holocaust victims. All of that's been a world-class scandal. They're trying to avoid this occurring with the museum, and, also, I like to think they might see that it's your moral right to have the Matisse in your hands after all these years.'

Rosa didn't speak. She couldn't, she was so touched. Again she shook her head wonderingly, and then she began to weep, totally overcome by the news.

Laura went and sat next to her on the sofa, took hold of her hand. 'A little bit of justice for you at last, Rosa,' she murmured.

Rosa looked at Laura through her tears. 'I can't believe it . . . that you did all this for me . . . Thank you, thank you. You've restored a piece of my soul, Laura, a little piece of my family's soul. I will be forever grateful, forever in your debt.'

30

'You did something really marvellous for my mother, Laura,'
Philippe Lavillard said several days later, when he had driven up
to Kent for a visit with Natasha. 'And I thank you for that.'

'Honestly, Philippe, thanks aren't necessary. I did it because
I had to, once I'd stumbled on the painting.'

He laughed. 'I know how you feel about Nazi-looted art.
You're like a dog with a bone. But very seriously,' he went on,
his voice changing slightly, 'I also know you're a very ethical
person, Laura. I admire your integrity.' His eyes settled on her
intently. 'Well, anyway, it's such a good feeling inside, knowing
that the Matisse is there, waiting for my mother at the museum.
Certainly it'll be satisfying to have it back in the family. But the
most important thing to me is that you've given my mother
something . . . something . . . rare. *Peace of mind.* And it's more
than likely the first time she's had that since her parents and
siblings were taken off to Auschwitz by those criminals so many
years ago.'

'I hope I have done that!' Laura exclaimed quickly, returning
his steady look. 'I love Rosa. She's the most remarkable woman,
and it truly pleases me to think I've helped to make her feel
better. God knows, her life's been hard, harder than most
people could ever imagine. So much loss and pain and fear

when she was a child. I can't help trembling when I think about it.'

'She's told you most of it, hasn't she?'

Laura nodded. 'Yes she has. But you sound surprised.'

'I was actually when she first intimated that to me. Not because it was you and Grandma Megan, but because she doesn't ever confide anything about her past. At least, she hadn't until she told both of you.'

'Why do you think that is, Philippe?'

He thought for a moment before answering, and then he said, 'Somebody once made a strange remark to her about professional Jews showing the numbers tattooed on their arms, and she said it made her shrivel inside because she couldn't imagine a Holocaust survivor being anything so crass as a *professional* Jew. The woman who said it offended her deeply, and it made her . . . protect her past. She held it to her, allowed no one to share it but my father and me . . . I'm certain you'll understand this . . . in a peculiar way her past became *sacred* to her. She didn't want it sullied by people's sympathy, indifference or scepticism. Those were her very words, and I do understand what she means, don't you?'

'Yes, I do. Her past is very private to her and so many people wouldn't . . .' Laura's voice trailed off. Clearing her throat, she finished, 'Wouldn't have the compassion to recognize the trauma it caused, the sense of dislocation she experienced.'

Philippe sat back, not responding. As she usually did, this woman had managed to touch and startle him yet again. That was her way, he supposed. At least it was the way she affected him. He tried not to dwell on Laura Valiant too much. He knew he was in love with her, but he was afraid to make this known to her because he didn't know where she stood. He supposed he would never know unless he made some kind of move towards her.

Laura remarked, 'Your mother is going to let me know when she can come to Vienna with me to collect the painting. Has she discussed it with you?'

'She has, and I think she's hoping that you'll be able to go at the end of this month.'

'I'm pretty sure we can ... and to tell you the truth, I'm as excited about the trip as she is.'

'We're all excited. Actually, Laura, what do you think about taking Natasha along with you? It's going to be such a memorable occasion, stupendous really, she shouldn't miss it.'

'You're right, I think she should come, Philippe.'

'I'm glad you agree. You won't mind if I tag along, will you?'

Although she was momentarily startled by his question, she was able to disguise this, and she said cautiously, 'No, of course not. After all, the painting will be yours one day. And I think you *must* be there to share your mother's joy.'

As she spoke Laura shrank inside, worried about travelling with him, staying in the same hotel as him, and having to be in his company for any protracted length of time. In fact, lately it had become an agony to be anywhere near him, feeling the way she did. To her amazement she had fallen in love with him. Once she had recovered from the shock, and regained her equilibrium, she had realized she was in an untenable situation. She had to spend time with him because he was Natasha's father and Natasha was in her care. But to see him was like putting herself on a rack. And so, finally, she had decided to make herself scarce whenever he was coming to visit his daughter. She invented business appointments, ran off to the office to work, and did as many other disappearing acts as she could. But eventually Natasha had become upset with her, and had insisted they all did things together; the girl had contrived to have them spend time together here at Rhondda Fach, and in the city. Oh well, she thought, I'll have to manage in Vienna. But deep down she knew it wouldn't be all that easy.

He said, 'I couldn't help thinking about the coincidences that happened to you, how you got onto the Matisse in the first place, and then all those documents that came your way. Just like that.' He snapped his fingers and smiled. 'You had lots of lucky breaks.'

Laura did not crack a smile. Her face was serious when she responded: 'I must tell you something rather strange, Philippe, there seems to be a lot of coincidence when it comes to tracking the purloined art of the Second World War. The Goodmans, two brothers now living in Los Angeles, just recently encountered *four* major coincidences when they were tracing art which their father had sought for forty years, art which had belonged to their grandparents in Holland. It seems to happen to everyone who is on the track of Nazi loot ... somebody finds an old record book or a document or a deed of title. Then someone stumbles on a painting in an obscure museum, hanging in an exhibition, or coming up for sale. It's quite uncanny really, all the coincidences.'

'Maybe God has a hand in it,' he said softly.

Laura glanced at him swiftly but didn't say anything. Maybe God does, she thought.

Philippe rose, walked across the library floor and stood at the window, thinking how peaceful the scene outside was: a long meadow, two horses grazing, and faintly, in the distance, the plop-plop-plop of tennis balls. Natasha and her friend Katie were enjoying a game on the tennis court. What a reassuring sound that is, he thought, just as the bucolic setting is also reassuring. A far cry from the sound of Nazi jackboots and prison doors clanging, the anguished cries of the victims of the Holocaust. Almost sixty years ago now, but still those terrifying memories haunted his mother. The past *is* immutable, he thought. She never escapes her past. It is with her always.

Laura startled him when she said, 'Your mother never confided much in Claire, I mean about her past, did she?'

He swung around to face Laura, feeling as though she had just tapped into his thoughts. 'No, she didn't. She just wasn't able to, as I told you a moment ago. I did explain a few things to Claire myself, but perhaps I didn't tell her enough. I've often wondered about that. I was nervous, I suppose.'

'What do you mean?'

'I was nervous about upsetting Claire, frightening her with the horror of it, the horror of my mother's tragic past. I mean, Claire led such a quiet sheltered life as a child, and she came from such a privileged and protected world.'

Laura was flabbergasted and before she could stop herself, she exclaimed, 'Privilege, yes! If you're talking about wealth, but protected, *no*! She wasn't protected.'

Philippe looked at her oddly, realizing he had touched a nerve, caught Laura on the raw. He came back and sat down near her in front of the fire, and said slowly, 'I'm not sure I'm following you.'

Laura shook her head, took a deep breath and said even more quietly than ever, 'There's something I've been meaning to tell you for a while now. Something about Claire that I think she would want you to know. But I was waiting for the right moment. I guess I've already started to blurt it out, so I might as well tell you the rest. Do you remember, you once asked me in Paris if I knew anything that would shed light on the reason Claire so hated men?'

'I remember.'

'Not long before she died, Claire confided in me, told me about her childhood, and what she told me was so horrific I don't know how she managed to live through it.'

Philippe frowned. 'Are you trying to tell me Claire suffered at the hands of her parents?'

'Yes, I am.'

'But why didn't she tell you before? Or me, when we were married?'

'Philippe, she was ashamed, embarrassed. That's what she said to me. You see, she was physically abused by her father. He used to beat her and her mother when he was drunk. Even when he wasn't. He treated her mother abominably. Aside from beating her, he was grossly unfaithful. Jack Benson was a regular dyed-in-the-wool womanizer. And at times he even sexually abused Claire. I suppose you could say she had plenty of reasons to mistrust and hate men.'

A terrible coldness had settled over Philippe as Laura had been speaking, and he could not shake it off. He felt icy inside and his heart ached for Claire. After a moment, he said slowly, 'I'd say she had more than enough reasons, yes. Poor Claire, poor darling. She was such a fragile, dainty little thing, and she must have been more so as a child. How could anyone beat her, hurt her? It's just horrendous, inhuman. Her father must've been a monster. Oh God, I can't bear to think of what she must have suffered.' He brought his hands up to his eyes, closed them for a moment, and when he eventually looked across at her Laura saw the tears glistening on his black lashes.

'She managed to hide it all very well,' Laura told him, speaking softly. 'And she managed to escape her father's hideous brutality when she was here at Rhondda Fach with us. In fact, she dealt with him very well when she was a little older. She threatened to expose him to my grandparents, and that curtailed his violent and disgusting activities.'

'If only she'd told me I would have understood. And perhaps I could have helped her in some way, Laura. How sad that Claire shut me out in the way she did. Perhaps . . . well, to be honest, I think she saw me as the enemy.'

'Oh I'm sure she didn't, not deep down. Not you, you're such a decent man, Philippe –' Laura stopped abruptly, cutting off her sentence, knowing better than to say another word.

Now wanting to change the subject, Philippe asked, 'Shall we walk over to the tennis court and see how the girls are doing out there?'

'Why not?' Laura answered, jumping up and heading for the door, no longer wishing to be alone with him.

Philippe had also risen, and as Laura passed him he caught hold of her arm, stopping her in her tracks. Staring into her bright blue eyes, he said, 'Thanks for telling me about Claire's childhood, it explains so much. I'm glad you had the trust in me to confide.'

Laura could only nod, wishing he would let go of her arm. His touch was like an electric current running through her. She knew she was vulnerable to him.

'It's been such a rotten year in so many ways, I don't really feel like having a birthday dinner,' Laura said to Megan, giving her a faint smile. 'Thanks, but no thanks, Gran.'

'But a birthday means you're actually starting a whole *new* year in your life, and perhaps it might be a wonderful year for you,' Megan pointed out, wondering how to make her change her mind.

Laura did not answer. She got up and walked over to the window and stood looking down the East River, her thoughts on Philippe Lavillard. She sometimes wondered if Natasha suspected something, realized how she felt about her father, and was trying to play the matchmaker. But it wasn't possible to be a matchmaker if the other person wasn't interested. And certainly Philippe wasn't interested in her. There was no special woman in his life, Natasha had announced that only the other day. Suddenly, Laura wondered why she had felt the need to say this. Perhaps the girl *had* tuned into the way she felt about her father. She was certainly bright enough. Thank God I don't have to spend more than a couple of days in Vienna, Laura thought. I can dash off to London once Rosa has received the painting.

'You seem very preoccupied with something, Laura,' Megan said, cutting into her thoughts.

Laura swung around and nodded. 'I am a bit, Gran. Lots of business is coming through the office these days. I'm really snowed under.'

'Oh dear, only business. And I was hoping it might be a young man you were thinking about.'

'Don't be silly.' Laura walked back to join her grandmother on the sofa. 'What time do I have for a man, young or old? I work like a dog, I have to travel constantly to London for Sir Maxim, and I'm bringing up a fifteen-year-old. Soon to be sixteen, actually. That's the birthday party we should be planning, Gran. Natasha's Sweet Sixteen bash.'

'We will, later. At the moment, I'm thinking of *your* birthday. And I do want to give this dinner. It'll be small. Just you and me and Natasha, and Rosa of course. Unless you'd like me to invite anyone else. What about Alison and Tony?'

'Alison and Tony won't come, they're not very social these days since Alison's pregnant again. No, there's nobody else I want.'

'Nobody else at all?' Megan pressed hopefully.

'Not really.'

'Definitely no young man.'

'No, Gran,' Laura said, and laughed for the first time in days.

'But you have agreed that I can give a dinner for you, haven't you, darling girl?'

'I guess you sort of trapped me into it, you wily old thing you, and why not? But please, no birthday cake.'

'Absolutely not. And no balloons either,' Megan quipped, keeping a poker face.

'When are you planning on giving this dinner, Gran?'

'That's up to you. Are you going off to see Sir Maximilian West this month?'

'No. He and his wife will be travelling. However, I do have to go to Vienna with Rosa. At the end of this month, so I can fit in with you.'

'Then I shall have your thirty-third birthday *on* your birthday. That's the way it's meant to be, you know.'

31

'Happy birthday, Laura!' everyone cried, lifting their champagne flutes and sipping the Dom Perignon.

Laura smiled and said, 'Thank you. And thank you, Grandma Megan, for my wonderful dinner party. Everything was absolutely beautiful.'

'My pleasure,' Megan said, and pushing back her chair she continued, 'now, let's go into the sitting room. It's time to open your presents, Laura dear.'

'Oh yes, let's do that!' Natasha cried, jumping up. 'Come on, Laura, come on, Dad.'

Not wanting to linger near Philippe, Laura got up quickly and hurried into the sitting room with Natasha. From the moment Philippe arrived at her grandmother's apartment, she had felt queasy inside, shaky. He had been a surprise. She certainly hadn't expected him to fly in from Atlanta for her birthday. In a sense, she was pleased he had made the effort, touched even; but the saner part of her told her not to be. After all, what did it signify? Tonight was Friday, and he frequently came to New York to be with Natasha at the weekend.

Natasha ran to her, caught hold of her hand as she was entering the room and said, 'Sit here, Laura, on the sofa. I'll sit next to you and hand you your gifts.'

'All right,' Laura answered, and did as she was told.

Megan and Rosa followed more slowly, escorted by Philippe. Once they were seated, he went and stood near the fireplace, watching the proceedings from this vantage point. He hoped Laura liked his gift which he had found in an antique shop last weekend when he'd been in New York. At the time he had been quite certain it would please her. Unexpectedly, he was no longer sure. But oh how he wanted it to be exactly right.

Automatically, his eyes were drawn to her, as they always were when she was in the same room. To him she was the most beautiful of women, not only on the outside but inside as well. Laura was a very rare being, a woman of integrity, understanding and compassion. There weren't many like her in this world.

He loved Laura Valiant. He had loved her for many months now, perhaps even longer than that, if he were honest with himself. That cold day in December, almost two years ago now, he had wanted to prolong his contact with her in the d'Orsay Museum. But his mother had arrived, and their conversation had been interrupted. And suddenly he was hurrying after Rosa, wondering when he would see Laura again. Now he wondered how to get their relationship on a different footing. Perhaps he could attempt it this weekend. If not, it would have to wait until he moved permanently to New York. He couldn't wait to be in the same city as Laura . . .

'Thank you, Rosa,' Laura exclaimed. 'The Renoir book is marvellous.' She went to kiss Rosa, then returned to her place on the sofa.

'This is from Grandma Megan,' Natasha announced, handing Laura a small package.

Ripping off the paper, Laura found herself holding a worn leather jewellery box. As she peeked inside she saw a narrow ring set with diamond chips, and taking it out she slipped it on her little finger.

'Oh Grandma, it's beautiful. Thank you!' Laura went to hug Megan.

'Your grandfather gave it to me many years ago,' Megan said, 'and I was sure it would fit you.'

'And this is from me.' Natasha presented her with a long slender box. Laura looked up at Natasha, who was sitting on the arm of the sofa, smiled, then tore off the wrapping paper. Out of the long cardboard box she lifted a white chiffon scarf handpainted with pink peonies. 'Why it's lovely,' Laura said, reaching for Natasha.

Natasha bent down and they embraced. 'I painted it myself, and I chose the peonies because they're your favourite flower. And now here's your final gift. From Dad.'

Laura's eyes flew to Philippe standing near the fireplace. He half smiled and nodded. 'I hope you like it,' he muttered, feeling suddenly awkward and a little embarrassed.

'I'm sure I will,' Laura responded, carefully taking off the ribbon and the paper. Again, it was an old leather jewellery box, and with a sudden rush of excitement Laura lifted the lid. She found herself staring at one of the most beautiful cameo brooches she had ever seen. 'Why it's exquisite, Philippe,' she exclaimed and rose, slowly walking across to the fireplace. She gave him a quick peck on the cheek, stepped away from him swiftly, and added, 'Thank you so much.'

Natasha said, 'I knew something was missing. And it's music. I won't be a minute.' She rushed out of the sitting room, humming under her breath.

Megan said, 'She's a whirlwind at times, but then I suppose I was too, when I was her age. Now, Laura, let me look at Philippe's gift.'

Laura took it over to her grandmother and showed it to her, and then to Rosa. They both exclaimed over it, and Laura said again, 'It's very beautiful, Philippe.'

He merely smiled at her.

The strains of music filled the room as Natasha came back and said, 'There, that's better, isn't it, Grandma Megan? You did say you wanted music tonight.'

'I did indeed, child, and it's perfect.'

Natasha, now standing next to her father near the fireplace, whispered, 'You should ask Laura to dance, Dad, it's her birthday after all.'

Philippe looked at Natasha and asked in a low voice, 'But where would we dance?'

'Out there in the front hall. Near the dining room.'

Philippe followed the direction of her gaze, and nodded. But then he hesitated, and did not move until Natasha squeezed his arm and whispered, 'Go on, Dad.'

Crossing the room, Philippe came to a stop at the sofa, looked down at Laura and gave a small half-laugh. 'Since the music's playing just for you, for your birthday, would you come and dance with me, Laura?'

'I'd love to,' she responded. Together they walked through the doorway of the sitting room and out into the front hall.

Taking hold of her hand, Philippe put his arm around her, and brought her closer, then slowly they moved around the marble floor, not saying a word to each other.

Laura was shaking inside. She could hardly breathe.

Philippe was as nervous as she was, but he managed to conceal this as they danced. When the music came to an end he said, 'There, that wasn't so bad, was it?' He dropped her hand, stepped away from her.

'No it wasn't,' Laura replied, also moving away.

They strolled back to the sitting room, only to find it empty. They heard voices and laughter coming from the library and turned to face each other in puzzlement. Just as they did so another disc started to play, and strains of a romantic ballad echoed throughout the apartment.

Philippe, looking down at Laura, said, 'Do you think we're the victims of a conspiracy?'

'I don't feel like a victim,' Laura murmured. 'Do you?'

'Not at all,' Philippe answered, and taking hold of her hand he led her out of the room, back to the front hall where, miraculously, the lights had been dimmed.

They stood in the middle of the marble floor, staring at each other. Their eyes locked. Neither of them could look away. And then before he could stop himself Philippe took a step closer and pulled Laura into his arms. Their mouths met; she clung to him. He kissed her passionately, and she responded ardently. When they finally pulled away, he said quietly, 'Dare I hope you feel the same way I do, Laura Valiant?'

'I think so. But how *do* you feel?' she asked, her eyes on his face.

'I'm crazily, madly, in love with you,' he answered.

'Then we feel the same way,' she said, and moved back into his arms. 'And that's the way I'm going to feel for the rest of my life.'

'The rest of *our* lives,' he murmured against her hair.

Where You Belong

Barbara Taylor Bradford

Valentine Denning is a courageous photojournalist on the frontlines in Kosovo. Her colleagues, Tony Hampton and Jake Newberg, are her comrades-in-arms – men whom she loves and trusts. One is her best friend, the other her lover. In a nightmarish ambush all three are shot, Tony fatally, and for Val an even worse nightmare begins.

For there are memories and lies – lies which force Val to find herself again by leaving her past life of heartbreaking war-danger for what seems like the gentler world of celebrity shots. But this too brings danger: a famous artist whose reputation as a playboy does not steel against a powerful attraction. Valentine's sense of searching for something leads her to retrace paths which she thought she had left behind.

'Few novelists are as consummate as Barbara Taylor Bradford at keeping the reader turning the page. She is one of the world's best at spinning yarns'   *Guardian*

ISBN: 0 00 651090 6

Everything to Gain

Barbara Taylor Bradford

Mallory Keswick is a woman with the world at her feet. Then out of the blue, that world is shattered by violent tragedy and she loses all that she holds dear.

Torn by grief, Mal knows that she must rebuild her life. She flees to a village on the Yorkshire moors where she learns to draw on the deepest reserves of her spirit, and to look life in the eye once more.

Returning to Connecticut, Mal opens a café and shop selling gourmet food and kitchenware and turns it into a highly successful venture. But there remains in her life an aching void, a grief that no individual, nor her new-found business acumen, can assuage. Then she meets Richard Markson, and once more, Mal's life has come to a crossroads. It is he who shows her that she has everything to gain – but only if she has the courage to take it.

Totally absorbing and heartrendingly real, *Everything to Gain* lays bare Mallory's life to expose powerful feelings that are startlingly familiar, because they are our own.

'Heart-rending stuff . . . *Everything to Gain* is truly uplifting'   *Today*

ISBN: 0 586 21740 1